"Immersive, cinematic, and exquisitely fun... ...d is the perfect debut, full of high-society hijinks, high stakes, and the joy of finding oneself. A delightful, transportive ride, and the New Adult book I was waiting for!"

—Ali Hazelwood, *New York Times* bestselling author
of *Love, Theoretically*

"With the glitz of *Gossip Girl*, the allure of vibrant and vivid Singapore, the glamour only the elite can bring, and the promise of a fake-it-till-you-make-it quest, *The Fraud Squad* is escapism at its finest. This book will swallow you right up and keep you awake until you turn the last page."

—Elena Armas, *New York Times* bestselling author
of *The American Roommate Experiment*

"*The Fraud Squad* is a cinematic and engrossing peek into the world of Singapore's elite, as seen through the eyes of its ambitious heroine, Samantha Song. As glamorous and page-turning as a glossy magazine, infused with sharp class critique, a vibrant cast of characters, and a poignant emotional core."

—Ava Wilder, author of *Will They or Won't They*

"This glittering gem of a novel is an incisive reflection on the perils of status and the callousness of wealth. Rich with clever charm and scandalous sparkle, *The Fraud Squad* introduces a delightful and daring new voice in Kyla Zhao."

—Emily Wibberley and Austin Siegemund-Broka, authors
of *The Breakup Tour*

"Zhao (not my cousin) showcases both glamour and grit in this thrill ride through Singapore's high society, balancing dazzling luxury with critiques of classism and inherited privilege!"
—Xiran Jay Zhao, #1 *New York Times* bestselling author of *Iron Widow*

"Lush, swoony, and delightfully exquisite, *The Fraud Squad* is an unputdownable debut that will transport you into the lavish world of Singaporean high society. With an irresistibly relatable heroine and a vibrant cast of characters, this book is perfect for fans of *Crazy Rich Asians* and *The Devil Wears Prada*."
—Amy Lea, author of *Exes and O's*

"Delightful and unpredictable, this drama is very *The Clique* meets *Crazy Rich Asians.*"
—*Cosmopolitan*

"Zhao updates *My Fair Lady* in her sparkling debut, a high-society farce set in Singapore. Zhao brings buckets of charm to her characters. . . . The author also gets plenty of mileage from arrogant socialite Lucia, who reads like she strutted off the pages of *The Devil Wears Prada*."
—*Publishers Weekly*

"Zhao's debut is a sparkly page-turner, with hints of *Crazy Rich Asians* and *The Devil Wears Prada*. . . . A delightful blend of emotion and aspiration."
—*Booklist*

"*My Fair Lady* meets *Working Girl* in Singapore. . . . There is sweetness to this story of glitz and glam."
—*Kirkus Reviews*

BERKLEY TITLES BY KYLA ZHAO

The Fraud Squad
Valley Verified

valley verified

verified

KYLA ZHAO

Berkley
New York

BERKLEY

An imprint of Penguin Random House LLC

penguinrandomhouse.com

BERKLEY and the BERKLEY & B colophon are registered trademarks of Penguin Random House LLC.

Library of Congress Cataloging-in-Publication Data

Names: Zhao, Kyla, author.
Title: Valley verified / Kyla Zhao.
Description: First edition. | New York: Berkley, 2024.
Identifiers: LCCN 2023022554 (print)
| LCCN 2023022555 (ebook) | ISBN 9780593546154 (trade paperback) |
ISBN 9780593546161 (ebook)
Subjects: LCGFT: Novels.
Classification: LCC PS3626.H38 V35 2024 (print) |
LCC PS3626.H38 (ebook) | DDC 813/.6—dc23/eng/20230616
LC record available at https://lccn.loc.gov/2023022554
LC ebook record available at https://lccn.loc.gov/2023022555

First Edition: January 2024

Printed in the United States of America
1st Printing

Book design by Daniel Brount

To my grandparents and parents,
for their unconditional love and belief in me.

author's note

Content warning: This book deals with emotionally difficult topics, including sexual harassment. Any readers who believe that such content may upset them or trigger traumatic memories are encouraged to consider their emotional well-being when deciding whether to continue reading this book.

valley verified

chapter 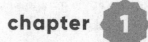 1

ZOE ZENG WAS having an absolute blast.

It was a balmy summer evening—the kind that showed Manhattan at its best. A slight breeze whipped around the rooftop terrace, but her braided updo didn't budge an inch thanks to extra-strong Alterna hair spray. In her Paco Rabanne dress and Charlotte Olympia wedges, she fit right in with the other guests at this party—a launch event for a.I.r, the hottest sustainable fashion brand as of late, whose claim to fame was turning mushrooms into leather.

The thumping electronic music—played by a DJ who was apparently "the next Diplo"—and the party chatter faded as Zoe walked closer to the railing and gazed out at the city. New York City was always prettiest at night, its blemishes disguised by the bright lights and flashing billboards. She took a deep breath of the calm evening air, her spirits lifting further as some other guest's sparkling perfume hit her nostrils. It was a welcome change from the rubbish stench that she still hadn't gotten used to after moving into an apartment right next to an alley with a nice selection of dumpsters.

A microphone-amplified voice boomed out. "Everyone, please join me at the front to welcome a.I.r's founder and CEO, Vladimir Trotsky!"

It wasn't clear to Zoe exactly where the front of the rooftop was, but somehow everyone else seemed to know. She followed them toward a patch of empty space right next to the refreshments table, but found herself squeezed toward the back, only just able to glimpse Vladimir Trotsky's beaming face over the crowd. A statuesque woman—probably a model—jostled past her, the pointy heel of her stiletto landing right on Zoe's right foot.

"Ouch!" But her pained exclamation was drowned out by Vladimir Trotsky's voice.

"Ladies and gentlemen," he began, a broad smile on his tanned face. "Thank you for joining me at the preview launch for a.I.r's second collection. My debut collection, Evoke, released last fall to great acclaim, and I am delighted to announce that we have taken everything people loved about Evoke and made it even better. This collection, Birth, celebrates the greatest creator of all, Mother Nature, for aren't we all birthed from her loving embrace?"

As he continued, Zoe could feel her concentration waning. Vladimir Trotsky was quoting a.I.r's press release word for word. She shifted from one foot to the other as twinges of pain shot through her ankle—these heels were the biggest she could find in *Chic*'s photo shoot closet, but still small for her size nine, extra-wide feet. Could she duck out now while it was still somewhat early enough that she could take the subway home alone without fearing for her life?

"Hey." A warm puff of air skated across Zoe's left cheek. "What did I miss?"

Zoe turned toward the source of the whispered question. A man was pressed close to her, squeezed on his other side by someone else. Instinctively, she took a step back and crossed her arms as she studied this stranger.

He wasn't very tall—about the same height as she was in her four-inch heels. His stocky build, like that of a former gymnast or wrestler, was rather incongruous with his young-looking face, as though someone had transplanted a toddler's head onto a grown man's body, clad in a tuxedo.

"I just got here and didn't catch the first part of his speech," he explained, catching Zoe's slightly startled expression. "What does a.I.r stand for?"

Something about his boyish looks made Zoe relax slightly and put down her arms. "Aspire, Inspire, Respire," she whispered.

He pulled a face. "Seriously? They sell clothes, not life coaching."

A snort escaped from Zoe's mouth. She winced apologetically as a blonde woman in front shot her a glare. "I think it's part of their whole *we love the earth* story," Zoe said, dropping her voice even further. "a.I.r uses sustainable materials and production methods to reduce carbon emissions. It's all in the press kit." She couldn't resist adding, "Guess someone hasn't done their homework, huh?"

The man chuckled under his breath. "Busted. So, why is only the *I* capitalized?"

Zoe shrugged. "Probably just to make themselves seem quirky and special. Could also be a symbolic middle finger to unsustainable fashion. Who knows?"

Now, it was the man's turn to laugh out loud. The woman in front whipped around again, but her annoyed expression quickly smoothed out into a coquettish smile when her eyes landed on his face. Zoe resisted the urge to roll her eyes.

She snapped back to attention as everyone around them started clapping and cheering. Great, she had just missed Vladimir Trotsky's speech. Not that she had really missed much if he was just repeating everything in the press kit.

"And now," the emcee said. "Vladimir will be taking questions. Who's first?" Zoe's arm shot up along with a dozen others. The emcee's eyes scanned the crowd. "Yes, that Asian woman in the back."

It wasn't until the mysterious man nudged her that Zoe realized *she* was the "Asian woman" in question. *Ugh.* Someone shoved a microphone in front of her face.

"I have a question about your sizing," Zoe said carefully, all too aware of everyone's eyes on her. "The clothes are one-size-fits-all—why's that the case?"

Vladimir Trotsky raised one perfectly plucked brow. "Well, mycelium is very expensive to make, and we'll have to use a lot of mycelium if the wearer has more . . . body real estate." He gave a small smirk as laughter rolled through the crowd. "And we don't want to make our clothes very expensive because we don't want sustainable fashion to be available only for the rich!" The crowd burst into another round of applause—even louder this time.

"But don't you think that only offering one size for all your pieces means your brand is available only to those of a certain size?" Zoe pressed.

"Miss . . ."

"Zeng," she supplied. "Zoe Zeng."

"Miss Zoe Zeng," Vladimir repeated, his smile turning earnest. "Please, help me understand. Is your question coming from, uh, personal experience?"

Heat rushed to Zoe's face. Her hand tightened around the

microphone as a hush fell over the crowd, their deafening silence only heightening her humiliation. In that moment, she would have given anything for a hole to open beneath her and swallow her, hiding her from everyone's stares.

Thankfully, the emcee came to her rescue. "We're running out of time so let's move along now. Who's next?"

THE MOMENT THE QUESTION-AND-ANSWER SESSION ENDED, Zoe made a move to leave, but the man beside her touched her shoulder lightly. "Hey, you okay?"

His kind tone made Zoe's chest tighten but she plastered on a big smile. "Of course," she chirped. "Why wouldn't I be?"

But he must have caught the overly bright note in her voice. The man leaned closer and said firmly, "Vladimir Trotsky is an asshole. Don't pay any attention to what he says. He's just jealous that you look far better in your outfit now than anyone can look in those raggedy designs of his."

Zoe couldn't help but smile. "Thank you." As she took in his warm expression, she was swept up by a sudden urge to confide in him. "Actually, this dress that I'm wearing—it's not even mine. I took it secretly from my magazine's wardrobe, which is full of clothes that we loaned from brands for photo shoots. I have to put this back tomorrow."

The moment the words left her mouth, Zoe wanted to smack herself. He seemed nice enough, but the fashion world was full of wolves in designer clothing, ready to pounce at the first sign of insecurity.

She braced herself for his judgment but to her surprise, his eyes lit up. "You work at a magazine? That's cool! Is it *Vogue*?"

Zoe held back a sigh. "Uh, no. It's a magazine called *Chic*; you probably haven't heard of it. We're pretty small." She bit her lip. "In fact, there are rumors that we might be shutting down soon."

"Oh." He seemed at a loss for words. "I'm sorry."

Suddenly, Zoe could no longer deny the truth: She wasn't having a blast. Actually, she wasn't having fun at all. This entire evening had just been a show she was putting on—for anyone watching her, but mostly for herself. When she moved to Manhattan after graduating from college, she had been so excited by the prospect of living and working in the mecca of the global fashion publishing industry. The chance to attend fashion week. To hobnob with up-and-coming designers and uncover new talent. To help expand the definition of what it meant to be fashionable, of who could be fashionable.

Four years later, she was a lot less starry-eyed. Living in a dingy apartment with three roommates, her own room so small that she had to store some of her clothes in the oven, could do that to a person. Meanwhile, she had barely made a dent in her student loans. No matter how carefully Zoe budgeted and saved, working in fashion demanded a certain look and lifestyle—one that her meager salary couldn't quite support, which resulted in plan Bs like "borrowing" photo shoot clothes. Sure, going to parties was fun, but that wasn't going to help her get to the front row at fashion shows where she was always stuck standing in the back, not even able to glimpse the runway.

The thought of returning to her cramped apartment tonight made Zoe's heart sink. She could see herself slumped on her creaky bed, since her room wasn't big enough to contain a desk, scarfing down instant ramen while rushing to finish her a.I.r article in time for her editor's review tomorrow, and knowing almost for certain that her efforts would be for nothing because Francesca would tear it apart anyway.

A lump of emotion welled up in Zoe's throat. The worst thing was, as much as she knew this wasn't sustainable, that working in this industry meant being paid peanuts for at least the first few years, she still couldn't imagine her life without fashion. It was her first—and greatest—love.

"It's okay," Zoe finally said, praying the man couldn't hear the tremor in her voice. "There've been a bunch of business consultants poking around lately, but nothing's been confirmed yet." She quickly pivoted. "*So*, you've heard my career story. What's yours?" He didn't seem like he worked in fashion, or at least not at a big brand or magazine—if so, she would have recognized him in a heartbeat. The industry was small, and the number of men in it smaller still.

The man stood up taller and straightened his tie. "I just realized I haven't introduced myself. I'm William, William Lawrence. And yes, I'm aware I have two first names. But you can call me just Bill."

Zoe mustered a smile. "It's nice to meet you, Just Bill."

That drew a chuckle out of Bill. "And my middle name is Maximilian. My name makes me sound a lot posher than I actually am, but you can imagine how long it took me to shade in the bubbles for my name on standardized tests."

He looked gratified when Zoe burst into laughter. "My full name isn't even as long as one of your names. I'm Zoe, Zoe Zeng with no middle name." She held out her hand, which Bill shook with a steady grip. "So what is it that you do?"

"I run an app called FitPick. Have you heard of it?"

He looked so hopeful that for a moment, Zoe was tempted to lie and say yes. But what if he asked for her opinion on it? "Uh, that sounds familiar. It's . . . that fashion app, right?" she hazarded. After all, they were at a fashion event, so this man must be connected to the industry in some way.

"Precisely!" He beamed. "Back in college, my then girlfriend was always asking me what she should wear, as if I could even tell the difference between two shirts of the same color. And the other guys in my frat would complain about the same thing. Their girlfriends would ask for their opinion but then not actually trust it because hey, we're guys—what do we know about women's style? And that gave me an idea—instead of just asking one person for outfit advice, what if you can take a photo of yourself in two different outfits, put it up on the internet, and get the public to vote on it."

His face shone as he spoke, the words rushing out of him in an excited stream, his hands gesticulating wildly for emphasis. "Over the past few years of working on it, I've gathered a small but mighty team. FitPick started off as an app that lets women crowdsource opinions on their outfits instead of relying on their clueless boyfriends, but we've really expanded our mission. We want to provide a safe space where people can have fun with their outfits and explore different styles, instead of being bombarded with photo after photo of everyone pretty much having the same look as what you see from Instagram influencers."

"Wow, I love the sound of that," Zoe exclaimed. Any effort to promote inclusivity in fashion was a plus in her book. "Why haven't I heard about it? I mean, why haven't I heard much about it?" she quickly amended, remembering just in time that she'd mentioned earlier the app sounded familiar.

Already, Zoe's writer brain was whirring: She hadn't read about FitPick in any of the major fashion magazines, so what if she was the first to break the news of this hot new app?

The next moment, the thought soured. Her editor, Francesca Fraatz, would surely shoot down the idea—like she had for the previous dozen ideas Zoe had pitched—on the basis that it wasn't aligned with *Chic*'s brand.

Bill scratched the back of his neck. "Oh, um, we are more of an up-and-coming company. Although our technology is really solid, we just haven't gained a lot of traction. And for apps like ours, the network effect is so important because the more people who use our app, the more helpful it becomes for anyone looking for fashion feedback. But because we don't really have a sizable user base yet, investors are wary about putting money in us. In fact, I'm only here at this fashion event because one of my board members told me it would be a good opportunity to meet potential investors." He frowned a little, his eyes swiveling absently around the rooftop. "I should probably be networking."

"We're technically networking," Zoe joked, before offering a sympathetic smile. "Sounds like your app and my magazine share a similar target audience, and the Gen Z–millennial fashion crowd is definitely a hard one to win over. It's not enough to just have an awesome product and assume the awesomeness would speak for itself. We have to convince them that we offer something different, something better than what they're used to." *And we can't, which is why* Chic *might get shut down soon.*

Bill snapped his fingers. "You know, that's exactly what the investor I was talking about earlier said when I pitched to him last month. Logan Horossen—you must have heard of him. He's a famous angel investor—someone who likes investing in young startups, which is riskier but also offers bigger rewards if those risks pay off. Have you heard of Uber? Or Rent the Runway? Spotify? All him. He's the real deal."

The light in Bill's eyes dimmed and his voice turned rueful. "At our pitch meeting, he said a bunch of nice things about the app itself, but also said that we aren't marketing it right. *I don't doubt you and your team have the coding skills*, Logan'd said, *But when I think of fashion, I think of glamorous, sexy. And right now, there's nothing sexy about this app."*

Zoe grimaced. "I hate to say it but he's right that marketing counts for a lot. If there's one thing working in fashion has taught me, it's that it doesn't matter how great something is if you can't make it look great." As she spoke, Bill narrowed his eyes appraisingly. "A two-thousand-dollar Dior dress can look frumpy if not styled right, but a cheap blazer dug out from a thrift shop bin can look like a million bucks if you know how to accessorize it."

"You!" Bill said suddenly, making Zoe startle. "You are a fashion writer at a hip New York magazine. If there's anyone who knows glamorous and sexy, it's you! And I can already tell that just like me, you care about creating a more inclusive environment in fashion."

He cleared his throat and spread his arms open like a television show host. "Zoe, what do you think about changing jobs?"

Zoe felt her mouth drop open in a most *un*glamorous and *un*sexy way. "Me?" she sputtered, eyes wide. "Are you asking me to join *your* company?"

When he nodded, she exclaimed, "But I know nothing about apps!" *Or tech. Or startups.*

Bill dismissed her protest with one wave of his hand. "Which makes you perfect to do marketing for us! My team is made up of some of Silicon Valley's brightest minds, but because we are so involved in the technical product, it's hard for us to assess our brand image objectively. But you—you are an outsider, one who happens to know our target audience very well. With your background and perspective, we can do a better job of promoting FitPick to women like you who care more about how the jeans look on their back end than the technology on the back end," he declared.

"Wow. Uh, I'm very flattered," Zoe managed. That, at least, was true—when was the last time her editor Francesca had even paid her a compliment? "But I'm happy with my current job," she finished, trying to ignore the doubt creeping into her mind. Was she really happy doing coffee runs for her editor and writing Pulitzer-worthy articles such as an incisive dissection of whether Meghan Markle or Kate Middleton looks better in maroon pantsuits? Was she really happy living with three roommates in an apartment that was so small the one bathroom had no sink and she had to brush her teeth at the kitchen sink—because that was all she could afford on a salary that was barely above minimum wage?

Zoe shook her head to dispel those thoughts. Fashion was what she had wanted to do her entire life; she couldn't turn her back on it now just because it was slightly challenging. After all, nothing that was worth it ever came easy.

"Of course you are," Bill agreed easily. "But I'll be giving you a much better title. Vice president of marketing, how does that sound?"

"Vice president?" Zoe echoed, a flicker of excitement stirring within her. At *Chic*, she was merely a small plankton in a sea of well-dressed sharks—not even a "fashion writer," as she liked to introduce herself as to other people, but a "*junior* fashion writer."

Bill nodded. "We're just a small startup, so there won't be anyone reporting to you. But you will be part of the leadership team and I guarantee you a lot of autonomy. I believe that it's the people who make or break a company and I see a great talent in you. As vice president of marketing, you'll be making a much stronger business impact than most people your age at their jobs."

Zoe had to press her lips together to keep herself from smiling too widely. "Talent" was how *Chic* employees referred to the celebrities and models featured in the magazine, and it was an unspoken requirement of her job to fawn over and boost the egos of said "talent." This was the first time anyone had ever referred to her as one, like a person with value to offer instead of being a dispensable cog in the machine that could be replaced at her editor's whim.

Bill's expression turned more solemn. "Look, I'm not going to sugarcoat it so I'll tell you now that working at a startup isn't for everyone. The perks are great, but the work is demanding. We'll all be working overtime quite a bit as we gear up for our second-chance meeting with Logan Horossen. He's giving us one quarter to boost FitPick's image. In three months, we'll meet with him again and if we successfully convince him of FitPick's business potential, he will agree to lead our Series A funding round. With Logan Horossen as the anchor investor, other VC firms are sure to come knocking."

Bill paused and took a swig of his drink. "But if we don't impress him, there's no way someone like Logan Horossen is going to give us a third chance. He doesn't even usually give out second chances. And without his funding, we'll eventually run out of money and be forced to shut down."

Zoe hesitated. She was no stranger to late nights and working on weekends given how notoriously fast-paced fashion publishing was. But now that they were no longer just talking about the great parts of the FitPick job, everything suddenly seemed a lot more real. A lot more uncertain.

"But can't you just look for other investors?" she asked.

Bill heaved out a sigh so big it seemed to run through his whole body. "News travels fast in Silicon Valley and people move as a mob. If a big investor like Logan Horossen is interested, then everyone wants in on the action. But if they hear he doesn't think we're worthy enough, no one will touch us with a ten-foot pole.

And I'm afraid team morale will run out even before our money does. Why would anyone want to work for a startup with no funding prospects when they can easily get a six-figure job at Google or Amazon?"

Zoe gazed past him and over the rooftop railing, sweeping her eyes again over the city skyline unfurling below. But this time, all the bright lights made her feel very small, and very alone. Was she really going to do this? Accept a job from a man she'd known for barely thirty minutes in an industry she knew nothing about and move to a city on the other side of the country, and more importantly, leave behind her family, friends, and the industry she'd dreamed of working in since she was young?

She met Bill's eyes again. "Can I think more about it?"

Bill nodded and pulled out a business card. "Take as much time as you need. You know where to reach me," he said, passing her the card. A grin slid over his face. "You know, I would say we are networking pretty well right now."

That broke the somber atmosphere. Laughing, Zoe carefully pocketed Bill's card, making a mental note to remove it before returning her dress to *Chic*'s closet. "That we are."

chapter 2

"BJORN, NO! ARE you serious?" Zoe exclaimed, staring at her best friend with an expression of mingled horror and amusement. It was ten on a Thursday morning, which meant it was their unofficial gossip session alongside Cassie, the last member of their work throuple. Bjorn believed that contrary to popular expectations, the week's juiciest events always happened on hump day and not the weekend ("People go batshit in the middle of the week because the weekend still feels too far away").

"Do I ever kid around?" Bjorn sniffed, but *Chic*'s junior lifestyle writer couldn't hide his pleased smirk at the reactions toward his recount of his dating shenanigans the previous night. Feeling friskier than usual, he and his paramour du jour decided to hit up a popular SoHo bistro while she was wearing a remote-controlled vibrator. Bjorn was relishing the power rush of being in control of said vibrator when he noticed in the app that there was a vibrator pattern labeled Mikey. When he asked about it, the woman had broken down, revealing tearfully that she had created it based on her late husband's last heartbeats.

"Let me get this straight," Cassie, *Chic*'s junior stylist, said slowly, lowering her voice even though the three of them were the only ones at the office section "reserved" for entry-level employees. "She enjoys having orgasms to the rhythm of his last moments?"

"She's just doing it to feel connected to him," Bjorn clarified. "I think the vibration's too slow to actually bring her over the edge, 'cos you know, I don't think a person's last heartbeats are very—" His voice suddenly rose. "Yes, Zoe, I'll forward you the press kit at once."

Zoe's heart sank. Editor alert.

Sure enough, a ring-studded hand soon landed on her desk. Zoe's eyes traced the line of the toned and hairless arm up to the immaculately made-up face of *Chic*'s fashion editor, Francesca Fraatz. To an outsider, Francesca's expression seemed perfectly pleasant, but those at *Chic* knew it was the result of years of monthly Botox injections and that her calm facade belied the imminent deliverance of bad news. Francesca Fraatz would never leave her perfumed office to hobnob with her subordinates at their desks unless she absolutely had to do so.

"Zoe, a word about your a.I.r article," Francesca said in her crisp German accent. "Why on earth would you include that bit about how you wish the brand could expand its line to cater to more sizes?"

From the corner of her eye, Zoe could see Cassie and Bjorn looking determinedly at their own computer screens. She swallowed. "Because it's one-size-fits-all, but we aren't all the same sizes. So what fits you won't fit me, for instance—"

Francesca's eyes flicked pointedly between her own size zero frame and Zoe's decidedly non-size-zero body. "Sure, but it doesn't look good if we're criticizing one of the world's hottest sustainable fashion brands now. Makes us look like we're not in on the green movement."

As if Francesca cared about anything green besides money and Bulgari emeralds. "But I didn't exactly criticize it," Zoe protested. "It's just that carrying only one size means bigger women can't wear their clothes, but a.I.r's founder was going on and on about how those who don't wear sustainable fashion are enemies of the Earth, and I just thought that wasn't very fair—"

"Zoe, I hired you to write, not to think," Francesca interrupted. "Why don't you just write out whatever they sent you in their press kit?"

"But then my—I mean, our—article will sound like what everyone else is writing!"

"And don't you think there's a reason why none of them are preaching about how a.I.r should be more size-inclusive? Rewrite it and send me your draft this afternoon." Not waiting for a response, Francesca swept away, a tinge of Chanel No. 5 in the air the only sign that she was ever there.

Zoe slumped in her chair. Great, this meant another day of skipping lunch so she could work on this article, then staying late to write the "Five Reasons You Should Steal Your Boyfriend's Ties" piece Francesca had asked her to submit by tomorrow. She used to keep a scrapbook of all her bylines, but she stopped doing so a few months ago when her articles began to sound more like a bullhorn for Francesca's ideas.

When the editor was out of earshot, Cassie murmured sympathetically, "I'm sorry, Zee. That was harsh."

"And so unfair!" Bjorn burst in. "It's not like you were wrong about any of it. And I read your draft—it was super matter-of-fact. Francesca made it sound like you were slandering them! Don't give in; preserve your journalistic integrity."

"I have to rewrite it," Zoe sighed, turning back to her computer. "She'll never let it get published otherwise. And I guess she has a point—a.I.r might be too pissed off to invite us to their future events. We can't get on the bad side of the It brand of the moment."

"Zee's right," Cassie said to Bjorn, who still looked disgruntled. "We have to put what the brands want before our personal opinions."

Before our personal opinions. The phrase swam around in Zoe's head the entire afternoon, even as she churned out a new eight-hundred-word report on a.I.r's launch that Francesca at last deigned to accept—though not without another pointed remark about how Zoe could have saved herself a lot of trouble if she just followed instructions from the beginning; as she packed up her belongings at the end of the day and got on the subway; as she clambered into bed without even bothering with her usual twelve-step skin-care routine; as she laid there staring up at the patch of paint flaking off the ceiling, the sounds from whatever Netflix show her roommates were watching seeping through the walls like mold.

She had gone to four years of fashion school, interned at numerous magazines for no pay, fetched coffee in subzero weather, and for what? A career of essentially being the mouthpiece for the brand du jour, slapping her byline above words lifted from press kits? Through all those late nights and weeks of eating cheap ramen and holding back tears when she was reprimanded in front of the whole crew at a photo shoot, the one thing that had kept her going was her love for fashion and the belief that this was how she could share that love with the rest of the world.

But how was she supposed to do that when she couldn't even share her own thoughts? Maybe this was a sign that she never really understood fashion at all, that she never truly belonged in the industry.

A white card popped into Zoe's mind. She lay still in bed for a few beats longer, then abruptly, like she'd been shocked, she leapt out and made a beeline for her clothes hamper. After a few moments of rummaging through the pile, she extracted a card from the pocket of her Paco Rabanne dress from last night.

BILL LAWRENCE

Founder and CEO, FitPick

Experiment, Explore, Excite.

blawrence@FitPick.com

She stared down at the white piece of embossed paper in her hand. Was she really going to do this?

Experiment, Explore, Excite. That sure sounded better than *Aspire, Inspire, Respire.*

Before her nerves could abandon her, Zoe opened the email app on her phone. She clicked on "Compose New Email" and began typing.

chapter 3

A NEW JOB?!"

Bjorn's shriek pierced the babble in the small bar where he, Zoe, and Cassie had gathered for their weekly happy hour.

Zoe's stomach tightened, and not just because of the annoyed look shot in their direction. She raised her cocktail glass and took a long sip to cover her crestfallen expression. But it was hard pretending not to notice how Bjorn had physically recoiled when she broke the news that she had accepted FitPick's job offer, or how Cassie gave him a none-too-subtle jab in the ribs that made him wince.

"Not that we aren't excited for you," Cassie said, setting down her own drink. "But I just never pegged you as someone who would work in tech. Tech is so cold and clinical, and Zee . . . you're *not*."

The knot in Zoe's gut eased slightly. The old guards in fashion publishing often spoke fondly of the past—when couture was made to be worn and admired in person (not viewed through pixels on a screen) and magazines were hefty nine-hundred-page tomes instead of pithy online pages that contained a dozen hyperlinks to influencers' Instagram accounts and retail platforms offering more affordable dupes of the featured clothes.

"Yeah, did you forget about the cover catastrophe from last September?" Bjorn whispered, as though the mere mention of the disaster would cause the roof of the hipster speakeasy to collapse.

Zoe and Cassie unanimously sucked in a sharp breath. *Chic*, like every other fashion magazine, had had to make the digital pivot with a host of new implementations, a few of which were more successful than others. The QR code in every photo spread that let readers use virtual reality technology to "wear" the featured clothes in the privacy of their own home was a hit, but it had all come to a head when the editor in chief got the idea of turning last year's September issue cover into an NFT. *Metaverse Magic* was the title emblazoned on the cover, featuring two nude models with their anatomy covered strategically with QR codes that would open up to an exclusive Jacquemus NFT design once scanned. Unfortunately, it had quickly spawned a tide of memes all over social media, and the cover became the worst-selling one in *Chic*'s history.

Zoe put her glass down. "Come on, you two, this would be an exciting challenge for me!" she said brightly, wondering if she was trying to convince her friends or herself. "I've been writing for *Chic* for two years, and it's really not typical for people in their twenties to stay at their first company for longer than that."

Bjorn's right brow shot up. "Girl, making denim on denim work is a new challenge. Getting a new job in an industry you have completely no experience with is a brain aneurysm."

"I have experience with technology," Zoe reminded him. "I handled *Chic*'s social media accounts when our digital coordinator was on her honeymoon a few months ago, and I worked with 3D printers during my 3D design elective in college."

"Everyone wears clothes but that doesn't mean they're qualified to make a living out of it like we do," Cassie said.

Zoe paused as Cassie's words sank in, hollowing a pit in her stomach. "So that's the real issue," she finally said. "You two don't think I'm qualified for this role."

"Of course not!" Cassie exclaimed.

"Well . . ." Bjorn started. "What?" he asked defensively when Cassie glared at him. "Friendship is all about tough love. Zee, you have an amazing eye for fashion and editorial, not to mention a kickass style. If you just stick it out for a bit longer, someone's bound to recognize your talent." His voice gentled. "Why do you want to throw that all away to start from square one, in an industry where you have no knowledge or connections?"

Zoe squashed down the niggling voice in her head that had been wondering the same thing on loop over the past two days. "That's the thing, Bjorn—I *can't* afford to stick it out for a bit longer. I've been saying that to myself for ages but you heard Francesca: I wasn't hired to think, just to parrot whatever those brand PRs tell us. That's not the fashion journalism career I want. And I'm not starting from square one: FitPick is a fashion app, so my fashion expertise will be very helpful for my new role as vice president of marketing."

"Vice president of marketing?" Bjorn yelped, his eyes bugging out of his head.

"Shhh," Zoe whispered, blushing as a man nearby glowered at them. "The title sounds way fancier than it is. There's a bunch of contracted engineers but only five full-time employees working there now. I'll be the only person in marketing, so I guess that makes me the head by default."

"Yeah but still, I bet your new fancy title comes with a fancy paycheck. We all know how much money is floating around in tech." Cassie nudged Zoe's arm. "Come on, Zee, admit you'll be making bank."

Zoe laughed, hoping her friends wouldn't catch the slightly forced quality behind it. It wasn't like the three of them had never talked about money before. Actually, they talked about it all the time, but always to complain about their lack of it and to day-dream what they would do if they ever won the lottery or—God forbid—if *Chic* decided to pay them even just a bit above mini-mum wage. But she had never been put in a position where she would suddenly be making over two times as much as her friends.

"The pay's not bad," she finally said, as if a six-figure salary could be considered just "not bad." "But it also means there's more pressure on me to actually do a good job at what they hired me to do. And if we don't succeed in impressing this hotshot inves-tor, we might have to shut down in a few months' time."

Bjorn sighed into his drink. "We've lost her already," he mut-tered to Cassie. "She's already saying *we.*"

Cassie shrugged. "*Chic*'s probably gonna get shut down soon anyway. At least going to FitPick means Zoe will be way better paid while she has a job."

"Hang on." Bjorn's face turned somber as he looked straight at Zoe. "This means you're leaving us."

Instantly, the noise in the bar seemed to fade, like someone had toggled an "Off" switch. Zoe shuffled along the booth bench and leaned her head against Bjorn's shoulder. "I'm not leaving you two; I'm just leaving *Chic*. But we'll still talk every day and watch *Love Island* together over Zoom and grumble about our jobs. Bjorn, you know I'm always just one text away to help you pick the best photos to post on your Instagram." Zoe turned to Cassie. "And I'll be on standby whenever you go on a Bumble date so that I can fake an 'emergency' phone call to you if your date goes badly. And we can continue to have our outfit huddles—over FitPick! Everything will still be the same."

"Except it won't!" Bjorn cried, almost upending their platter of fries with his flailing hands. "We won't be able to gossip together at work or ogle the hot male models who drop by. And if it's just Cassie and me going to bars, we will just look like a couple and no one's going to hit on us. And how am I supposed to find the motivation to go to Pilates without you coming with me? You know Cassie doesn't like to sweat." He gestured out the floor-to-ceiling window next to their booth. "And how can you possibly think of leaving the greatest city on Earth?"

Zoe looked pointedly at the pile of trash bags on the sidewalk right next to the bar. A well-dressed lady stepped daintily over a smaller heap of food scraps that had spewed out from an open hole in one of the bags. The moment she was a safe distance away, a pigeon flew down and began rummaging through the discarded waste. It quickly took flight as two blaring car horns boomed out in quick succession, followed by a stream of colorful shouts from somewhere on the road that was thankfully muffled by the bar's thick glass windows.

Zoe raised one brow at Bjorn, *I rest my case.*

He rolled his eyes. "Yeah, but at least the city is walkable. Good luck surviving without a driver's license in California, where the nearest grocery store is probably twenty minutes from your house. And it might be messy here but that just shows us New Yorkers know how to have a good time. I can't say the same for those tech geeks and suburban moms in your new neighborhood."

Cassie placed a gentle hand on Zoe's arm. "What Bjorn means is, we will miss you a lot, Zee. Very, very much. But we're still really happy and excited for you that you found such a great opportunity. Go, save yourself from the dumpster fire that will erupt when *Chic* is shut down and we all get laid off. Just . . . give us some time to process the fact that our best friend will be on the other side of the country."

Bjorn looked suitably chastised. "I'm sorry, Zee. I didn't mean to rain on your parade. You deserve so much better than what *Chic* and Francesca Fraatz can give you. It's just really hard to imagine life without you here and not knowing when I'll see you again. Cass and I can't be a throuple without you."

Suddenly, Zoe's heart was gripped in a painful squeeze. New York City was where she had attended college and worked her first (and only) job; how was she ever going to survive in California where she knew no one, while her best friends continued on at *Chic* without her? With whom was she going to gossip about celebrities in the office break room or play What Would You Rather Wear? when walking past mannequins in storefront windows? As much as she wanted to pretend everything would stay the way it was, the cold hard truth was that this would be the last time in a long while the trio would all be together. In just two weeks, while Bjorn and Cassie made their way to *Chic*'s office in Tribeca as usual, she would be on a plane across the country.

She quickly turned away from her friends and fixed her attention on the street as a wet pressure built up in the back of her eyes. Her gaze caught on the rubbish heap on the sidewalk. Even that looked prettier now, more like a uniquely New York sculpture of sorts than a breeding ground for vermin.

The table quieted as her friends clocked the change in mood. Finally, Bjorn wrapped an arm around Zoe's shoulders and said fiercely, "You are going to be the best fucking thing that's ever happened to Silicon Valley. Just promise me you'll never lose your style and become part of the Patagonia Posse. You're a Prada girl through and through."

The idea of herself wearing one of those odd-looking Patagonia fleece vests made Zoe shudder. "Please give me more credit than that," she told her friends firmly. "There's no way I'm going over to the dark side."

chapter 4

ZOE PROPPED HER phone up against the mirror on her bedroom vanity and confirmed she was in frame, before doing a pirouette. The fringed hem of her maxidress danced around her legs, in sync with the tasseled hairband she had looped through her hair. "Is this good enough for a first-day outfit? I don't know how many people at FitPick have heard of *Chic* before, so I really want to make a great first impression and show them that I'm the right person to make their app seem more fashionable."

Bjorn clasped his hands together, his broad smile bursting through the screen. "Girl, stop worrying! You look absolutely fabulous. I'm glad you went with our suggestion."

Zoe had to strain her ears to catch her friend's response. Cassie and Bjorn were currently taking an extended "bathroom break" at work to hop on this last-minute outfit check. In reality, they were hiding in separate restroom cubicles, whispering so they wouldn't be caught by a prowling Francesca, who had a preternatural sixth sense for when anyone on the fashion team wasn't working.

Zoe curtseyed her thanks. "And I'm glad that seventy-eight percent of the voters on my FitPick poll agreed with your suggestion. Look at technology helping us stay connected even from opposite coasts," she couldn't resist adding.

The last time the three of them had been in the same room was at her send-off dinner three days ago on Friday. It probably hadn't been a good idea to stay out past midnight when she had a cross-country flight twelve hours later, but Cassie and Bjorn had insisted on sending her off in style at Cipriani, one of the city's hottest restaurants. Cassie had asked her well-connected Goldman Sachs banker ex to help get them a table with just a week's notice, and Tomas (who Zoe and Bjorn both suspected was still hung up on Cassie) had come through beautifully. And when Zoe had offered to pay for her share (less of a financial pinch now thanks to her new tech salary), she had immediately been shut down by her best friends even though Cipriani's four-dollar-sign price range was definitely an eye-watering splurge for most *Chic* employees.

Zoe had resolved not to drink too much but Bjorn and Cassie wouldn't stop toasting her, their toasts growing steadily more ridiculous ("To all the times you helped me squeeze out my blackheads!" Bjorn had cried out at some point, to the horror of the other well-dressed Cipriani diners). And when Zoe proposed a toast to their Friday night tradition of wining and whining, Cassie started weeping, only stopping when Bjorn reminded them that every minute spent at Cipriani cost at least three dollars and they couldn't afford to be sad there.

Cassie broke into a loud yawn. "Oh God, I'm sorry," she said, clapping her hand to her mouth. "But I've been up since four for that Grand Central Station photo shoot and I'm so tired right now."

Zoe's smile froze. She had helped plan the photo shoot, working with Francesca to come up with the concept, then with Cassie to pair the right models with the right outfits. It had taken twenty-seven emails before she finally secured the city council's permission to host the photo shoot at Grand Central Station. But now, the project that she'd labored over for so long was moving on without her.

She pushed aside those thoughts. "Oh yeah, I forgot about the time zone difference." Her eyes snapped to her phone's time display. "Damn, you've been awake for eight hours. No wonder you're tired. Go get some coffee, Cass. We can talk more tonight."

"I've got that Tiffany and Co. event at night," Bjorn said, pulling a face.

"And I'm going as his plus-one," Cassie said.

The hollow sensation in Zoe expanded. She, Bjorn, and Cassie grumbled all the time about the evening and weekend commitments that came with working at a fashion magazine, but now that she never had to go to a Tiffany and Co. event again, it suddenly seemed a lot more appealing. After all, not everyone got invited to cool parties hosted by the world's most popular brands.

"Why don't we call you instead when we're done?" Cassie suggested. "And here's to hoping you have a better work-life balance at FitPick than we do at *Chic*."

As her friends went offline, a disconcerting sensation ballooned in the room. It took Zoe a moment to place it.

Silence.

Other than the faint rumbling of vehicles in the far distance, her apartment was completely quiet, made even more obvious now that her friends' chatter wasn't filling it up. No roommate watching television; no creaking and clatter from old pipes; no neighbor stomping around in the apartment above; no drunkards stumbling down the streets outside and vowing to get revenge on their exes.

In her Manhattan room that wasn't really a room, she would have sold her left kidney for this peace. But at this moment, standing stock-still in the center of an apartment that was all hers, the peace was deafening, drawing one's attention not to what was there, but to what wasn't—the friends and laughter and vibrance that had made New York home through four years of college and two years of work.

Giving her head a slight shake, Zoe switched off her phone and tossed it onto the couch, where it sank gracefully into the velvety-soft upholstery. Back in her New York City apartment, the surface of the two-seater was so hard that her phone might have bounced right off.

She kneeled down and opened one of her still unpacked suitcases. With less than forty-eight hours in her new place, she only had time to unpack the most important things: her bedsheets, toiletries, and clothes. But it only took a few moments of rummaging before her hand found what she had been searching for—a framed photo wrapped in a thick faux-fur Sandy Liang coat for protection. Carefully, Zoe placed the photo onto her new mantelpiece, then stepped back to assess that it was perfectly centered.

The photo was slightly blurry; the diner it was taken in was not grungy-cool, just pure grunge; and just a moment before, Zoe had accidentally upended their entire ice-cream sundae onto herself, and Bjorn was laughing so hard that a bit of his milkshake dribbled out of his nose—all captured by Cassie with a perfectly well-timed selfie, though only half of her face could be seen since it was smushed against the camera.

But as she studied the photo, Zoe's heart swelled until she had to take a deep breath to push down her emotions. The photo was objectively unglamorous, but it had preserved one of her most favorite New York memories, made with her favorite people. It gave her the strength she needed to pick up her purse and walk out the door, steeling herself for her first day at her new job.

chapter 5

AS ZOE MADE her way to the reception counter in FitPick's office—a two-story building in Palo Alto called The Nook—she found herself swept up in a steady trickle of people, though none of their faces looked like the headshots on the "Who We Are" page of FitPick's company website. Bill had told her that they shared The Nook with three other startups, with each occupying its own wing.

"AnotherYou is a virtual reality game company," he'd written in an onboarding email a few days ago. "And Man's Best Friend is an artificial intelligence company that claims to use deep learning to decipher canine language, but they're all bark and no bite if you ask me. Then there's Dreamcatcher that supposedly analyzes and controls dreams—sounds like some hippie shit. They have crystals and stuff everywhere in their office."

The receptionist, a young woman with pale blonde hair in a simple ponytail, squinted at Zoe. "Hi, do you have an appointment?"

Zoe shook her head.

"We don't take visits without an appointment. Would you like to—"

"I'm not a visitor," Zoe quickly said. "I'm a new employee." She tucked one of her headband's tassels behind her right ear. "Zoe Zeng . . . vice president of marketing at FitPick." A flicker of pride darted through Zoe as she uttered those words, even as her tongue tripped over the unfamiliar, lofty title. "Bill—William Lawrence told me to meet him here at nine?"

The receptionist flicked her eyes down Zoe's body, then up to her face again. "Miss Zeng? Right, Bill is expecting you and he'll be down here shortly. I'm Priscilla, the building's receptionist, and let me be the first to say, 'Welcome to FitPick.'"

"It's wonderful to meet you, Priscilla," Zoe said absently as she did a reciprocal scan of the receptionist's outfit. Black skinny jeans and a plain linen blouse, and were those . . . New Balance shoes on her feet? Zoe swallowed as her eyes roamed the reception area, lingering on the employees from the other startups making their way to their own offices. It was jeans and sports shoes and Birkenstocks galore—with socks! And either a Patagonia fleece or a North Face vest layered over their respective company shirt. The biggest deviance she could see was a man who had put on a blazer over his AnotherYou tee.

Something brushed against Zoe's face—her headband's tassel had escaped back in front of her ear again. She pushed it back into place with a growing dread. As far as she could tell, no one was wearing any sort of accessories except wedding rings and Apple Watches. Even the bags they carried were either nondescript black purses, slouchy JanSport backpacks, or messenger bags emblazoned with their company logo.

As inconspicuously as possible, Zoe pressed her arm against

her Paul Smith satchel to hide as much of its rainbow-striped print as she could. Hopefully the other FitPickers would be dressed more like herself since they worked at a fashion app.

"Zoe, welcome to FitPick!" Bill's voice boomed out. He rounded a corner, blinking as he neared her. "Wow." Zoe clutched her satchel strap tighter. Was she just paranoid or had she also imagined the slight widening of Bill's eyes as they gave her a once-over? "I know you worked in fashion but it seems like I underestimated your sense of style."

Is that a good thing? With a pang, Zoe found herself suddenly missing her old coworkers at *Chic.* They were all competitive about their dressing, vying to see who could get their hands on a limited-edition item or uncover the most vintage piece of Galliano, but they were also accepting and encouraging of sartorial experimentation. People showed up wearing sports bras under blazers, feathery gloves with slip dresses, and Bjorn once won an office challenge for finding the greatest number of ways to wear a scarf (that was also how everyone found out about his nipple piercing).

"Thank you?" Zoe laughed nervously. "I like your outfit too."

Bill struck a comical pose as he caught Zoe eyeing his Patagonia jacket embossed with FitPick's logo. "You like? I've prepared one for you, too, as a welcome gift."

"Oh, that's nice of you!" Zoe said, trying to imagine the scratchy-looking plain fleece jacket overlaying the delicate lace of her maxidress. Bjorn and Cassie would suffer an aneurysm if they ever caught her in one of those.

Bill clasped his hands together. "Priscilla, I've got it from here. Zoe, let me show you around."

chapter 6

FITPICK'S SECTION OF the building was a huge loft with exposed brick walls and a network of metal pipes running over the ceiling. Sunlight streamed in from the floor-to-ceiling windows, lighting up the dozens of colored Post-it Notes stuck on them to form the word *FITPICK*. There was a conspicuous lack of rooms in the FitPick office. Instead, a long desk rolled through the center of the room like an airport runway, though only five of the spots appeared to be taken.

"Ah, The Hook," Bill said as he caught where Zoe was looking. "This is where we all work."

"Why is it called The . . . Hook?"

"'Cos it's where we all hook up and have wild orgies." Bill chuckled at the horrified expression Zoe wasn't quick enough to hide. "I'm just messing with ya. We call it that to remind ourselves that we need to create a unique hook to set ourselves apart from other fashion apps."

"Oh! I thought it was called that because you were going for the same rhyme scheme as The Nook," Zoe joked.

Bill beamed. "Ding ding ding! Besides The Hook, we also have a conference room in the far right corner where we have our company meetings twice a week. We call that room The Rook after the chess piece, because it's basically like a fortress for the front line. We like to say that what's said in The Rook stays in The Rook. And then there's the pantry, called—"

"Let me guess, The Cook?"

"Right again! I knew from the very start you were a FitPicker at heart."

Zoe returned his smile. Or just someone who could decently guess words that rhymed.

"We don't cater lunch, but everyone gets a fifteen-dollar daily food stipend that you're welcome to spend however you want," Bill continued, gesturing for Zoe to put her bag down on an empty chair at The Hook. "If you bring your own food, there is a state-of-the art refrigerator, microwave, and an oven. We also have a good selection of snacks: every flavor of LaCroix, kombucha on tap, Chobani yogurt, Quest protein bars, and fruit cups. The Cook isn't big but it offers what we need now."

Zoe was sure her jaw had dropped to her Jeffrey Campbell heels by this point. The only thing more incredulous than what Bill was saying was how casually he said it, as though it was all just run-of-the-mill. It seemed like the only perk *Chic* offered over FitPick was the thirty percent discount on designer sample sales, but that was a moot point since it wasn't like she could have afforded any of the pieces anyway, even with that discount.

Zoe ran her eyes over the personal knickknacks scattered across the surface of the long table in The Hook. At one end was a light box with the quote "Move fast and break things" spelled out in big block letters. "Mark Zuckerberg said that," Bill informed Zoe, catching where she was looking. "Great guy."

"You know him?" Zoe gaped.

"Not personally," Bill admitted. "Not yet. But I feel a strong affinity with him, you know? We're both college dropouts. We both saw a chance to create something that would make an impact and disrupt the status quo." He patted the light box fondly like it was a child, then tossed his unzipped Patagonia jacket onto the table, nearly knocking over a framed photo.

Bill let out a yelp and quickly reached over to grab the photo before it fell off the table, visibly exhaling in relief as his fingers closed around it. He adjusted it so that Zoe could see the black-and-white photo clearly and used the corner of his sleeve to rub away a fingerprint smudge. "I put this right next to my laptop as motivation."

Zoe stooped down to take a closer look. Bill was standing on the far right of the photo, almost half cut off—clearly an afterthought. He also seemed to be the youngest one there; the other half dozen men in the photo looked to be in their forties or fifties. All wore headdresses and various kinds of eyewear ranging from goggles to monocles to sunglasses. Towering far above the group in the back was a metal statue of a woman that was at least thirty feet tall, her eyes a pair of circular disks that glinted in the sunlight.

"That's me at Burning Man this year," Bill said.

"Burning Man?"

"It's this cool art and culture festival that lasts eight days in some godforsaken desert. Think of it as Coachella for the tech crowd. It used to be pretty hippie—very anti-consumerism, live in tents and no Wi-Fi and all that. But after Sergey Brin brought along a private chef one year, all the other billionaires began doing that too. And soon enough, tents were replaced with air-conditioned Gulf Stream RVs. Now, Burning Man is just where the who's who of Silicon Valley swans around in a dick-measuring contest in which people don't brag with Instagram photos, but with how many shares they have in Instagram."

Zoe looked back at the photo of the seven men in their grungy outfits, faces streaked with dirt and hair in varying states of disarray. Behind the rather shoddy appearance was a collective net worth that could probably rival the GDP of certain nations. Her eyes fell on the man in the center. "Oh my God. Is that Elon Musk?"

"Yup. Get this: I struck up a conversation with Eric Schmidt while we were both waiting in line for the porta-potty." Bill grinned. "Burning Man is a tech person's networking wet dream—that's the only reason I went. I'm not usually one for roughing it out in the desert and going an entire week without showering, you know?"

"Having a private chef at your beck and call? I'd love to be roughing it out too," Zoe joked.

"Oh please, I'm nowhere near Elon Musk's or Sergey Brin's level. I wasn't even planning on going to Burning Man—the cheapest ticket is more than two hundred dollars, and that's only if you can prove you need financial assistance. I'm trying to get a young startup off the ground—I don't have that kind of personal money. I only went because Drew Macklemore"—he pointed at the bald, strapping man next to him in the photo—"invited me along."

"As in the CEO of Macklemore Corporation?" Zoe exclaimed.

Bill gave a pleased smile. "Yup, his son Dune was in the same college frat as me and one of my best friends. Dune also happens to be an early and enthusiastic user of FitPick 1.0," Bill said with a chuckle Zoe couldn't quite understand.

"After I dropped out of college to run FitPick, Dune introduced me to his dad, a well-known venture capitalist. Drew really liked FitPick's concept, so he bought a stake in the company and now sits on our board. He was the one who recommended I attend that a.I.r event—I think one of his mistresses was modeling so that's how he heard about it. He's also very chummy with some of the Valley's top VCs and offered to make some introductions while I helped them with their Burning Man art projects."

Zoe shifted from one foot to the other, not quite sure how to respond to Bill's casual comment about Drew Macklemore's adultery. "Sounds like summer camp," she finally said.

"Summer camp for the ultra-wealthy. None of those lame Popsicle sticks and origami paper stuff for those tech billionaires; everything has to have *symbolism*. See this?" He pointed at the giant metal statue in the photo's background, careful not to let his finger touch the glass. "It's got some lofty name like *Eye on the Future*, or something. Its body is made up of a super-lightweight alloy that was recently invented for Elon Musk's space shuttles, but its eyes are made of CD discs. It's supposed to be ironic, you know? Mix a futuristic material with an ancient object that no one uses anymore."

"Is that why you're all wearing those eye accessories? To fit the whole Eye on the Future theme?"

"Yeah, billionaires can be corny too. And you know what's the wildest thing? At the end of the event, we tore down this structure and threw out everything like it was garbage." Bill shook his head. "That was made from a material that took the world's top scientists and engineers years and millions of dollars to develop. And it ends up being treated like Play-Doh."

Zoe let out a low whistle. "Dang. Those people are nuts."

"True. But very rich nuts. I can't tell you how many times I accidentally hammered my own fingers, but I did get a whole bunch of business cards from the world's most powerful people, so a swollen thumb is worth it, eh?" Smirking, Bill pointed at a man to Elon Musk's left, whose face was mostly hidden by a pair of comically large sunglasses. "That's Logan Horossen, the VC I was telling you about," he said reverently. "If he agrees to fund our Series A—"

Bill dropped his hand back down by his side with a small sigh. "Big if. We just have to hope our second meeting with him in ten weeks goes better than our last meeting with him."

"It's already really impressive that you managed to secure a meeting with him!" Zoe said, trying to sound encouraging. "Someone like Logan is too important to meet with just anyone who pitches him."

"Or maybe he's just doing it as a favor for Drew Macklemore. But thank God we have Drew's connections—at least he's able to introduce me to the top dogs like Logan Horossen. Meanwhile, Keira White, another one of our board members—I honestly don't know why Drew recommended we bring her on when she doesn't actually know tech."

"I've heard of her!" Zoe said of the former supermodel turned philanthropist, who had once turned down *Chic*'s invitation to be their cover model. "Didn't she found that nonprofit, A Perfect 10, to encourage girls to code?"

Bill snorted. "She told me once that when her business adviser suggested the name, she didn't understand at first it was a reference to binary code. Just because she's funding a charity kind of related to tech doesn't mean she actually understands what we're trying to do. She's just a pretty face who was lucky enough to marry a tech genius and got half his fortune when they divorced, and now she throws money at causes like A Perfect 10 to repair her gold-digger reputation. I bet Drew only recommended her because it looks good to have a female board member these days, especially since we deal with fashion. And I bet she accepted the board invitation so she can make herself seem smarter by associating with legit tech people."

"I think it's a great sign that Logan wants to meet you twice," Zoe said, keen to change the subject to something more pleasant. "It means he genuinely believes in FitPick's potential."

"I sure hope so!" Bill said, looking marginally more cheerful as he turned away from the framed photo. "That's why I hired you, so that I can show Logan Horossen I am taking his advice to heart when I meet with him again once he's back from the desert."

"Is he going to another festival?"

"Nah, he's in a bunker somewhere, training for his space expedition. Didn't you hear—he's joining Elon Musk on his space shuttle to go to Mars in 2026? Oh, and Zoe?"

"Yeah?"

"It's considered pretty disrespectful to call someone as important as Logan Horossen by their first name only. You don't hear anyone saying Steve or Mark, do you? It's always Steve Jobs, Mark Zuckerberg." Bill held up his hands. "I don't have a problem with you calling them whatever you want. But thought I should let you know in case you do that in front of someone else and they aren't as nice about it as I am."

Zoe forced a smile onto her face. There were still so many hard and soft rules about Silicon Valley that she had to learn. "Right."

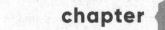

chapter 7

THE SPOT TWO chairs down from Bill's was much more austere in decor. Besides a giant monitor looming over a compact ThinkPad laptop, a Kleenex box that looked untouched, and a stationery holder that contained a lone stylus, there was only one personal artifact. A framed photo of a woman with a tidy black bob and perfectly painted lips, eyes crinkled in the corners as she smiled, her arm around the broad shoulders of a man with cropped black hair.

"She's out right now at an offsite meeting with a potential investor," Bill explained. "But she'll be back at noon."

The "she" in question was Lillian Mariko, FitPick's chief operating officer, as Zoe had gleaned from combing through the company website. A quick Google search had turned up no social media presence for the thirty-one-year-old COO except an extensive LinkedIn profile. Lillian Mariko had graduated from Stanford University with a 4.3 GPA in computer science, scoring internships at Facebook, Tesla, and Google in the summers before her sophomore, junior, and senior years, respectively. After graduation, she'd become a product manager at Google, securing a string of quick promotions until she ascended to senior director in just seven years, at which point she'd jumped ship to FitPick.

Zoe smiled. "I'm really excited to meet her." FitPick's website had revealed that Lillian was the only other woman on the team. It was rather daunting going from the female-dominated environment at *Chic* to the tech industry, but at least having Lillian around meant having a friend she could gabble about clothes and exchange style tips with and bum tampons off if necessary.

"Good, because your spot is right next to hers." Bill patted an empty station at the long desk. "Oh, and even better: You get a direct view of our mascot."

It was then that Zoe noticed the naked full-length mannequin in one corner. Bill beamed fondly at it. "It's Louise on Tuesdays and Thursdays, and Luka on Mondays, Wednesdays, and Fridays, because we believe in gender equality. And," he said loudly as Zoe opened her mouth, "before you ask how is it equal when it's a two-three split, that's only for this month. Next month, we switch the days."

Zoe nodded, hoping she seemed impressed that there would be a faceless figure staring at her every minute while she was at work. A mannequin looked a lot creepier when it wasn't dressed in designer clothing like the ones strewn over *Chic*'s office. She quickly dragged her eyes away from Luka's soulless ones.

"So this is where the business side of our team sits, and"—Bill led Zoe to the other end of the long table—"here is where the engineering side sits." Even if Bill hadn't said so, the giant split-screen monitors were a dead giveaway, as were the fancy keyboards, strange-looking mouses, and the pair of Bose headphones hanging over the corner of one monitor. Two black Hydro Flasks stood side by side, identical except one carried a sticker that read: *My love language is C++*. There was a potted plant that Zoe took a moment to realize was made of Lego. And right next to it was a glass figurine shaped like a lightning bolt and emblazoned with the word "Tesla." Someone had put a string of fairy lights into it.

"Is that a Tesla paperweight?" Zoe asked.

Bill looked to see what she was pointing at. "Nah, that's Bram's Tesla Tequila bottle. Bram's one of our two app developers, by the way, and vice president of product design. The other being Austin, vice president of software engineering. They tend to come in around noon."

"You're okay with them starting work late?" Zoe asked cautiously.

"Engineers tend to be night owls, so they start work later but also end work later. And here in Silicon Valley, we don't care about the traditional nine-to-five. People are productive at different times of the day and they should do what works best for them. So if you want to come in later or leave earlier for a Barry's class or whatever, be my guest. All's cool with me as long as you meet your deadlines."

"Oh wow." The work hours sounded much more stable than what she had at *Chic*, where she had once woken up at 3 a.m. to manage a photo shoot on the Brooklyn Bridge and then got back home only at 1 a.m. the next day after covering a store opening that night for the magazine. But as much as she appreciated the flexibility, Zoe doubted she would actually take Bill up on his offer to come in late. After years of waking up at seven so she could reach the office earliest to snag the only computer in the junior employees section with decent internet speed, she couldn't fathom just rolling out of bed and casually strolling into the office at lunchtime.

"Bram and Austin report to Damien, the chief technology officer. Absolute wizard—a find of Lillian's. Oh, speak of the devil. Damien, come over here! There's someone I want you to meet."

Zoe turned around to where Bill was gesturing. It took her a few moments to recognize the tall figure walking toward them. *Goddamn.* Damien Scott's website photo had done him no justice at all.

About six feet tall, he sported a buzzcut that was just beginning to grow out, giving Zoe the urge to run her fingers over his scalp. There was something vaguely East Asian about his features, but it was his chin that caught her eye—she had always had a weakness for strong chins with a cleft. It looked even better with the sprinkling of dark stubble that covered it.

Zoe tucked her long hair behind her right ear as Damien walked over, his lanky frame clad in a flannel shirt and a black messenger bag slung across his chest. "Nice to meet you," she chirped. "I'm Zoe."

His face expressionless, Damien nodded. Just a single up-and-down motion of his head. Another beat of silence passed before he grunted, "Hi."

Damien had what Bjorn would call "erotic vocals"—low and gruff, with a hint of gravel underlying it. But Zoe had to fight to keep her expression from faltering. Would it kill him to say a full sentence?

She continued smiling at him as he stared back at her, his eyes roaming over her face. Until he said, "You're standing in front of my desk."

Oh. "Sorry!" she squeaked, scrambling out of his way as her face heated up. *Way to make a first impression, Zoe.* Desperate to change the subject, her eyes flitted around the room, finally landing on Damien's desk as he sat down. Lined up beneath his monitor was a row of paper cranes in different shades of pastel. Those delicate paper figurines seemed so incongruous with Damien's big hands.

"Are you into origami?" Zoe asked.

"Yes." A beat of silence passed, with both Zoe and Bill staring at Damien. Begrudgingly, he added, "Folding paper is calming and helps me think."

"He can go through a hundred pieces of origami paper in a week," Bill chimed in, beaming at Damien. "This man's a thinker."

Wordlessly, Damien turned on his computer, the black screen instantly giving way to the default Microsoft wallpaper. Zoe sent the universe a silent note of thanks that she hadn't bothered to change her FitPick laptop's screensaver yet. She wondered what Damien would make of the cluttered collage of photos with Bjorn and Cassie that was her *Chic* computer wallpaper.

Damien pointedly looked up at Bill and Zoe, then back at his computer screen. Bill got the hint. "Zoe, let's continue your tour! Right this way."

With Bill leading the way, they breezed past The Nook—a rest area of sorts with two sleeping pods. Zoe couldn't help but gape as she took in everything. Forget sleeping pods; at *Chic*, their office was a coworking space shared with another magazine, and between the two publications, there were enough PR packages and shoe boxes and clothes bags piled up to violate every fire hazard regulation.

From the corner of her eye, Zoe saw Bill wave his hand. "Lillian! Come meet our new FitPicker!"

Instinctively, Zoe straightened up and smoothed down the pleats of her dress as a woman stepped through FitPick's office entrance and walked toward them, a black structured tote purse of indiscriminate brand dangling from the crook of her right arm. Lillian Mariko, FitPick's chief operating officer, wore a black turtleneck tucked into gray cigarette pants and plain black flats. Her hair was pulled back into an unfussy ponytail and she sported no accessories as far as Zoe could tell. As Lillian neared, Zoe couldn't decide whether the other woman had fully mastered the art of the no-makeup makeup look or wasn't wearing any makeup at all. Either way, she was the epitome of corporate chic.

Smiling brightly, Zoe held out a hand. "Hi! It's wonderful to meet you at last. I'm Zoe."

Lillian's eyes fell on the tasseled laces of Zoe's heels. "Hey," she said, her right brow rising slightly. "Your outfit's so . . . vibrant. How did you manage to drive in those?"

"Oh, I took the bus today." Zoe laughed. "I've never learned how to drive. There was never really a good reason to in New York, since my legs and the train would bring me to most places." Cassie had coined the phrase "No sober Ubers" for their trio, insisting that the only time they were permitted to shell out their hard-earned money for a cab ride was if it was too late to take the train safely and they were too drunk to walk home after a wild night out.

"Oh. That's very eco-friendly, but the public transit here is really unreliable. You live pretty near our office, right? Maybe you could try biking instead."

"Maybe," Zoe said doubtfully. That would mean giving up all her high heels and long skirts. She shuddered as an image popped into her mind of the hem of her favorite flapper-like slip dress getting caught in the bike chain.

Bill clapped one hand on Zoe's shoulder and the other on

Lillian's, looking between the two of them like a proud patriarch. "Zoe, I'm going to leave you in Lillian's capable hands. Gotta run. I have a coffee chat with a potential investor."

Zoe gave Lillian a bigger smile as Bill sped away. So what if the introduction had been a little awkward? They would have plenty of time to get to know each other. "I love your turtleneck! It's very Steve Jobs–chic."

Lillian looked blankly at her as though she couldn't decide if that had been a compliment. "Thanks, but I chose it for convenience, not chic-ness." She pronounced "chic-ness" the way Bjorn would say someone was "nice." "I wear turtlenecks every day to save myself from having to spend any energy on deciding what to wear so I can focus on work."

"That's smart," Zoe said, even as question marks danced through her head. Wasn't this a little ironic for the COO of a company whose app was about promoting outfit diversity? And wasn't the most fun part of fashion the outfit planning? Some of her best memories in New York were going to Cassie's apartment so they could get dressed for events together—her holding up different pairings of tops and bottoms to her body so Cassie could offer her critique, then returning the favor for her friend. Discovering new, better clothing combinations was infinitely more interesting than settling for a default.

Zoe cleared her throat. "Anyway, I can't wait to dive in. What should we cover first?"

Lillian set her purse down on the table. "I haven't had time to plan your onboarding yet. I didn't even know we had a vice president of marketing role until Bill remembered to tell me two days ago that he brought you on to help improve our brand image and impress Logan Horossen."

Zoe's smile faded. What did it say about her or her new job that Bill hadn't bothered to inform the other FitPickers when she'd accepted the job two weeks ago?

Lillian let out a small sigh. "Damien." She waited until the CTO looked up before continuing, "Why don't you get Zoe up to speed on our technology? She's doing marketing, but it would be good for her to know more about the tech behind the app. After all, we're a tech startup; what would help us succeed is GitHub, not . . . Gucci."

As Damien nodded, Zoe made a mental note to look up GitHub on Google later. The term sounded familiar—she'd probably come across it in the book *How to Speak Tech*, which she'd speed-read last week to prepare for her big career switch. But regardless of what GitHub was, wouldn't Gucci be just as important for a *fashion* tech startup?

Lillian, who seemed very used to Damien's economical communication, gave a nod of her own. "Good. I need to run. Zoe, I'll schedule a one-on-one for us to catch up at the end of this week. Hope you and Damien have a good discussion."

Lillian was already ten feet away by the time Zoe registered her words. *Wait, that's it?* It was like someone had just doused her in cold water. She fingered her tangle of necklaces, suddenly feeling like a kid playing too hard at dressing like an adult and still getting everything wrong. She knew work at FitPick would be fast-paced and they wouldn't be standing around all day making flowery small talk. But she'd figured they might take half an hour or so to get to know one another better over coffee, perhaps discuss their favorite fashion brands. But Bill had passed her off to Lillian, and now Lillian had passed her off to Damien, as though she was some pest no one wanted to handle.

Damien stood up. "Are you free now?" he asked. "I have a meeting with the engineering contractors in forty-five minutes, but that should be enough time for us to cover the fundamentals."

Zoe pulled her coat tighter around herself, a familiar smell wafting off the wool. Back in her New York apartment, because she had no space to store her outerwear but in a cabinet right above the stove, there was always a tinge of smokiness to her clothes that she could never entirely cover despite placing lavender-scented sachets (a thoughtful gift from Cassie) in the cabinet.

But now, as the faint mix of lavender and smoke drifted to her nose, Zoe felt a little spark burst into life within her. Made her stand up straighter, lift her head higher, look her new co-worker in the eye.

If she could survive the brutal fashion industry in New York, she could do anything.

Meeting Damien's gaze, Zoe smiled. "Yup, I'm ready."

chapter 8

ORTY-FIVE MINUTES LATER, Zoe walked out of FitPick's conference room, her head swimming with tech jargon and startup lingo. Damien had stayed back in The Rook to take his meeting, and Bill and Lillian were still gone when she arrived back at The Hook. But there were two new men sitting in the engineering section—one white and one Indian.

The Indian man closer to Zoe had a pair of Bose headphones clamped snugly over his ears, blaring EDM music so loud that Zoe could hear it from a foot away.

She summoned the last dregs of her energy. "Hi, I'm Zoe."

The man remained staring at his monitor, his finger tapping against the desk to the beat of the music.

She stepped closer and raised her voice. "Hi! Hello! Can you hear me?" Still, no response.

Finally, she reached forward and touched his shoulder. The man jumped so sharply that he nearly upended his cup of black coffee. "Jesus! What did you do that for?" He looked at her warily. "Are you a new employee at Dreamcatcher? They are on the other side of this floor. Just follow the trail of crystals."

"Oh, no. I'm Zoe, Zoe Zeng. The new VP of marketing."

The man scrunched up his face. "Oh, right. Bill mentioned something about that last Friday." He narrowed his eyes. "Um, so what would you be doing exactly?"

Before Zoe could answer, the other man raised his head and chimed in, "Dude, you have the manners of a barbarian." He stood up and extended his hand to Zoe with a flourish, giving her a firm handshake. He had a cheerful voice and twinkly brown eyes that made Zoe warm to him immediately. "I'm Austin, VP of software engineering. And this is Bram, VP of product design."

Zoe smiled for what felt like the millionth time that day, her cheek muscles basically calcified by this point. "Nice to meet you both. And marketing—well, it's . . . making FitPick seem more fashionable before our second pitch meeting with Logan Horossen in three months."

Austin and Bram exchanged a look that Zoe couldn't quite decipher. "We've never had any marketing folks here," Bram said after a moment. "I don't think Lillian believes in paying for ads. She believes in good old-fashioned word-of-mouth publicity because a great product should speak for itself."

Zoe's stomach sank. She really had her work cut out for her here if the second most senior person at the company didn't think she should even be here. As a strained silence reverberated around the room, Austin looked like he didn't know whether to punch Bram or disappear through the floor from secondhand embarrassment.

Bram looked between Zoe and Austin. "What? Was it something I said?" At that, Austin clapped a hand to his face and groaned, which only deepened Bram's bewildered expression. "Austin, can you not communicate like a normal human being?"

"*I* can't communicate? Do you even hear half the things that come out of your mouth?"

Sensing Bram gearing up for a snippy retort, Zoe jumped in. "So," she said brightly, "How long have you two been working together?"

"Just slightly over a year—" Austin began saying.

"But every day feels like a drag with this guy," Bram interrupted. "So it feels way longer."

Austin shot him a look. "What Bram means is that we've actually known each other a lot longer. We met at a coding boot camp when we were in high school."

A memory stirred in Zoe's mind. The first Friday afternoon every quarter at *Chic* was always Fashion Boot Camp. Everyone would gather in the biggest conference room, and any employee could go up to give a presentation on anything related to fashion. It had taken Zoe six months before she finally mustered the courage to volunteer, delivering a presentation about the symbolism of boots in Hollywood chick flicks that was titled "Putting the Boot in Boot Camp." The whole room—even Francesca Fraatz—had burst into laughter and it was the first time she'd felt in on the joke.

"We didn't come from the same high school, but it was a boot camp for high schoolers," Bram clarified. "And we didn't get along. At all. He was the programming prodigy who coded his own game when he was six, took college-level computer science classes in elementary school, and enrolled at MIT when he was only sixteen—"

"And meanwhile, Bram was the classic self-taught programmer who thought he knew it all just because he could solve all the problems on LeetCode and looked down on those of us who went to school for 'playing it safe' and not 'thinking outside of the box'," Austin retorted.

Bram rolled his eyes. "There you go again thinking you're so much better, just because you know the x86 assembly language."

"And there *you* go again thinking you're so much cooler just because you can code in Rust, which everyone with half a brain cell knows is a language that's all hype but no substance."

"*Okay,*" Zoe cut in, raising her voice to be heard above men's squabble. "So you two met in high school and somehow ended up working for the same startup years later. How did that happen?"

Austin at least had the decency to look slightly ashamed of their bickering. He straightened his polo shirt. "I was fired from my last job," he said with dignity.

Zoe winced. "I'm sorry."

Austin chuckled. "It's actually a funny story. So, I was working at another startup as a software engineer, and one day I got bored and made a program that tracked the takeoffs and arrivals of all registered private planes. Pretty silly, right? But I linked the program to Twitter and my account would broadcast the flights of planes owned by celebrities. And that was how the wife of a certain billionaire discovered he was flying to Portugal a lot even though he has no business there. Turns out he was keeping a mistress in Madeira."

"Wait . . ." Zoe said slowly. "Is that Keira White—"

"And her ex-husband, Malcolm? Yup." Austin rubbed his hands gleefully. "Malcolm lost his shit and got me fired. But then Keira took a shine to me—she was already on FitPick's board then—and told Bill to check me out. That's how I ended up here. Then a few months later, I saw Bram's Facebook post saying he was looking for a new job, so obviously I took pity on him and gave him a referral."

"Oh please," Bram scoffed. "You're just afraid you can't handle the work and need me to come clean up your mess."

"Nah. I just wanted that fat referral bonus."

Zoe looked down to hide her twitching mouth. There was something so endearingly familiar about this scene unfolding in front of her. For a moment, it almost felt like she was back at the *Chic* office with Bjorn and Cassie, listening to them argue about whether ghosting men on dating apps was self-love or selfish. Maybe, just maybe, she could find something like that in Silicon Valley too.

FOR WHAT FELT LIKE THE DOZENTH TIME IN FIVE MINUTES, ZOE'S eyes darted to the time display on her computer. It was already almost seven, so why was everyone still at their desk, click-clacking away at their keyboards? What happened to leaving at 5 p.m. for Pilates?

Zoe reached over to tap Bram on his shoulder. He turned around, lifted one side of the headphones away from his ear, and raised an eyebrow, *Yes?*

"Um, just checking, working hours are from nine to six, right?"

"Technically, yeah."

Technically? "So why's everyone still around? Is there a big launch coming up or something?"

"Nah. But FitPick provides free dinner and also comps your cab fare home if you work past eight. If we aren't here, we'll just be working at home anyway, so might as well get a free meal and ride." Bram glanced at his own computer's time display, then did a little fist pump. "Only forty minutes to go."

Zoe stifled a sigh and leaned back in her chair. She'd been hoping her coworkers would leave soon so she could catch Cassie and Bjorn at a lull during their Tiffany and Co. event and give them an office tour over FaceTime. Bill said the working hours were flexible, but it didn't seem like the work-life balance here was any better than at *Chic*. Still, the comped dinner and cab fare at least counted for something, much better than when she had to shell out exorbitant amounts for a late-night Uber after a particularly long day at work because she didn't feel safe taking the subway home alone at 1 a.m.

Zoe turned her computer off and began shoveling her belongings into her tote. "I think I'll head home now." There was still a mountain of boxes she had to unpack.

Bram's eyes darted again to his computer's time display, then back to Zoe. Even though he said nothing, Zoe felt her face warm. "It's only my first day anyway, so I don't have much to do right now besides onboarding, and I could just do that at home," she hastened to explain, hearing and hating the defensive note that had crept into her voice. It wasn't like she was committing a crime by leaving an hour *after* the workday was supposed to have ended, so why was she trying to justify herself to him?

The product designer nodded. "Oh, sure. Yeah, I guess marketing is . . . more thinking than actually doing any hands-on work, so you don't have to be in the office for that. See ya tomorrow." With that, Bram snapped his headphones back into place and turned back to his own work.

For a few moments, Zoe simply sat still and stared at him. Did he think she was lazy just because she wasn't staying until eight like everyone else was? If only he knew about all those times at *Chic* when she had crawled home past midnight because they were closing an issue or there was some industry event she had to cover. And when New York Fashion Week rolled around—what even was sleep anymore? She would be out and about so much that her feet would be a blistered mess by the time fashion shows moved on to London (which *Chic* didn't have the budget to send her to).

Instead, Zoe just muttered a quick farewell that Bram didn't hear, before making a swift escape out of the office. As she walked out the doors and into the still, silent night, the rhythmic sound of fingers pounding keyboards ringing behind her, no one stopped her to say goodbye.

chapter 9

BACK AT *CHIC*, everyone took the term "fashionably late" extremely seriously. Bjorn, in particular, was a serial offender, arriving perpetually late for their weekly 9:30 a.m. all-hands because he "simply *had* to pop into Starbucks for an Americano first." And God forbid anyone *rush* to be on time—Chanel Mary Janes were not made for pounding the pavement.

But if there was anything Zoe had learned from her first day at FitPick, it was that nothing worked the same way it did at *Chic*. So at exactly five minutes to nine on Tuesday, Zoe gathered her things and made her way to The Rook for her first-ever biweekly company meeting.

Last night at 11:27 p.m. (when did the woman even sleep?), Lillian had emailed them all with the meeting agenda, but this was the first time Zoe had seen a meeting adhere so strictly to its schedule. Bill opened with a quick summary of recent meetings with prospective investors (sadly, no positive updates), before giving the floor to Lillian, who walked them through the app's privacy policy updates. Austin's debrief about his debugging sessions was even more succinct.

"Nice work, team. We have made big strides in our app development over the past few months," Bill announced. "And Zoe is here to make sure more people, especially Logan Horossen, know about what we've been doing. Zoe, over to you." He swept one hand out toward her.

Her legs shaking, Zoe got to her feet. At *Chic*, one of her proudest works had been a retrospective of the power suit and how modern women were redefining the concept of #girlboss dressing. *Structured lines*, *head-to-toe cohesion*, and *statement jewelry* were just a few of the tips she had offered in the article on how to power dress. So for this meeting, she'd decided to practice what she preached. A floral Veronica Beard blazer over a silk jumpsuit, a pair of pointy Sergio Rossi heels whose four-inch height gave her an extra boost of confidence, topped off with her favorite statement accessory: a metallic vintage Ann Demeulemeester bib necklace. Power dressing with a Zoe Zeng spin.

Squashing down her nerves, Zoe summoned her brightest smile. "Hi, I just want to say again how thrilled I am to be working with you all. My greatest passion in life is fashion, and I'm so excited to be combining that with tech. FitPick is a product I strongly believe in, and like Bill said, I'm here to make sure more people believe in it too."

"Zoe, not to put you on the spot or anything," Bill said, "but you mentioned you have some great marketing ideas inspired by your fashion background?"

Zoe swallowed. There was a rustle as her coworkers shifted into more comfortable positions, all eyes fixed on her. "My ideas, right. Well, um, like any social media platform where personal photos are shared, there's a high likelihood that users will be editing what they post. And I just think, you know, that's really bad for mental health. There's a whole bunch of studies that show that—"

"Yes, we all know the criticism against Instagram. But we *aren't* like Instagram," Bill interrupted. "What's the point of people posting edited photos on FitPick? That's not going to show how the clothes look on them in real life—which is what they are interested in getting feedback on."

"Precisely! So I was thinking maybe we could add in a feature that would flag if a photo has been manipulated. That would encourage users to not do that."

Lillian raised her pen. "But why do we need a flagging feature when, as Bill just said, it's unlikely users will be editing their photos in the first place?"

"People on dating apps edit their photos all the time even though they know they will be seen in real life," Zoe said. If there was one thing she knew from years spent in the fashion industry, it was how closely people scrutinized their appearance—and their single-minded desire to buff away any self-perceived flaws like coffee stains on a table. The *Chic* office had a Wall of Shame that featured Photoshop fails from their magazine competitors; they had to take down the photos every fortnight to make space for new ones.

"That's just how photo-sharing sites work," she continued. "If people are going to be uploading their photos, they will feel the pressure to look a certain way. Especially when they see photos uploaded by other users. They might even think people would be likelier to click on their photos and check out their polls if they fit a certain standard of beauty. I like how FitPick wants to democratize fashion, and I think we should start with democratizing the beauty standards upheld by users of our app."

Zoe held her breath as silence fell upon the room. Beads of sweat started gathering under her arms at the sight of Bill's furrowed brows, the thin line of Lillian's mouth, the look being exchanged between Austin and Bram like a neon sign screaming out the words: *What is she doing here?* Her Veronica Beard blazer suddenly felt two sizes too small.

"I think it wouldn't be hard to implement a feature like that," Damien said suddenly, leaning forward and resting his elbows on his knees. "Might take a few weeks to test and iterate, but straightforward enough."

"Yes, it can be done," Lillian conceded with a frown. "But we already have a list of features planned for our product road map that we need to prioritize for this quarter. This flagging feature won't help us attract new users; it's an unnecessary detail that will only make us seem too uptight and turn people off."

As Lillian pursed her lips, Zoe switched tack, aiming to appeal to the other woman's highly practical side. "If it were me, I wouldn't keep using an app that makes me feel lousy about myself for not living up to some conventional ideal of beauty. Preventing unrealistic standards from taking over the app can go a long way toward creating a safe space for everyone that will keep them coming back."

Zoe's chest tightened as memories flooded her brain. Of the sales assistant who had shepherded her toward a black dress, telling her sincerely, "Black is a very slimming color." Her college roommate, who had once heaved a long-suffering sigh before saying, "I wish I had your boobs. Mine are so big that men keep hitting on me even though I have a boyfriend." Her mother, who would remind her to stay away from skintight clothes that showed her pooch, which never shrank regardless of how many sit-ups or juice cleanses she did.

Lillian's voice jerked Zoe back to attention. "We can add this to our product road map, but it's a nice-to-have, not a must-have. Given our limited manpower and our *very* long to-do list, we need to focus on making the changes that will *significantly* improve the user experience."

"But—"

"*Oh-kay.*" Bill held up a hand. "We're running out of time here. Zoe, any other ideas?"

Zoe racked her brain, trying to pull together the ideas she had been mulling over for the past week. But beneath Lillian's assessing eyes and the FitPickers' blank stares, her brain felt as holey as a Balenciaga chain mail dress, all her threads of thought leaking out before they could be strung into a cohesive whole.

She reached up to finger the bib necklace that covered almost her entire décolletage, the chill of the metal giving her a jolt of fresh confidence. Zoe took a deep breath. There was a reason she had worn the statement accessory in the first place—she had a statement to deliver and she was doing so today, regardless of whether Lillian liked it or not.

"Another idea I have is to establish partnerships with a few fashion influencers—get them to use our app and share their FitPick polls to social media to attract their followers' attention. And instead of using the typical influencer, I think it will be better to engage micro-influencers who occupy narrower niches, like Primrose van Harper, who's known for their cottagecore dresses, and Ishani Chandra, who has the most amazing collection of saris." Zoe's voice grew stronger as the names and sartorial lingo rolled off her tongue. This, at last, was a language she spoke fluently. "That will show the public that there's a place for everyone's fashion sense on FitPick, as opposed to the typical Brandy Melville basic style that is all over Instagram and Pinterest these days."

There was a long moment of silence, then Bill asked, "What's cottagecore?"

"Uh, something soft and—"

"Won't it be better to hire celebrities instead?" Austin interrupted. "I've never even heard of any of those women before."

Bram rolled his eyes. "That's because all you do is code and go on Reddit."

Zoe looked straight at Austin. "They might not be Kardashian-level famous but they are all style icons. Primrose van Harper isn't a woman actually, and they've done a lot in spotlighting the non-binary community in the fashion industry."

"You know them because you worked in fashion," Austin said. "But we haven't, and neither have most of FitPick's target users. If we're going to do a celebrity campaign, I say we go with someone like . . . Kylie Jenner."

"But the whole point is to not use someone already super famous," Zoe countered, but her words were drowned out as Bram shouted across the table.

"Dude, do you think Kylie Jenner's going to be dropping by our office to shoot her lingerie posts or something?"

Austin crossed his arms, his face pulled into a long-suffering expression. "Bram, for once can you just get your mind out of the gutter?" he snapped. "I'm only trying to help Zoe brainstorm here."

"It's so obvious that you aren't thinking with your head but with your—"

Zoe shot Bill a helpless look. How had she managed to lose control of the situation so quickly? Austin and Bram were now lobbing insults at each other across the table, and the ideas she'd painstakingly worked on for the past two weeks were now buried beneath the colorful names flying around the room.

Catching her pleading gaze, Bill clapped his hands together

loudly. "Okay, enough. Let's move on. Zoe, thanks for sharing your ideas. Next, we have Damien to take us through . . ."

No one reached over to pat her on the back or whisper "good job" as she slunk back to her seat, feeling like she had lead weights on her feet instead of strappy stilettoes. The room was quiet as Damien spoke, everyone hanging on to his every word, their heads bobbing in unison to the stream of unfamiliar terms pouring out of his mouth. Even Bram was so busy taking notes that the tip of his tongue stuck slightly out of his mouth as his pen flew across his notebook.

Would she ever get to a stage where she could command attention and respect as effortlessly as he did? Was that something she could gain through experience, or was it an innate quality that people like Bill, Lillian, and Damien possessed, and that she didn't?

"All right, back to work, everyone!" Bill announced as Damien wrapped up at nine-thirty on the dot. The Rook bustled with activity as everyone snapped their laptops closed and picked up their now empty coffee cups. Zoe nudged her way past Austin and Bram to approach Bill. He was talking to Lillian but their conversation came to an abrupt stop as she neared.

Lillian raised one brow but Bill smiled warmly. "Zoe, congrats on surviving your first FitPick meeting."

Why did she feel like she was closer to sinking than to surviving? But Zoe returned Bill's smile. "Do you both have some time now? I would love to circle back to my proposal about flagging edited photos, but my other idea about partnering with fashion influencers is probably more time-sensitive. It would be good to launch that in time for New York Fashion Week, with fashion influencers using FitPick to get their fans to pick their street-style outfits."

Lillian exhaled deeply and massaged her temple. "Zoe, I didn't want to say anything earlier in front of everyone, but we definitely don't have the budget to hire someone like Kylie Jenner—"

"I never said we should hire Kylie Jenner," Zoe said, trying to keep her voice even. "In fact, she's exactly the kind of person I want to avoid. Many social media influencers basically follow the same Instagram fashion trends, but I want to show the public that FitPick is a safe space for them to explore and experiment with fashion. That's why I want to hire micro-influencers—people who aren't famous-famous but have a very distinctive style. And because they aren't super well known, it won't cost as much to engage them."

"We still don't have the budget for any sort of influencer marketing campaign. Your hire was, uh, quite a surprise," Lillian said diplomatically. "And the budget for this quarter was determined even before you came on." She turned to Bill, her mouth tight at the corners. "Look, you were the one who set our targets for improving image quality and app agility. The budget is stretched thin enough as is and the engineering team needs every dollar of it to have a chance at meeting your targets. We need to be strategic about our priorities."

Zoe swallowed. "Of course, I get that," she said. In front of her eyes, Lillian's face seemed to morph into Francesca Fraatz's. She'd moved across the country, changed industries—to get the same kind of treatment?

Lillian's face softened by the tiniest fraction. "Zoe, it's nothing against your ideas. I think you are very creative and obviously know more about fashion than any of us here. But when we did our budget planning, we didn't account for a new VP coming on board and starting an entire marketing campaign involving third-party spokespeople. Marketing *is* important, but first we have to make sure our product is good enough to justify such pricey marketing. Why don't you start off with SEO marketing and email campaigns before transitioning to more big-budget ideas?"

Search engine optimization? Zoe's fingers dug into her palms. Why did Bill even bother bringing her all the way from the opposite coast to do something that didn't even tap into her fashion expertise? He could have easily found a random person off the Palo Alto streets to write those customer emails.

Her heart sank when Bill nodded. "Zoe, you've only been here for just over a day," he said, not unkindly. "No one's expecting you to jump into the deep end immediately. Maybe book a weekly one-on-one with Damien so he can continue teaching you about the technology you're promoting. Let's regroup next week and talk more about any SEO marketing ideas you have."

Without waiting for a response, Bill clapped his hands together. "Excellent discussion, team. I've got to run to another meeting now."

"And I have an app update to review," Lillian said. "Zoe, talk to Damien about getting set up with Eloqua, our marketing automation platform. You'll need it to send out and track email campaigns. And get him to walk you through how to pull email contacts from our database. Any questions?"

A million of them, but Zoe could tell Lillian's thoughts were already on the app update review. And no matter what she could say, Lillian wouldn't change her mind, so what was the point of harping on it? Zoe forced a smile on her face. "Nope, I'm all good."

THANKFULLY, THE OFFICE restroom was completely empty when Zoe ducked in. She headed straight for one of the cubicles, her shoulders relaxing once the door clicked shut behind her. She loosened the sash of her dress, feeling her stomach expand as she inhaled deeply. The sharp scent of Clorox disinfectant hit her nostrils like a truck and a dull ache throbbed in her jaw—no doubt from how hard she worked to swallow her protests.

Zoe wasn't a stranger to the bathroom hideout. She and Cassie would often meet up in *Chic*'s, exchanging office gossip or comments on male model sightings beneath the potpourri air freshener and the lingering traces of their coworkers' perfumes. But a bathroom *escape*—on the second day no less—was something else altogether.

She stiffened as two pairs of footsteps entered the restroom. Next came the sound of running water and the rustle of paper towels being pulled from the dispenser.

A man's voice broke the silence. "Did you see her face?"

Zoe's head jerked up. It was Bram speaking! She then remembered Bill had told her that the building's restrooms—shared among the four startups—were all unisex. Which gorgeous woman was Bram crushing on now?

"Stop yakking away and help me clean up the mess you made," came Austin's voice.

"Dude, your shirt's so lame that the coffee I spilled on it only made it more interesting." More paper rustling. "But did you see her expression when Lillian said that?" Bram asked a moment later.

Zoe's mouth dried. The "her" wasn't about some gorgeous woman after all.

"Yeah, I felt bad for her. But she seems kinda naive if she didn't expect Lillian to respond like that."

"I don't think she even gets what we are trying to do at FitPick."

Although she was alone in the restroom cubicle, Zoe drew her shoulders up around her ears and hunched over, wanting to make herself as small as possible. Just a few steps away, her co-workers were talking about *her*. No, not just talking, but *criticizing*.

"Well, she doesn't. What?" Bram exclaimed over the bellows of the hand dryer—Austin must have just shot him a look. "You've seen her resume too. She studied *fashion merchandising*. While we were grinding over code, she was going to fashion parties. And then she comes here and acts like she knows the app so much better than the rest of us even though *we* are the ones who have been working on it for over a year."

The hand dryer stopped. Austin's next words seemed to fill up the entire restroom: "She did seem kinda know-it-all, preaching to us about beauty standards and mental health."

There was a dangerous prickling of wetness at the corners of

Zoe's eyes. While Bram had seemed snarky even when she first met him, she'd thought Austin looked kind. But here he was, barely a day later, saying these things behind her back.

"Maybe that fake-woke mumbo jumbo worked on her magazine readers," Bram said, "but tech is the *real* stuff and it's obvious she doesn't know shit about it. How did she even get hired?"

An audible sigh rang out from Austin. "I heard Bill met her at some party and hired her on the spot. Didn't even bother to interview her or check her qualifications or anything."

"She's probably one of those founder-hounders," Bram snorted. "Trust Bill to fall for a pretty face and now we're the ones stuck working with her."

"Yeah, I don't see how she can help us impress Logan Horossen and get his investment."

"It will be a miracle if she doesn't set us back further. Dude, are you done yet?"

"You're the one who spilled coffee on me," Austin huffed. "And it's somehow my fault that I have to clean this stain up?"

"I spilled coffee on you because you bumped into me," Bram retorted. The bathroom door opened again, and their voices grew fainter as they walked out, then finally disappeared as the door blissfully swung shut.

It felt like an eternity had passed before Zoe finally found the energy to stand up, clean herself off, and totter out of the bathroom stall. Her legs were shaking in her high heels. When she went up to the sink, her pale face stared back at her from the mirror, the two spots of blush she had dabbed on that morning standing out in sharp relief. Besides Austin and Bram, did everyone else at FitPick look down on her too? Did Bill regret hiring her?

In a daze, Zoe wandered out of the bathroom, her arms hugged close to her body like a shield. Thankfully, Bram and Austin weren't at their desks when she got back to the office. There was no way she could stand to be near them now, having to pretend everything was all fine and dandy when she now knew what they really thought of her.

"Hey, Bill, can I work from home for the rest of the day?" she asked weakly. "I think I'm coming down with something."

She must have looked as terrible on the outside as she felt on the inside, because Bill didn't even hesitate. "Of course! And don't bother working—just take the whole day off."

Zoe shot Bill a small, grateful smile before quickly gathering up her things and leaving. Even if her coworkers looked down on her, at least her new boss was way better than her old one. Francesca Fraatz once made her stand for hours in the line of an Alexander Wang sample sale to help the *Chic* editor hold a spot. And that was on a wintry November day when she was still getting over a cold.

For the rest of the day, Zoe busied herself with unpacking the rest of her belongings and sprucing up her new home. The hours flew by and it was only around five in the afternoon that she finally took a break to check her phone. There was a text message from Austin.

Heard you weren't feeling well.
Hope you get better soon!

Zoe's hand tightened around her phone. Her new coworkers at FitPick might seem to care about her. But they didn't, really. Not the way her real friends did.

Before she knew it, Zoe found herself pulling up her WhatsApp group chat with Cassie and Bjorn. Some of her melancholy ebbed away at the sight of their group name: *Make throuples chic again!*, followed by three emojis: a dancing girl for Zoe, a nerd for Cass, and a grinning devil for Bjorn. Even if she was all alone at FitPick, at least she could always count on them to have her back even from across the country.

Hey, you guys free to talk? she sent.

A few moments later, an audio message came in from Bjorn. When Zoe played it, she had to strain her ears to catch his slurred words over the thumping beat of music in the background. "Yo, Zee! You're missing the party of the century here. Oof, Cass, stop hitting me!"

A smaller voice chimed in on the message: "Bjorn, you're *so* drunk. Get off the phone now."

Zoe furrowed her brows as the message ended. What was this about a party? How come they hadn't told her they were going to one? And how could Bjorn be partying and drunk at 5 p.m. on a Tuesday night?

Then she remembered: New York was three hours ahead, so it was already nighttime there. It was basically a whole different world.

Her phone dinged with a message.

CASS: Hey, sorry, Bjorn's pretty out of it now. I popped out of the party for a sec. Wanna call?

Gratefully, Zoe dialed Cassie. Her background was much quieter, though when Zoe pressed her phone tight against her ear, she thought she could pick up the faint refrain of Cardi B crooning about being a certified freak.

"Hey! What party are you two at?"

Cassie's voice lowered to a conspiratorial whisper. "Oh my

God, you have to keep this to yourself. Remember when we saw that Hearst Media guy coming out from Francesca's office and thought it was because they were shutting us down?"

"Uh-huh."

"Turns out it's the exact opposite! Apparently some trillion-aire or whatever wants to invest in *Chic*! Isn't that crazy? They just told us the news today, so a bunch of us decided to hit up Balthazar tonight for a spontaneous celebration!"

It took Zoe a few moments to absorb the news. "That's amazing! Congratulations! I'm so happy for you guys." And she meant it. But even as she uttered those words, her heart twisted. If she hadn't accepted the FitPick job, it would have been her at Balthazar with her best friends and *Chic* coworkers, toasting to their magazine's success. She could have continued writing about the topics that Bram and Austin considered "dumb crap" but that she adored.

"Apparently the investor is some Indonesian media magnate who grew up in a small village. He told Francesca he really likes our focus on sustainable style, especially your May issue piece about Southeast Asia's heritage weaving artisans—his grand-mother was one! He wants us to do more human interest stories like that."

Zoe's hand tightened around her phone. Fashion was what she knew best; fashion journalism was what she did best. Her working at a tech startup was almost as unfathomable as Rick Owens designing colorful prints. What made her think it was a good idea to forsake what came so naturally to her?

"And guess what: We'll all get a three-month bonus! Isn't that nuts?"

"It's the least they could give you guys!" But no matter how bright she made her voice, Zoe couldn't quite ignore the niggles of unease squirming through her—was that a flicker of envy she felt?

Cassie giggled. "Oh please, I bet you earn more than our three-month bonus in just one month. Anyway, how are things with you? I can't believe your office has five different flavors of kombucha on tap and literally every single brand of protein bar in your pantry. Seriously, how lucky are you?"

A hollow feeling crept into Zoe. On paper, it seemed like she was working at the dream place, with an undeniably good salary and more office perks than one ever needed—the exact factors that had convinced her to move to Silicon Valley and work at Fit-Pick in the first place. But at this moment, all alone in her apartment after fleeing her office and coworkers, Zoe would have given it all up in a second to return to *Chic*, for a job that might not pay as much but that she knew she could do well, and where people actually liked her.

But how could she bring herself to tell that to Cassie? How could she complain about her six-figure-salary job without sounding completely ungrateful?

So Zoe made her voice breezy as she said, "Yeah, the office is great! Super fun! I've tried four of the kombucha flavors already—I think my favorite is elderberry." She could hear the note of false cheer underlying her words and was thankful Cassie wasn't standing right in front of her, or her best friend would have noticed something amiss immediately.

"I totally knew you would love it there. So, what are your coworkers like?"

Zoe swallowed. "Everyone is really . . . passionate. Super smart and driven." *And they don't think I'm like that at all.*

On the other end of the line, Cassie gave a loud cheer. "But hey"—her voice turned more solemn—"there can only be one work throuple in your life, okay? Tonight, Bjorn and I kept looking over at each other and saying, *If only Zoe were here.* So no matter how cool those FitPickers are, you can't like them more than you like us."

"Trust me, there's no danger of that happening," Zoe said, completely honest for the first time in the entire conversation.

A loud crash rang out from Cassie's end. She let out a muffled curse and shouted, her voice sounding fainter to Zoe, "Bjorn, what the hell! Don't put your glass over the candle!" Then she must have put her phone to her ear again because she sounded clearer as she said, "Zee, sorry, I gotta go. Bjorn is being Berg again," citing the name for Bjorn's drunk alter-ego that she and Zoe had invented two years ago.

Before Zoe could respond, Cassie had already hung up. Zoe tucked her phone back into her skirt pocket and looked around her empty apartment, starkly aware of her solitude, her *otherness*, once more.

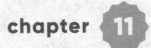

OE? ZOE?"

Zoe startled out of her reverie, her eyes snapping to Damien. Halfway through her second weekly one-on-one with Damien, she'd started thinking about how she could promote her latest FitPick poll—a Thakoon tie-dye sheath pitted against a Mukzin blazer dress—on social media.

"Sorry, you were saying?" She sat up straighter to prove her renewed focus. After all, it was generous of the company's CTO to sit down with her and impart his knowledge.

"I'm sorry my lecture about our tech stack isn't interesting enough for you," Damien said drily.

Her cheeks turned pink. "No, it's interesting! Well, I mean, it's definitely good to know," she amended as he raised a brow. "And you're obviously an expert in this." But that was the thing, wasn't it? It seemed like everyone at the company besides her knew what they were doing and were the best at what they did. Wasn't there the saying that a chain is only as strong as its weakest link? Was she going to be the one to drag the entire FitPick team down and waste their talents?

"Have you always been this sure of what you want to do? Have you ever doubted yourself?" Zoe blurted out.

Before he could answer, she gave a small shake of her head. "Forget it, that was dumb." Just because he was the only one who hadn't shot down her idea yet didn't mean he wanted to deal with her existential crisis. And what if he reported this to Lillian?

Zoe attempted an airy laugh. "Ignore me. I think I just need more coffee or something."

"Yes."

Her flush deepened. "I didn't mean to be like that—"

"No. I mean, I've felt that way before—not knowing if I'm actually doing what I like. Not even knowing what I like."

Zoe's eyes grew round. This was the first time Damien had revealed anything remotely personal about himself. He always seemed so steady and unruffled that it was impossible to imagine him not like that.

Now frowning slightly, he eyed her. "Is that how you feel?"

"Yes, sometimes," Zoe admitted, bolstered by Damien's honesty. A now familiar thrum of anxiety squeezed her insides as her eyes fell upon The Hook: everyone's heads were bent over their laptops, brows furrowed in concentration. She wanted to be among them, but they didn't think she deserved to be. "I don't . . . really know what I'm doing here, to be honest."

Damien's frown deepened. "For your weekly lesson on our technology."

Zoe couldn't help but laugh. "I know *that*. I meant I don't really know what I'm doing at FitPick, in Silicon Valley." One corner of her mouth quirked up. "You know, back in college, when almost everyone took the Intro to Computer Science course to fulfill the tech requirement, I took a class on the history of the sewing machine instead and persuaded my dean that sewing machines were a hallmark of the industrial revolution."

She almost fell out of her chair when Damien shook his head and half smiled. "That's some high-level bullshitting right there."

Zoe's heart began thudding extra fast. Holy shit. Damien Scott just let out a smile because of something *she* said. Well, just barely a smile, but same thing. It added an unexpected softness to his face, making him look much closer to his actual age of twenty-seven than his stoic demeanor would suggest.

Zoe gave a little cough to reset her head. "I just never imagined ending up in the tech industry of all places. I don't even know how to set up my iCloud storage—an ex did that for me. Every day, I wake up feeling completely in over my head."

"It's only your second week here."

"But what if I just don't have what it takes?" Zoe whispered, even though they were the only ones in the room. Lillian Mariko probably had supernatural hearing for confessions of incompetence.

"Everyone else here, including you, studied computer science or engineering, then worked at top tech companies." Her face burned as Bram's voice drifted into her mind, every word laden with derision: *She studied* fashion merchandising. "And yesterday, Austin told me that he used to be a contractor at NASA. NASA! He was working on the next frontier of advancement for humankind while I . . . wrote about DIYing belts from necklaces."

Damien looked straight into her eyes. "Firstly, there's nothing wrong with writing about accessories if that's your passion. And secondly, you've written about plenty of other stuff too. Your series on how transgender people use fashion to explore their gender identities was interesting."

Zoe swallowed. "You . . . you read my articles?" The thought that Damien had gone searching up her past, getting a glimpse of the Zoe pre-FitPick—the Zoe who had been so in her element and nothing like the bumbling mess she was now—made her feel even more exposed than the time she wore a Versace leather top slashed to the navel. Even though her time at *Chic* had only ended a few weeks ago, it already felt like it was from a different lifetime altogether.

Damien shrugged. "Just doing my due diligence on my co-worker."

Oh. A strange twinge of disappointment darted through her. *Coworker, right.* Zoe cleared her throat. "It's not that I'm embarrassed of my fashion articles." On the contrary, she took great pride in pitching stories and seeing them through. There had been a stretch last year when she produced *Chic*'s most-read article for four months in a row. "It's just—that doesn't fit into my life here."

"It sounds like you really loved your previous job, so why did you leave it?"

"One, because I didn't like the direction the magazine was headed in. And two, well"—she hesitated—"because of money." Zoe shook her head and laughed. "I sound like a sellout, don't I?"

Frustratingly, Damien's expression didn't change. "What do you mean?"

"After years of unpaid internships, I thought I was prepared for how tough working in the fashion publishing industry would be. I was ready to grit my teeth and slowly work my way up the ladder, but my student loans still aren't going down after a few years and my parents aren't getting any younger. What if I never make my way to the top of the ladder and can't repay my parents for everything they've done for me? They supported my dreams to become a fashion writer and it's supposed to be my turn to support them now. I want to buy them a house and a car and send them on nice vacations, but I can't even do that for myself." She bit her lip. "I miss working in fashion, but how happy my parents looked when I bought them a new TV with my FitPick signing bonus—that means so much."

Zoe broke off, a lump swelling in her throat as she caught the rawness in her words, the naked emotion in her voice. A chill ran over her skin and she pulled her cardigan sleeves down over her hands before forcing herself to meet Damien's gaze. Her breath snagged at the sight of an unfamiliar softness flickering in his eyes.

"I think it's admirable that you want to do so much for your parents," he said quietly.

"They never asked that of me," Zoe hastened to add. Even Cassie and Bjorn—the two people she trusted most—had been mystified when she admitted after too many mojitos at happy hour once that what she wanted above all else, even more than a limited-edition Moncler x Craig Green parka, was to give her parents everything they wanted. Even if her Ma and Ba would never dream of asking her to do so. To her best friends, it was the parents' job to care for the kids up until the child turned eighteen, at which point everyone would lead largely financially independent lives; Cassie even still Venmo-requested her mother's share when they went out to brunch together. "My parents always said they would be happy as long as I'm doing what makes me happy."

But with a pang, Zoe recalled how her parents had only started humble-bragging about her to their relatives and friends after she accepted the FitPick job. They photocopied every *Chic* article she had ever written and even framed a photo from the *DailyMail* where she had been snapped at a fashion show (Ma had put masking tape over the cleavage of the model posing next to Zoe). However, no matter how supportive they were of her fashion career, that was ultimately an industry they did not understand. *Vogue* meant nothing to them, but Silicon Valley, technology, and six-figure paychecks—that was a language they understood very well.

"I understand what you mean," Damien said, never taking his eyes off her. "I wish—" His voice was pressed low, but there was a hint of wistfulness running through it that caused Zoe to lean forward, wondering if she had imagined it. "Back in college, I actually wanted to become a writer, but my mom said I could never make a career out of it. So I decided to follow what she said—after college, instead of going to Northwestern to get an MFA, I found a job at Microsoft, and now I'm here. And I don't hate tech; I like it very much, actually, and I'm lucky that I'm good at it. But it's just . . . I'm not sure it's what I would have chosen for myself."

He scuffed a hand over his head, leaving his hair sticking up in tufts that made Zoe itch to smooth them back. "Still, I know my mom's just looking out for me—after my parents' separation, I lived with her and our financial situation was . . . tricky. So financial security has always been top of mind for her."

Zoe stared at him, something soft and warm stirring in the depths of her chest. In him, there was that same odd mix of distance and protectiveness toward his parents that she felt toward her own. The same awareness that he and his mother were from different generations with different outlooks, but also the same desire to put her happiness first, the same willingness to defend her against outsiders and not hear any criticism against her—even if it was on his behalf.

"You sound really close to your mom."

"We are." His eyes crinkled at the corners, the fondness in his voice undeniable. "After my dad left, I actually wanted to take her last name. But she convinced me to keep his—she thought people would take me more seriously at work if I had a white last name."

"Your mom isn't white?"

"Nope, Chinese."

So that explained the vaguely Asian curve to his features that Zoe couldn't quite put her finger on previously. "That sucks—that people would respect you more if they think you're white."

He shrugged. "You'd think that the industry that claims to be pushing mankind forward would be more progressive, but no. Big tech is just like every other industry."

Memories long buried resurfaced in Zoe's mind. The one time a couple of models on a photo shoot started pulling back the corners of their eyes to show off their best fox-eye looks. The time she had shown up to a New York Fashion Week event and a photographer had given her a once-over and said none-too-quietly, "I thought Asian chicks are supposed to be skinny." The time she pitched a story about a makeup artist who specializes in monolid makeup, only to have her editor Francesca shoot it down with "Zoe, most of our readers don't have monolids. We need to write with our audience in mind."

Since she was young, she had loved fashion and longed to work in the industry, but the industry didn't always love people like her. But she had forgotten that until Damien's words unlocked something in her brain. Or maybe it was that she had chosen to block out the less-than-savory parts, instead holding on tightly to everything that made fashion fun and breezy and what her current job was not.

A featherlight touch skimmed the back of her hand, causing Zoe to look up with a start. "You okay?" Damien asked.

Zoe's eyes traced the line of his brows, down his nose, and

landed on his stubbled chin. His five-o'clock shadow made him seem older and gruffer, but his eyes—two pools of molten brown, calm and placid—gave her the involuntary urge to move closer, to open up. It was then that Zoe caught how closely they were sitting. At some point, she had turned to him such that they now sat directly facing each other, their knees almost touching.

Zoe jerked back in her chair, dusting off a piece of imaginary lint from her shirt lapel to disguise the suddenness of her movement. She inhaled deeply, willing her pounding heart to slow down. There was no way she was developing a crush on Damien; he was so . . . stoic and gruff and serious, so unlike the guys she'd liked in the past. She was probably just grateful that he was the only person besides Bill to have been nice to her so far.

"Yeah, I'm okay," she managed, hearing the high-pitched edge to her words. She cleared her throat. "So, you're a fellow writer, huh? Can I read anything you've written?"

Now it was Damien who drew back, the sudden loss of his body heat against hers leaving Zoe's skin mourning. He crossed his arms over his chest. "Um, it isn't very good."

"I don't believe that," Zoe said. There's no way someone as self-assured as Damien wouldn't be the best in anything he chose to put his mind to—much less something he was so passionate about.

Damien paused. "My writing is kind of . . . personal."

Heat pooled in Zoe's cheeks. Of course, Damien was just trying to be polite as he rejected her, his deflection simply a more roundabout way of saying: *No, I don't trust you enough.* And why should he? They were just coworkers, their relationship nothing like the easy camaraderie she had with Cassie and Bjorn, no matter how attractive his stubble was. It had been she who was too dense to pick up on what he was really saying.

"Of course! I understand," she said in her brightest voice. "Back at *Chic*, I didn't even like showing my editor my articles until I had revised them at least three times. Sharing your writing, especially if it's about a personal subject, feels like revealing a piece of your soul."

Damien's folded arms relaxed back down to his sides. "Exactly. I've never told anyone at work about my writing before. Even outside of work, only my childhood best friend knows."

"Oh." Against her will, Zoe felt her heart lifting, the same buoyant feeling in her chest tipping up the corners of her lips into a smile. "And thanks for hearing me out about my parents. My friends don't really get it."

"Yeah," Damien said. "You know, you shouldn't have to suppress how passionate you are about fashion. That's why Bill hired you. It's okay if you don't know the technology—we have plenty of people who do know that. But it takes all kinds of talents to make a successful business, and there are things you can do that the rest of us can't."

Zoe found herself nodding along to every word. Damien spoke so simply that it made everything he said sound so indisputable. "You're right. I need to stop trying to be like you and just focus on my own strengths."

"You wanted to be like me?"

Was it her imagination or did he suddenly lean just a bit closer to her? Zoe wiped her clammy palms against her skirt and crossed her legs. Once more the picture of corporate studiousness. "I meant you in the broadest terms, as in engineers and techies," she said quickly. "Anyway, what were you saying about the app's back-end infrastructure?"

He looked at her for a beat longer, his mouth twitching as if he wanted to say something else. But in the end, Damien simply nudged his computer until the screensaver mode flickered, revealing his PowerPoint deck about FitPick's engineering frameworks. "Right, so as I was saying . . ."

Forty minutes later, Zoe walked out of the room, her journal stuffed with her copious notes from Damien's lesson. She made a beeline for her desk, a fresh wave of excitement surging within her. If she dropped some of the tech jargon she'd just learned into her proposal, that would make her ideas sound more GitHub than Gucci, maybe enough to win Lillian over. It was time to get down to business.

As Zoe cracked her knuckles, she grew starkly aware of the jumble of beaded friendship bracelets circling her left wrist, their frayed edges trailing on the tabletop. She had made those during a Friday night hangout with Cassie and Bjorn.

Zoe quickly stuffed her left hand under her thigh, hoping the voluminous folds of her crushed velvet skirt would hide the colorful accessories from view. Someone like Lillian Mariko would never wear friendship bracelets or a crushed velvet skirt in the office. If she wanted her ideas to be taken seriously, she needed to start dressing more seriously too. But she had limited herself to only three suitcases when she moved to California, which meant leaving a significant portion of her clothes behind to Cassie and Bjorn. The ones she had allowed herself to keep were all her favorites—featuring bold colors, loud prints, and interesting cuts and textures. Nothing that Lillian Mariko would be caught dead in.

A small spark of excitement bloomed within Zoe. This situation definitely called for a shopping trip—her first since she moved to California. But . . . there would be no Cassie hyping her up as she tried on the clothes, no Bjorn making snarky remarks about the designs in the store. With an effort, Zoe pushed those thoughts out of her head and turned her attention to her proposal. But for the rest of the day, she couldn't quite ignore the inkling of loneliness simmering in the back of her mind.

chapter  12

THE MOMENT ZOE stepped over the threshold of Nordstrom in Stanford Shopping Center, she closed her eyes and took a deep breath of the delicately perfumed air. Even without Cassie and Bjorn, being surrounded by beautiful clothes never failed to lift her heart. And she had the whole Saturday ahead of her to find a completely new, *work-appropriate* wardrobe.

She scanned the racks of clothes, stretching out across the cavernous store as far as the eye could see, grouped into sections by their respective brands. *Ah!* Zoe's eyes lit up as they landed on a fuchsia ruffled shift dress with shimmery silver embroidery. It would pair brilliantly with the pair of similarly colored platform heels she thrifted a few months ago—

No. Zoe forced herself to look away. This was a shopping expedition for work, not for herself. She strode down the aisles, resolutely ignoring the siren call of all the gingham and polka-dot prints, and keeping her eyes peeled for business casual clothes only. She stopped in front of a Calvin Klein rack and fingered one

of the sleeveless dresses. It looked . . . promising, with its simple
A-line cut that ended slightly above the knee, square neckline,
and deep blue color all over. Even Lillian Mariko wouldn't be
able to find fault with it.

But she could hear Bjorn's voice niggling in the back of her
mind. "This is a Kate Middleton outfit," it sniffed, referencing the
modest and straight-laced style the duchess had to abide by. "This
is *not* Zoe Zeng."

"Good morning, can I help you?" a melodious voice chimed
in from behind her. Zoe whirled around, her eyes meeting the
ones of a statuesque brunette who looked to be in her late twenties. Her black pantsuit with power shoulder pads managed to
show off every curve, with the blazer jacket unbuttoned just the
right amount to reveal a glimpse of cleavage. A pair of black suede
mules made her long legs appear even longer. Both her red lipstick and full blowout were immaculate, the honey-blonde high-
lights in her hair gleaming beneath the bright fluorescent lights.

"Bernadette Dubois," the woman announced, brandishing her
right hand out with a flourish. Her handshake was just as firm as
Zoe imagined it would be. "I'm a Nordstrom personal shopper.
And how should I refer to you?"

"Zoe, Zoe Zeng."

Bernadette's smile broadened. "Pleasure to meet you. At Nordstrom, we offer free styling sessions to put together outfits for our
clients." She nodded at the Calvin Klein dress Zoe had been assessing. "Are you interested in that piece? I can have a dressing
room set up for you."

"I'm not sure yet." Zoe pulled the dress off the rack and held
it up against her body. "What do you think?"

A faint wrinkle appeared between Bernadette's brows. "I think
it looks good on you, but it just doesn't seem very . . . you." Her

eyes scanned Zoe's flowy paisley dress and turquoise bead belt, lingering briefly on her cowboy boots. "Your style seems more free-spirited to me while this dress screams Stepford Wife. But perhaps with the right accessories . . ."

A surprised laugh bubbled out of Zoe's mouth. Huh, this was the first time she had ever heard a saleslady say anything less than profusely gushing.

"You're right," Zoe admitted. "I don't feel like myself in this. But my current wardrobe isn't exactly work-appropriate . . ."

Bernadette considered the clothes on the Calvin Klein rack. "These are all fine, but if you don't think you'll feel like yourself in them, you won't feel good. And if you don't feel good, you won't look good no matter what you wear. Tell me a little more about your job so that I can pull together some pieces for you that are office-friendly and still suit you."

"I work in marketing at a tech company—"

"Ah, say less," Bernadette said knowingly. "I could throw my Louboutins in any direction in the Bay Area and nine times out of ten, it would hit someone working in tech. Isn't it frustrating how those engineers get away with wearing T-shirts and jeans, while someone working in a more customer-facing role like you has to dress up more?"

It wasn't the customers who had an issue with her sartorial choices, but Zoe kept that to herself. "I love dressing up though. I don't like having to dress a certain way like everyone else." She sighed. "Especially when that way of corporate dressing just doesn't fit my personal style."

Nodding, Bernadette began browsing through some nearby racks. "I know what you mean. I used to work in consulting and lord knows how many people have the same Ann Taylor pantsuit or Ferragamo loafers."

"You used to work in consulting? What made you switch to a job that's so different?"

"The work-life balance was shit," Bernadette said as she pulled a silk green blazer off the rack and held it up against Zoe's body, squinting to assess the fit. It had the most fantastic paintbrush-esque streaks of color that caught the light perfectly. "I was working twelve hours every day and flying across the country every week. The pay was great but the lifestyle was messing up my health and stopping me from having a family—"

Bernadette broke off, a guarded look coming over her face. "Not that a woman has to have children. My fiancé's cousin is some boss lady at her company and says she never wants to have kids—and I fully respect that. I know that's not for everyone, but I grew up in a big family and I want to have one of my own too."

Zoe nodded sympathetically. "It sounds like your old job was a lot, so I totally understand why you needed to cut that out of your life. Regardless of whether you want to have kids or not."

A look of relief flitted across Bernadette's face and she resumed walking. "Exactly. But I felt *so* guilty when I put in my two weeks' notice! It's like I was setting feminism back by ten years or something. My best friend at work joked, 'How can you leave me alone in a sausage fest?' I hadn't even realized that after I left, she would be the only woman on the team." She paused to eye a blush-pink Erdem dress, then plucked it decisively off the rack and added it to the expanding pile of clothes in her arms. "I told her it was because I wanted to start a family and she told me that it's the twenty-first century and women didn't need to choose between their careers and their families. Bless her."

Scurrying to catch up with Bernadette's long strides, Zoe winced. "Ouch."

"Ouch all right. I mean, I want to believe that too and buy

into Sheryl Sandberg's *Lean In* spiel, but my worsening endome-
triosis was telling me a different story. Still, that was better than
what my male coworkers said. I didn't tell them about the family
thing, just said I was switching careers to become a personal
stylist. One of the partners looked me up and down and said—I
kid you not: 'Of course a woman who looks like you wants to shop
all day long.'" Indignance swelled in Bernadette's voice. "Like
what's that supposed to mean? A woman who looks like what?"

Zoe hurried to catch a blouse that was slipping out of Bernadette's hands, scooping it up just before the poplin garment hit
the ground. "I hear you. I used to work in fashion and I don't
think my current tech coworkers take me seriously because
of that. They think fashion is somehow an inferior industry, which
makes me . . . inferior. That's why I'm hoping that wearing more
serious clothes will make them take me more seriously, especially
since I only have one last shot at convincing them of my ideas."

Bernadette's footsteps screeched to a halt. She shifted the pile
of clothes in her arms so she could look Zoe dead in the eye. "Just
because those people think Birkenstocks and Patagonia are the
height of style does *not* make them better than those who like to
experiment more with fashion. They just like to think of themselves as being too busy 'disrupting the system' to care about
how they look. I know men like that and the only way to get them
to respect you is to stick to your convictions. Not to be some sort
of Disney sap or whatever, but you have to be yourself."

Bernadette's self-assurance was infectious. "You're right," Zoe
heard herself saying. "And that begins with what I put on my
body. Life's too short to waste any time on things I don't love,
including my clothes."

"Exactly." With her free hand, Bernadette pushed open the
door to a dressing room. "And now, what we're going to do is

have you try on these clothes I've picked out just for you. This Anna Sui lace blouse and those Maeve floral silk pants will go great together." The massive sparkler on her left ring finger shone beneath the flattering overhead lamp as she gestured at each clothing item. "And just look at this striped jersey knit dress from Christopher John Rogers—throw on a little shrug over it and you'll look classy but far from boring."

Zoe's heart did a little leap as she looked over the selections. Every garment in the mix was one she would have chosen for herself. "Bernadette, it's like you've read my mind," she marveled, running her finger reverently down the ruched detailing on a Nanushka sweater. "You're a fashion fairy godmother."

Bernadette shook back her hair and let out a throaty laugh. "Well, I've always believed dressing up isn't about turning someone into a different person, but bringing out the best person they can be."

"THANKS FOR MAKING THE TIME FOR THIS," ZOE SAID, HER heart thudding as she looked between Bill and Lillian in The Rook. Hopefully, only she could hear the slight tremble in her voice. "I know I only put this on your calendar yesterday, so I appreciate you two being so flexible."

Bill smiled kindly. "Of course. You've been here for almost two weeks, right? How are things going? The work isn't too much, I hope."

That gave Zoe the perfect opening. She adjusted the bow on her Anna Sui blouse that—tucked into the Maeve silk pants that Bernadette had also recommended—was just the statement-making outfit she needed for such a moment. "Not at all. In fact,

I'm hoping to do more, which is why I want to bring up my fashion influencers idea again."

Zoe could almost hear the sigh that Lillian was holding back. "I thought we agreed to table the idea because we don't have the budget for that now and it's not a priority on our road map," Lillian said. For the dozenth time, Zoe wondered how the other woman had such unblemished skin despite her propensity to furrow her brows. "We should make sure the foundation of the house is rock-solid before we add any bells and whistles."

Zoe's fingers dug into her palms. Why did Lillian always have to make it sound like marketing wasn't a serious job, merely the "bells and whistles" to the technical team's oh-so-important foundation-building work?

Instead, she channeled her inner Damien—unruffled and self-assured—and looked Lillian straight in the eye. "We could make the app a few fractions of a second faster, but that's not what's going to win us new users. No one goes around telling their friends, *Hey, you should download this app because it loads really quickly.* Instead, what gets people talking *are* the bells and whistles. People will get excited when they see their favorite influencers using the app, want to use it, and convince their friends to get it too."

"Even if improving product stability and reducing latency doesn't 'win us new users,'" Lillian replied, pointed air quotes in her words, "it will keep our existing users satisfied. If they go around complaining about how buggy the app is, that's going to turn off prospective users. No amount of marketing can cover that up."

"Fashion is all about making people buy into an illusion." Zoe stood up taller, hoping that her painstakingly crafted outfit conveyed an illusion of cool, calm, and collected. "At New York Fashion

Week last year, I decided to conduct a little experiment: I started carrying around a reusable bag from Trader Joe's, babied it like it was a Birkin, and told everyone who asked that it came from a little boutique in Athens. So many people, even Margot Robbie's stylist, wanted to know the name of that boutique." She detailed her social experiment in an article titled "The Anatomy of a Fashion Week It-Accessory" that ended up going briefly viral. "If there's one thing I know, it's how to dress something up to make people believe it looks like more than it is."

Bill burst into laughter, but Lillian cut in. "Except, we're not talking about a five-dollar bag from Trader Joe's. We're talking about an app that we hope Logan Horossen would want to invest millions of dollars into."

"And I'll help build up its public image so that people like Logan Horossen think it's worth even more than that," Zoe swiftly replied, making sure to enunciate every word loud and clear. "Even if the app isn't perfect, good marketing will highlight its strengths and cover up the not-so-great parts. It will convince people that we can address their pain points—so much so that they are willing to overlook the occasional bug."

The groove between Lillian's brows only deepened. However, Bill was the CEO, the person who had the final say over everything. That he hadn't said anything against her pitch yet might be a good sign, so Zoe turned to him.

"Bill, you hired me for a reason. I might not know coding but I know your target audience; I *am* your target audience. And I know what they want to see. Just give me a chance to try this idea out."

Bill leaned back in his chair, his eyes darting between the two women. "Zoe, I get where you're coming from and your Fashion Week stunt is genius. *But*, to Lillian's point, an influencer campaign would require quite a bit of money," he said, ever the diplomatic boss. "I'm just not sure we can spend so much just for 'a chance to try something out'."

Zoe's hand tightened around her meeting notes. If she gave in now, she would be back at square one. No, scratch that—it would be even worse because Bill and Lillian would assume she didn't have the gumption to stick to her ideas and might be even less welcoming toward her future suggestions. If she didn't dare to fight for herself, then who would?

Zoe pulled herself up to her fullest height and made her final pitch. "Bill, you told me that Logan Horossen is all about going big or going home. Do you think SEO marketing is his idea of going big?"

She held her breath as she stared anxiously at Bill, every fiber of her being willing him to shake his head. She didn't think she had ever wished so hard for something at work before, not even when *Chic* was given one—just one—slot to cover last year's Met Gala and all the writers were fighting for it.

Bill pinched the bridge of his nose and exhaled loudly. "Okay, I'll set aside thirty thousand dollars for this project. As Lillian said, there are plenty of app updates we hope to make in the near future and that the money could be spent on, but I trust you'll put it to good use."

"Yes, definitely!" A typical influencer marketing campaign would cost more than thirty thousand dollars, but just getting this amount was more stressful and painful than getting teeth pulled. Ignoring Lillian's pursed lips, Zoe nodded her thanks at Bill, too drained to come up with a more verbose response. But that didn't matter anyway. She would let the results of the campaign do the talking for her.

chapter  13

THE MOMENT SHE reached her desk in The Hook, Zoe collapsed on her chair. All she had done was sit for a meeting with Bill and Lillian, but it felt like she'd run an entire marathon. The hard work would begin soon, but first, she was sorely in need of some caffeine.

Before she could muster the energy to stand up again and head to The Cook, Bram scooted his chair toward her. "Zoe, do you think we could order some Tupperware?"

Zoe pressed her lips together, her body stiffening. How could Bram have the nerve to speak so normally to her now after saying such hateful things behind her back? If she hadn't overheard his bathroom conversation with Austin, she might have even fallen for his friendly act.

"Why do you need it?" she asked, eyeing him warily.

"I recently read that Twitter's founder Jack Dorsey does intermittent fasting to improve his concentration, so I'm trying that now. I only eat between the hours of noon and six, which means I can't take advantage of our catered dinners anymore. So my idea is to bring home food in Tupperware containers and have it on weekends," Bram explained, looking immensely proud of himself.

"Wow, um, that's very resourceful of you," Zoe managed. Intermittent fasting had hit the fashion industry a decade ago and became an easy euphemism for dieting. But trust workers in Silicon Valley to do it for productivity's sake.

"So can we get some Tupperware containers for the office?"

"I guess so. You don't need my permission."

Bram gave her his best show of puppy dog eyes. "I was hoping you could help me order them?"

In a flash, it became clear to Zoe what was happening. Maybe it was because she was new, maybe it was because she was a woman, but for some reason, Bram thought that of all the people at FitPick, it fell on her to order office supplies.

"I think it'd be better if you do it yourself," she said as pleasantly as she could. "Since you would be the only one using them."

"I would but I'm rushing to finish debugging this in time. I'm trying this new thing called high-intensity interval programming. I code nonstop for an hour, take a break for five minutes, then rinse and repeat. Sundar Pichai says all his best engineers at Google do this."

A grudging "okay, fine" was on the tip of Zoe's tongue. The faster she agreed, the sooner she could get back to work, and it wasn't like it would take more than a couple minutes to make a one-click purchase on Amazon with her company credit card.

But it wouldn't take Bram more than a couple minutes either. He had a debugging deadline, but she had her own work too. And just because his work was more technical didn't mean his time was more valuable than hers.

"I have work too," Zoe said, trying her best to keep her tone cordial. Even if they would never be friends, they were still coworkers on a very small team—hardly the place to be burning bridges. "My influencer campaign idea just got approved, and there's a million things I have to start doing for it."

Bram blinked. "Oh, wow. Uh, that's great," he said, unable to hide his astonishment. If Zoe weren't still riding a post-meeting high, she might have been offended by how Bram clearly didn't expect her ideas to ever succeed.

On Bram's other side, Austin looked up from his laptop. "That's really wonderful, Zoe," he said, doing a much better job than Bram of sounding sincere. "It's definitely a . . . unique idea, but it sounds like something ValleyVerified would dig."

"What's that?" Zoe asked.

"You haven't heard of ValleyVerified before?" Bram asked, his voice hushed like he was in church. He exchanged a look with Austin as Zoe shook her head, the now familiar sensation of being the outsider rushing back to her.

"ValleyVerified is a news aggregation site," Lillian spoke up from the other side of the table.

Bill snorted. "Let's call a spade a spade: It's a gossip site that focuses on Silicon Valley and ninety-nine percent of its posts are about tech companies. ValleyVerified breaks the news about upcoming IPOs, mergers, acquisitions, and bankruptcy filings, but even more importantly, it's the first to dish the dirt on any personal drama happening at companies. Founder fights, employee lawsuits, divorces, and pregnancies." He spread his arms like a host welcoming his guests to a grand feast. "The good, the bad, the ugly—everything ends up on ValleyVerified."

"That's their tagline," Austin added.

Zoe let out a low whistle. "I thought people in Silicon Valley were too serious to bother with gossip." Not that she was a stranger to gossip, since fashion was an industry built on who you knew and what you knew.

"Ha! When I was at Burning Man, good old Drew Macklemore told me that every morning, his assistant prepares a summary for him of all the top headlines in *The New York Times*, *The Wall Street Journal*, the *Financial Times*, Bloomberg, TechCrunch, and . . . ValleyVerified," Bill said grandly.

"*Everyone* in Silicon Valley reads ValleyVerified," Lillian agreed, and there were nods all around the table, even from Damien. "A company's stock performance is very much affected by news completely unrelated to the product, so any investor would want to monitor what's going on at the companies they have their eyes on. Think about it: When Yahoo! CEO Marissa Mayer announced in 2015 that she was pregnant with twins, Yahoo's share prices fell immediately because investors were afraid her going on maternity leave would negatively impact the company. And when ValleyVerified revealed that Desk Step's CEO was seeing his executive assistant—"

"The public totally blew that one up," Bill chimed in. "And it's ridiculous—they are two adults having a consensual relationship. Who cares who he wants to sleep with?"

"But she was his assistant," Zoe said. "There's a power imbalance so we don't know for sure if it was consensual."

"Oh, she totally wanted it," Bill said. "It's so obvious from her leaked text messages. She was always telling him what an awesome boss he was and confiding really personal stuff to him."

Lillian's mouth tightened at all the interruptions. "As I was saying," she said loudly, drawing all eyes back to her. "ValleyVerified is the most well-known non-mainstream media within Silicon Valley. If we can get featured on there—*positively*, obviously—we could attract a lot more investor attention instead of putting all our eggs in the Logan Horossen basket."

"I agree," Zoe said, jotting down a reminder in her notebook to look up ValleyVerified and see how she could tailor her campaign to be more aligned with the site's angle. "Thanks for telling me about ValleyVerified. I wouldn't have known about it otherwise."

Bill held up a hand. "Not so fast. ValleyVerified has a reputation for skewering young startups. They even have a section on their site called "Fab or Fad," where they review and rate startups, and most of the time, ValleyVerified goes *hard* on the companies. Just ask Dreamcatcher—" Bill nodded in the general direction of the other startup's wing in the building. "They were absolutely slaughtered by the columnist Rebecca Stiles and because of her verdict, there are rumors they're headed into a down round." His voice was hushed, as though fearing that someone from Dreamcatcher was right outside FitPick's office, eavesdropping.

"A down round is when a company's value decreases in their new funding round compared to the previous one," Damien said. Zoe sent him a silent note of thanks. His timely interjection saved her from the embarrassment of having to ask yet another question about a piece of Silicon Valley jargon she didn't understand.

"Dreamcatcher was flying high after their Series A funding, which gave them a thirty-million-dollar valuation," Bill said. "But after Rebecca Stiles's verdict on them came out in ValleyVerified, apparently their Series A lead investor got spooked and no longer wants to stay on for the next round. So if Dreamcatcher can't find a suitable replacement, they will be forced to decrease their Series B valuation, and that's basically a death knell for a young startup."

"Let me get this straight," Zoe said slowly, her mind whirling from the deluge of information. "So the only thing worse than not having enough money is having too much of it at first?"

"Yup." Bill beamed at her. "You're a quick study. Most people would have simply become sucked in by Dreamcatcher's high Series A valuation, but Rebecca Stiles isn't afraid to go against the grain. And unfortunately for the startups she puts on blast, her instincts are usually correct. According to the industry grapevine, Dreamcatcher's AI technology has a much higher error rate than what they're advertising."

"Which is why," Lillian cut in, "we need to make sure our product is foolproof before we think about marketing it too widely and appearing on ValleyVerified's radar."

Zoe resisted the urge to roll her eyes. Of course Lillian would find a way to keep harping on that. Whoever this Rebecca Stiles at ValleyVerified was, there was no way she would be harder to please than FitPick's COO.

WHEN SHE GOT HOME THAT NIGHT, ZOE TEXTED BERNADETTE, who had given her number in case Zoe had any questions about the clothes.

> ZOE: I LOVED the outfit you put together!
> It made me feel so confident.

Her phone *ping*-ed with a reply almost immediately.

> BERNADETTE: Yay!! I was wondering how
> your meeting went.

> ZOE: I survived, which is all I can ask for.
> I was so nervous I might have sweated
> right through that Anna Sui blouse.

BERNADETTE: Lol! Thank god silk is sweat-
wicking and temperature-regulating.

Before Zoe could respond, another message came in.

BERNADETTE: Speaking of sweat, wanna
join me for my workout class some day?
I have a one-free-session referral I can
give to a friend.

Friend? Zoe smiled.

ZOE: Sure! What are the details?

BERNADETTE: It's this place called Desk
Step—super cool and has an ultra-long
waitlist. When are you free?

As they started discussing times, Zoe pulled up Google Calendar on her phone to schedule her Desk Step class with Bernadette. A field of perfectly white squares greeted her. In New York, she barely had any free time, between all the overtime work, after-work events, and maintaining some semblance of a social life outside work. But now, in this new city where she knew no one, her schedule was completely empty.

But as she clicked "Enter" and watched her newly made appointment—no, *hangout*—bloom into life on her Google Calendar, Zoe felt her mood lift. It would take some time to build a life for herself here, but at least she was taking a step—a *Desk Step*—in the right direction.

ZOE RAISED HER arms over her head and gave a deep stretch, relishing the sound of her stiff joints cracking. Breathing out a satisfied sigh, she switched off her computer and started packing her bag.

"Heading home?" Bram asked, his eyes still fixed on his monitor.

"Yup." She glanced at the clock on the wall. 7:42 p.m. "Wow, this is the latest I have ever stayed back here." And on a Friday, no less. But today had been her most productive workday so far—she'd done a good bit of research into which group of micro-influencers would make up the best representation for FitPick's marketing campaigns. She had even drafted cold emails to the short-listed micro-influencers, scheduled to go out first thing on Monday morning.

Bram finally lifted his eyes from his screen, his face scrunched in thought. "I think the latest I ever worked was—Oh, there was that period right before our Android rollout last year when there were a million bugs to fix. My record was staying in the office three nights in a row—I brought in a sleeping bag and would sneak in a power nap every six hours."

Zoe's mouth dropped. "No way." As far as she knew, no restroom in the entire building contained showers, which meant . . .

"Yes way. I was the reason why Bill decided to install those sleeping pods in the first place," Bram recounted with no small amount of pride.

"Does anyone even use them? I looked at one the other day and there was still a price tag left on the pillow."

"Sleep before the year of a potential Series A? Why, I barely know her," Bram joked.

"I barely even know my girlfriend anymore," Austin said from his seat, looking uncharacteristically glum. "She keeps complaining about how I'm not 'present enough' and never take her on dates anymore. But I don't hear her complaining when I bring her to Nobu for her birthday or Maldives for our anniversary last year. I don't mind paying because I like making her happy, but I wish she would understand that the money doesn't come easy."

"I think the busiest time in my life was New York Fashion Week three seasons ago," Zoe said, hoping to distract Austin. The conversation that had started off in good fun was now quickly dissolving into bitterness. "Once, I had to attend two dinners, one fitting, one launch event, and an after-party at Soho House." She fanned herself theatrically. "Whew, I remember wishing I could clone myself—"

Her mouth clamped shut as Bram and Austin looked at each other.

"I don't know," Austin finally said. "Dining with celebrities and going to glamorous parties every day—that sounds a million times more fun than what we do here."

"Yeah, you're basically being paid to party."

"It's not all about partying," Zoe quickly said. "I mean, yeah I was there as a guest, but I had to be super alert all the time because the whole thing was just a big industry networking event. It was nonstop socializing and sucking up to people for a good ten hours. I got back home at three in the morning and I still had to stay up to write my daily summary of Fashion Week for my magazine's website, my daily report of my favorite fashion show looks, and my *other* daily report of the best street style I saw. And then I had to plan my three outfits for the next day and be up again at six. It was . . . a lot of hard work," she finished weakly as the two men exchanged another look.

Zoe would give anything to have Cassie and Bjorn with her again. They would understand and commiserate because they had experienced the craziness of the fashion world too. Cassie even got a UTI once because she was so busy rushing around the whole day from one event to the other that she didn't even have time to use the bathroom or hydrate herself.

Austin scratched the side of his nose. "Um, sure. That sounds like a lot."

"But even now, your work is basically going on social media. You were on Instagram and TikTok for basically the entire afternoon," Bram said.

"I was doing research for my influencer marketing campaign," Zoe protested. "It's important to choose influencers whose personal brands are aligned with FitPick. Trust me, marketing hinges on brand image." God, the note of defensiveness in her voice made her sound like Bjorn every time he showed them the Instagram account of his latest crush and insisted, "I swear he just doesn't photograph well but he's way cuter in real life."

Bram opened his mouth again but stopped when Austin gave

him a none-too-subtle jab in his ribs, which Zoe pretended not to see. "Well, you're the marketing expert here," Austin said. "Have a good weekend, Zoe."

"Yeah, see you on Monday," Bram echoed, rubbing the side of his waist.

"See you guys," Zoe muttered, leaping to her feet and shoving her chair toward the table. In just one conversation, all of her previous elation and pride in her work had been erased into nothing more than a distant memory.

"IT'S UNFAIR HOW GOOD YOU LOOK EVEN AFTER 'WORKING out,'" Zoe huffed as she jammed her laptop back into her gym bag after completing her first Desk Step session with Bernadette.

Desk Step was the latest fitness trend to have hit the Bay Area. Touting itself as the solution for the millions of tech and finance workers who complained about being too busy to exercise, its most popular class was an hour-long treadmill desk session. The treadmill varied its speed at regular intervals—ranging from a leisurely stroll to a light jog—all while the user cooked up their next money-making scheme on the attached laptop. From her research, Zoe gathered that Desk Step blew up after Larry Page was seen sauntering out of a class two years ago, and it'd since become so big that it'd even branched out to Stairmaster Desk, Trampoline Desk, and Bicycle Desk workout classes. According to Bernadette, its star instructor in Palo Alto, a hunky brown-haired man by the name of Craig, now had almost half a million followers on Instagram. Whenever her eyes needed a break from the laptop screen, Zoe busied herself with counting the number of suburban moms in her class ogling Craig's bulging calf muscles.

Bernadette laughed as she tucked her own iPad back into her Louis Vuitton holdall. "What are you talking about? I'm all sweaty."

"Yeah, but not in the gross way like me. Yours is more like a post-O glow—"

"A post-O glow?" Bernadette asked with one lifted eyebrow.

Zoe's cheeks turned pink. "Oh, you know what I mean. It's a term my friend in New York came up with." Bjorn had been much too proud of his wordplay, but the phrase—which Zoe and Cassie initially used in jest—soon became a part of their daily vernacular.

"Ah. We have a similar phrase here—the post-IPO glow." Bernadette quickly spritzed some hair spray to tame her postexercise curls. "A startup founder never looks more radiant than the day they take their company public. And they say money can't buy happiness."

Zoe flattened herself against the wall of the locker room to make way for a gaggle of ladies beelining for the showers. "You have the post-IPO glow while I look like I just drowned." Grimacing, she lifted a piece of hair stuck to the side of her face with sweat. "And you chose the harder incline mode too."

"You did really well for your first session," Bernadette said kindly. "Besides, you were actually hard at work on your laptop, while I was just watching a crafts video."

"A crafts video? You don't strike me as someone into arts and crafts," Zoe said as the two women walked out of the locker room.

"Hey, what's that supposed to mean? What does someone into arts and crafts look like?" Bernadette was smiling, but Zoe thought she could detect a faint trace of hurt in the other woman's voice. Shame wormed through her. Hadn't she just done the same thing to Bernadette that her coworkers did to her—made a snap judgment about a woman based on her appearance? Just because she liked wearing vintage tea dresses didn't make her less qualified to work at a tech startup, and just because Bernadette looked like she should be sauntering down the streets of Paris like they were her personal catwalk didn't mean she couldn't tinker around with polymer and beads.

"Sorry, I didn't mean anything by that. I've just never heard you talk about it. Do you like crafting?"

For the first time since Zoe had met her, Bernadette looked a little embarrassed. "Kind of. It's just a little hobby . . . I mean, yes, I'm interested in it," she said more firmly. "I like the idea of being able to create something that's entirely my own vision, instead of working for someone else's vision like I did in consulting and still do as a stylist."

"So, you want to create your own startup?"

Bernadette was quiet for a moment as she stared down at the tiled floor of Desk Step's locker room. "I don't know," she finally said, her voice so low that Zoe could barely catch it over the sound of the hair dryers in the background. "I haven't thought that far yet. I don't even know what I want to create—embroidery or pottery or something else. For now, it's just a casual hobby that makes me happy. I don't like the Silicon Valley culture of having to turn every passion project into some sort of hustle. In the past, it wasn't enough to do something if you couldn't find a way to monetize it. These days, even that's not enough if your hustle doesn't become a unicorn or a super-unicorn."

Zoe's hand tightened around her laptop case. No wonder Bill and Lillian were so stressed out about FitPick. How could they not be when anything short of major success was considered a failure? But she was also a FitPicker now; the company's success was hers and vice versa. By hook or by crook, she would make sure Project Influencer exceeded all expectations.

Then again, the bar was low since everyone was expecting it to fail.

After changing into their street clothes, Zoe and Bernadette walked out of Desk Step, swept up in a pack of women whose sports bras and matching leggings revealed a strip of rock-hard abs. They put on their sunglasses, all bearing interlocking letter logos—Gucci, Celine, YSL—and peeled off one by one into their respective cars—Teslas, BMWs, Porsches.

Zoe followed Bernadette's line of vision as the other woman stared at a Range Rover reversing past them out of the parking lot. On its rear window were three stickers: *My son is a Gunn High School scholar!; Proud parent of a Fairmeadow Elementary superstar; Precious cargo on board*—above the silhouette of a baby. Bernadette's throat bobbed as she swallowed.

"Bern, do you want to get a drink with me?" Zoe blurted. She still had a lot of work to finish before Monday, but at least her question successfully drew Bernadette's attention away from the family car with its proud gallery of children-themed decals.

"Sure," Bernadette said, though Zoe could tell half her mind was still somewhere else. "There's a good juice shop around the corner."

When they reached Rejuice, Zoe quickly realized the place was filled with fellow Desk Step devotees as well as weekend workers who had popped over from the Work Hive building next door. In a stroke of genius, Desk Step had set up their flagship studio right next to one of the Bay Area's most popular coworking spaces so that people could easily go from their work desk to Desk Step's workout desks.

"Two Radiance Reboosts, please," Bernadette said to the Re-juice worker at the counter and handed over her credit card. "This is on me," she said as Zoe made a sound of protest. "To thank you for coming with me to Desk Step."

Zoe smiled her thanks as she accepted her smoothie and the accompanying bamboo straw. It was icy-cold to the touch, making her long to hold it against her sweaty face. But she settled for taking an extra-long sip of the lemongrass and raspberry concoction (which promised every health benefit under the sun short of immortality).

"Hey," she said softly as she noticed Bernadette staring blankly down at her own juice, not making any move to drink it. "You okay?"

"Yeah," Bernadette said immediately, then shook her head. "Actually, no." She half smiled at Zoe's look of bemusement. "One of the personal goals I set for myself after quitting my job was to be more honest with myself and others. So to be frank with you, I've not been feeling too great lately."

"Why don't we take a seat and finish our smoothies?" Zoe suggested, gently leading Bernadette to an empty table in a corner of the shop. She waited quietly as Bernadette fiddled with her straw, not wanting to rush her friend in any way.

"This was actually my first Desk Step class since I quit my job," Bernadette finally said. "Having you there made me feel more comfortable, but I almost felt like I didn't deserve to be there because I wasn't working like all the other Desk Steppers."

"Let me know if I'm overstepping," Zoe said carefully. "But Bern, do you ever regret quitting your job?"

"No," Bernadette said, then paused. "Well, I don't know. I don't *think* I regret it because I know it's the best decision for my health and my dreams of starting a family. But I was good at consulting; I loved my job and the people there. It was such a big part of my life and now I don't quite know who I am without it."

"It's very normal to feel that way," Zoe started saying, but Bernadette shook her head.

"The thing is, I don't think other people know who I am outside of my job either. After I quit, my old coworkers still invited me to company parties and happy hours, but it just felt like they were all tiptoeing around me. There was once when one of my former teammates was complaining about a project he just got staffed on and how lousy the hours were, and the person sitting next to him jabbed him in the ribs. And I had to sit there and smile and pretend like I didn't see them glancing in my way, as though they were scared my ovaries would combust the moment I heard them say the word 'work'." Bernadette jabbed her straw into her smoothie cup, piercing the plastic film cover with a loud *pop*, then sucked up a mouthful with an extra-vehement slurp.

Zoe laid a gentle hand on the other woman's arm. "I'm sorry. I'm sure they meant well, but I get why you would be frustrated." It couldn't be easy for a strong woman like Bernadette to be forced by circumstances beyond her control to give up her career.

Zoe shot Bernadette a reassuring smile, but there was a weight in her chest. Since her teens, she had made working in fashion her goal in life. Who was she outside of that? But now, she was working in an entirely different industry, at a company where everyone constantly doubted her and drove her to constantly doubt herself. Her teenage self would surely be disappointed by where she ended up in life.

chapter 15

"**U**GH."

Zoe slumped forward on her desk, burying her face in her hands. The marketing automation platform Eloqua had shown her three days ago that Nicola Harper, who had over half a million Instagram followers, had opened her campaign pitch email. But there was still no response nearly seventy-two hours later. At least Nicola (or more likely, Nicola's agent) had seen her email; most of the influencers she had reached out to hadn't even done that.

At Zoe's frustrated groan, Lillian looked up from her own work, her right eyebrow raised in a perfect arc. "What's wrong? Anything I can help with?"

Zoe quickly sat up straight and plastered a smile on her face. *Of course* Lillian would assume she had done something wrong; the COO loved nothing more than a chance to show how she could have done everything better. "Everything's great!" she chirped. "My internet's just a little slow right now."

Lillian did a few clicks on her own laptop. "My internet seems to be fine."

"Uh, I'm opening up a pretty large spreadsheet so maybe that's why," Zoe said weakly. "But don't worry about me. The campaign's absolutely peachy!"

She couldn't blame Lillian for looking skeptical. *Absolutely peachy?* Who even says that? After a beat of silence, the other woman smiled. "That's great. I really want your first project to be a success, you know?"

Lillian sounded friendly enough, almost genuine, but even her smile couldn't cover up the barely veiled threat. *It'd better succeed, or else.*

Zoe looked down at her laptop with what she hoped was a convincing display of delight. "Great! My file finally loaded. Back to work now!"

She made a show out of typing furiously until she was sure Lillian was no longer paying attention to her, then immediately went onto Instagram. She needed a meme break before she had to return to the disaster that was her campaign project.

But the moment the Instagram webpage loaded, the first post that greeted Zoe was an Instagram Reel uploaded by Amirah Amin—another New York–based influencer who hadn't responded to her pitch. In the clip, Amirah was slicing open what looked like a cross between a muffin and a Scotch egg. Creamy yellow yolk oozed out onto the white plate. *They made a vegetarian version for me* 😍, the influencer had captioned.

Zoe bit back a groan. Why couldn't Amirah take just one minute out of appreciating her yolk porn to check her inbox?

But Zoe couldn't even blame Amirah and Nicola for ignoring her campaign pitch. FitPick was young with no reputation to speak of—nothing that would catch the eye of a social media influencer who got upward of a hundred pitches every day. Her email and follow-up probably didn't even make it past their spam filter. At least when she was working at *Chic*, she could count on her emails being read and responded to most times; while *Chic* wasn't quite at the same level of *Vogue* or *Elle*, it was still considered legitimate and established.

Absently, Zoe picked up a fidget clicker that had come in the welcome box Bill had given her on her first day. The steady bobbing of her thumb against its buttons and the rhythmic clicking sounds were soothing but couldn't stop her mind from churning. At this rate, the campaign would be over before it'd even begun, they would be nowhere closer to impressing Logan Horossen, and she would have failed to fulfill the biggest—the only—reason why she'd been hired in the first place.

"Stressed out?" Austin asked, wheeling his chair toward her. "I was also using my fidget clicker nonstop back when I was trying to figure out how to do push notifications on Android. My stress-clicking drove Bram nuts—that's why he got his fancy noise-canceling headphones. I only stopped when he told me it looked like I was clicking on nipples."

Zoe looked up to make sure Lillian had her headphones on, but still lowered her voice. "My campaign isn't going well," she admitted, too tired to think of how to put an optimistic spin on the situation. Not that there was even a way to frame a zero percent response rate positively. "Actually"—her voice turned glummer—"it's not going at all."

"That's okay, Zoe," Bram said, walking up from behind them as he returned from The Cook, a cold brew in one hand. "I don't think people are swayed by social media influencers anyway."

"Of course they are—*What is that?*" Zoe gaped, torn between amusement and horror as her eyes landed on her desk mate. Bram was wearing his hoodie backward, with the hood in the front, hanging halfway down his chest. Nestled in his hood was an open bag of Cheetos.

Unperturbed by her outburst, Bram settled himself into his chair and began typing away. His hood rested perfectly on the table, and every few seconds, Bram would absently reach one hand into the bag to grab a handful of Cheetos and shove it into his mouth, while his other hand continued jabbing away at his keyboard. Crumbs flew off his fist and onto the hoodie like orange snowflakes.

"What does it look like?" he grunted, spewing more Cheeto dust out of the corners of his mouth. "I'm working."

"But what's with this"—she waved one hand at his torso—"snack situation? Can't you just put it on the table?"

"Nah. It's not ergonomically efficient enough." More Cheeto flecks floated down onto his hoodie.

"Dude, don't you have a date tonight?" Austin asked, looking both disgusted and reluctantly impressed.

Bram finally looked up at them to roll his eyes. "Cheetos obviously aren't filling enough. Don't worry, I'm saving stomach space for steak later."

Austin gave Zoe a long-suffering look. *See what I have to put up with?*

"What happened to intermittent fasting?" Zoe asked.

"Nah, I'm on the keto diet now."

Bram swept his tongue out and curled it around his left index finger, sucking up the orange remnants and leaving a glistening layer of saliva in its wake. Zoe's stomach turned.

"Zoe, what were you saying about influencers?" Austin asked, resolutely turning away from Bram's make-out session with his own finger.

Zoe eagerly jumped on the change of subject. "SEO campaigns and ads might pique people's interest, but no one wants to download yet another app. So it doesn't matter how amazing we say our app is. They need to hear it from people whose opinions they will actually listen to—influencers."

Zoe pulled up a mock-up she'd created of what a FitPick poll by style icon Amirah Amin would look like, featuring two images she'd pulled from Amirah's Instagram of the fashion darling in different red dresses.

"Even if Amirah's fans don't plan on using FitPick for their own outfits, they will still join our app so they can vote on Amirah's polls, because who wouldn't want a personal say in what their favorite influencer wears? And they also get this exclusive inside look into Amirah's wardrobe and styling process! But the more time they spend on the app and see for themselves how useful outfit polls are, the more encouraged they will be to set up polls for themselves. This is the power of influencer marketing."

Bram looked up at her with a derisive snort. "That might work for tweens, but most people are too smart to do something just because a semi-famous person does it."

Translation: *You, Zoe, aren't smart enough to not fall for it.*

Zoe raised a brow. "You literally bought Tesla Tequila because Elon Musk made it."

A flush rose on Bram's cheeks that rivaled the orange coating on his fingertips. "I bought it as a joke!"

Austin scoffed. "Two hundred and fifty dollars per bottle? Pretty expensive joke. And didn't you code a program that would help you snag one of the front spots in the checkout line?"

"Yeah, and you only started doing intermittent fasting because Jack Dorsey did it," Zoe pointed out.

"Nice one," Austin said, raising his hand out to Zoe for a high five that she happily returned. For once, she wasn't the odd one out.

"But that's Jack Dorsey," Bram retorted as he shoveled another handful of Cheetos into his mouth. "The founder of two of the largest tech companies in the world."

"Bram, I guarantee that to our target audience, someone like Amirah Amin and Nicola Roberts matter much more."

Bram popped another handful of Cheetos into his mouth. "For the sake of my company stocks that I'm still waiting to vest, I really hope you're right."

"There's a chicken and egg problem though," Zoe sighed. "I'm confident we can attract more users with a successful influencer marketing campaign. *But* micro-influencers are picky with who they work with because their personal brands are so specific, so they wouldn't want to put their name to FitPick unless we already have a lot of users."

Austin winced. "Damn, that's tough. Hey, you've been working on this all day—why don't you take a break now and go get some dinner first? Maybe some distance will help you come up with ideas. Bill ordered in Mediterranean food from DishDash today and it's already in The Cook."

Zoe's eyes shot to her computer's time display. Time had flown by without her realizing and it was already twenty minutes past eight. This was the first time she had worked until late enough in the office to get the catered dinner. The thought of free food made her stomach rumble, especially since she hadn't eaten anything after lunch nearly seven hours ago.

As Zoe trudged toward the pantry, she pulled out her phone and clicked the first contact in her speed dial. The Cook offered the solitude she needed for a call to Cassie, where she could *finally* unload all her worries about work. The other FitPickers would judge her incompetence, but her best friend would understand.

Thankfully, Cassie picked up almost at once. "Zee! What's up?"

Just hearing her friend's voice was enough to make Zoe's heart lift. She pushed aside the stack of to-go boxes on the pantry island so she could lean against it, making herself comfortable for a long phone call. "Hey, Cass. Oh God, I have so much to complain about—" There was a sudden burst of laughter in the background from Cassie's end—a cackle that was all too familiar. "Wait, is Bjorn there too?"

"Yup. We're binging *SNL* and he's already polished off half my rosé."

In a flash, it came to Zoe. It was Wined Down Friday—her weekly tradition with Cassie and Bjorn where they spent the evening winding down the workweek with wine (Bjorn had been very proud of his wordplay). But over time, it had devolved into Whine(d) Down Friday, where they would get together at someone's apartment to commiserate about how tedious work was over cheap alcohol.

Right on cue, Cassie said, "It's Wined Down Friday, remember?"

"Of course I do," Zoe said, but her mouth filled with a sour taste. A part of her hadn't expected—had maybe even secretly hoped—that her friends wouldn't continue their tradition without her.

Cassie, perceptive as always, must have sensed the sudden shift in tone. Her voice softened as she said, "Zee, we miss you so much."

"*Is that Zoe?*" Bjorn shrieked. There was some rustling and then Bjorn's voice boomed out in Zoe's ears. "Zoeeeeeeee my babyyyyyy. It's not the same without youuuuuu. Come back to us, bitch." He gave a small hiccup and added brightly, "Wait, I think that was a haiku. Five-seven-five. Oh my fucking God. I'm fucking Shakespeare."

Zoe burst into laughter, the genuine joy in the sound taking even herself by surprise. Bjorn's words were slightly slurred but the excitement in his greeting was unmistakable. It was like returning home after a long and tiring day and being greeted by an affectionate golden retriever. She might be on separate coasts from them now, but at this moment, she almost felt like she was in her New York room with them, slugging out of cheap bottles without the demand to impress anyone.

"Trust me, I wish I could be back there with you two," Zoe sighed.

There was an indignant yelp from Bjorn, and then it was Cassie's voice coming out from Zoe's phone again. Zoe guessed she must have wrenched the phone from Bjorn. "Zee, what's up? You sound kinda down."

"Cass, you ass, put her on speaker!"

Bjorn's interruption gave Zoe an extra moment to collect her thoughts and make sure her laugh sounded believable enough as she replied, "Me? Down? Nah, I'm just . . . a little tired." She shifted her weight to her other foot and propped her chin on her phone-less hand.

"Yeah, why would Zoe be unhappy?" Bjorn asked Cassie. "Not when she's getting that sweet dough at her new job. That check makes me want to sell out too."

Zoe gripped her phone tighter. There was no way Bjorn meant those words negatively, but was that really what her fashion friends thought of her? A sellout whose passion for fashion paled in comparison to theirs, so much so that she ran away at the first sign things were tough?

"It's not just fun and games," Zoe said, the edge in her voice surprising herself. "I was only hired to help impress this one potential investor and if I don't succeed, I'll be fired or the company will run out of money. Either way, I'll be out of a job. And the perks aren't *that* great," she continued, her voice growing small as she eyed the mountain of takeout boxes in front of her. "I mean, yeah, there's free food, but I think it's just a trap to get us to stay in the office and do more work. And there are free Uber rides home, but it's only after eight p.m., which means working even more—"

Bjorn cut her off with another loud hiccup. "Girl, do you even hear yourself? All I had for lunch today was black coffee—"

"That's 'cos you went to that Vivienne Westwood sample sale and spent all your money on a pair of boots," Cassie said, and Zoe could almost hear her eye roll.

"*Platform* boots," Bjorn corrected pompously. "With the most wicked studs. You'd sell your left kidney for that. And did I tell you about the flasher I saw on the subway last weekend? Zee, I'd kill for your free cab rides and those other 'not that great' perks. And I don't hear you saying anything bad about your six-figure paycheck!"

"Zee, you don't have to play them down to make us feel better," Cassie said gently. "We're *happy* for you that you found such a great job."

"I'm not playing down anything. It's all true—"

"Just a teeeeeensy-weensy bit jealous," Bjorn slurred. "But mostly over-the-moon excited for you and your new successful career!"

On the other end of the line, Zoe swallowed the rest of her protest. Even Cassie and Bjorn—the two people who knew her the best in the world, who knew the name of the cute bodega owner she had a crush on in college and the secret Poshmark account she used to sell freebies she got at *Chic*—could only see the shiny dollar signs and glossy facade of Silicon Valley. And if she ever tried to say otherwise, she would only seem like an ungrateful brat.

"Well, the next time I grab a LaCroix from the office pantry," Zoe said, wanting to cringe at how overly chirpy she sounded, "I'll think of you two when I drink it."

After a few more minutes of small talk about FitPick's work perks, the call finally ended. With a soft sigh, Zoe turned to the food, ready to drown her work frustration in falafel, only to collide with a warm, cotton-clad chest.

"You okay?" came Damien's deep voice as he reached out one hand to steady her, the warmth of his palm jolting Zoe out of her stupor.

"Sorry, I'm so tired I'm basically a zombie right now."

"Want me to make you some coffee?" He gestured at the espresso machine. "I came to get some for myself."

"Thanks, but I'm trying to cut down on my caffeine." Zoe scanned the takeaway boxes on the pantry island. "What's good here?"

"No idea. I brought food from home because there's a bunch of leftovers I have to finish before tomorrow."

Zoe flipped open the cover of one of the boxes, her senses instantly engulfed by the toasty aroma of golden-brown pita bread and hummus. "Why do you have to finish the leftovers today?"

"Every Saturday, I visit my mom in San Francisco and she always makes me bring home tons of her cooking. I'm talking half a dozen Tupperware containers. She knows I get free food at work but she's still convinced I'm a growing boy who needs proper nutrition. I just finished the last of her spinach soup today."

"You can store creamy soups for a week?"

"My mom makes the clear, Chinese-style kind. She uses Chinese spinach and anchovy-flavored broth, then adds goji berries and ginger root for their anti-inflammatory properties."

"That's how my mom makes it too!" Zoe exclaimed. "And I love when she adds century eggs."

Damien smiled. "My mom sometimes swaps out century egg for salted duck egg, which I think might be even better."

Zoe's chest tightened. The long hours at *Chic* and expensive plane tickets meant she only got to fly home once a year to see her parents in Michigan. Sometimes, she was even grateful to have work as an excuse to not visit them so that she wouldn't have to go through another round of questioning about her job. Her parents only asked about her career because they cared, but it was hard explaining to them why it seemed like she was making no progress, hard getting them to understand that fashion publishing's strict hierarchy required junior-level employees to pay their dues for years before they could move up the ladder.

But at this moment, standing in her office pantry at half past eight on a Friday evening, Zoe would have given anything to be back in her childhood home again, sitting down with her parents at their dining table—a cozy size perfect for just the three of them—and enjoying a hearty homemade meal. A bit of familiarity, comfort, and the knowledge that there was someone else—*real* adults—she could depend on.

"I miss my mom's cooking," she said quietly, unsure why she was suddenly spilling out her thoughts to Damien but too drained to filter herself. "I know the Bay Area has lots of amazing Asian food, but it's just not the same as a home-cooked meal. But I feel so tired lately that even on weekends, all I want to do is watch Netflix and order DishDash. I tried looking around for Chinese ingredients, but I think they're only available at Ranch99 and the closest one is still pretty far from me and I don't have a car."

"You can find Ranch99 on Instacart," Damien suggested.

"The prices are super jacked up on that app. It's not a big deal anyway. It's not like I'm starving or anything." She started spooning beetroot hummus into her disposable bowl.

"I can show you where to find fresh Chinese spinach," Damien said. "There's this booth at the California Avenue Farmers' Market that sells Asian vegetables. Also has organic kai lan and bok choy if you like those."

"I would love that!" It must be the prospect of replicating her mother's vegetable stir-fries that was making her heart suddenly beat faster, and *not* the prospect of spending time alone with Damien outside of work. "Are you sure it's not too much trouble to bring me around?"

"Not at all—I go there every week. Does this Sunday work for you?"

"I'll have to check but I think so," Zoe said casually, as though her schedule had not been completely open ever since she moved to California and made no new friends except Bernadette.

"Great. I'll text you the details."

"I guess it's a date then."

There was a beat of silence as Zoe processed what had just left her mouth. Heat rushed to her face. "A date as in a hangout. Sorry, I always say that to friends, so it just came out as a force of habit," she quickly said, throwing in a laugh for good measure. She squeezed her box of pita bread, hoping she could just squeeze herself into blissful oblivion instead. Why did she always seem to lose her head around Damien?

He shrugged, looking far more unbothered. "I'll let you get to your dinner then. See you on Sunday," he said, stepping aside to let her leave the pantry.

"See you," Zoe called over her shoulder as she walked away, a new spring in her step.

chapter 16

SUNDAY MORNING DAWNED bright and crisp—the perfect opportunity for Zoe to bring out her tangerine-print maxi-dress from Color Me Courtney. Something about wearing citrus fruits on her body in fall just felt so right, and she decided to round off the outfit with teal feather earrings and a white-and-brown rattan tote. At the last minute, she tossed in a rolled-up shopping bag, in case any of the produce at the farmers' market ended up catching her eye.

The weekly California Avenue Farmers' Market was already packed with couples and families when Zoe arrived. Tarp-covered booths lined both sides of the road, their stands hawking anything from fresh produce to potted succulents, floral-infused cheeses to gleaming crystals like the ones scattered all around Dreamcatcher's office. A harpist was basking in one corner of the street, her melodious tunes the perfect backdrop for the market's hustle and bustle.

"Zoe!" A voice called out from behind her. Her dress swished around her legs as Zoe turned around to find Damien walking up to her, an SF Giants cap casting shadows on his face. Her mouth dried. He was clad in a white shirt so thin that beneath the noon sun, it looked almost translucent in places, showing off the curves of his muscles. She'd been proud of her accessorizing, but Damien managed to make a simple tee and rugged jeans look good. Life was so unfair.

"Hi," she squeaked once he was in front of her. How had she never noticed that he basically towered over her? She cleared her throat and was relieved her voice sounded more normal as she said, "I'm so excited to be here! Where should we start?"

"I don't know about you, but the first thing I need is some coffee," he said, leading the way confidently through the throngs. Zoe hid a smile when she noticed he was shortening his strides so she could keep up in her espadrilles.

"Sir, hi!" A flower booth owner called out, gesturing toward the profusions of blooms displayed, from giant tea roses to dainty baby's breath. "You two are the best-looking couple I've seen to-day! Buy a bouquet for your lady?"

A flush crept up Zoe's face. "Oh, we aren't a couple," she blurted.

As they beat a hasty retreat, Damien chuckled. "I bet he says that to every couple that passes his store just to get them to buy his flowers."

"Yeah, anyone can clearly see we don't belong together." Zoe laughed too, trying to ignore the sinking feeling in her stomach. Why was she always more flustered than he was?

Damien came to a stop in front of another booth. "Anyway, this is my go-to coffee place."

The booth owner swooped in. "Hi, folks! We have a special today: Buy a drink and you get a pastry half off."

Damien's eyes lit up. Zoe mentally filed away this new discovery—it seemed like her coworker was a bit of a foodie. Either that or he loved a great discount.

He bent down to take a closer look at the glass case of pastries and made a sound of pleasure. "This pastrami croissant looks good."

But Zoe's attention was drawn to another item. "I just saw that yesterday on someone's Instagram story!" she exclaimed, pointing at a split-open muffin that exposed the soft-boiled egg nestled within.

The booth owner, a silver-haired man wearing a gingham beanie and matching apron, grinned toothily at her. "That's our most popular item, The Rebel Within. A savory cake containing pork sausage, scallions, different kinds of cheese, and when you cut into it, the most amazing, perfectly runny golden-yellow egg yolk oozes out. We've recently been experimenting with a vegetarian option made with Impossible sausage."

Zoe's eyes flew up to the sign on the booth's awning. "*Craftsmen and Wolves*," she read out. "Is your shop some sort of franchise?"

"Nope. We only have one store in California."

Something prickled in the back of Zoe's mind. "Wait, so you don't have a store in New York?"

"Not that I know of. Just that one in San Francisco, and we set up a booth here every Sunday."

But she had clearly seen Amirah Amin devouring one of these on her Instagram two days ago, which meant it couldn't have been a recycled video. Was the muffin in that clip a knockoff? But Amirah had even sprinkled a small vial of pink salt over the dish, which looked just like the cluster of salt vials in a canister by the booth's cash register.

Or maybe—

Zoe whipped out her phone and went to Amirah's Instagram, clicking on the section of photos the New York–based influencer had been tagged in. The most recent was of Amirah beaming in a selfie next to a girl with spiky green hair. Caption: *I met the Amirah Amin today!! SCREAMING is this my life?!*

Geotag: San Francisco

Dimly, Zoe registered the booth owner inviting Damien to sample a chunk of lemon poppy seed muffin and orange poppy seed muffin, explaining that the store was testing the two flavors out on customers to see which one they ought to sell. But all she could focus on was the one thought racing through her mind: Amirah Amin was just an hour away from her.

While Damien chewed thoughtfully on the two muffin samples, Zoe quickly typed out a message.

> Hey Amirah! I've been a big fan of yours for a long time, starting from back when I was a fashion writer at Chic in New York. I now work at a fashion startup called FitPick, and our app lets users poll the public on their OOTDs. We believe in creating a safe space for people to explore and experiment with fashion, which is very aligned with your own ideals. I heard that you're in SF now—any chance you would let me buy you coffee and tell you more about the app?

Holding her breath, Zoe hit "Send," watching as the words crystallized in her Instagram chat with Amirah.

"Zoe, you have to try this banana bread!" Sounding more

animated than she'd ever heard him, Damien proffered a golden-brown slice, so moist that Zoe could see the oil glistening in the sun. It looked divine and smelled even better, and was so soft it crumbled once he placed it in her palm. In her mind, Zoe updated her previous suspicion of Damien: *definitely* a foodie.

Zoe took a big bite, her eyes fluttering shut as she savored the sensation of the buttery-smooth bread melting on her tongue. The next moment, her phone pinged, and she almost dropped her banana bread in her haste to click on the Instagram notification that just popped up.

> Hey Zoe, thanks for reaching out. I'm in
> SF now but flying out later this afternoon.
> If you can come up before 3pm, I can meet
> you for coffee at Starbelly in Mission. Let
> me know.

"Damn it."

It was only when Damien asked "What's wrong?" that Zoe realized she had cursed out loud. With a sigh, she recounted her exchange with Amirah Amin to him. "Demoing the app in person to Amirah is the best way to convince her of what we can do and how we can work with her. But—"

"Go," Damien interrupted. "You should go now."

"I can't just ditch you!" Not after Damien had so kindly offered to show her around the farmers' market based on one offhand remark from her about missing home-cooked Chinese vegetables.

"The farmers' market will be here every Sunday and we can always come another time. But this meeting could be the big break you need for your campaign."

A faint glimmer of hope sparked within Zoe, though it quickly flickered out when she glanced at her phone again. "There's no way I will make it there in time," she groaned. "My entire campaign proposal is on my work laptop, so I have to go back home to get it, then go to San Francisco. And I doubt I'm going to get an Uber easily on a Sunday afternoon." She could feel beads of sweat rolling down the back of her neck, plastering her hair against her nape and soaking into her dress's Peter Pan collar. Great, now she had the frazzled appearance to match how she felt on the inside.

Damien checked his watch. "I'll drive you. My work laptop is in my trunk because I was planning to do some work at Blue Bottle after this. If your proposal is on SharePoint, you can access it on my laptop."

"But you just went up to San Francisco yesterday. I could be there for hours."

Damien was already retrieving the car keys from his pocket. "I'm sure my mom won't mind seeing me again while you have your meeting. Tell Amirah you'll be there by two. That gives you one hour to make your case before she has to catch her flight."

Zoe had the sudden urge to hug him, but she settled for saying, "Oh my God, thank you. You're a lifesaver! Please, let me pay for your coffee at least."

But the booth owner was already shoving each of them a steaming hot cup. "It's on the house. Good luck for your meeting," he said with a wink. "Go knock 'em dead."

***

"DAMN, THIS DOESN'T LOOK GOOD," DAMIEN MUTTERED, TIGHTening the grip of his right hand on the steering wheel. If this were any other time, Zoe's eyes might have lingered on the bulge of his bicep against his shirt sleeve, or the thick vein running down his forearm.

But with only twenty minutes until her meeting with Amirah, Zoe followed Damien's gaze to the road. Her heart sank. She'd been so absorbed in reading her pitch deck on Damien's laptop that she hadn't noticed traffic had slowed to a crawl. Stretching ahead of them, as far as her eye could see, was a long line of cars, their windows gleaming beneath the afternoon sun. The 101 was so packed that the car procession was moving even slower than they would be in a parking lot.

"I'm so screwed." Zoe leaned back in her seat, unable to stop her left index finger from tapping incessantly against the center console. All the caffeine from her free coffee—which she'd gulped down in the first five minutes of getting into Damien's car—must be sinking in now. Not that she could entirely blame the coffee for what a frazzled mess she was.

"We'll get there in time. You just focus on preparing for your meeting."

With a sigh, Zoe shut Damien's laptop. "It's okay, I've been rereading the same slide heading for the past five minutes. I'm too nervous to take in anything right now. This is basically my last shot because Amirah Amin is the only influencer who hasn't completely shut me out. Actually, she ghosted my email, too, like all the other influencers I contacted, but for some reason decided to respond to my Instagram DM."

Her hands tightened around the edges of Damien's laptop. "Bill could have hired anyone else, even someone who has never worked in fashion before, and they would probably be able to come up with better ideas," she continued, her voice growing smaller. A roadside billboard flashed past her eyes: *Cover your SaaS with Haloed Solutions.* "I'm just not sure I have the right background for this—" *Role. Job. Company. Industry.*

Damien was quiet for a moment as he deftly changed lanes. "Do you know that Bram is a big soccer fan?" he suddenly asked.

Zoe blinked. "Yeah." Going by the half dozen Cristiano Ronaldo jerseys he wore on a rotating basis. "But what does that have to do with anything?"

"Last year, he was following the Champions League, an international tournament that uses a bracket system. So thirty-two teams are divided into groups of four. The winners of Group 1 and Group 2 face off in the next round, while the winners of Group 3 and Group 4 face off. And then, the winners of those two matches face off in the round after that. And it goes on until one team becomes the overall winner. And that got Bram thinking: Could a similar system be applied to our app?"

Damien raised his voice to be heard above the rumbling of a passing truck. "That's what inspired Austin and me to add voting logic that lets users create a sequence of polls using a bracket system in FitPick."

"*Bram* came up with that?" Zoe asked. The man who ate Cheetos out of his hoodie came up with one of her favorite FitPick features? The night before she left New York, she'd set up a poll for her airport outfit, asking users to help her pick between a sweatsuit set and a slouchy jumpsuit. Once they'd made their selection, they were then directed to a follow-up poll asking them to choose between two pairs of sneakers for the sweatsuit set, or between a pair of sandals and a pair of slides if they'd picked the jumpsuit. In this way, she'd gathered multiple outfit combinations into one winning outfit—the entire process a welcome distraction from the inevitable reality that she'd be in a new city twenty-four hours later.

Damien glanced over at Zoe, his face tanned and golden as the afternoon sun shone through the window behind him. "Yeah, that was all Bram. My point is: Good ideas can come from any-where, even soccer. FitPick's lucky to have you and your fashion knowledge."

Zoe shook her head. "No, I'm lucky Bill believed in me enough to offer me this job when it was obvious I didn't know anything about tech. Most CEOs wouldn't have done that."

"Just because you've never worked in tech before doesn't mean you can't come up with great ideas. "

Zoe snorted. "Right, and that's why my campaign idea is go-ing soooo well."

"That's not a reflection of your abilities but of how tough this job is. You are the first and only marketing person at FitPick, which means you have no lead to follow. You're single-handedly developing our entire marketing program."

As the highway traffic became glutted again, Damien turned to face her, his expression completely serious. "And even though this is all new to you, you still go above and beyond in everything you do. You're rushing to another city on a Sunday afternoon just on the off chance you might talk one person into partnering with FitPick. You deserve to be here, you know. As much as any of the rest of us."

His eyes slid back to the road as the vehicles in front of them started cruising again. Zoe gazed unseeingly at the road, her mind racing. *You deserve to be here.* When was the last time someone had said that to her? When was the last time she had genuinely believed that?

"Thank you," she said quietly, something soft stirring in the depths of her chest. She hugged Damien's laptop closer to herself, suddenly feeling oddly exposed. How had he managed to see into her so clearly, at once grasping her fears and insecurities?

"Enough about me," she said, clearing her throat. "What brought *you* to FitPick?"

Damien switched his driving hand and rested his right hand on the center console. "Just wanted a change. Worked at Microsoft for a few years but didn't feel like I was making an impact—"

"Weren't you made a senior engineer when you were only twenty-five?" Zoe asked, then blushed when Damien turned to her, one eyebrow lifted. "I read your LinkedIn profile," she admitted.

"Huh, I forgot I had that. I only created it because my director at Microsoft asked me to reshare some post he wrote."

"Well, I created LinkedIn to stalk you FitPickers when I was debating whether to take this job. Back in New York, no one in fashion used LinkedIn. Instagram, Getty Images, the society pages of magazines—that's how we checked if someone was—"

"Cool enough?"

"It's not that we're shallow," Zoe said, shifting in her seat. She didn't work in fashion anymore, but it was hard not to take his judgment of an industry she had loved since she was a child as a judgment of herself. "If a magazine writer wants to stand out, they need to bring something other writers can't to the table. Like scoring an invite to a really exclusive event so that your magazine can be one of the first to cover it. The way to get on those VIP invite lists is to be popular, and a person's social media following is a good measure of that."

"It's a good thing that's not how software engineering works or I'd never get a job."

"Back to your job. Why do you say you weren't making an impact even though Microsoft obviously valued you a lot?"

"I just felt like I wasn't making a *big* impact." Damien blew out a breath, making the curl lying over his right eye flutter. "It's hard to do when you're just one of thousands of software engineers at one of the world's biggest tech companies. And there was so much office politics to deal with that some days I could barely get any real coding done. Then I got an email from Lillian one day that she was looking for people to join FitPick. I didn't know anything about FitPick but I trusted Lillian's judgment, so I ended up becoming employee number three."

Her eyes wide, Zoe jerked upright in her seat. "You knew Lillian before FitPick?"

"She was a teaching assistant for one of my computer science classes back at Stanford."

Huh. Zoe popped a breath mint into her mouth as she pondered this revelation. Damien obviously liked and respected Lillian a lot to follow her to a budding startup. Why did it seem like she was the only one who had trouble working with Lillian Mariko?

"Working at a startup is definitely very different, but I like it. I feel much more involved in the high-level planning instead of just carrying out the instructions of some C-suite executive I probably would never meet. Hey, check that out." Damien jutted his chin toward her car window.

Rolling hills loomed ahead of the highway, stretching across the horizon. Nestled in the hillside right before their eyes was a sign, its stark white letters standing out against the green and brown landscape:

SOUTH SAN FRANCISCO
THE INDUSTRIAL CITY

Maybe it was the big, blocky letters that screamed more functional than fun. Or maybe it was the word *INDUSTRIAL*—a clear reminder that this city and its Silicon Valley vicinity flourished because of companies whose products had become household names around the world. Nothing about this was glamorous the way fashion tried to make everything look, but those companies didn't care as long as the job got done. Function over form.

Zoe gnawed on the inside of her cheek. Maybe her influencer campaign idea—which might have worked in Los Angeles, the City of Angels, or New York, the City of Dreams—just wasn't suited for a company birthed in the Industrial City. And maybe Lillian was right all along that tried and tested search engine optimization and email marketing would have been the best path for FitPick.

As if of its own accord, Zoe's left index finger started tapping against the center console again to the rhythm of her pounding heart. If only she had her FitPick fidget clicker right now so she could do one last bout of stress-clicking. But according to Damien's car GPS, they were less than twelve minutes away from Starbelly, the café Amirah Amin had suggested. In less than twelve minutes, she would be sitting down to hawk her influencer marketing campaign.

Instead of cold leather, her tapping finger touched something warm and soft. The next moment, what felt like an electric shock ran up her arm, leaving a trail of goosebumps in its wake. She quickly whipped her hand away from Damien's on the center console.

"Sorry," Zoe muttered, feeling a warm flush creep up the back of her neck. "It was an accident."

"No big deal," Damien said easily, placing his right hand safely back on the steering wheel.

But why were the hairs on her left arm still standing on end? For the rest of the ride, Zoe kept her arms firmly planted on her lap. Once they got off the 101, the highway tapered into narrower side roads that curved up and down and side to side like a roller coaster. As they crawled up a particularly steep incline, Zoe dug her shoes into the floor and gripped her seat belt extra tight, her wide eyes trained on the truck in front of them.

Damien glanced over. "You okay?"

"Of course I'm completely okay with the possibility that the brakes of that truck are gonna fail and it's going to slide backward and crush us into pulp. My own mother wouldn't even be able to recognize me."

"They can do DNA analysis on your teeth."

Zoe shot Damien a glare that only made him chuckle. "Is that supposed to make me feel better?"

"No, but the view at the top might."

The car inched slowly toward the top and as it crossed the crest, a maze of houses unfurled before their eyes like a Polaroid whose colors were slowly coming to life. The sky, calm and cloudless, stretched out to the horizon, where it met a sparkling strip of deep-blue ocean—the two blending at the edges until it became hard to tell where one ended and the other began. And just behind a rolling hill came a glimpse of a tall metal structure, its red hue a stark contrast against the landscape.

"The Golden Gate Bridge," Damien said quietly.

Zoe's stomach unclenched at last as she took in the view. "You're right, it's beautiful," she breathed out, her eyes drinking in every detail. From this high up, it felt like the entire city was laid out in front of them, sprawled open like a treasure chest, serving up its hidden gems and secret spots for their eyes. "But gosh, these roads are so windy. I feel like I'm about to be sick."

"Take a deep breath," Damien instructed as he started driving downhill, straight into the crush of the weekend city traffic. "Pre-meeting nerves are completely normal. But if you are free after your meeting, we should check out Lombard Street, supposedly the crookedest street in the world. At Stanford, every freshman goes on a scavenger hunt during orientation week, and one of the items is to streak naked down Lombard Street."

Do not think of Damien Scott naked, Zoe commanded herself, praying her cheeks weren't red. "Did you actually do it?"

"I was too terrified I'd accidentally run into my mom."

By some miracle, the traffic cleared and they pulled up in front of Starbelly at five minutes to two. The moment she opened the car door, a gust of cold air rushed into the warm car interior, making Zoe flinch as her hair flew in front of her face.

Damien held out his jacket to her. "Take this."

"It's okay," she managed to say over her chattering teeth. "I'll be in the café soon."

"Starbelly is very popular and it's going to be noisy. If you want a good discussion with Amirah, you should ask to be seated outside. So just put on my jacket, even if it clashes with your outfit."

Damien looked so serious that Zoe couldn't help but laugh. She accepted his offering and shrugged it on. "Thanks! Will you be okay though?"

"I'll just head over to my mom's place and she always has the heater on full blast. Good luck," he called out as Zoe rushed out of the car, almost dropping her (technically Damien's) laptop and notebook in her haste. "Text me when you're done."

Zoe nodded, too pumped up on adrenaline and nerves to speak. *It's showtime.*

chapter 17

AS ZOE NEARED Starbelly's entrance, a wall of noise hit her immediately. The bottomless brunch trend was still clearly booming in San Francisco since all of Starbelly's outdoor tables were already occupied, and most of the café's indoor area was also filled. It would be a miracle if she and Amirah could even hear each other over the din; how was she supposed to give a full presentation? At least she still had a few minutes to settle her nerves before Amirah arrived.

Except, the influencer was already seated at a table. Even more unfortunately, she was facing the door and caught Zoe's eye immediately. *Damn.* Why hadn't she fixed her windswept hair and touched up her makeup *before* walking in? Meanwhile, Amirah looked just as chic in real life as she did on Instagram in a white sweater tucked into patchwork jeans and paired with cowboy boots. Her sunglasses (with the distinctive Celine logo) were perched atop her pink headscarf, which matched perfectly with her sweater's pink embroidery.

Zoe had met her fair share of celebrities while working at *Chic*, but she couldn't help but be slightly starstruck as Amirah flashed the winsome smile that had won her an Invisalign endorsement. Amirah Amin had almost single-handedly popularized hijabi fashion and shown that Muslim women could have fun with their outfits. She was the perfect choice to front FitPick's campaign, but this was a woman who had worked with Tory Burch and Stella McCartney—there was no way FitPick's thirty-thousand-dollar budget could compare.

"Hey, thanks for coming up here on such short notice," Amirah said, her voice somehow even more melodious than it sounded in her TikTok try-on hauls. She nodded down at the two cups of foamy coffee on the table between them. "Hope you don't mind that I went ahead and ordered cappuccinos for us. I heard the coffee here is pretty good."

"Thank you! But I was supposed to be buying your coffee." Thanks to the two oversized coffee mugs, there was barely any open space on the already small table. Zoe clutched her laptop and notebook in her lap, feeling like a student being lectured in the teacher's office. How was she supposed to access her pitch deck when the table wasn't even big enough for her laptop?

Amirah waved a hand nonchalantly through the air. "It's no big deal. Princess Polly flew me out this weekend and they said all my expenses for this trip are on them."

"Wow, Princess Polly?"

A mischievous twinkle entered Amirah's eyes. "Keep this to yourself, but I just finalized my contract to design my own capsule collection for them."

"Oh my God!" Zoe shrieked, though her words were drowned out by the brunch babble. "Congratulations!"

"Thank you," Amirah said, smiling graciously. "I love clothes, obviously, but designing them is a new challenge." She lowered her voice, her expression becoming somber. "I understand how huge this is for representation, so I'm afraid that if my collection doesn't sell well, it will make Princess Polly and other big brands more hesitant to work with Muslim women or other creators from marginalized communities in the future. I don't want to fail and give people a reason to believe that only clothes designed by white women have an audience."

"But so many people adore your style! Didn't you just cross four hundred thousand followers on Instagram?"

Amirah let out a soft sigh. "That's true, but there are so many decisions I must make, even down to the nitty-gritty details like sleeve length and fabric print. I just wish I had a way of know-ing what people would actually love enough to buy." She sat up straighter and dialed her smile up a notch. "Anyway, enough about me. Let's talk about you and your work."

Zoe straightened up too. "As I mentioned in my DM, I work at a fashion startup called FitPick and we've got an app that lets you crowdsource opinions on your outfits." A group of women sat themselves down at the next table, and Zoe had to raise her voice to make herself heard over their chatter about a guy named Rick. "I actually have a slide deck on my laptop about the app, so maybe it's just easier if I walk you through it and you can—"

She broke off as Amirah held up a hand. "That's fine. I actu-ally read your email about it."

Zoe held the steaming cappuccino to her mouth to cover her look of surprise. "The one I sent a few weeks ago? I thought it might have gotten buried in your inbox since I'm sure you get tons of emails every day."

"No, I saw it on the day I got it." Amirah paused, looking as though she was trying to pick the right words. "Frankly, when I first read the email, I thought what you wrote about *creating a safe space* and *exploration and experimentation* was just buzz-words. You wouldn't believe the number of pitches I get every day from brands who claim they and *only* they know what people really want. So no offense, but I kinda thought you and your company were also just talking a big talk."

"None taken," Zoe said, straining to hold on to her smile.

"But if I had realized the Zoe at FitPick was you, I wouldn't have been so quick to close the email." Amirah leaned forward. "I only opened your Instagram DM and agreed to meet you to-day because I've been following your work for quite a while, ever since I came across an article you wrote two years ago about this New York woman with alopecia."

Zoe's mind flashed back to one of the first articles that she had pitched instead of it being assigned to her. An article that almost hadn't seen the light of day. When she had first proposed interviewing the indie musician with alopecia who performed twice a week at the speakeasy that she, Bjorn, and Cassie frequented, her editor Francesca had made her explain over and over again what alopecia was. And when Zoe had described how the musician would rotate among different neon-colored wigs, Francesca exclaimed, "Why don't you compile a list of Kylie Jenner's best wig moments?" The editor had finally okayed the article when Zoe agreed to feature the indie musician alongside a bona fide celebrity who also had alopecia—in that case, Jada Pinkett Smith.

"I just found it so refreshing to finally read a hair story that had nothing to do with how to get summer-ready beach waves or the perfect hairstyle for every face shape. It made me feel like I don't owe anyone an explanation for what I choose to do with my hair and why I cover it up with my hijab. Afterward, I set an alert on *Chic*'s website for every article you wrote and went to check out your Instagram. I guess your Instagram handle must have stuck in my mind, so I clicked on it when I saw it in my inbox today. Everything you've written for *Chic* shows me you genuinely support those from marginalized communities who might not fit in with conventional beauty standards. And now that I know you're the one who sent that email, it makes me think that maybe FitPick really does practice what it preaches."

Zoe couldn't nod fast enough as excitement coursed through her. "We do! Bill, our founder and CEO, really believes in challenging the stereotypical look that social media sites like Instagram and Pinterest are constantly pushing. We want our users to feel comfortable in their personal style and share that with others, instead of creating an echo chamber where everyone looks and dresses in the same few prescriptive ways. And unlike Instagram, where people feel the pressure to only post flawless images, FitPick makes fashion fun because our users aren't afraid to ask for advice. It encourages people with different styles and preferences to bond over a common love for fashion."

Amirah took a long sip of her cappuccino, letting out a soft "ah" as she set her mug down. "That's why I started my fashion blog—I love fashion but for the longest time, it didn't seem like there was a seat for me at the table. As though I can't be considered fashionable just because I have to be covered up and can't wear certain trendy styles."

She adjusted her pink headscarf and steepled her hands. "Look, to be straightforward with you, the engagement fee you mentioned in the email doesn't quite match what I usually charge, and the FitPick app is still very new. But your company's mission sounds very aligned with my personal brand, so I want to see if there's a way we can meet in the middle."

Even though she had already suspected that was the reason for all the rejections and no-responses, and even though Amirah had tried to phrase it as delicately as possible, Zoe's stomach still clenched. There was no way Lillian would give her a bigger budget for this. "I understand where you're coming from, Amirah," she said, hoping she seemed calm and collected even as her mind raced for a solution. She could feel sweat dotting her upper lip and gathering on her arms. Just in time, she managed to tighten her grip before Damien's laptop slid out of her clammy hands.

Thankfully, Amirah was distracted for a moment as a waiter came up behind her. "Miss, sorry, do you mind moving your chair in so I can squeeze past you?" he asked apologetically, balancing a plate of fried chicken and waffles in his left hand and a platter of muffins with three different condiments in the other.

As Amirah obliged, a memory flashed into Zoe's mind of the farmers' market this morning, which almost seemed like a lifetime ago. The booth owner for Craftsmen and Wolves inviting Damien to sample two different kinds of muffins, crowdsourcing feedback from the market patrons to determine which might sell better. The glimmers of an idea began to take shape.

"Amirah, I think we can offer you something even more valuable." Zoe paused, waiting until Amirah's attention was completely on her before continuing.

"Data," she declared, dropping her voice so Amirah had to lean in to catch the word. "More specifically, data for your target audience because FitPick lets you set country, age, and gender limits on whom your polls are shown to. You said earlier you wish you knew what kind of clothes your audience liked, and you can use FitPick to find out. Let's say you want to know if they prefer long sleeves or short sleeves, so create a poll where you're wearing two blouses of similar colors and style but different sleeve lengths, and see which receives more votes."

Zoe's voice grew stronger as she spoke, possibilities tumbling into her mind faster than she could voice them. "In fact, what you learn from FitPick can be helpful beyond your Princess Polly collection. Let's say you notice that across multiple polls, people are showing a preference for maxidresses. That's your cue to write a blog post of your favorite maxidress brands, or create an Instagram Reel of different ways to style them. The sky's the limit for what you can do with the results of your FitPick polls. So besides the engagement fee, this is one thing FitPick can offer you that other apps can't: a way to conduct user research that's quick, free, effortless, and most importantly—fun for both you and your followers."

Zoe's voice trailed off as Amirah gazed off into the distance, her face creased in thought while her finger tapped absently against her coffee mug. Zoe reached for her own cappuccino, but the contents in her mug were in a sorry state—the milk foam largely dissolved and the cup lukewarm. Still, she made herself gulp down every last drop to soothe her parched mouth, trying not to make a face as the bitter coffee coated the back of her throat.

Was it the coffee making her heart rate skyrocket until it almost felt like her heart would leap out of her chest? If only she could be like one of those women at the next table having a carefree afternoon gossip session over good food. Instead, she was laying all her cards on the table—one marked with coffee stains— her whole plan hinging on Amirah's response. If the influencer said no, well, that was that then. A dead-end street. There was no way Bill and Lillian would give her another chance.

"I'll do it."

Zoe's eyes snapped back to Amirah. "Really?" she asked breathlessly, searching the other woman's face for any hint that she was joking.

"Yup," Amirah said, the *p* sound popping extra loud. She glanced down at her phone, tossed back the last of her cappuccino, and slid her sunglasses back onto her face. "I'll have my people reach out to yours once I'm back in New York, and we can discuss the deets. But I have to run now—got a flight to catch!"

Oh. My. God. Still stunned, Zoe remembered her manners just in time to offer her cheek to Amirah for the customary goodbye air-kiss. The moment the influencer disappeared through the doors, she sagged back into her chair, her tightly coiled muscles finally unspooling. She dumped her belongings onto Amirah's vacated chair and cracked her knuckles. Her fingers, stiff from being locked in a tight grip around Damien's laptop for the past half hour, creaked so loudly that the women at the next table looked over, annoyance written all over their faces at the disruption to their discussion.

Zoe smiled apologetically, her heart so light that their glares slid off her like a silk negligee. It didn't matter that she had no "people," unlike Amirah, that FitPick's influencer marketing campaign was essentially a one-woman show. At long last, something was going right.

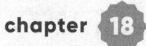
BRAM THREW HIS phone onto the table. "Ugh. Another one."

"Another what?" Zoe asked, not even looking up as her fingers flew across her keyboard, carefully documenting the profit-loss statement for her marketing campaign, which she'd since named See Yourself. Four years of studying communications and two years of fashion journalism had not prepared her for working so extensively with numbers.

"Let me guess," Austin cut in. "Another referral digger."

Bram let loose a heavy sigh. "Yeah, the third one this week."

Zoe clicked "Save" on her Excel spreadsheet, letting slip a smile at the neat rows and columns of numbers on her screen. "What's a referral digger?"

"Someone who hits you up on dating apps not because they're actually into you, but because they're into the company you work for and want to get a referral from you," Bram explained glumly.

Zoe winced in sympathy. "Ouch. That sucks. *They* suck."

"Bram, you set yourself up for it though," Austin interjected.

"You still listed Microsoft as your employer because you know it will attract more people than FitPick."

A hint of red bloomed on Bram's cheeks. "No, it's because my BaeArea account is connected to LinkedIn and I forgot my LinkedIn password so I can't go in and update my employer."

"Really? 'Cos I could have sworn I saw you comment on Bill's LinkedIn post a few days ago—"

"What's BaeArea?" Zoe asked before another squabble could break out.

"The latest hit dating app in the Bay Area," Austin answered, a heavy dose of *duh* in his voice.

"But instead of matching people based on physical appearance or hobbies or whatever, the algorithms are based in psychology," Bram eagerly explained, pouncing on the change of subject from his LinkedIn activity. "When you create an account, you take a test to assess your love language and attachment style, and you're matched with people from compatible backgrounds."

"Ah," Zoe said. And people thought New York's dating scene was whack.

"But it's not working for me," Bram lamented, his mouth turning down at the corners. "It doesn't matter what my love language is when the only language I really speak is C++, Java if I'm feeling kinky. No woman is going to want an engineer like me when there's millions of us here. I'm sure they'd rather go for a cooler guy like Bill."

Zoe turned her chair around to look at him fully. "Hey, don't knock yourself down like that. Some women will prefer Bill and some women will prefer you. Different strokes for different folks."

"Where are those different folks then? I've only gotten a dozen matches in the last six months and half of them ghosted me the moment I told them I've left Microsoft and now work at a startup they've never heard of."

"If my marketing campaign goes well, more people will know of FitPick," Zoe joked.

A brief pause, then: "Yeah, that'd be awesome." Bram smiled, but Zoe could tell he wasn't actually confident it would happen. Maybe no one did except Damien. And maybe he was just being nice when he said he had confidence in her.

"Dude, if you want women to stop thinking of you as just an engineering geek, change up your profile a little," Austin said.

Bram crossed his arms. "What's wrong with being an engineering geek?"

"Nothing. I'm a software engineer. But like you said, there's too many of us here. You should try to show off a different side of you." He turned to Zoe. "Zoe, back me up here."

"Uh—"

Bram pushed his phone in front of her, his BaeArea profile pulled up on the screen. "Yeah, what am I doing wrong?"

Zoe shifted in her chair. Jesus, she should have just kept her attention on work. Why did they think her being a woman made her an automatic expert on what all women wanted? But as she flicked her eyes over Bram's dating bio, she had to work hard to hide a grimace. Austin had a point—everything Bram put on there *did* make him seem like the caricature of a software engineer. The cover photo was of him at his work desk in his typical combo of flannel shirt and jeans, holding up a mug that read: *Have you tried turning it off and on again?* ("Hey! I took that shot," Austin said, poking his head over Zoe's shoulder to look.) The next photo was a selfie taken at what she guessed was a hackathon, judging from the word *TreeHacks* on the front of his shirt. To the prompt that asked what he was looking for, Bram had written: *Someone to grab a byte with.*

Ouch. No wonder Bram was getting lost in the BaeArea shuffle. Someone else might have been able to pull off the quirky responses in an ironic way, but Bram's awkward smile and poses in his photos made him seem more like the butt of the joke than in on the joke.

Bram peered at her anxiously. "Is it that bad?"

Zoe gnawed on her lower lip. She could lie to him that his profile was great and he should definitely keep it. He would continue to make a fool of himself on BaeArea and on his dates (in the rare scenario in which he actually scored one with that profile)—just what Bram deserved after all the jibes he took at her behind her back.

But what if his failed love life meant a relentless stream of complaints at work? Putting up with his presence as her seatmate for fifty hours a week was hard enough without having to hear more about his online dating woes.

"Well, this does kind of make you seem like just another tech guy," Zoe finally said. Against her will, a small prickle of sympathy darted through her as Bram's face fell.

"But I really do love my work," he said in an uncharacteristically soft voice. "What's wrong with that?"

Zoe shrugged. "Nothing at all. But I bet there are at least a dozen other tech people you know with that same exact mug."

Bram nodded slowly. "Yeah, that mug was actually a welcome gift when I started at Microsoft," he admitted. His eyes swiveled over his own profile again. "You're right. I'm really not doing myself any favors, am I? If I change my profile, could you look over it again?"

Zoe smiled, a tinge of smugness itching to poke its way out. Guess there was something she did "know shit about" after all, contrary to what Bram had said about her in the restroom. And it felt good to be on the receiving end of a plea for help, after weeks of always being the one with questions to clarify. "Of course! I also know you love Formula One and watching improv shows, and you're learning Mandarin now." It was amazing the things one could pick up about another person just from sitting one foot away from them fifty hours a week. "Those are interesting facts you might want to mention since they make you more memorable."

"And dude, you gotta change up your wardrobe too," Austin piped up. "All you have are flannel shirts and company tees, and yes, I know that's how I dress too, but I already have a girlfriend. You can't go on dates looking like you just came straight from work. And that Cheetos hoodie has got to go."

Zoe clapped a hand on Bram's shoulder. "I know who can help. Just leave it to me."

Bram furrowed his brows. "But what if the new clothes don't make me look like me anymore?"

Zoe was already dashing off a quick text to Bernadette to ask if she could squeeze Bram into her styling schedule. "In the words of my very wise friend," she said, fingers flying across the keypad, "Dressing up isn't about turning someone into a different person, but about bringing out the best person they can be."

"SO, YOUR FRIEND SEEMS RATHER NERVOUS ABOUT SHOPPING," Bernadette said that evening as she and Zoe walked out of their Desk Step class together and trod the now familiar path to Re-juice. "I'm trying to arrange a time for him to come by Nordstrom for a personal styling session, and he asked if he could bring snacks and use the restroom if the session goes on for too long."

"That sounds like Bram all right." Zoe chuckled, but her mind was stuck on one word. *Friend.* She and Bram weren't friends, just coworkers who had to be cordial due to circumstances outside of their control—mainly the seating arrangement. Her real friends were still back at *Chic*, on the opposite end of the country.

Except . . . for the first time since she could remember, she had kept something back from them in their last phone call. She hadn't told Cassie and Bjorn about her issues at work because they didn't believe she could have any.

Zoe swerved to dodge a frazzled mother carrying her toddler in one hand and an Hermès Kelly bag in the other. "Hey, Bern, uh, speaking of friends"—*real smooth, Zoe*—"How often do you see your old friends from work?"

"I've barely seen them since I left." A note of wistfulness entered Bernadette's voice. "Then again, I used to see them almost twelve hours every day, five or six days a week. Compared to that, any other frequency would seem too low. Besides, they're all very busy with work now, while I'm just busy shopping for other people, walking on treadmill desks, and watching DIY craft videos."

Zoe chose to gloss over Bernadette's self-deprecating jab. "But you would still call them friends, right?"

"If you asked me this just two months ago when I was still working there, I would have for sure said yes. I saw those people way more than I saw my own fiancé. But in hindsight, maybe we were friends only because we spent so much time together that we had to get along."

Zoe swallowed. "What do you mean?"

"When we met up after I quit, we barely had anything to talk about. All the awkward silence made me realize how much our conversations used to revolve around work. And they would ask me what I'm up to, but after they cracked one too many jokes about how they 'long to pull a Bernadette and just kick back with champagne on a Wednesday afternoon,' I started holding back more on what I told them. We've been drifting apart and maybe"—Bernadette shrugged—"we're just not friends anymore."

Zoe absently followed Bernadette into Rejuice, her mind roiling over Bernadette's words. What the other woman had described sounded just like what she was going through with Bjorn and Cassie. But at least Bernadette was still in the same city as her former coworkers; meanwhile, she was on the complete opposite coast from her friends. How was she possibly going to rescue their friendship?

As they joined the end of Rejuice's snaking line, Bernadette asked, "Speaking of work, what were you working on at Desk Step? You looked so caught up in it."

"I had a pitch meeting in San Francisco on Sunday, for that marketing campaign I was telling you about." Zoe couldn't hold back the smile that tugged at the corners of her mouth, thoughts of Bjorn and Cassie falling to the back of her mind—at least for now. "And that gave me a million ideas for how to take the project I'm working on to the next level."

Bernadette swept her sweat-soaked bangs off her face and peered at Zoe in surprise. "Wow, I don't think I've heard you this enthusiastic about work before. The meeting must have gone well then."

"Very well," Zoe confirmed with a grin, not bothering to try to act humble. God knows how much she had put in to make the meeting happen in the first place. "Better than I dared to let myself hope for, to be honest. I was so happy afterward that we went to this cute café—"

"*We?*"

"Me and a coworker. He offered me a ride there and visited his mom, who lives in San Francisco, while I had my meeting." Her eyes crinkled at the memory. "When he came to pick me up after the meeting, his backpack was bursting with Tupperware containers from his mom. It's really cute—they are obviously close."

"Let's do . . . two Mindful Matchas?" Bernadette said to the Rejuice girl, looking to Zoe for confirmation. Zoe nodded. "You like him, don't you?"

A few seconds passed before Zoe realized Bernadette's second question had been directed at *her.* "Me? Like Damien?" she sputtered. "We're just coworkers!"

"Ah, so he has a name," Bernadette said, a gleam in her eyes. "Now, I don't usually go around assuming that any man and woman hanging out are into each other. But you should have heard the way you were speaking about him."

Zoe shook her head vehemently. There was no way she liked Damien. She had only just stopped being intimidated by him, for crying out loud. Although . . . they did have a really good time at the farmers' market before their time was cut short. And the car rides to San Francisco and back had been surprisingly devoid of awkward silences. And the expression he had made when she started rhapsodizing about The Rebel Within muffin afterward while celebrating at Craftsmen and Wolves had been quite unlike his usual stoic mask—a mix of bemusement and wryness with a tinge of . . . softness? It had felt like a glimpse into the side of Damien Scott that he never showed at work.

A burst of laughter broke into Zoe's thoughts. "All right, all right. I'll stop." Bernadette smirked, accepting two matcha smoothies from the Rejuice girl and passing one to Zoe. "You should see your face though—it's so red."

"Because I just did a Desk Step workout," Zoe protested, but her voice sounded weak to her own ears. She could feel a layer of heat emanating off her cheeks that hadn't been there when she got off the treadmill. As she followed Bernadette to two stools by the window-facing counter, she resisted the urge to press her smoothie cup against her face.

Bernadette took a long sip of her matcha smoothie. "I'll let you off this time. Anyway, I'm really happy for you that your marketing campaign is going well. That's the one with the influencers, isn't it? Have you found your people yet?"

"Yes! On Sunday, I secured my first campaign spokesperson, Amirah Amin. And since then, four more have signed on. It's a really diverse bunch too—different genders, ages, ethnicities, and body types—which captures what FitPick represents really well."

"That's amazing! Quite a change from just a few weeks ago when you were so worried that you wouldn't get anyone."

Zoe flipped her hair over one shoulder. "Social media influencers move like a mob. All I had to do was name-drop Amirah Amin when I followed up with the others, and voilà—half of them said yes."

Grinning, Bernadette clinked her smoothie cup against Zoe's. "The good old name-drop. Nicely played."

Zoe took a big gulp of her refreshing beverage, a sweet respite after a tough workout. Things were looking up all right.

chapter 19

TWO WEEKS LATER, one night before the launch of the See Yourself campaign, Zoe was starting to feel like she might have played herself. With less than twelve hours to go, it was absolute chaos trying to coordinate with five popular fashion influencers who all had their own busy schedules and strong ideas about when and what to post. Jasmine Nguyen had asked at the eleventh hour if she could announce the app using a different photo of herself than the one her agent had submitted two weeks ago and that had been approved by Bill, Lillian, and the freelance graphic designer Zoe had contracted to create the campaign graphics.

There was also the issue of making sure the campaign would get good press coverage. Bill had wanted features in all the major tech publications, but Zoe had been forced to tell him that Fit-Pick was too new and small to get anyone at those media outlets to take note. Instead, she had aimed for the fashion sites, sending a dozen of them a missive teasing that an exciting new app fronted by major fashion influencers was dropping on Thursday. But all her emails had been ignored, as she'd predicted when Lillian decided that the influencers' identities should be kept under wraps and revealed only at the campaign launch for maximum impact. Those fashion media outlets surely got hundreds of emails a day promoting all kinds of "influencer-endorsed" products.

As a last resort, Zoe reached out to *Chic* yesterday. She hadn't wanted to take advantage of her connections there (read: Bjorn and Cassie), but desperate times called for desperate measures. Cassie agreed to pass on her email to Francesca, and now Francesca's response was sitting in her inbox. Zoe took a deep breath and clicked on it.

> Zoey, nice to hear from you. Unfortunately, we have
> a full plate right now and are unable to fit in your
> announcement. Hope the launch goes well.
> -Francesca F.

Zoe's shoulders slumped. Not only had her former boss managed to misspell her name (for the millionth time), but now her last hope was also gone. She would have to rely purely on the campaign itself to drum up attention once it'd been launched. But in this age of media oversaturation, the chances were slim. And while the band of fashion micro-influencers she had assembled were well known in their respective domains, their brands might be too niche to catch the mainstream eye.

"Do you think it's possible for anyone at a growth-stage startup to have a decent social life?" Austin asked to no one in particular.

Zoe looked up from her computer, glad for the distraction. "Is your girlfriend mad at you for canceling date night again?"

Austin breathed out deeply. "Yeah," he admitted, massaging the back of his neck. "But I really have to stay back tonight to finish debugging this." He waved his right hand at the lines of squiggly code on his laptop screen that made Zoe cross-eyed just looking at them. "It's not like I'm out partying or something! Does she think I *want* to be stuck at work this late instead of eating pasta and cuddling with her?"

Zoe shot him a sympathetic smile. "Try speaking to Damien. I think he'd understand and let you go home to finish up."

"Yeah, he would. Damien's a good guy." Austin cracked his neck, then his fingers. "But the whole team's here getting ready for tomorrow's grand unveiling; I can't just ditch you guys. Anyway, this will all be worth it once we get that sweet Logan Horossen money."

Zoe had to strain her cheek muscles to keep her smile intact. *Thanks, Austin.* No pressure or anything.

"Honestly, this makes me relieved I'm not in a relationship," Bram chimed in as he worked away on his own roster of programming bugs. "I wonder how Lillian does it."

"Right? She works more than any of us, but still finds the time to get a boyfriend during our most stressful period."

Zoe's ears pricked up. "What do you mean?"

"You've heard about the first Logan Horossen pitch meeting, right?"

"I know it was super stressful because Bill really wanted him to invest in us. But I didn't realize Lillian got into a relationship then."

After a quick scan of the vicinity to make sure Lillian wasn't within earshot, Bram lowered his voice and beckoned Zoe and Austin to draw in closer. Austin waved him off. "I know this story, dude. It was all we could talk about for days. Anyway, I have to get back to work."

Bram scooted his chair closer to Zoe's. "We didn't even know Lillian was seeing anyone. And then two days after the Logan Horossen meeting, a photo of her and her boyfriend appears on her desk. When Austin and I saw it, we both went—" His eyes widened and he pantomimed his head exploding. "She's a dark horse, I tell you. But I think being in a relationship has changed her—made her less of a workaholic."

Catching Zoe's doubtful look, Bram laughed. "Believe it or not, she used to be even more of a workaholic than she is now. She would stay back every evening for brainstorming sessions with Bill. But now, she'll leave the office around the same time as the rest of us—probably to have dinner with her boyfriend or whatever. But I still get emails from her super late at night, so she's probably back on her laptop the moment dinner is over. I think she's only staying back this late today because all of us are here."

Zoe snuck a peek in Lillian's direction. As always, the other woman was sitting with perfect posture at The Hook's long table, fingers flying across her keyboard as she nodded along to whoever was speaking on the other end of her headset. Without slowing her typing, she took a quick sip out of the green juice carton next to her, before saying something into her headset Zoe couldn't hear but was no doubt superbly intelligent.

Zoe turned back to her own computer and gulped down the remainder of her significantly unhealthier hot chocolate. There was Lillian, juggling both a thriving career and a thriving relationship. And meanwhile, she couldn't even seem to maintain her friendships with her closest friends.

Zoe jumped in her chair as Austin stood up and poked his

head over her shoulder. It'd been about two months since she started at FitPick and she still hadn't gotten used to the office's open-floor layout. He ran his eyes over the See Yourself campaign mock-ups Zoe had been tinkering around with on her computer. "Woah, these look good," he finally said.

She tried not to let the tone of surprise get to her. "I sure hope so, seeing as the campaign launches tomorrow." As the words left her mouth, a now familiar squeezing sensation entered Zoe's stomach again. The thirty thousand dollars allotted to this campaign was the most FitPick had ever spent on a single project, and also the most amount of money she had ever been put in charge of—a significant step up from the ten-dollar bill her *Chic* editor Francesca would give her to fetch her cigarettes and coffee from the corner shop.

And thirty thousand dollars could go up in smoke if the campaign opened tomorrow to a terrible reception. Her Sandro dress suddenly felt too tight around her midriff as visions of her deepest fears flooded her head. The photos getting only a few pity Likes on Instagram; the comments beneath them swarmed with question marks and laughing emojis; the influencers she'd taken so long to convince telling her they never want to work with FitPick again because the campaign they'd put their name to had tanked so badly.

Bill being disappointed but trying his best to hide it—which would only make Zoe feel worse; Lillian wearing a *I told you so* expression; and worst of all: the gut-wrenching realization that she didn't have what it took after all to make it in this industry, just as it had been the case back in New York.

Austin straightened up. "I'm heading to The Cook. You two want anything?"

"Can you grab me a LaCroix? Surprise me with the flavor."

"Sure. Zoe?"

Zoe shook her head. "I don't think my stomach can handle anything."

Bram nodded knowingly. "Ah, are you hopping on the Meal in a Pill bandwagon too?"

Both Zoe and Austin stared at him. "The what in the what?"

"You know how we get hit with a food coma after a large meal? What if you didn't have to eat an entire meal to get all your nutrition? What if there was a small pill that would give you all the proteins, carbs, fats, and fiber you need? It's amazing, really. Ever since I started replacing dinners with Meal in a Pill, I can keep working like a machine." Bram beamed.

Zoe resisted catching Austin's eye, knowing she would crack up the moment she did. "I thought you were doing the keto diet," she said.

"A pill isn't food," Bram said defensively. "Anyway, Jack Dorsey is using Meal in a Pill too," he added, like that settled matters. "That's how I heard about the Pill in the first place—I read in ValleyVerified that Jack Dorsey just invested ten million dollars in them."

Austin made a strangled sound in his throat, as though trying to prevent laughter from exploding out of his mouth. "Zoe, do you want any *real* food?"

"Uh, that sounds interesting, Bram," Zoe said. "And thanks, Austin, but I just can't eat anything when I'm freaking out. I want to finish reviewing the campaign materials first before dinner."

From the other end of The Hook, Bill looked up, a sympathetic grin on his face. "Oh Zoe, working at a startup means you never stop freaking out. It's like being a parent and always worrying about your child, even when they already have children of their own. But don't overthink it—it's too late to change anything about the campaign, so just grab some dinner, sleep early, and mentally prepare for tomorrow. We'll cross the bridge when we get to it."

Zoe swallowed, the topsy-turvy feeling wringing her guts anew. "I guess we will."

THE NEXT MORNING, AT TEN MINUTES TO NINE (ALMOST NOON on the East Coast), a scheduled email in Zoe's name went out to five fashion influencers.

It's go time.

chapter 20

WHAT'S—WHAT'S GOING on?" Zoe asked when she walked into The Hook the morning of the See Yourself campaign launch. Everyone was huddled around Bill, staring wide-eyed at his computer screen. Even Bram and Austin had arrived before noon today. At the sound of her voice, every pair of eyes snapped to her.

"Zoe." Bill's Adam's apple bobbed as he swallowed. "We've been written up in ValleyVerified."

Zoe rushed over to the group, her heart in her throat. Bill must be a ValleyVerified subscriber—his screen showed an email with the title: *Valley Verified: What's New in the Valley.* His cursor hovered over the very first item in the newsletter: *Fab or Fad—FitPick.*

She'd been up all night worrying about how the campaign would unfold, consequently only getting three hours of fitful sleep. She'd even woken up so late that she had missed her bus and was forced to Uber to work. But at Bill's words, Zoe's stupor instantly vanished. "No way. I didn't even send them a press release because you didn't want to attract their attention this early on."

"This is ValleyVerified—they always know what's happening on the ground. And we're their 'Fab or Fad' pick for the month. And even worse"—Bill gulped—"our reviewer is Rebecca Stiles."

Everyone sucked in a breath, even Zoe. After two months in the Valley, she had gotten a better understanding of the key movers and shakers. Rebecca Stiles had been the editor in charge of the Games section at *Entertainment Weekly*, then moved on to write about tech for *The New York Times*, before ValleyVerified poached her. "Fab or Fad" had a roster of reviewers, but Rebecca Stiles was notoriously harsh. In her three years there, she'd only awarded two *Fabs*—to Instacart and Figma.

Lillian clapped her hands together. "It's okay. Let's just read it. This is only what one person has to say," she said in an admirably calm voice. No one pointed out what everyone was thinking—it might be just one person but it was Rebecca Stiles, and her words would be read by millions.

"Okay." Bill took one last deep breath before clicking on the article. "Here goes nothing."

FitPick asks: Can style be crowdsourced?

BY: REBECCA STILES

'd be the first to admit I am a jaded, cynical soul. Every company these days claims they support "diversity." Yes, I see you rolling your eyes already—"diversity," the buzzword to end all buzzwords.

But when I saw the new marketing campaign from fashion tech startup FitPick this morning, a faint inkling of optimism that I'd previously thought was extinct stirred back into life. FitPick is an app that allows users to upload polls of their outfits and get their followers to vote on which one they should pick. On their website, FitPick's founder Bill Lawrence declared: "We want to give everyone—not just those whose physical appearance fits conventional ideals—a safe space to explore their style. Most photo-sharing apps pit users against one another in an algorithm-driven rat race to see who can rack up the greatest number of Likes, and that inevitably favors those who fit the current Eurocentric beauty standard. And before you know it, your entire feed is filled with women who all look a certain way and dress like one another, which alienates those who don't fit their mold. But on FitPick, the only person the user is being compared to is themselves in another outfit."

Unlike most other companies, FitPick actually seems to be putting its money where its mouth is. Its marketing campaign features the most diverse representation of campaign spokespeople I've seen coming from the fashion world in a hot minute—or should I say, haute minute. It eschews the usual skinny white cisgender female influencer with their preppy Y2K aesthetic honed in the hallowed halls of the Brandy Melville institution. Instead, three-quarters of its campaign cast is people of color. Amirah Amin, who runs the fashion blog *Amirah's Latest*, poses proudly in her extensive collection of hijabs; silver-haired actress Patricia Fields shows fashion isn't just a young person's game; and how can you not adore how Paralympian Holly Ngo accessorizes her walking stick to complement her outfits?

Even better, unlike most other social apps that are largely one-sided in nature—putting the influencers on one side and their admiring followers on the other—FitPick bridges this chasm. When Holly Ngo uploads photos of herself in two different Alo Yoga sets, her fans can now have a personal say in picking her workout look by voting on the OOTD of their choice. In her latest poll, Alo's Match Point tennis skirt (which I also voted for) edged out the Accolade shorts in a tight 52–48 split. Everyone gets one vote, and every vote counts.

It's impressive how FitPick manages to stand at the forefront of both the fashion and tech circles—arguably two of the world's biggest and most valuable industries. But these are also two of the most mercurial arenas, where what's hot one minute is not the next. The verdict's still out on whether FitPick will be little-black-dress-classic or go the way of low-rise jeans.

But in the meantime, here's my verdict: *Fab*. At least for a haute minute.

Check out my profile on FitPick at @stilishrebecca and tell me which Topshop co-ord set I should wear out on my next date. (Read my "Fab or Fad" review here of BaeArea, the latest in the wave of psychology-driven online dating apps.)

"Fucking amazing!" Bill's exclamation made them all jump. He scrolled back up to the paragraph that mentioned his statement. "This totally sounds like something I would say." He turned to Zoe, his face shining. "Zoe, you did a fantastic job of capturing my voice and FitPick's mission when you wrote our website landing page."

Zoe could have cried with relief, but all she did was say, "I'm really happy you like it." All that hard work chasing down influencers, pitching them FitPick, putting together the campaign and its press kit had finally paid off. She let out a long exhale, relief soaring through her. She did something valuable for the company. She finally showed she belonged.

She finally felt like she did.

Bill's words seemed to be a key unlocking the floodgates. Zoe felt two thumps on her back. "Let's fucking go!" Bram shouted, pumping his fist against Zoe's before she could even react.

"Zoe, you the man—I mean, woman!" Austin said just as exuberantly, his face lit up with a maniacal grin.

Damien moved his head closer to Zoe. "Good job," he said, much more quietly than anyone else did so that only Zoe could hear him. But something about the low timber of his voice only enhanced the sincerity of his words, making Zoe's cheeks warm.

Even Lillian smiled. "Hopefully, Logan Horossen will see this. I'm sure he's subscribed to ValleyVerified, but we should alert him just in case."

"Great point!" Bill immediately turned back to his computer. "I'm going to forward this to Logan Horossen right this second."

Zoe looked down as her phone began buzzing rapidly in her hands, having finally connected to the office's sometimes spotty Wi-Fi. A dozen messages squeezed one after another into her work inbox. "Oh my God. People want to interview us! They must have all just read Rebecca's article." Her eyes landed on the only email address she recognized—Bjorn's.

Zee, I just saw an online article about FitPick. This
is what you've been working on, right? IS MY BEST
FRIEND THE COOLEST OR THE COOLEST?! Mega

congratulations on pulling this off! Hopefully you can take the evening off and celebrate with some champagne. 😉

This sounds right up the alley of *Chic* readers. I'd love to interview you and your CEO about FitPick. We'll make it the core feature on *Chic*'s website and in our next issue! What do you think?

Congrats once again!! No one else but you could have scored this coup. Cassie says congrats too. Drinks on us the next time we see you!

"One of my former coworkers at *Chic* wants to do an exclusive feature on us!" Zoe exclaimed, her heart ballooning. She had come full circle from doing the reporting for *Chic* to now being the one reported on. And all in nine weeks. No one, least of all herself, could have predicted this.

Because of the campaign, she'd been working late into the night almost every day lately, which meant it would be almost midnight in New York by the time she left the office. But after weeks of missing Bjorn and Cassie's calls, she could finally afford to kick back, take a breather, and catch up with them.

"What does exclusive mean?"

"He wants to make it the core feature on *Chic*'s home page and the September issue, and that's *huge*. The September issue is the most important issue for any magazine, so we—I mean, they—wouldn't have promised that unless they are certain they're getting a scoop no one else has. Rebecca Stiles might have broken the news, but I think *Chic* wants to dive much deeper into our fashion use cases, the challenges of creating the app, and our future direction. And there's going to be a photo shoot too. You'll be in it for sure, and *Chic* will probably want a few of the campaign influencers or their own models to appear—"

Bill held up a hand. "Let's not rush into that. No offense, but *Chic* isn't the most well-known publication." He said it in his kindest tone, but even so, a wave of heat rushed to Zoe's cheeks.

"You said we're getting lots of interview requests, right? So if we're going to offer any publication an exclusive, I want it to be the splashiest deal possible," Bill said. "I'm thinking *Vogue* or *Vanity Fair*. And we definitely want to break into the Asian market. We should try to get featured in one of the popular publications there—there's one called *S*, I think, in Singapore. Do you know anyone working there?"

"Yeah, *S*—I read their Socialite Whisperer column every month. Okay, I'll go through all the interview requests and shortlist the best ones." But how was she supposed to respond to Bjorn? Everyone back at *Chic* would see her turning down the exclusive interview request as a personal betrayal. They might gossip about her becoming too big for her Charlotte Stone boots now that she worked in tech—and would Cassie and Bjorn even defend her when she hadn't spoken properly to them in a good few weeks?

A DAY LATER, WHEN ZOE WALKED INTO THE ROOK FOR FITPICK'S biweekly company meeting, she found Bill wearing a Cheshire cat grin on his face, squirming in his chair like an impatient child before dessert. "Don't bother asking," Austin said as Zoe opened her mouth. "I tried and Bill just said he wanted all of us to be here when he shared his news."

Zoe rolled her eyes good-naturedly as she took her seat between Lillian and Damien. At least it was clear that Bill's news was good.

When Bram still didn't show up at a quarter past nine, Bill huffed. "Well, I can't wait anymore, so Austin, you'll just have to catch him up later. Everyone, guess what? Logan Horossen responded and he wants to set up a second meeting with us as soon as possible!" His beam broadened as everyone burst into cheers. "I knew it was a good idea to email him! The meeting's going to take place this weekend in SF, so just wait for the good news on Monday—"

Pounding footsteps cut him off. The next moment, Bram rushed into The Rook and flopped into the only empty chair. "Sorry I'm late," he panted. "Traffic on the 101 was ass."

A hush descended over the room as everyone stared at him, their mouths hanging open. Zoe recovered her vocal faculties quickest. "Bram, the blue shirt looks great on you!" she exclaimed, sweeping her eyes over his outfit.

Gone was the plain black hoodie Bram always wore backward and that was permanently speckled with orange Cheeto dust, as well as his jeans that were so faded it was hard to tell what the original color was. In their place was a formfitting blue button-down that brought out the light flecks in his brown eyes, ending at just the right length above a pair of well-pressed tapered black pants.

He sat up straight and brushed off an invisible piece of lint as Bill and Lillian voiced their admiration too. "Really? I threw this on at the last minute. Didn't even have time to check how I look because I was running late," he said casually, but the pleasure in his voice was unmistakable.

"Damn." Austin whistled. "You look so fine right now that if we were out in public together, I might actually admit I know you."

"It's all thanks to Zoe's friend, actually," Bram said, sending a smile Zoe's way. "I finally went for my styling session with her last night. I was only intending to buy one shirt and one pair of pants, but somehow she convinced me to buy four button-downs, one blazer, two casual shirts, one pair of jeans, and two pairs of slacks. Oh, and a Henley because she said ladies dig that. She even taught me to roll my sleeves up because apparently women like looking at forearms?"

Zoe stifled a grin as, from the corner of her eye, she spotted Austin jotting down Bram's last note. Bernadette's charm was an undeniable force of nature.

"And I'm also signed up for Nordstrom's monthly styling sessions now," Bram continued. "Austin, if you ever want a wardrobe overhaul, I've got a ten-percent-off coupon I can give to new members."

Austin bristled. "Why would I need to change *my* clothes?"

"Have you seen your clothes?"

Thankfully, Lillian broke up the squabble before it could begin with a question about whether an artificial intelligence feature Damien was building would be ready by this weekend. The meeting seamlessly moved to other topics before wrapping up half an hour later.

As The Rook emptied out and Zoe began gathering up her materials to head back to her desk with everyone else, Bill gestured for her to come closer. "Zoe, you should come to the Logan Horossen meeting. His biggest issue last time was that we weren't attracting enough users, but we will now thanks to your marketing campaign. And who better to walk him through our progress than you?"

Zoe studied Bill's face to see if he might be joking, but his eyes were wide and earnest. "But I've never spoken to any VCs before," she squeaked out. "Much less Logan Horossen." The man with the Midas touch known for killing dreams and making top executives cry. Just seeing his signature deadpan stare was enough to make grown men quake.

"Don't worry." Bill gave her shoulder a hearty pat. "I'll be there with you the whole time. And because the meeting will end late, we'll stay overnight in SF at one of the top hotels—all paid for by the company. And think about it: How many people your age can say they have been in the same room as one of the world's most powerful men?"

A spark of excitement flickered to life within Zoe. "I only have to present the marketing part, right?" she clarified.

"Hang on." Lillian's voice snaked into their space as she approached them, making Zoe startle. She hadn't even heard the other woman approaching. It was like the COO had a sixth sense for when she would be with Bill and didn't want her enjoying any one-on-one attention from the CEO. "What's this about Zoe presenting?"

"Lili!" Bill threw an arm around Lillian's slim shoulders and pulled her close, making her stiffen visibly. "I just had the great idea of asking Zoe to come along with us to the Logan Horossen meeting."

Zoe's heart sank. She had forgotten that as the COO, Lillian would definitely be at the meeting too. That meant spending an entire weekend with Lillian, as though it wasn't enough being near her frosty demeanor for fifty hours during the workweek.

Without waiting for Lillian's response, Bill turned back to Zoe. "Don't worry about presenting. I'll do most of the talking for our business, and Lillian will cover the upgrades we've made to the app since the last meeting. I just want you there in case Logan Horossen has any questions about the marketing. Oh, and since marketing is what shapes a company's image, dress up in something nice. Maybe that V-neck top you were wearing on Monday, paired with this skirt?" Bill nodded down at her legs. "I'm sure Logan Horossen would appreciate the effort you put into your outfit," he finished with a chuckle.

Zoe shifted her weight from one foot to the other, resisting the urge to pull down the hemline of her skirt. It was nice that at least someone at FitPick was taking note of her style, but she hadn't realized the CEO had been paying so much attention to what she wore.

She looked at Lillian, waiting for the COO to dish out a reason why Zoe shouldn't go. But Lillian must have thought trying to convince Bill would be a futile effort because she kept silent. However, her narrowed eyes and pursed lips made clear her disapproval.

Well, even if Lillian didn't want her there, at least Bill valued her enough to bring her along. So Zoe squashed down her niggles of unease. "I can't wait! Logan Horossen is going to be so blown away."

"Fingers crossed." Bill grinned. "Well, I'll let you get back to work then. Lillian, I have a suggestion for the presentation deck."

As she walked to The Hook a few steps behind them, Zoe could hear Bill saying, "I was thinking we could replace the screenshots we have in the deck now with screenshots of polls featuring more attractive users. I know, I know—it's awful, but guys like Logan Horossen dig that stuff."

"Zoe!" Austin beckoned from his seat. "Come here, Bram has big news to share."

As Zoe hurried over, Bram whacked his coworker on the arm. "Why are you such a bigmouth?"

"Whatever, dude. So now that Zoe's here, what's your dramatic announcement?"

Bram gave a little cough and sat up straighter. "I, uh, might be going on a date tonight."

"That's awesome!" Zoe said. "So that's why you switched up your look today."

Austin smirked. "She knows you don't work at Microsoft, right?"

"What's that supposed to mean?" Bram huffed. "That the only reason why women would be interested in me is my career?"

"Nah, dude. I just want to make sure you go out with someone who genuinely appreciates you and isn't another referral digger," Austin said with an unexpected sincerity that made Zoe do a double take.

Bram blinked. "Man, that might have been the nicest thing you've ever said to me."

"Okay, enough with the mushiness. Show us who this unlucky lady is."

Grumbling, Bram nevertheless pulled out his phone and clicked into his BaeArea app. Austin studied the screen, then raised a brow in grudging admiration. "Damn, dude. She's fire."

Zoe leaned over for a look too. "Oh yeah, she's really pretty."

Austin scoffed. "Not fire as in hot—"

"But she is," Bram interrupted. "Very pretty, I mean."

"FIRE as in being a part of the Financial Independence, Retire Early movement. Also known as, living the dream."

"How can you tell that from a dating profile?" Zoe asked.

"It says here that she's a product manager at Amazon, so easily a six-figure salary—"

Bram made a face. "Do you think that's a deal-breaker, her working at Amazon?"

Austin paused to think. "No, because she's planning to retire early, which she can since she says she's also a personal finance influencer on TikTok with over two million views, so another six-figure income stream. And since she's famous for her budgeting and saving tips, I'm guessing she's really frugal as well. Definitely on the FIRE track." Austin gave a firm nod, as though daring anyone to disagree with his character assessment.

"I've never seen anyone make Roth IRAs sound so sexy," Bram said dreamily, making Zoe burst into giggles.

chapter 21

AFTER WORK, ZOE immediately texted Bernadette the news about the Logan Horossen meeting, though she was careful to leave out his name and simply refer to him as a big investor due to FitPick's confidentiality requirements.

As she watched a checkmark appear below her message, indicating it had been delivered, a sudden pang struck her. In the past, the first people she would have texted about any news—good or bad—would have been Bjorn or Cassie. But besides comments left on one another's Instagram posts, the three of them hadn't spoken in weeks. Although Bjorn had responded with an understanding message to Zoe's apologetic one about having to turn down *Chic*'s exclusive feature, Zoe thought she could sense a distance behind his words that hadn't existed before.

The sudden ringing of her phone jolted Zoe. When she picked up, Bernadette's throaty voice poured out of the speaker. "Zoe, that's wonderful news! I was so excited that I simply had to call you. You should be so proud of yourself—you helped turn your company's image around."

"Thanks, Bern. But gosh, I'm so nervous," Zoe said, letting herself admit what she hadn't dared to voice in front of Bill and Lillian. "I mean, this guy is *huge* and I've never even met a VC before, much less have to pitch to one. I know I won't be doing much of the pitching, but still."

"There's no need to be nervous," Bernadette said soothingly, and Zoe could imagine her giving an airy wave of her hand. "VCs will throw money at any app that sounds even semi-legit. When I was still in consulting, I helped a messaging app get acquired by Facebook for two million dollars. And all it did was let you send "Wassup?" to your friends once a day. Literally, that was the only word you could send."

Zoe's mouth fell open. "Seriously? Facebook believed in it enough to give *seven* figures?"

"Yes, and Facebook wasn't the only big company interested. Point is: If you believe in your company's app, then walk into that pitch meeting and just make it clear that you won't accept anything less than what your value is."

Although Bernadette was talking about FitPick, Zoe felt an ember of pride spark to life within her. Even if Logan Horossen decided to pass on funding FitPick, other potential investors had reached out to Bill after seeing the See Yourself campaign featured in various media outlets. No matter what happened at the pitch meeting, she had already surpassed her own expectations and many other people's too with how well her campaign had turned out. She had proven all the naysayers *and* herself wrong.

THE NEXT DAY, ZOE ARRIVED AT THE OFFICE BRIGHT AND EARLY to work on her portion of the meeting presentation. With no one else around, she could rehearse her part out loud without feeling self-conscious. But after less than twenty minutes, footsteps sounded behind her.

"Hey, Zoe. Do you have the image specs for Amirah Amin's scheduled post next week?" Damien asked.

"Uh, yeah," Zoe said absently, switching from PowerPoint to Canva to look for the campaign materials. "But it might take me some time to find them. Can I send them to you la—" Her words died as she finally lifted her head to look at Damien. She blinked. Damien, who usually donned a black FitPick polo shirt to work every day, was wearing a button-down in almost the exact same shade and cut as Bram did yesterday.

"Did I miss some fashion memo? Is FitPick turning into the Blue Button-Down Brigade?" Zoe joked.

Damien glanced down at his torso as though surprised to see the shirt on himself. "Oh, I just grabbed it randomly out of my closet this morning. Should I, uh, wear it more often?"

Yes! Zoe wanted to scream. Bram looked great in it, but on Damien, it looked like the button-down had been made for his body, the material hugging his chest and the rolled-up sleeves highlighting the muscles in his arms. Turned out Bernadette had been spot-on about the allure of a guy's forearms. And the shirt's deep blue shade only made Damien's hair and eyes appear even darker.

However, it was one thing to compliment Bram, because it was Bram after all. But how was she supposed to give Damien a compliment and make it seem casual, when it was anything but?

Zoe coughed lightly to clear her head of any indecent thoughts concerning Damien and his chest-clinging shirt. "That's up to you. Fashion is a very personal choice."

"But you're the fashion expert here, so you'd know better than me what looks good," Damien pressed.

"You should wear whatever makes you feel good," Zoe said, giving herself a mental pat on the back for her successful non-answer answer. But was it her imagination or did a slightly disappointed look cross Damien's face at her response?

But his usual stoic expression was back on his face as he said, "That's true. Anyway, you can just shoot the image specs to me over Slack once you have it. Thanks," before walking away.

Zoe stared after him for a moment longer, bemused by the odd exchange. Then she gave herself a tiny shake of the head and forced herself to focus on her presentation again. The only man she should be thinking about now was Logan Horossen.

THE REST OF THE WEEK PASSED IN A HAZE OF COORDINATING with the five influencers to remind them to continue posting on FitPick and promoting their polls on social media, fending off more feature requests from fashion and tech sites alike, and working with Bill and Lillian to perfect their presentation deck. And before Zoe knew it, it was Friday evening, with just twenty hours to go before the Logan Horossen meeting. For once, both Lillian *and* Bill had left early to get some rest before the big day tomorrow.

Bill had asked Zoe to sleep early today, but being alone in her apartment meant having nothing to distract her from all her nerves about tomorrow. Bram and Austin had also disappeared at 5 p.m. sharp for their weekly board game night with a few mutual friends. And so she was all alone in FitPick's office. Technically, Damien was there, too, just a short distance away. But he was so absorbed in his own work and so quiet that even Luka/Louise the mannequin had more presence than he did.

Zoe clicked "Save" on her latest draft of FitPick's press release and leaned back in her chair, stretching her arms above her head with a long exhale. A loud *crack* echoed through the silent office as she flexed her right wrist, stiff from hours of pounding away on her keyboard.

"Impressive," Damien deadpanned, not looking up from his own computer. "I don't think my bones are as nimble."

Zoe snorted and rolled her chair toward him. "You should take a stretch break too. You've been at it longer than I have."

"Soon. I'm almost done validating my model."

"How's it looking?" Without a technical background, she didn't understand much about the artificial intelligence feature Damien was constructing. She only knew that it was meant to detect the clothing items in a FitPick poll so that if users clicked on any of the items, they would be directed to a list of dupes at varying price points.

"Ninety-one percent accuracy."

"That sounds really good! If it were a test grade, that'd be an A."

The corners of Damien's lips tilted up slightly as he met Zoe's eyes. "Depends on what domain you're talking about. If my model was about fraud detection, for instance, even a ten percent accuracy would be great because that means it's catching one out of every ten fraud cases. But if I was using AI in a surgical context, the accuracy should be as close to perfect as possible because even one mistake could mean a person losing their life. In this case, ninety-one is good, but still not great."

He scooted his chair back slightly from the desk, allowing Zoe to move closer. She breathed in deeply as she came to his side, hoping it wasn't obvious that she was taking in his scent. Damien always smelled clean, not in an artificial Febreze way, but more of a subtle cotton scent that made Zoe long to bury her face in the crook of his neck.

With an effort, she squashed down her inane thoughts and

focused on Damien's screen. It was filled with lines and lines of code in different colors—all of which she didn't have the slightest inkling of. "Okay. What am I supposed to be looking at?"

"Right now, my model has trouble identifying the clothes if the person is holding something that obstructs part of their outfit. But I've just incorporated body posture information into the latest round of testing and hopefully that creates a normalizing effect on the issues I just mentioned."

"You know AI really well," Zoe remarked. Even machine learning model testing sounded interesting when it was Damien doing the talking.

"I specialized in the AI track within Stanford's computer science major." He glanced at his computer, then made a few clicks. "Actually, AI was what motivated me to minor in English creative writing."

"How come?"

Damien turned back to her, and it was then that Zoe became aware of how close they were. Her knees were touching his, his rugged jeans the only thing between their skin. He leaned forward and clasped his hands together in the empty space between his legs. She quickly lifted her eyes back up to his face, a layer of heat pooling in her cheeks. The air around them suddenly felt much heavier than just moments ago.

"I was doing a group project for an AI class, and one of my groupmates was complaining about an essay he had to write for a mandatory writing class. He kept saying things like 'Why do we have to learn how to write an essay anyway? That's a useless skill when I can just code a program that will write it for me.'"

The distaste Zoe was feeling must have shown on her face, because Damien chuckled. "Trust me, I was pissed, too, then. But mostly because he wasn't even doing what he was supposed to do for the group project. So I argued that there was no way computer-generated content could ever match up in terms of creativity and emotional depth. Honestly, I was just arguing for the sake of arguing."

"And then what happened?"

"Nothing. We were just dumb sophomores—we finished that project, somehow got an A, then never spoke to each other again. But that conversation got me thinking about whether machines can ever perfectly imitate humans, so I started exploring more into natural language processing—that's the AI domain focusing on human linguistics. Do you know how AI works?"

"Not really," Zoe said truthfully. But even if she did know, she would have given anything to hear Damien talk about something he was obviously so passionate about, his face lit up with a rare smile.

"Basically, you build a computer program, feed it lots and lots of data, and gradually the program begins to spot patterns, learn them, then use them to construct its own database."

"So it works best when the data it's studying has distinct patterns?" Zoe asked.

"Right!" Damien said, his eyes bright against his tanned skin. "But the thing is, writing is so much freer than people think it is. In high school, my teachers taught me to follow the three-act structure, to show not tell, to never use adverbs. But my English professors in college taught me to forget those rules and write whatever *feels* right for the story I want to tell. So yes, computer programs can write—but it would do better at writing how-to guides than epic novels because the former is much more formulaic. There's an entire universe out there those computers still can't fully capture."

"Even if they can, I think people would still want to read things written by other people, just to celebrate what humans can achieve,"

Zoe mused. "It's like how we still hold the Olympics even though cars are so much faster than humans."

"Or how factories can churn out fast fashion designs but there are many people who would still pay a premium for handmade couture."

Zoe did a double take. "Excuse me, did you just make a *fashion* analogy? You know *couture*?"

Damien rolled his eyes but smiled. "Just because I wear jeans and hoodies every day doesn't mean I'm sartorially illiterate."

Zoe wanted to scoff but without warning, a loud yawn bubbled out of her mouth. Mortified, she clapped a hand to her face. "Oh my God, I'm sorry. It's not you—I just haven't been sleeping well lately because I'm up all night thinking about the Logan Horossen meeting."

"That's okay. You should head home now though; it's late."

Zoe bit her lip. "Being alone will just make me think more about tomorrow and freak out."

Damien took one look at his monitor screen, then swiftly clicked out of his coding page. He snapped his laptop shut and stood up. "Come on. Let's get out of here and go for boba."

"You said last week that you hate boba pearls because they're too squishy."

"But you love them. And you're the one who could do with a distraction that's not just more work. So come on. Pack your things and let's go. It's my treat."

"Okay, thank you!" Zoe looked down to hide her flushed cheeks as she shoved her belongings into her purse. Her heart was beating too fast for her to focus on whether she was slotting her items into the right compartments within the bag. This display of bossiness was rather out of character for Damien, but she couldn't say she didn't like it.

chapter 22

ZOE SHIFTED IN her seat, her eyes darting up to the clock on the wall for the dozenth time in five minutes. Logan Horossen was running late, and she could tell that she wasn't the only one on edge because of the delay. Bill was now pacing back and forth in the small holding area adjoining Logan Horossen's meeting room—technically a conference room in the Ritz-Carlton in San Francisco, the very same hotel the FitPickers would be staying at that night. The hotel was one of the fanciest buildings Zoe had ever seen, but she was too busy mentally running through their pitch to admire it properly.

This, after all, would be the cumulation of all her efforts over the past few months. The event that determined if Bill had been right to hire her, had been justified in thinking he saw something in her.

And while she squirmed and Bill wore a hole in the hotel carpeting with his relentless pacing, Lillian sat calmly in her chair, her face impassive as she watched the replays of *Late Night with*

Jimmy Fallon on the television in one corner. As Zoe took in Lillian's wrinkle-free, well-pressed A-line dress, she quickly reached up to smooth down the ruffles along the collar of the V-neck blouse Bill had suggested she wear.

Bill whipped around, his forehead creased in a frown. "Do you think he forgot—"

His voice died as a slim brunette in a skirt suit entered the room. "Mr. Horossen will see you now." Her gaze fell to Zoe's feet. "Would you like me to put that anklet in a jewelry box for you?"

Although she had on sleek Larroudé mules that anyone with taste would approve of, the scrutiny made Zoe long to tuck her feet out of sight. "Um, what?"

Bill clapped a hand to his forehead. "Shit. I forgot to warn you about this."

"Warn me about what?"

Zoe soon found out. As the large double doors to the conference room were thrown open, four desk treadmills came into view, arranged in a ring and all facing inward. A stocky man with a platinum-blond man bun was pounding away on one of them, swinging his arms up and down vigorously like one of those grannies brisk-walking in Sunset Park, near Brooklyn's Chinatown. Whenever he lifted his arms up, it exposed a tattoo of a serpent on his ribs through the gaping hole of his muscle tee.

He didn't slow down even when he caught sight of the newcomers. "Join me," he said in a deep voice that contained a trace of an Australian accent.

Wide-eyed, Zoe looked around at Bill and Lillian, but they were both swapping their shoes for brand new socks and Nike sneakers that the brown-haired lady was handing out. Bill caught her eye and whispered, "Just go along with this." Go along with what? What sort of twilight zone was this where one of the world's most powerful venture capitalists was just casually taking a stroll on a treadmill during a pitch meeting?

When it came to a man like Logan Horossen, the wisest path was that of least resistance, so Zoe clamped her mouth shut and accepted the socks and shoes given to her. Then the assistant asked her quietly, "Miss, would you like us to store your anklet for you? We have a jewelry box that comes with a built-in dehumidifier and is lined with proprietary material that's a newly developed hybrid of velvet, silk, and alpaca wool. It's the new frontier for storage of fine valuables."

"Um, thanks, but it's okay," Zoe whispered back. The anklet was a five-dollar purchase from Claire's. She tightened the laces of her Nike sneakers, which were a perfect fit, of course. So that was why Bill had asked for her shoe size a few days ago; she'd thought he wanted to get customized shoes as company swag, but he must have then passed the information to Logan Horossen's team.

Gingerly, Zoe stepped onto one of the treadmills. Thanks to Bill's suggestion that she wear her Saloni bandage skirt, it would be impossible for her to go any faster than one and a half miles per hour. Was this Logan Horossen's idea of a survival-of-the-fitness test, and he would only give FitPick funding if all three of them aced the treadmill?

She startled to attention as Logan Horossen's voice boomed out, "Young lady, I believe we have not met."

"Hi—" Shit, should she call him Logan? Mr. Horossen? She settled for not calling him anything at all and instead summoned her brightest smile. "Hi, it's so nice to meet you. I love this setup. Reminds me of the Desk Step classes I do with my friend."

He smiled serenely even as sweat dripped down his ruddy cheeks and splattered onto the conveyor belt beneath his feet.

"That's why I had these treadmills brought in. I'm considering investing in Desk Step and I want to test their products out personally. See if their business can keep up with my expectations," he said with a small chuckle.

Bill and Lillian immediately laughed as though that was the wittiest thing they'd ever heard, and after a beat, Zoe joined in, feeling one step behind everyone else. "So far, it seems to be going pretty well," Logan Horossen continued. "I've calculated that big decisions are made in 1.67 fewer minutes and small decisions are made in 3.31 fewer minutes in meetings where everyone is on a treadmill instead of sitting around a conference table. I guess everyone just wants to end it as quickly as possible. So it's a great fitness tool, but there's incredible potential here as a workplace productivity tool as well. Desk Step just has to pitch it right and it can capture a new market."

Zoe bit back the urge to point out the ableism at play as Bill exclaimed, "That sounds like a great idea. Well, we know you're extremely busy so we can go straight into our presentation if you'd like."

Logan Horossen inclined his head. Bill adjusted the laptop on his treadmill's desk so that the screen was directly facing the famous investor, took a deep breath, and launched into the presentation.

Somehow, he managed to keep his voice so level that it sounded like he was merely taking a stroll on a beach instead of moving on a treadmill at three and a half miles per hour, which Zoe guessed he deliberately set to match Logan Horossen's. And even though Zoe had heard him rehearse this spiel at least a dozen times, it somehow sounded different this time as she tried to look at the many diagrams and charts through the investor's eyes. It was Bill giving the presentation, but her fingerprints were all over it. While Lillian, meticulous and detailed, was tasked with putting together all the product road maps and usage data, Zoe had been asked to use her "eye for aesthetic" to create the visuals and her creativity to develop the overarching presentation narrative.

And then, Bill arrived at the See Yourself campaign's section. Zoe's stomach clenched. But just then, Lillian shot her a small smile. Seeing this rare phenomenon smoothed out some of the knots in Zoe's gut. They were a team. Team FitPick.

"The See Yourself campaign is just one of our marketing efforts to put our brand in front of Gen Zs and millennials—the two generations that are steadily accumulating a greater share of the population's overall spending power," Zoe began, making sure to enunciate every word clearly over the sound of everyone pounding the treadmill. "Social media is the best way to reach them, but people are increasingly finding those big-name influencers unrelatable and inauthentic, and that's the opposite of what FitPick represents. That's why we engaged micro-influencers who might not be household names but occupy a specific fashion niche—they represent the diversity and inclusion that FitPick champions above all else. After the launch of See Yourself, we have amassed almost a quarter of a million installations and a twenty-two percent daily active user rate, with the average runtime being—"

"Why should I care?"

Zoe's steps faltered, forcing her to jog in a most unglamorous manner to catch up with the treadmill's speed. Once she was sure she wouldn't face-plant on the Ritz-Carlton's carpeted floor, she glanced quickly at Bill and Lillian for help, but they looked just as dumbfounded by the interruption as she was. "I'm not sure I understand—"

Logan Horossen spread his arms open. "Why should I care

about how many downloads you have? Those numbers mean nothing to me. The only number I care about is how profitable you are, and I'm hearing nothing about your business model. You have two hundred and fifty thousand users, but what you're not telling me is how that will translate into profits."

"Well, we're taking things one *step* at a time," Bill jumped in, moving his legs on the treadmill with an extra big swing to emphasize his pun. His joking expression faded as Logan Horossen gazed back at him blankly.

Looking more subdued, Bill tried again: "We want to attain a critical mass of users first so that we have a solid foundation to monetize—"

"You have over fifty thousand active users daily, Bill, so what are you still waiting for?" Logan Horossen demanded. He jabbed the "Stop" button on his treadmill, and Bill and Lillian promptly followed suit. Zoe stopped hers one beat late, but everyone was too busy looking at Logan to notice.

"You have this hot app on your hands but you'll be letting it go to waste if you don't come up with some sort of monetizing call to action for your users now. What if someone else comes up with a similar app tomorrow? You'll regret not doing something to generate profits now while you're the only player in the market."

chapter 23

THE MEETING WRAPPED up not long after. Zoe was grateful she could blame her flushed cheeks on the treadmill and not because Logan Horossen had just exposed a critical gap in FitPick's business. After thanking the venture capitalist profusely, she, Bill, and Lillian must have come to the same unspoken decision that they were too drained to discuss Logan Horossen's critique right then and there. Instead, after a half-hearted "Good job team" from Bill, they all wandered back to their own rooms on the eighth floor of the hotel.

Zoe collapsed onto the hotel's perfectly made bed, not even bothering to take off her heels. Now that the adrenaline rush from the meeting was wearing off, she grew aware of a dull pang in her stomach. Right on cue, it gave a little growl, which she could only be thankful hadn't happened during the meeting itself. But it was a jarring reminder that except for the cup of weak coffee she had made earlier with the hotel coffee machine—the only thing she could stomach in her nervous state—she hadn't eaten anything the whole day and it was already past eight.

She counted to three, then mustered the energy to push herself into an upright position and reach for the room service menu. FitPickers were given a forty-dollar daily stipend on work trips, and she planned to spend every last cent of it. Just as she was trying to decide between the seared scallops and the steak frites, her phone chimed.

> BILL: Zoe, celebratory dinner at
> the hotel restaurant tonight—great
> Chinese food. You in?

With her stomach rumbling, Zoe didn't even hesitate. Of course!

> BILL: Sweet. Good thing no one has
> to drive tonight 😊 I've got my eye
> on a bottle of Dom Perignon 2010.

Zoe snorted. There was no way their combined budget of one hundred and twenty dollars for three people was going to cover a bottle of Dom Perignon. She looked up the hotel restaurant, Ophelia, on her phone. Damn, it had a Michelin star; Dom Perignon was probably the cheapest thing they had on the menu. Since Bill suggested it, he'd probably cover the cost of dinner, but what was she supposed to wear to a place this fancy? The restaurant's website said the dress code was *Elegant*, but all she brought on this trip were pajamas and the sleeveless blouse and tight skirt she had on now. And some fine-dining restaurants didn't allow sleeveless tops . . .

But Lillian might know. She had stayed at this hotel with Bill for their previous meeting with Logan; they might have dined at Ophelia then too.

Zoe fired off a quick text to Lillian: Hey, what are you wearing to dinner at Ophelia? Is sleeveless okay? This was almost like texting Cassie and Bjorn back before one of their infamous paint-the-town-red nights out in New York, when they would start planning a whole week beforehand the optimal outfit combo that would score them free drinks but still be comfortable enough for doing the walk of shame to the kebab food truck when they finally left the clubs at three in the morning. Not that Lillian Mariko would ever be caught partying out late or inhaling greasy food truck fare.

Her phone chimed again after barely a minute, but it was a message from Bill.

> BILL: Dinner's in five minutes, btw. Managed
> to scope a last-min cancelation. A miracle
> considering they're all booked out for
> another month.

Damn. Zoe straightened her blouse, cursing herself for lying down in it and causing it to wrinkle. She quickly pulled on her heels and ran to the bathroom to polish her makeup and dab on a little perfume. This would have to do.

THANKFULLY, THE MAÎTRE D' DIDN'T EVEN BAT AN EYE AT ZOE'S outfit when she showed up. Very politely, he escorted her to a table in the corner of the room. The restaurant was already filled with diners in their best fineries, clinking champagne flutes against one another and laughing in the way only people self-assured in their status and appearance could.

Bill was already at the table, having swapped out his own meeting blazer for a more relaxed dinner jacket. Zoe breathed out a sigh of relief. It would have been slightly nerve-racking if she had gotten there first and had to sit at the table alone while waiting for Bill and Lillian to show up. Or God forbid, if only Lillian was there and they would have to make small talk. Come to think of it, she had never spent time alone with FitPick's COO before.

Bill's eyes lit up when they landed on her. "Zoe, you made it!" he exclaimed. He flagged down a passing waiter. "Could we have two menus, please?"

"Three," Zoe corrected as she slid into the chair opposite Bill's. "We have one more person joining us soon."

"Lillian isn't coming."

The moment the waiter left after depositing two leatherbound menus, Zoe leaned forward and lowered her voice. "Is she not feeling well? Should we go check up on her?"

Bill chuckled. "No, no. I just figured she'd say no if I invited her." He waved one hand around the room. "This isn't exactly her kind of scene, you know? I don't think she enjoyed it much when we came here last time."

Zoe gave a small shrug, but she saw what Bill meant. Ophelia carried a rather club-like feel, with its dim cove lighting, the dark red lantern lamps hanging over every table, and its gold-inlaid walls. The pièce de résistance was an open bar smack in the center of the room, with a cocktail cabinet decorated to look like a Chinese herbal shop. Zoe could already imagine the look of aghast bemusement that would cross Lillian's face when she spotted the giant gold dragon statue undulating above the restaurant's entrance or the small koi pond in the far-right corner. It would be all too kitsch for the COO's taste.

Bill pushed one of the menus toward Zoe. "And if she were here, she'd probably want to go over how the meeting went and brainstorm next steps. That would make it feel like a work dinner. I kinda just want to chill and have fun, you know? I know the meeting didn't exactly end on the best note, but I think we still managed to impress Logan Horossen with our progress and that's definitely worth celebrating."

Zoe accepted the menu with a smile but unease wormed through her. It felt odd having a post-meeting celebratory dinner without Lillian, who had played such an integral role throughout. But Bill had known Lillian far longer, so who was she to presume she knew better about what Lillian wanted to do on her night off? Resting in her room, putting on a moisturizing mask while ordering room service and Netflixing sounded pretty damn good.

A bottle of Dom Perignon came to their table a few moments later—Bill must have ordered it before she even arrived. Bill poured them both a generous amount, before holding his glass aloft. "To FitPick!"

Pushing away all thoughts of Lillian, Zoe smiled and touched her glass to his. "And to new opportunities!"

Bill leaned toward her. "And to new friends."

There was a slight dip in his voice on the word "friends" that made Zoe take a second look at him. But he was already reading his menu so she flipped hers open as well. "Everything looks so good here," she remarked. "Maybe you should just order for us."

Fifteen minutes later, there was more than enough food on the table for just two people. Lobster rangoons, slivers of raw yellowfish doused in a light yuzu sauce, rock shrimp ceviche, crab gyozas, and chicken satay. There were also two complimentary cups of green tea whose leaves had been harvested just yesterday from Alishan Mountain in Taiwan and airfreighted to San Francisco, as the waiter informed Zoe and Bill before taking his leave.

"Do you realize this is the first time it's been just the two of us since that New York party?" Bill asked as he deftly welded his chopsticks to pick up the plumpest slice of yellowfish and deposit it on Zoe's plate.

"Wow, you're right." It had only been three months since that rooftop event—although it was hard to tell the passage of time in the Bay Area thanks to the absence of the four seasons—but so much had changed since then. She had to adapt to a new job, new industry, new city, and even a new group of people. When was the last time she had had a proper conversation with Cassie and Bjorn?

Zoe quickly took a sip of the scalding-hot tea. At least the burning temperature distracted from the guilt thrumming through her.

But her mood lifted as Bill enthralled her with juicy anecdotes of Silicon Valley, most of which he'd gleaned from ValleyVerified. Like the chairman of a well-known social media company who kept accidentally clicking "Reply All" until one of his assistants was forced to tell him that everyone in upper management could see what he was saying about them behind their backs. Or the founder of a health tech startup who was worth a few hundred million dollars but still made his girlfriend Venmo him her share of gas money when they went out on dates. "And yet they just recently got engaged," Bill commented wryly, pouring himself another glass of champagne. "I heard he's rushing to complete his IPO before their wedding day so that those IPO stocks are considered his property only."

Zoe waved away his offer to top up her glass. "Poor woman. She has no idea what she's in for."

"I think she knows very well what she's getting out of it. Those IPO company shares aside, she still stands to get at least nine figures if they divorce. Every woman wants to be the next Mac-Kenzie Bezos—"

"Scott," Zoe corrected. "She goes by MacKenzie Scott."

Bill looked slightly taken aback by her interruption but simply replied, "Sure. Anyway, Zoe, have more champagne. You just finished your first ever VC meeting—with a man known as the Shark of Silicon Valley. You deserve to relax tonight and treat yourself."

"Oh, it's okay. I—"

Just then, Bill's phone gave a loud chime. Zoe breathed a sigh of relief as he immediately put down the bottle to check the notification—she didn't know how to turn down his offer for admittedly very good champagne, but the last person she wanted to get drunk with was her boss.

"It's from Logan Horossen! Well, from his assistant, technically, but I bet he told her what to write." His eyes flitted across the screen, and gradually, an incredulous smile spread over his face. "He had one of his guys run some projections for FitPick and he said if we can find a way to monetize our user base, things are looking really good for us. He was totally negging us earlier!"

"Negging?"

"Being super critical to assert his dominance, but I bet he thinks we're on the right track. He also said in this email that if we continue doing what we are for marketing, we would be able to corner a sizable portion of the market. Zoe, let's go up to my room. I need to show you these numbers."

Excitement surged within Zoe. "Can't you just show them to me now?" Logan Horossen heard dozens of pitches every week, but she doubted many of them interested him enough that he would get his personal team to look further into it. And he had singled out and praised *her* marketing ideas. This one email instantly made all the late nights and moments of tear-her-hair-out frustration worth it.

Bill shook his head. "Not good to discuss company matters in a public setting. And this seems like a pretty big file so I want to open it up on my laptop."

"Why don't I just grab us a conference room? There are a few on the fifth floor. Your room might not be big enough for us and Lillian."

Bill was already signaling the waiter to bring the bill. "Oh, there's no need to call Lillian. We can just go over the marketing stuff now since it's more of your domain anyway. And my room feels more private, no?" He shot her a big grin that showed all his teeth. "It's definitely big enough for us two. And we can polish off the rest of the bottle up there."

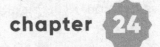

chapter 24

ZOE HAD NO choice but to follow Bill out of the restaurant. He was walking so fast in his excitement that she could barely keep up with him in her heels. At least Damien had slowed down for her at the farmers' market.

They had just stepped out of the elevator on the eighth floor when a familiar voice rang out: "Zoe, there you are."

Zoe turned around to see Lillian striding down the hallway, still looking as fresh as she did at the start of the Logan Horossen meeting. From the corner of her eye, she spotted Bill quickly covering the champagne bottle in his hands with his jacket, which he had taken off halfway through dinner.

The dinner Lillian hadn't been invited to.

Shit.

"Lillian, hi!" she exclaimed, wanting to cringe at how overly perky her voice sounded. "How are you?"

How are you? Zoe longed to kick herself. Next, she would be babbling on about the weather.

Lillian stopped in front of Zoe and Bill. "I'm good," she said, sounding a touch wary. Not that Zoe could blame her after that weird opener. Lillian's eyes swiveled between the pair. "Where were you two? I wanted to touch base about the next steps based on what Logan Horossen said."

Bill shot Zoe a look that managed to convey both *See, I told you so* and *Let me handle this*, which she was only too happy to acquiesce with. "Zoe and I ran into each other at the hotel restaurant. What a coincidence, eh?" he said brightly.

Zoe dialed her smile up a notch when Lillian turned to her, hoping the uneasiness she felt wasn't written all over her face. Everything just felt . . . wrong. When Bill first texted her, he had made it sound like a dinner celebrating a meeting that all three of them had worked so hard for. But now it felt like something that had to be hidden, a crime that pitted her and Bill on one team against Lillian on the other.

"Yeah, um, actually, Bill was just saying I should go—"

"Rest," Bill cut in. "I'm sure we're all beat after a long day."

Zoe's mouth clamped shut. She was about to suggest they go to Bill's room to check out Logan Horossen's latest email—at least this was a safe topic they could all talk about. But it was clear from Bill's interruption and the warning glance he shot her that that was something she was supposed to keep to herself. Now, she didn't even feel like she was on the same side with Bill. This conversation felt laden with land mines and no matter what she said, she was on the cusp of triggering an explosion.

"Yeah, I'm about to head to bed soon," Lillian replied. "Zoe, I wanted to ask if you could give me some makeup wipes? I forgot to bring mine."

"Of course." At this point, she would have agreed to just about any request from Lillian to put a stop to this odd exchange.

"Great. Can I follow you to your room to grab it?" Lillian asked before Zoe could offer to just bring the makeup wipes out.

"Uh, sure," Zoe said, not knowing how else to respond. If they were quick about it, she wouldn't have to be alone with Lillian for too long and there wouldn't be any time for awkward questions she couldn't answer without outright lying.

Bill shot them a big smile. "I'll see you two ladies tomorrow morning then. Remember, checkout's at eleven." He swiftly dashed off to his own room, leaving Zoe and Lillian standing in the hallway, staring at each other.

Zoe headed toward her room, keenly aware of Lillian's heels click-clacking after her. A muscle behind her right eye twitched as she fumbled with the lock, which for some reason refused to recognize her key card. It was like when the office printer always broke down just when she had an important document to print. Now, just knowing that Lillian was scrutinizing her made Zoe feel younger and clumsier—a bumbling anxiety that the door must somehow be picking up on. Even Logan Horossen had nothing on the woman whose eyes were currently burning a hole through her back.

Finally, the door clicked open. Zoe breathed a sigh of relief as she walked into her room. Thank God she hadn't left her underwear lying around *and* she had tossed away the wrappers of all the gum she had been stress-chewing earlier before the meeting.

She quickly grabbed an unopened bag of her best makeup wipes from her bag and handed it to Lillian. "Here you go. It's really gentle on the skin." It also happened to cost twenty dollars, but she didn't think a woman like Lillian Mariko would ever use Neutrogena, so her best Patchology wipes it was.

"Thanks," Lillian said, but made no move to leave. Zoe could feel a bead of sweat rolling down the back of her neck. How was it that the other woman managed to make her feel like an out-sider in her own room?

Lillian raised one perfectly plucked brow. "So, was there some sort of dinner plan that I missed? I was in the shower when your text came so I couldn't respond in time, but it sounded like you thought we were getting dinner together."

Zoe swallowed. *Shitshitshit.* She could confess the truth, but that would be throwing Bill under the bus.

"My mistake," she squeaked. "I just thought you might be go-ing to Ophelia for dinner, too, since it's the only restaurant in the hotel and wondered if you knew what the dress code was. It seemed like a really fancy place so I was afraid I would make some sort of mistake, but thankfully Bill was there and it helped to have a familiar face." Everything she said was technically the truth, but her heart thudded wildly as Lillian examined her face as though trying to spot a lie.

"I see. It's a good thing you had Bill looking out for you," Lil-lian said lightly. "He does tend to pay more attention to certain employees than others."

Oh God, was Lillian jealous of *her* for having Bill's favor? That wading-through-a-minefield feeling was back again. "He's probably just concerned about me since I'm so new to all this," Zoe said weakly.

Lillian nodded. "And you know you can come to me any time if you have any questions, right?"

"Definitely," Zoe said as she crossed her fingers behind her back and her toes in her Larroudé mules.

Lillian moved toward the door. "Well, thanks for the makeup wipes. I'll see you tomorrow."

Zoe couldn't nod quickly enough. In just a few moments, she would be free to change into her comfortable pajamas, jump into bed, and not worry about either of her two bosses for a full twelve hours.

Lillian's hand paused on the door handle and she turned to face Zoe again. "But it helps to be more alert so that you won't be caught in any"—she paused—"*compromising* situations in the future. Good night." And then she was gone, closing the door so softly behind her that it barely made a sound.

Zoe stood rooted to the floor, heat crawling up her face even as her blood ran cold. Lillian's parting message had been a thinly veiled warning to . . . what exactly? To be more careful about the text messages she sent so that they didn't cause any misunderstandings? Or did Lillian somehow sense that Zoe was lying and wanted to let Zoe know that she knew?

Zoe sank down on her bed and buried her face in her hands, all of her earlier excitement from Logan Horossen's meeting going up in smoke. No matter what she did, it seemed like Lillian managed to always find fault with it. With her.

chapter 25

ZOE STRAIGHTENED UP as Bill took his spot at the head of the table in The Rook. It was the Monday after the pitch meeting. FitPick's biweekly meetings were every Tuesday and Thursday, but Bill had called this "emergency session" to brainstorm what to do with Logan Horossen's critique.

Despite the somber situation, a flush of pleasure darted through Zoe as she looked around the room. Back at *Chic*, she'd been too far down in the pecking order to do any strategizing beyond whether to feature the JW Anderson puffer jacket in plum or black. But Bill must really trust her to include her in this discussion with Lillian and Damien, where she was the only non-C-suite executive.

Bill stood up. "Okay, team. I've already caught Damien up on what happened at the meeting. Logan Horossen did send a supportive email afterward, but he could easily forget about us tomorrow once a new startup catches his eye. So the main item—well, the only item on today's agenda—is to figure out how we can start monetizing FitPick." He leaned forward and splayed his hands on the table. "Here's what I'm thinking—a subscription model."

Zoe gnawed on the inside of her cheek as she pondered the idea. A subscription model could be tricky—*Chic*'s online readership plummeted the moment they started putting their articles behind a paywall, forcing them to lift it after advertisers complained about the sharp drop in number of impressions. But at least *Chic* produced original content; meanwhile, FitPick's only content was created by the users themselves, which would provide even less incentive for people to pay to use the app.

Lillian coughed lightly. "Bill, I don't think we have the numbers to support a subscription model yet."

"But you heard what Logan Horossen said—we have over fifty thousand users daily! We need to start making money off them."

Zoe shifted in her seat. Bill wasn't wrong per se, but did he have to word it quite so callously?

"Yes, but that's still not an adequate membership base," Lillian said. "We're still so young, so there's no app loyalty. The moment we make people pay to use our app, they will just go back to posting *this or that* outfit photos on Instagram or TikTok. Maybe in the future, we can do a . . . freemium model, where users have to pay to use some higher-level features, like the chance to have their polls be shown to more people or maybe even personal styling sessions."

Zoe's ears pricked up. Perhaps she could find a way to bring Bernadette on board as a contracted consultant if they started offering styling services.

"But we would probably need at least four hundred thousand daily active users for that," Lillian added.

Bill pursed his lips. "Well, what do you suggest we do in the meantime then? How am I supposed to convince Logan Horossen we can make him money?"

"Ads," Lillian said. "Fashion ads obviously—"

"Yes, obviously," Bill muttered under his breath, clicking his pen then releasing it with a loud *twang*. Zoe's eyes darted around the table, wondering if she was the only one who heard his utterance, but Lillian was continuing as if she hadn't.

"Ads of clothes and accessories and maybe even fashion-adjacent items, such as suit bags and shoe inserts. We can even tailor ads based on—"

"The user's appearance!" Bill pounded his hand down on the table. "We can use AI to detect their physical traits, like body shape, height, skin color, and so on, then recommend them clothes to buy. If you're short, we'll show you petite bottoms; if you have pale skin, we won't show you white clothes 'cos wearing them makes you look washed-out; if you're plus-size, we'll—"

Memories flooded into Zoe's mind, of the Macy's salesperson who told her very helpfully that the cropped denim jacket she was eyeing wouldn't flatter her pear-shaped body; of that stranger at a *Vanity Fair* event who had complimented her on how her "fleshy round hips" allowed her to "rock that sexy dress," not knowing that those words would cause Zoe to shy away from skinny jeans for a year; of the countless comments that had told her what to and not to wear because of her body shape and size.

Shame wormed through her as Zoe recalled all the "advice" she herself had doled out to *Chic* readers over the years on how to dress to cover up their hip dips and make their legs look longer with the right sponsored shapewear.

"Um, I don't think that's a good idea," Zoe cut in. "Recommending what to buy means we're pushing some ideal about how people should dress—that goes against what we stand for. We want people to explore and experiment with clothes instead of implying they should pigeonhole themselves."

A beat of silence passed, then Bill said, "That's a good point, Zoe, but I just don't think Logan Horossen would care." He spoke slowly and patiently, like how an adult would explain to a child why they couldn't have another piece of candy. Zoe felt her face burn. "All that matters to businessmen like him are the dollar signs. If we have to put up some ads that aren't the most aligned with our brand values but would help us make more money, then—" He shrugged. "At least we would get the funding to keep FitPick running while we strive toward our long-term mission."

"Actually, Zoe has a point," Lillian interrupted. Zoe almost fell out of her chair. Had she stumbled into a twilight zone where she and Lillian Mariko actually agreed on something?

"Bill, your suggestion is . . . very interesting, but I'm afraid of the litigious potential," Lillian continued. "What if our ads recommend maternity clothing to a woman who's not pregnant but just has a fuller figure? What if the woman is actually pregnant but ends up miscarrying and has to keep seeing ads for maternity clothing or baby outfits? And skin color—we shouldn't touch that with a ten-foot pole."

Bill groaned out loud. "Shit, I didn't even think of that. Any potential lawsuit would be a death sentence for a young startup like us."

"But I like your idea of incorporating AI into targeted advertising," Lillian continued. As Bill's expression relaxed back into a smile, Zoe felt a reluctant glimmer of awe. In just a few clever sentences, the COO had managed to change Bill's mind *and* soothe his ego with a subtle compliment. "We could use AI to assess usage behavior. What are the features of the clothes a user tends to upvote more often? Is it long or short? Dark or light colored? Plain or with print? We can then show them ads for clothes that fit their fashion preferences."

Zoe tried not to make it seem like she was staring as Lillian spoke, every word coming out firm and strong and punctuated with sleek hand gestures. She'd seen the COO's LinkedIn resume, but a written list of accolades couldn't adequately capture that charisma that made Lillian Mariko one of the most lauded young executives in Silicon Valley. Just like how Virgil Abloh saw the high-fashion potential in streetwear and helped transform the perception of sweatpants from lazy to luxe, Lillian saw diamonds where others only saw dust.

"The AI technology shouldn't be too difficult to implement," Damien spoke up, twirling a pen between his fingers. "But there's one issue: Our app's entire feed is dominated by images, so clothing ads would compete with our users' photos. The interface might be too cluttered and that could turn users off."

Lillian leaned back in her chair with a deep exhale. "You're right," she said, massaging her temples. "Ads might be a bit too overwhelming."

Frowning, Bill clicked his pen over and over as he looked up at the ceiling, lost in thought. The loud *ping*s of the pen-clicking echoed throughout the small room and pounded in Zoe's head. She snuck a surreptitious glance at her phone. It was almost eight, and if she didn't leave now, she would be late for her dinner with Bernadette.

Damien stretched his arms over his head, his shirt riding up and flashing a strip of tanned skin that made Zoe's face warm. She quickly looked away as he said, "I've got to go now, but I'll keep thinking about this tonight."

"Yeah, sure. See you tomorrow, Damien," Bill said absently. "Lillian, maybe you and I could stay back—"

"I can't," Lillian said, looking down as she shuffled through her notes. "I have dinner plans with my—my boyfriend."

Bill blinked. "Right, your boyfriend." He turned to Zoe with a playful smile. "Well, Zoe, looks like it's just gonna be you and me—"

"Bill, it's late on a Monday evening and we were all working hard over the weekend," Lillian cut in as she closed her laptop. "It might be better if we all head home now and regroup tomorrow with fresh minds. Maybe Austin and Bram can add some new perspective."

A twinge of regret welled up in Zoe as Bill threw up his arms and muttered, "Okay, okay. Y'all enjoy your evenings." She did have a dinner to get to, but trust Lillian to make sure that if she couldn't have one-on-one time with the CEO, then no one else could. Lillian had great ideas, so why was she so insecure that a great idea might come from someone else?

chapter 26

HEY, I'M SO sorry I'm late!" Zoe exclaimed as she rushed up to Bernadette, who was standing outside Stanford Shopping Center's Pacific Catch and chatting with its maître d'.

"No worries. Robert and I were having the most interesting conversation about lobster recipes," Bernadette purred. "Weren't we, Rob?"

Looking slightly dazed, Robert nonetheless nodded most enthusiastically. "Oh yes. Your knowledge of crustaceans is incredible."

"Crustaceans? Bern, seriously?" Zoe whispered to Bernadette as Robert led them to the best table in the restaurant, which Zoe was sure was usually reserved for VIPs. She shook her head and stifled a smile as Bernadette merely winked in response. Trust even Pacific Catch's stern maître d' to fall under her friend's spell.

"Sorry again," Zoe said once they were settled down and Robert had given each of them a menu. "A work meeting ran very late."

"Don't worry about it. It's not like I had anything better to do," Bernadette replied with an airy little laugh.

There was a fragility in Bernadette's voice that gave Zoe pause, but she saw no way out of asking the natural follow-up question: "Oh, how was your day?"

"Went for my monthly facial after my morning shift at Nordstrom. Did grocery shopping at Whole Foods—they have an amazing deal on avocadoes right now, by the way. Did some crafting in the afternoon for my goddaughter's birthday present; I'm making her some enamel pins, which are apparently the height of tween fashion. And then I went for my Desk Step class, and now I'm here." Bernadette spread her arms open in a *ta-da* way. "Really working my butt off here, as you can tell. Anyway, tell me about your meeting—sounds like you had a much more productive day than I did."

Bernadette's tone was light but a shadow passed over her face so quickly that Zoe might have missed it if she wasn't looking straight at her friend. With a start, Zoe realized: Bernadette was *envious*. Not of Zoe, but of her job. Even though Bernadette had made the decision to leave consulting for her health, it couldn't be easy transitioning from seventy-hour workweeks to a part-time styling stint. No one to boss around, no benchmarks for success to hit, no thrill of closing a deal.

But now didn't seem like the time to broach such a sensitive subject with Bernadette. So instead, Zoe obligingly recounted how the strategy discussion with Bill, Lillian, and Damien went—though she kept the details vague—pausing only to place her order for a mojito and grilled steak while Bernadette requested white wine and braised sea bass. Pacific Catch wasn't cheap, but a delicious dinner with a good friend was just what Zoe needed after the weekend. Even dinner at Ophelia, which was meant to be celebratory, had ended up being unexpectedly stressful.

"So yeah, that was my Monday," Zoe said. "And now my back aches from sitting all day. I keep resolving to use my standing desk more, but then I get too comfortable and before I know it, an entire day has flown by and my tailbone hurts."

"Come to Desk Step with me tomorrow. You can do all your brainstorming while moving your body."

With a sigh, Zoe reached for a complimentary breadstick. "Ugh, I'm jealous of Desk Step—at least they know how to make money." *And* Logan Horossen seemed to be a big fan of their treadmill desks. "Meanwhile, I have zero idea how to monetize FitPick without compromising what we stand for."

Bernadette wagged her own breadstick at Zoe. "Now, now, great ideas take time."

"Yeah, but it's just—" Zoe hesitated. "I feel like I'm the only one without any ideas," she forced herself to admit in a small voice, fixing her eyes on a faint smudge on her water glass as she put her deepest fear out into the open at last. "Bill is always the first to throw out a suggestion and get the ball rolling. Damien is responsible for all our technology and he'll implement the AI stuff once we get to that stage. And Lillian is Lillian—she seems to think of everything. I bet she'll have a twenty-page proposal ready by tomorrow. And the whole time, I just sat there, not contributing anything valuable. I bet Bill regrets including me in the discussion."

I bet he regrets hiring me.

Bernadette opened her mouth just as the waiter arrived with their drinks and dishes. Zoe picked up her cutlery listlessly. Her grilled steak was so succulent it was oozing juices onto her plate, but she barely had an appetite anymore. The Logan Horossen pitch meeting was supposed to be a culmination of her—no, the whole team's—hard work, but all it did was create even more questions they didn't have the answers to.

"You're being much too hard on yourself," Bernadette said, drizzling miso glaze over her sea bass. "You aren't giving yourself enough credit for even being asked to that strategy meeting in the first place. Your marketing ideas and efforts impressed your boss so much that he *wanted* you there. And I know it's important to figure out the monetization strategy, but Zoe"—Bernadette leaned forward and looked her in the eye—"FitPick wouldn't even have a user base to monetize if not for your See Yourself campaign."

"But what if that was the best I could do?" Zoe whispered. Glumly, she drew circles in sauce on her plate. "I don't know tech and I don't know business. Lillian comes up with good ideas every other minute, but I feel like I just got lucky with that See Yourself campaign—a lightning bolt of inspiration that won't strike twice."

Bernadette threw her head back and let out a throaty laugh. "Babe, do you even hear yourself? A lightning bolt of inspiration that won't strike twice?"

Her laughter was so infectious that Zoe couldn't help but join in. "Okay, that sounded pretentious. But the point stands. It was beginner's luck—"

Bernadette placed her cutlery down and held up her hand. "Stop right there. You. Did. Not. Get. Lucky." Her eyes bore into Zoe's. "Your campaign succeeded because of your hard work, your fashion knowledge, and how well you understand FitPick's target audience."

Zoe's cheeks turned pink. "You really think so? I mean, I do have more experience in fashion, but it doesn't seem that valuable compared to, you know, knowing how to code or how to pitch to investors."

"If all FitPick had was talented coders, it would never get anywhere. *You* complete the team; you make it better. You might not know tech as well as Damien, or business as well as Bill and Lillian, but you know fashion and you know what people want—sometimes before they know it themselves. Okay, take Winnie Hu for instance. I didn't know who she was, but one of my friends forwarded me Winnie's FitPick poll for some gala—"

"Oh yeah, the S Gala in Singapore?"

Bernadette pointed her knife at Zoe. "Yes, that! She was asking people which septum ring to wear with her gown. And I was like, wow, who is this girl who can rock a buzzcut and septum ring with a princess gown? So I went to stalk her social media and now I'm obsessed with her punk princess style. In fact, I'm getting Nordstrom to order in the whole of Junya Watanabe's latest collection because Winnie said he's her favorite designer. I've already reserved three items for myself." She tipped her glass of white wine toward Zoe. "So thanks to your campaign, I'm learning about fashion brands and expanding my wardrobe. My fiancé isn't happy about the second part though."

Zoe's spirits lifted. Bern was right—while the work was still far from over, it didn't mean her work for the past few months was for nothing. At least for this evening with her friend, she would allow herself to celebrate.

"I'm so happy to hear that," she said as she dug into her steak with renewed relish. "I didn't expect that the campaign would actually help introduce brands to—"

Her fork paused midway to her mouth as a new idea crystallized in her mind. The piece of steak on her fork slipped off the tines and fell back onto the plate, splattering sauce all over Zoe's cream top and making Bernadette exclaim out loud. But Zoe noticed none of that as her mind raced and churned.

"Oh my God," she breathed out. "Bern, you are a genius. You just gave me a great idea."

"That's very nice," Bernadette replied absently as she rummaged through her purse. "Aha!" She whipped out a pen and brandished it toward Zoe. "This Tide to Go pen will get those stains out in no time."

chapter 27

BRAND SPONSORSHIPS."

Bill tilted his head to one side. "Huh?" His confused expression was mirrored on the other FitPickers' faces.

Zoe took a long sip of her lukewarm Americano as she tried to think of a way to rephrase her thoughts. Subpar as the coffee was, at least it kept her awake. After dinner with Bernadette last night, she'd rushed home and stayed up until three in the morning to put together a proposal for FitPick's company meeting this morning. Now, she could barely keep her eyes open. Even the fuchsia Lilly Pulitzer sweater and matching lipstick she threw on couldn't distract from her heavy under-eye bags.

"Remember how we realized yesterday that ads would compete visually with the users' outfit polls?" Everyone nodded. "But what if the outfit photos *are* the ads? Think about it," Zoe rushed on as Lillian opened her mouth. "We will approach brands and pair them up with our campaign influencers. The brand will provide the clothes, and the influencer will create a poll comparing one item from the brand to another. Like: *Should I wear this Princess Polly dress or that Princess Polly blouse on my date?*" We will give a cut—let's say twenty percent—of whatever the brand pays us to the influencer as their commission."

"Ohhh," Bill breathed out. "So this way, there won't be any tension between user content and ads because they are one and the same."

"Except there *is* still tension though," Lillian pointed out. "There are regulations that any advertising must be openly labeled. Why would users bother voting on a poll for sponsored clothes when they know the influencer might not actually wear them?"

"That's true—the influencer will have to disclose that," Zoe said. Thank God Bernadette had asked her this exact question over dinner. "*But* there's tons of research that social media users have an increasing tendency to just scroll past sponsored ads. However, putting the clothes into a poll format helps to engage the user. By gamifying their viewing experience, they are far more likely to pause and participate in the poll—and the few seconds they take to process and vote on it will increase their awareness of the brand. And fans will be more willing to ignore the fact that the clothes are sponsored if they are involved in deciding what their favorite influencer wears next."

Austin raised his hand like he was in a classroom. "But why would the brands want to advertise with us when they can turn to Instagram, Facebook, and Google Ads?"

"Same reason as earlier—advertising on FitPick is much less in-your-face." Zoe slid a copy of her proposal to each person. "If you flip to page three, you'll see a section on how millennials and Gen Zs—our target audience—hate being bombarded by ads. Almost everyone I know has an ad blocker on their phone, so just running paid ads on social media is less effective than integrating the ads into user-generated content like we can do on FitPick."

She flipped to the next page, waiting until everyone else had done the same before continuing, "Also, people want to feel like they are being engaged instead of just getting blasted with content—the research supporting that is on page four. So while a user might just scroll past a sponsored post they see on Instagram, they are more likely to pause and engage with a poll, increasing the number of impressions on a FitPick post."

Bram snapped his fingers together. "What if we add a feature that allows users to tag the fashion brands in their outfit photos? Like that tagging function Instagram has."

"I love that!" Zoe could hear her words pouring out faster now. It was like a fire had been lit within her, the same kind she would feel back at *Chic* on the rare occasions her editor accepted one of her long-form article pitches instead of making her write yet another listicle about Coachella fashion.

"And finally, just like how I pitched the campaign to the influencers as a chance to do market research about what their target audience likes, the same goes for brands—especially small fashion businesses that don't have the resources to do product research. If they are debating between two designs, they can test them out in a poll and see which one is more popular. That way, they won't accidentally manufacture too much of a design that doesn't sell well and leave them stuck with tons of inventory."

Silence stretched across the room, punctured only by the ticking of the clock on the wall. By now, Zoe was wide awake, her heart pounding as she looked between Bill and Lillian. The CEO was gazing up at the ceiling, lost in thought; the latter was flipping through the proposal, lingering on certain pages more than others.

If only she could read their minds. Zoe's brain whizzed through all the research she had done, but maybe she had missed something, somewhere. In the very next moment, Lillian could point out an angle she hadn't considered, a gap in her plan that she couldn't account for, somewhere where the numbers didn't add up. And she would have to go back to the drawing board all over again.

Something bumped lightly against her knee beneath the table. It was Damien's leg—a comforting strip of warmth in a room that was otherwise so cold she could feel goosebumps prickling her skin. When she caught his eye, the stoic set of his face softened slightly. A fluttering sensation swept through Zoe's stomach. With an effort, she forced herself to look away first.

She startled to attention as Bill put his pen down. He leaned back in his chair and clasped his hands behind his head. "You know, I think this could actually work."

His words had barely landed before Lillian spoke up, her forehead creased as she studied page six of Zoe's proposal. "Hang on. Why would the brands come to us first? Why wouldn't they just cut us out and go directly to the influencers themselves?"

Zoe's mouth dried. She hadn't prepared for this question, and damn, this was a legit one. She took a long sip of her coffee as her mind raced for an answer. The Americano tasted even worse now, but the bitter edge sent zings straight to her brain, sparking a flicker of inspiration.

"As part of the brand sponsorship package, we can offer perks like boosting the poll so that it's seen by more people. The brand can also control who gets to vote on their polls so that the results come from their target audience only. Besides, influencers receive so many brand pitches every day that they won't have time to read through them all, but we can get the brand directly in front of the most suitable FitPick campaign influencers."

"That makes sense," Bill said before Lillian could respond. He put both hands on the table and pushed himself back into a standing position. "Zoe, I love this idea. You have *my* permission to start contacting brands."

"Just run them by us first before we confirm the sponsorship," Lillian said, her brows still furrowed. "We need to make sure all the brands and influencer partnerships are aligned with our image."

Zoe nodded, too fired up by Bill's approval to mind the other woman's grudging tone. It was clear Lillian wasn't fully convinced but couldn't contradict Bill. But Zoe would take what she could get from the high-brow COO, and hopefully Lillian would come around once she saw how much better the app was doing thanks to See Yourself 2.0.

A twinge of worry darted through Zoe. This idea *had* to work as well as she pitched so Lillian couldn't toss out any *I told you so*s. The stakes were even higher now that everything was being assessed through the lens of dollar signs—the only thing Logan Horossen cared about.

A gentle nudge against her elbow cut into her roiling thoughts. "Hey, I really like your idea too," Damien said, bending his head closer to hers. "I can help with the tech specs for some of the new features you suggested. We could get together to work through those."

More alone time with Damien? Zoe's heart skipped a beat. "I'd love that," she said, feeling her anxiety settle as his deep, even voice wrapped around her like a warm blanket.

"Wonderful work, team," Bill announced. "I think this is our clear next step, and Zoe, you can take the lead on this. Does anyone have anything else they'd like to discuss before we disband?"

Bram's hand shot up in the air. "I have a suggestion," he said before Bill could call on him. "I think we need to replace our chairs with exercise balls. Like those big, bouncy ones you see at the gym."

Everyone stared at him. "What, pray tell, is wrong with our state-of-the-art, top-of-the-line Herman Miller chairs?" Bill finally asked.

"Ryan Holmes, the CEO of Hootsuite, uses an exercise ball as his office chair," Bram replied. "It's apparently great for posture and reducing fatigue."

Bill pinched the bridge of his nose. "Bram, we bought those standing desks because you said Zillow's CEO uses them, and I haven't seen you use one after the first day. Our Herman Miller chairs cost nearly two thousand dollars each; I'm not replacing them just on a whim. Okay"—he raised his voice as Bram opened his mouth again—"this meeting is over. Back to work, team."

"OH YEAH, DUDE, HOW WAS YOUR BAEAREA DATE?" AUSTIN asked Bram as they settled back at their desks after the meeting.

"Did she dig the new digs that Bernadette chose for you?" Zoe added teasingly, still riding the high of her successful proposal.

"Good." Bram shrugged. "I had fun."

Austin sucked in a breath. "Woah. You mean a woman actually likes you?"

Bram flung a paper clip at him. "Shut up, dude. I just decided that instead of always worrying about whether I'm impressing my date, I should start focusing on whether *I* am having a good time.

We went to this cool café that she suggested, but although I enjoyed the date and her investment tips, I didn't really feel a spark with her. So I told her afterward that I'd like to continue hanging out with her as friends, but I didn't want to waste her time if she's looking for something more."

Zoe stared at her coworker. Something about Bram was . . . different. And not just because he was wearing a plain but well-tailored Oliver Spencer shirt that Bernadette must have pulled for him. He was also sitting up taller, his fingers not as fidgety as before, and even his voice sounded slightly deeper. Damn, Bernadette must have worked some true magic on him with those clothes.

Austin gaped at Bram for a few moments, his lips parted as though poised to voice his incredulity. But all he said was "So, uh, what's this cool café she showed you?"

As Bram's shoulders instantly loosened at Austin's question, an unexpected tenderness entered Zoe's heart. Bram was more nervous about his new wardrobe and dating life than he was letting on, and thankfully Austin hadn't asked something that would undermine his newfound confidence. After all, it took courage to start doing something different.

"It's this board game café with pretty awesome drinks, including—get this—*spiked boba*! Another couple there invited us to play Catan with them and I blame my taro-flavored tequila for how badly I played."

"What's Catan?" Zoe interjected.

There was a beat of silence. Then Austin said, "Please tell me you're kidding about not knowing the greatest game in the world."

"The best game is *Kim Kardashian: Hollywood*, and I'll have you know I kicked ass. I got to A-list status."

Her two coworkers sighed loudly in unison. Bram shook his

head. "Zoe, you're so missing out. We need to rectify this, pronto. You're coming to play Catan with us after work today."

"No *buts*," Austin said firmly as Zoe opened her mouth to protest. "It's embarrassing that you've been living in the Bay for over two months and you have no idea what Catan is. Tonight, you're losing your Catan virginity."

Zoe had planned on spending her evening fleshing out her proposed business model, but faced with Austin's not-taking-no-for-an-answer expression and Bram's pleading puppy dog eyes, she felt her resolve waver. Her mind flashed back to that fateful Wednesday two years ago when Bjorn—then only *just* a coworker—had asked the editorial team if anyone wanted to go with him to a stand-up show that he was supposed to attend with his boyfriend before finding him in a compromising position with their landlady. Only Zoe had agreed, reasoning that free entertainment was never bad. At the comedy club, they had run into Cassie, one of *Chic*'s newest stylists. The show had turned into late-night drinks and then plans to go to a flea market in Central Park that Sunday, and soon they were officially a work throuple.

Austin and Bram weren't Bjorn and Cassie, but that didn't mean they couldn't be more than coworkers. "Okay, I'm in," she said, smiling as the two guys cheered.

Then, as though guided by some magnetic force, Zoe's eyes slid toward Damien, typing away on his laptop in his corner of The Rook. "Should we invite Damien to come too?" she whispered.

"You can try," Austin said, squinting doubtfully in the CTO's direction. "We've tried asking him out before and he says no every time."

"Damien!" Zoe called out, waiting until he'd looked up from

his screen before continuing. "Do you want to come to a board game café and play Catan with us?"

The moment the question left her mouth, Zoe felt an urge to take it back. From what Austin had said, a no sounded like Damien's typical response, but she didn't want to hear it coming from him—directed at her.

Before he could reject her invitation, she forged ahead. "Both Bill and Lillian are leaving early today and it's rare for them to both be gone before five. So we should take this chance to get out early, too, and do something fun. Team bonding!" she coaxed in her chirpiest voice, hoping no one could detect her selfish ulterior motive for asking him along.

After a moment, Damien shrugged. "Yeah, I'm down."

As Austin and Bram exchanged a look of shock, Zoe gave an internal cheer. Thank God she was wearing a floral Rachel Antonoff dress today that worked just as well for a hangout as it did for the office.

"Perfect!" She beamed at the three men. "This is going to be so much fun."

chapter 28

THIS *IS* ACTUALLY really fun," Zoe said, grinning as she placed a city block on the Catan board. She popped a piece of Korean fried chicken into her mouth with one hand while her other hand passed the dice to Damien for his turn. "I wish more people I knew back in New York played this. I've never even heard of Catan before today."

"Of course you'd find it fun. You just got another point," Austin huffed.

Bram sucked up the last of his tapioca pearls, letting out a small satisfied burp as he drained his Matcha Rum Royale boba. "My family and friends back in Wisconsin don't know Catan either." He paused, scrunching up his face in thought. "Maybe Catan is so popular here because everyone in the Valley is obsessed with having their own empire like Bezos or Gates. But if we can't do it with a startup, the next best option is to do it with plastic blocks in a world-building board game."

"Huh, you might be on to something."

Wordlessly, Damien rolled the dice. "Damn it," Austin cursed, looking down at the seven produced by the sum of the dice. "Damien gets to play the robber."

"What's that?" Zoe asked.

"He gets to take a card from a player of his choice—"

"Rob Zoe!" Bram said loudly. "She's in the lead, so take one of her resource cards."

Zoe clutched her cards close to her chest as she awaited Damien's decision. She could almost see the cogs whirring in his head as he studied the board, then counted the number of cards she had in her hand. He was so smart that he would have surely pieced together her strategy by now based on the resource cards she'd been gathering. She needed all five of them to build a city on the next turn, and he could dash her plans by taking one of them.

Damien met her eyes and half smiled. "I'm going to rob you, Bram," he said, extending his hand out toward the product designer.

"What?" Bram shrieked as Austin chortled in glee. "That's so unfair. Why didn't you rob Zoe?"

Zoe looked down at the table so no one would see her smile. Was Damien looking out for her?

"For God's sake, Bram, it's just a game," Austin tutted.

The smile slid off Zoe's face as heat pooled in her cheeks. Austin was right—they *were* playing a game. Damien must have gone for Bram because he had a strategy that no one else was sharp enough to spot yet. And for her to imagine it was about herself was just a dumb little fantasy. Thank God no one at the table could read her embarrassing thoughts.

Bram's snappish retort to Austin was cut off by Zoe's phone ringing. She put down her cards as Bjorn's name popped up on the screen. Why was he calling her? When had they last spoken? "I should probably take this."

"No, don't go!" Austin whined. "It's my turn next and I was about to ask you for a trade. Would you like some of my wood?"

Zoe hesitated, her hand still clutched around her ringing phone. It *was* rude to answer a call in the middle of a game and hold up everyone else, especially since Bjorn tended to be chatty on the phone. Besides, this was the first time she was hanging out with Austin and Bram outside of work, and even more surprisingly, she was actually having fun with them—something she would have never imagined way back when she overheard them in the office restroom.

But what if it was an emergency? Granted, this was a man who considered his celebrity crush Shaun White dating Nina Dobrev an emergency, but maybe it was a genuine one this time. Maybe it had something to do with Cassie.

"This will be a quick call," Zoe assured Austin and Bram as she leapt to her feet, her phone ringing away furiously in her hand. "I'll be right back."

In a quiet spot outside Boba and Board, Zoe answered the video call. "Hey! What's up?"

Bjorn's familiar voice boomed through the speaker: "Zee! Cassie's here too. We just want to know what our tech gal has been up to lately."

Something in Zoe warmed the moment Bjorn's and Cassie's faces appeared on the screen. Grinning, she launched into a summary of everything that had happened since the launch of the See Yourself campaign. As she spoke, she was surprised by how much was pouring out of her. Had she never told her friends any of this? Just how much had gone unsaid between them over the past couple months?

"Right now, Damien, our CTO, is working on this feature that uses computer vision—that's a kind of artificial intelligence—to detect what a person's wearing in a photo. He trains his model to recognize the key features of that clothing item, then our neural network combs through millions of images pulled from every clothing retailer and selects those that have similar features. So let's say, Bjorn, you upload an outfit photo right now. FitPick would be able to tell that you're wearing a black hoodie with white strings, and if another user—say, Cassie—clicks on your hoodie in the photo, she would get suggestions for look-alikes at different price points. From Shein to AllSaints—everyone can find a dupe in their budget . . ." Her voice trailed off as she finally noticed her friends' slack-jawed expressions. "Am I making sense?"

"Yeah," Cassie answered. "It's just . . . you sound so . . ."

"Techy," Bjorn finished. "Computer vision? Artificial intelligence? Neural networks? Girl, what are all these big words you're throwing around?"

"Oh, thank you," Zoe said, trying to hide her pleasure. At last, she was starting to sound like a *real* tech worker. "Anyway, what's up with you two? How are things at *Chic*?"

An inkling of dread welled up in her as her friends exchanged a look, as though trying to decide who should break the news. "Not good," Cassie finally admitted. "There's been a recent round of layoffs."

Zoe's breath caught in her throat. "Are you two—"

"We're okay," Cassie hastily reassured. "But remember Mel?"

"Of course I do!" Zoe said, stung. "I've only been gone for three months, not three decades." And then, Cassie's words sank in. "Shit. Has she been fired?" she whispered, thinking of the office "mom" who often showed up with homemade pastries so delicious that no one even minded they were made with real flour and whole milk and not some "healthier" substitute. On Zoe's last day at the office, Melanie had brought in her special olive oil cake, with *Zoey* written on top—an inside joke about how Francesca would consistently misspell her name—in beautiful cursive using lemon-flavored buttercream.

Cassie nodded somberly. "Yeah, along with Bethany and Grace."

"*No.*" Zoe inhaled deeply, her former coworkers popping into her mind. Bethany Larkins had an aristocratically high nose bridge, which she'd gamely revealed was a high school graduation present, and a snarky wit ("Now, *that* is all-natural"). Grace had a penchant for floaty, feminine dresses (it was through her that Zoe discovered LoveShackFancy apparently had a special VVIP tier for their most devoted customers) and three tattoos of citrus fruits. "What happened? I thought things were going great after the acquisition by MediaCorp."

"MediaCorp's publishing division head thinks we're just bumming around. He says we take too long to produce content," Bjorn spat out.

"Is he for real?" Zoe exclaimed, outraged on her friends' behalf. "We were each writing two to three articles a week."

"That's still not fast enough for him. He says that readers want lots of content instantly. Like, one listicle every hour, one best-dressed roundup every day, one what-to-buy guide every other day."

"That's ridiculous. No one can do that."

"Precisely. No *person* can do it, which is why he's introducing a new AI writing bot, or an *A(I)ssistant*, as he called it," Cassie said. *"Developed by the brightest minds in Silicon Valley,"* she continued, her voice turning gruffer in presumably an imitation of this mysterious publishing division head's. "He threw out the same jargon you just did, Zoe—neural network, machine learning, all that jazz."

"This A(I)ssistant is *scary,*" Bjorn said, his voice dropping to a whisper as if the bot was a real person standing right behind him. "Ralph—that's the MediaCorp guy—demonstrated it for us, and holy shit, it literally created an article from scratch within minutes on how to accessorize for fall. Hell, it suggested this funky paisley-print blazer that *I* went to buy online the moment the demo ended. Yeah, there were a couple of awkward sentences, but it honestly read like something that could have been written by you or me. And then Francesca asked if the A(I)ssistant could create gallery posts—"

"Of course she would," Zoe muttered. Francesca adored listicles full of photos because every photo viewed by a reader would be considered one unique view, so just one person reading one listicle could yield dozens of impressions. They were easy enough to write, mostly because there was barely any writing to be done, just a lot of scouring of Instagram and Getty Images for good photos. Quick and easy, for sure, but it wasn't exactly the most intellectually stimulating work, and Zoe had rarely felt proud of the ones she was tasked to write.

"And it could! Thalia went to the restroom at some point during the demo and by the time she came back, it had produced a gallery of Hailey Bieber's top twenty Princess Diana–inspired looks. And Ralph said that to make the article feel personable, we should put a person's name on it, so I suggested my name as a joke," Cassie said. "And when Thalia saw it, she didn't realize it was written by the bot, so she praised *me* and said I chose great photos."

"Woah, that's amazing," Zoe breathed. To think she was at the heart of where all the world's most advanced technologies were being developed. "That bot's using machine learning, maybe even deep learning, to mimic human thinking and linguistics— it's kind of like what Damien was doing back in college."

Bjorn raised a brow. "It's not amazing," he said, an edge in his voice. "Bots don't have to be paid. They don't suffer Sunday scaries or Monday blues or complain when the Nespresso machine breaks down. If MediaCorp has bots that can produce articles that seem like they've been written by us but take much less time, we would all be replaced by bots. Cassie and I could lose our jobs soon because of these whacky new technologies *developed by the brightest minds in Silicon Valley.*"

Zoe flinched at Bjorn's sharp tone. Most days, she didn't even feel like she belonged in the tech industry, but Bjorn sounded as though he was holding her responsible for all the "whacky new technologies" just because she happened to work at a startup based in Silicon Valley.

"That's not true," Zoe managed. "Damien says that the field of natural language processing is still pretty new, and it might take decades before machines can capture the intricacies of the human language. Besides, the writing is only half the battle— coming up with the idea is just as important. Machine learning just means they are learning from the data we feed them, but us humans are the ones developing fresh ideas. We're still miles ahead when it comes to creativity."

"Natural language processing? Zee, all the tech jargon is rolling off your tongue as easily as you used to say fashion brand names like Ermenegildo Zegna." Bjorn chuckled but the laughter fell flat. "And all that might be true, but I don't think you'd be saying that if you were still here, knowing *your* job might be on the chopping block."

The remark sounded teasing enough, like an inside joke between friends. Bjorn had even used his longtime nickname for her. But even though they were looking at each other, Zoe had never felt further away from him and Cassie.

Bjorn looked like he was about to say something else but stopped short as Cassie shot him a look. "There's no point speculating about *what-ifs*," she said firmly. "We're lucky we weren't caught up in the layoffs—"

"*Yet*," Bjorn mumbled, which Cassie chose to ignore.

"—So let's just focus on doing our jobs well."

Bjorn snorted. "While we still have them."

The conversation seemed to return to normal again as Cassie made a smooth segue into talking about a celebrity brawl at a brand launch party she recently attended. Bjorn swore up and down that he always knew one of the actors involved in the fight had "small dick energy" because he made his leggy supermodel girlfriend wear flats around him so she wouldn't be taller than he was. Meanwhile, Zoe was aggrieved on the brand founder's behalf that what should have been a celebration of her hard work had now been overshadowed by a silly squabble between two men over—per Cassie's account—whether Cristiano Ronaldo or Lionel Messi was a better soccer player.

"Men," Zoe said, rolling her eyes. And her friends both rolled their eyes in agreement, Bjorn making his extra-theatrical as if to compensate for his fellow men's shortcomings.

By the time they hung up, it felt like old times again—the three of them clustered in some dingy bar, pounding back cheap shots, and gabbing away about anything and everything. But as

Zoe switched off her phone, her wallpaper of her, Cassie, and Bjorn at her farewell dinner instantly fading into black, niggles of unease ate at her. She'd hoped she would feel more comfortable in her new home and job, but the closer she got to that, the further she felt from her old self, her old life back at *Chic* and in New York, and her old friends.

chapter 29

THE SERIES OF eight polls by Imani Singh for Jawara Al-
leyne's spring collection is launching this Wednesday and
happening for the next eight weeks—one poll per week," Zoe read
off her notebook in FitPick's biweekly company meeting. "I'm
also in talks with a designer called Somdusca, who makes jeans
in the funkiest prints. He seems excited about my suggestion of
connecting him to Linkin Mitts, the mom influencer known for
her quirky style. I think she can help him tap into the trendy
mom market and show other moms that having a baby doesn't
mean you have to stop having fun with fashion. And that's all
from me."

She snapped her notebook shut and was about to sit back
down, but Bill's voice stopped her. "Great progress, Zoe. I also
saw in your project tracker that a request from the brand Mana-
tee came through yesterday. What's the status on that?"

"I'm gonna pass on that. They are adamant about bringing in
their own spokesperson, Aisha Monroe—"

"Holy shit." Bill's jaw dropped. "*The* Aisha Monroe? As in last year's Rookie of the Year for *Sports Illustrated*?"

"And apparently she's appearing in the magazine this year too! In the body paint spread," Austin chimed in, his eyes wide. His cheeks turned a mottled red when Bram raised one eyebrow at him. "I follow *Sports Illustrated* for their baseball news," he mumbled.

Bram rolled his eyes. "Yeah, tell that to your girlfriend."

Lillian held up a hand. "Back to Zoe. What's your concern with them bringing in Aisha Monroe? Are you worried they might not be able to engage her because she's such a big name?"

"But she's already their spokesperson, no?" Bill interrupted. "She appeared in their Super Bowl ad this year, in that T-shirt with those two manatees stretched over her, um, torso. And then she looks into the camera, winks, and says—"

Both Austin and Bram joined in: "*Do you like my manatees?*" The latter tried for a wink that probably was modeled after Aisha Monroe, too, but it came out looking more like a muscle spasm.

"It was the most-watched Super Bowl ad this year—two guesses why," Bill chuckled before his voice turned serious. "Since she's already with Mana-tee, there shouldn't be a problem with bringing both her and the brand on board."

Zoe grimaced. "It's an open secret within the fashion industry that she's very difficult to work with. My friend at another magazine once did a photo shoot with her and she kept the whole crew waiting around for hours because she said she was too bloated to be on camera. She makes magazines edit her photos until they fit her standards and refuses to work with those that don't allow her to do so. I have nothing against Mana-tee, but working with Aisha could be more trouble than it's worth."

"Surely we can keep one influencer in line," Bill tutted. "And who cares about how much of a diva she is? Steve Jobs was a diva too." He clasped his hands together. "Look, forget Mana-tee; Aisha Monroe will be by far the most popular person using our app. Do you know how many people watched her Super Bowl ad?"

"Yeah, baseball lover Austin here probably contributed half those views," Bram snickered.

Bill raised his voice above Bram's heckling. "We could reach a whole new stratosphere of publicity if she mentions us just once on her Instagram."

"But we've already been featured in ValleyVerified with a positive review from none other than Rebecca Stiles. Didn't you say that was a sign we've made it?"

"ValleyVerified is for the clickeratti, but I want to win over the glitterati too. Like my Kappa Sigma bros—they will be way more impressed by a mention of Fifth Avenue or Sunset Boulevard than by Sand Hill Road. You get my drift? I doubt most of them have even heard of ValleyVerified, much less read it on a regular basis." Bill grinned. "But they *definitely* read *Sports Illustrated*, and I assure you they are very intimately familiar with Aisha Monroe. Can you imagine the look on their faces once they learn that *the* Aisha Monroe is a spokesperson for *my* app? They will download FitPick immediately just to check her out."

Bill held up a hand as Zoe opened her mouth to protest further. "I hear your concerns, Zoe, and I completely understand where you're coming from. But I can't possibly tell Logan Horossen that we passed on what could have been a game-changing business opportunity because we're afraid some influencer might get the better of us. Anyway, she isn't our problem to deal with—she's

Mana-tee's. Aren't they the ones coordinating with her on everything? So long as her outfit polls go up on our app, then all's Gucci. Tell Mana-tee we're excited to work with them."

Zoe's mouth clamped shut at the note of finality in Bill's voice. Biting back a sigh, she plopped down in her seat and opened her notebook again to jot down a reminder to email Mana-tee back.

AFTER THE MEETING, ZOE WALKED TO THE COOK TO GRAB SOME coffee, only to find Bram swiping the last Nespresso pod for himself. "Sorry, Zoe," Bram said cheerfully with a shrug, "But you snooze, you lose."

Too tired to come up with a retort, Zoe simply turned on her heel and headed to the building's general pantry one floor above. It was shared by all four startups and pretty much never used since the coffee there was so insipid it tasted more like flavored dishwater, as Bill had kindly warned her in her first week. But it was either that or pay nearly seven dollars for a puny cappuccino at the Blue Bottle a couple blocks away.

Zoe peered warily into the coffee maker on the pantry counter. It wasn't the fancy machine in The Cook, but at least there was no mold.

"Hello."

Zoe jumped at the sudden voice. She whirled around to find a short, slim man right behind her, his bald head gleaming like an egg beneath the pantry's unflattering fluorescent light. His eyes were so big they gave his face a vaguely bullfrog-like quality. "I'm Wylan Watts. Charmed."

"I know you! You're the CEO of Dreamcatcher." Dreamcatcher, which occupied the other wing on the same floor as

FitPick, was a startup selling ear plugs that allegedly allowed users to control their dreams.

Wylan recoiled like he'd been slapped. "At Dreamcatcher, we don't use titles like CEO because we don't believe in hierarchy. Everyone in this world is absolutely equal, even you and me, because dreams are universal."

"So you guys don't have managers and stuff?" Zoe asked, flummoxed.

"Don't even say the *m*-word around me," he sniffed. "That word is highly sexist. Beginning a word with 'man' implies the male species is superior, which goes against Dreamcatcher's core value of equality, because dreams are—"

"Universal," Zoe finished warily. "Right. So, uh, what's your role at Dreamcatcher then?"

"Chief Dream Evangelist."

Zoe waited a beat to see if he was joking, but Wylan the Chief Dream Evangelist looked steadily back at her.

"Um, doesn't the word 'chief' imply some sort of hierarchy?"

"No, because we're all dreamers," he said slowly, enunciating every word like a preschool teacher would when speaking to a toddler. "If we all believe in the same dream—building Dreamcatcher—that makes us all—"

"Equal." Zoe raised a hand to her mouth to hide her yawn. "So you've said."

But she must not have done a great job of covering her tiredness, for Wylan only looked even more affronted, his toothbrush mustache quivering as though to show his upset. "And who are you?" he asked, drawing up to his full height—two inches shorter than Zoe in her pumps.

Zoe quickly lowered her hand. "I'm Zoe, Zoe Zeng. The vice president of marketing at FitPick."

Wylan's already enormous eyes grew even rounder. "Zoe Zeng? The one who created that fashion campaign that everyone in the Valley is talking about? That was *you*?"

If Zoe wasn't so surprised herself, she would have been offended by Wylan's incredulity. "How did you know it was me?"

"Because the chairman of my board forwarded me the ValleyVerified article and told me to check out what creative marketing really looked like." From his sour expression, Zoe guessed that chairman probably said a few other things about Dreamcatcher's marketing, none of which were positive. "I ran into your COO, Lillian Mariko, in the building lobby two days ago and asked her who came up with the campaign. She said it was all you."

In the reflective door of the microwave right next to Wylan, Zoe saw her mouth hang open. Lillian said something *nice* about her? Actually praised her work to someone else? Well, not exactly praised, but at least the COO acknowledged her contribution. She could feel her exhaustion fading away. A compliment from Lillian Mariko was more invigorating than any cold brew.

"Oh, you think this is funny, do you?" Wylan snapped, his features twisted into a scowl.

Zoe jerked back at the sharpness in his voice. Clearly, he must have misunderstood her expression of incredulous delight as one of smugness. "Uh, I'm sorry, but I wasn't thinking of you—"

"Look at you, acting so high and mighty and like you're better than me just because you got lucky on this one project. Meanwhile, because of what Rebecca Stiles wrote about my company three months ago, we're headed into a down round. That's right," he said vehemently as Zoe blinked. "I bet that makes you happy to hear how much better your startup is doing compared to mine."

"No, no. Of course not—"

Suddenly, Wylan's expression crumbled and he let out a wail. "I'm already thirty!"

Zoe froze, torn between wanting to comfort the crestfallen man and hightailing it out of the pantry. "Okay . . . What does that have to do with anything?"

"This is my last year to be on *Forbes* 30 Under 30, but I'm officially in my flop era instead of my Forbes era. I've poured all my time, energy, and savings into Dreamcatcher but everything's falling apart. Meanwhile, all you do is hire a bunch of wannabe models and ask them to pose in trendy clothes and somehow that's considered 'creative marketing.' Who the hell cares what they put on their bodies?" He jabbed a finger in Zoe's direction, forcing her to back away. "I bet you bribed Rebecca Stiles to write that good review, didn't you? How much did you pay her? Maybe I can use the last of our funds to do the same," he muttered under his breath, almost to himself.

Through her shock, a tendril of sympathy rose within Zoe. People said Silicon Valley was a pool of sharks all vying to be the biggest shark of all, but it was only at this moment, staring into Wylan's expression of mingled despair and fury, that it finally struck Zoe just how high the stakes were in this startup world. Millions of dollars were on the line, to be won and to be lost. And even though there was plenty of money being tossed around the tech industry, it was ultimately still a finite amount—every dollar given to one startup meant one fewer dollar left for others also vying for funding, for survival.

At the end of the day, what could any of them do except their jobs, as well as they could? Except . . . it was the venture capitalists and investors who determined what "well" meant, and they would give their money to whoever outperformed the others.

Zoe slowly backed out of the pantry, not wanting to startle Wylan, who was still muttering to himself. The sheen of sweat on his forehead made it look even shinier. "I think I'm gonna head out," she said awkwardly, unsure if he was even still aware of her presence. "Uh, you have a nice day. And good luck with everything."

Then, she turned around and dashed out, making a beeline for the comfort and safety of FitPick's office one floor below.

chapter 30

ARE YOU KIDDING me," Zoe muttered, leaning back in her chair forcefully enough to send it sliding away from the desk.

Next to her, Bram lifted his headphones off his right ear and cocked an eyebrow. "Did Teaspoon's delivery fees go up again? You know all that sugar will give you early-life diabetes, right?"

Zoe exhaled deeply. "Aisha Monroe just emailed to say she doesn't want to send her FitPick poll to me for review before she uploads it next Monday. She thinks needing to get it reviewed and approved takes away from her authenticity."

"Sounds reasonable to me," Austin chimed in. "Isn't being authentic on social media a good thing?"

Zoe chewed on her lower lip. He had a point, except Aisha Monroe had never been known for being authentic. It was well known in fashion circles that she'd faked having mono last year so she could stay at home and recuperate after her nose job. Once, she was caught applying a skin-smoothing filter to her six-year-old niece's face in an Instagram photo.

"Why do you have to approve her photos anyway? Aisha Monroe is a model," Austin said. "She knows how to upload good photos—that's how she makes a living. If it's good enough for *Sports Illustrated*, it's good enough for us." Bram nodded firmly in support.

"But a good campaign post is so much more than just the model looking pretty. And doing a pre-posting review is to make sure everything is consistent with *our* brand."

Bram lowered his headphones back over his ear, already losing interest in the discussion. "Just tell Bill, then, if you're so worried."

She could, but it was unlikely Bill would agree. He and everyone else were bending over backward to keep Aisha Monroe happy since she was by far the biggest star FitPick had ever worked with. Zoe swallowed a sigh. Working at a startup and having to juggle a million things at once meant picking your battles, and she had bigger ones to tackle at the moment.

A loud yawn cut into her thoughts. Zoe glanced up to find Damien getting up from his chair. He rubbed a hand over his face and frowned. "Damn, I forgot to shave today." He met Zoe's eyes. "I'm gonna get some coffee. Want anything?"

"No, thanks. I'm good," she said, hoping he hadn't caught her eyes tracking the curve of his stubbled cheeks, wondering what they would feel like against her palm.

"What if I offer boba instead?" he asked, a teasing smile playing around the corners of his mouth. "We can swing by Teaspoon. Might be good to pop out of the office for a minute and get some sun."

Every fiber in Zoe's being screamed at her to accept Damien's invitation, but she couldn't justify a boba run when there was an avalanche of emails demanding her attention—chief of which was Aisha Monroe's. "I'll pass," she sighed. "Too much work to do."

Zoe Zeng rejecting free boba? If Bjorn and Cassie were here right now, they would think she had been replaced by a doppelgänger.

Zoe couldn't help but let her eyes linger on Damien's retreating profile as he made his way to The Cook. For some reason, her heart now felt just a tad lighter after that short conversation with him. Smiling softly to herself, she pulled up Aisha Monroe's email and began to type a response.

THE MOMENT ZOE STEPPED INTO FITPICK'S OFFICE ON MONDAY, Bill rose from his seat and waved at her. "We've all been waiting for you!"

She hurried over to join them in The Hook, excitement flushing through her at the eagerness in Bill's voice. She'd reached the office later than everyone else because of a morning meeting with a prospective brand partner in San Francisco. Aisha Monroe's poll and her Instagram promotion post were scheduled to have gone up a few hours ago, though Zoe had been so caught up in her meeting that she hadn't had a chance to see them yet. But judging from the bright expressions on everyone's faces, the public reception must have been good.

"Rebecca Stiles wrote another article about us!" Bram blurted out before Zoe could take her spot in the cluster around Bill's seat.

"Bram!" Bill huffed out. "I wanted to be the one to break the news to Zoe." He cleared his throat officiously. "But yes, it's true. I saw the item in my daily ValleyVerified email, but I wanted to wait until we were all here to read it together."

"It must be about the Aisha Monroe post," Austin said. "My friends have been texting me about it for the past hour."

"Mine too," Bill said, his face lighting up. "All my college buddies are mega-jealous. They all seem to think that Aisha Monroe is just hanging out in our office. How many other startups do you know with a freaking supermodel as their ambassador? This is a level of cool that the nerds in Silicon Valley rarely see."

Everyone's excitement was infectious. Zoe beamed, adjusting her position to get a better view of Bill's monitor. "Let's read it then."

———

FitPick . . . or NitPick?

BY: REBECCA STILES

Fashion app FitPick—which allows users to upload two outfit photos and get the public to vote for their favorite—has quickly become the latest hot thing to come out of the Valley. Everyone you know is probably on it, either evaluating other people's outfits and/or having their own assessed by the rapidly growing community of FitPickers on the app (nearly four hundred thousand at the time of publication). Even my own grandmother participated in my poll for a slinky date night dress, though she did message me through the app to say, "Darling, more is more. You might want to show less cleavage."

But the higher you climb, the harder you fall. And just like how Cinderella's ballgown devolved into rags again at the stroke of midnight, FitPick suffered a rude awakening this morning when its latest and arguably most famous campaign star to date, Aisha Monroe, was caught allegedly photoshopping one of the images in her FitPick poll, which featured her in a white tank dress from Mana-tee that hugged all her famous curves.

An eagle-eyed user by the name of @mrsjensenackles08 spotted some suspiciously wavy-looking floor tiles in the photo's background and reshared Aisha's post on their own Instagram Story (using the same @mrsjensenackles08 handle), with the caption: *When she tells women to get their ass up and work for the ass they want but photoshops a smaller waist for herself* 😏 *#ladyboss*

The caption is a thinly veiled reference to the comment that Aisha gave in an April interview with *Grazia*: "I have the best advice for women who want my ass. Get your f****** ass up and work out. It seems like nobody wants to work out these days." Very bravely or very foolishly or both, @mrsjensenackles08 tagged Aisha in her Instagram Story post, and within an hour, Aisha has reshared it on her own Instagram Story with this caption: *Baby doll, don't project your insecurities onto me. Working out might make you look better on the outside, but nothing can change how ugly you are on the inside.*

However, the wave of backlash she received prompted Aisha to take the Story down within an hour. Unfortunately for her, her words live on in the screenshots that quickly began making their way across social media. Netizens are slamming her for her hypocrisy in promoting her fitness influencer image when her curves (which have earned her over four million Instagram followers) might not entirely be the result of her fitness routine.

Aisha has since apologized for her words in an Instagram post, where she explained that she never edits her photos but was directed by FitPick to upload photos of herself looking her best. She had eaten a burrito prior to the photo and felt under pressure to edit away her slightly bloated stomach shown off by her skintight dress. Aisha mentions she is currently working on a new line of stomach bloat–detoxing teas that will be available as part of her Move with Monroe line at the end of this month. FitPick was not available for comment at time of press.

Influencers and Photoshop are a love story as old as time. The real question we should ask is: Why are we giving apps like FitPick the platform to promote unhealthy behaviors? Did we really expect any better from an app whose entire premise rests on people letting themselves be rated for how they look and what they wear? So much for FitPick's lofty mission of giving everyone "a safe space to explore their style," as stated on their website. It talks a big talk, but the only walk it walks is the same catwalk of size zero fashion as most other photo-sharing and image-rating apps.

Is it possible for anyone on FitPick, much less an influencer whose livelihood rests on public reception to her appearance, to escape the pressure of making sure they always look their best? And is its founder, Bill Lawrence, the compassionate fashion messiah he makes himself out to be, or just another techbro more concerned with metrics than ethics?

It might be time to retire FitPick and its contemporaries once and for all. I'm sure my grandmother will just find another way to keep up with my outfits and tell me none-too-subtly to stop flashing so much skin.

Verdict (revised): *fad*

GRADUALLY, ZOE BECAME AWARE OF A DULL RINGING IN HER ears. Her head swam as she tried rereading Rebecca Stiles's words, but they melded together on Bill's monitor until a haze of black dots filled her vision. When she dragged her eyes away, she saw identical looks of disbelief on the other FitPickers' faces that mirrored her own shock. For once, even Lillian looked at a loss for words.

Bill slumped back in his chair. "Fuck."

A dull and heavy weight settled in Zoe's gut. Well, that just about summed up the situation.

The CEO groaned out loud. "*Another techbro more concerned with metrics than ethics.* They make me sound like a bloody hypocrite. People judge a company by its leadership, and they are going to think I'm some ponce. Fuck! Logan Horossen would laugh me out of his office. How could this have happened?" he asked, looking between Zoe and Lillian with an expression of wild incredulity.

Zoe bit her lip. Was that a rhetorical question? Because even if it wasn't, she didn't have the answers.

"We just expanded a little too fast," Lillian said after a moment. "We made some decisions and invested our trust in people who aren't the most aligned with FitPick's values."

Lillian didn't look at Zoe once as she spoke but every word pierced Zoe, flinty-sharp. She could feel her face burning as she stared down at the floor, her throat choked up with every retort she wanted to fire back but couldn't because Lillian was her boss. It wasn't even her fault. She hadn't wanted to work with Aisha Monroe in the first place. And months and months ago, hadn't she pointed out the risk of this kind of photo engineering and suggested they put together checks and balances to prevent that?

And yet, Lillian was now turning it around on her.

"It's okay," Damien interjected. "This is just one article. It will become old news once Elon Musk posts another tweet."

"No, it won't be okay," Bill said. "Look at the comments section." He jabbed his index finger at the screen so hard that it left a fingerprint on the surface. "People are comparing me to Mark Zuckerberg, and they're definitely referring to the dorky version of him back when he was still at Harvard, and Facebook was still called The Facebook and used for rating girls. *Ew, another Mark Zuckerberg wannabe,*" he read out loud, before sputtering, "What the hell? At least I have social skills. I was voted Best Flirt by my college frat!"

There was another long silence in which everyone looked at everyone else, as though hoping someone besides themselves would respond. Then Lillian broke the stillness by clapping her hands together. "Okay, here's what we can do. Bill, it would be good if you could personally contact Logan Horossen and our brand partners to explain the situation. I'll put together a press statement. Damien, Austin, Bram—just carry on with your work as per usual. And Zoe—" Lillian took a longer look at Zoe and frowned. "You look really pale. Do you want to go home and get some rest?"

Bram peered at her. "Yeah, Zoe, your face is kind of white. If I ran into you at night, I would think you were a ghost."

Zoe tossed back her hair and lifted her chin. "No, I'm okay. What can I do?"

Lillian hesitated, her eyes scouring Zoe's face. "I think you really should go get some rest. You're shaking." Her voice gentled slightly. "I know this seems terrible, but the startup life is a never-ending series of ups and downs, and the ones who succeed are those who learn to ride the waves. One of my friends was a vice president at Facebook when the Cambridge Analytica saga broke out—now that was a *real* mess. This is just a minor bump in the road. So go home, lie down, and come back stronger tomorrow, okay?"

Zoe felt a hand touch her shoulder. "Hey, I can give you a ride home," Damien said.

Still staring at the Mark Zuckerberg comment on his computer screen, Bill sighed. "Yeah, Zoe, you should get some rest."

Zoe looked around the circle, but except for Damien, it seemed like no one would meet her eye. Finally, she picked up her bag and allowed Damien to lead her away. As they headed toward the exit, she could hear Lillian saying in her crisp, clear voice, "Damien has a point—we just have to wait for another piece of news to break out to distract people from this." And Bill replying, relief clear in his voice, "Thank God I have you, Lillian. I would hate to be handling this alone."

Soon, Zoe and Damien were out of the building, the noon sun caking their shoulders as they made their way to Damien's car in the parking lot. But despite the sunshine, chills ran down Zoe's spine. Lillian had managed to make her seem weak and useless in front of Bill, sidelining Zoe and letting herself play the hero. Now, Zoe was heading home while Lillian stayed behind, taking it upon herself to put out the fires as Bill watched on admiringly.

Even though this shouldn't have been a competition, even though she and Lillian were supposed to be on the same side, Zoe couldn't help but feel like somehow, she'd lost.

chapter 31

IN DAMIEN'S CAR, Zoe slumped in her seat and leaned her head against the window. She watched silently as Damien put her address into his car's GPS, having gotten it when he gave her a ride back home after the Amirah Amin meeting in San Francisco. That drive seemed like a lifetime ago. Then, she'd spent the entire ride back to Mountain View gabbling away about all her ideas for the campaign now that she had secured its first spokesperson. She'd been brimming with hope and excitement, so eager to go into the office the next day to announce the good news.

The atmosphere in the car now couldn't be more different.

"This sucks," she muttered, not even caring that Damien could overhear.

He took one look at her, then put his shift stick back into park. "You want to talk about it?"

Zoe stared down at her hands so she wouldn't have to look at Damien. What FitPick needed right now was all hands on deck to try to put out the Aisha Monroe fire. But instead, she was being sent home because everyone thought she would be more helpful gone than present. And Damien, who would have otherwise been in the war room with his steady, calm presence, was being dispatched to play her chaperone and therapist.

"I'm so sorry," she said softly, her fingers twisting together in her lap. "I made a mess out of everything."

"It's not your fault Aisha Monroe did that," Damien began, but Zoe shook her head.

"I was the one who came up with the campaign idea. And it worked well for a while, but I was too naive. I should have insisted that Aisha let me review her post, or been firmer when I explained to Bill why she wouldn't be suitable. Instead, I decided to take the easy way out . . . and this happened."

Wetness prickled at the back of her eyes, threatening to spill over. "I just set FitPick back even further than where it was before I joined. I bet Bill wishes he had never offered me the job. I wish I never took it and stuck with what I know I'm good at. I didn't know the first thing about how to market an app, and because I thought it would be good to make a gamble, I just gambled our company's prospects away."

For a few moments, the car was quiet except for the gentle whirring of the air-conditioning. Damien opened his mouth then closed it again.

Zoe let out a small laugh. Then again, what could anyone say in this situation? No words could make things right. "You know, I still remember my very first company meeting. When you stood up and began talking, everyone was so attentive because you clearly knew what you were talking about. I didn't understand most of what you were saying and even I was completely absorbed. And in that moment, I thought to myself, *Damn. I wish people would think that of me someday. I wish I had my shit together as much as this man does.*"

She broke off, suddenly embarrassed at having rambled on for so long to a silent audience. "Forget it. This is all ridiculous, sorry."

"I don't have my shit together," Damien said suddenly. He was looking straight out the windshield, his right arm braced against the steering wheel so tightly that a tendon was bulging. "I'm still trying to figure stuff out too."

He turned to face her. "But the only way to learn and grow is to do something different, to step out of our comfort zone. It sometimes feels horribly uncomfortable, and that's okay. You never once took the easy way out, Zoe. If you did, you would still be at your magazine in New York. But you took a chance on yourself and you should be proud of that."

There was something soft swimming in the dark pools of Damien's eyes, a gentleness that made Zoe long to lean in closer. "But does going out of your comfort zone mean much if you don't have anything to show for it?" she managed to say, her voice barely above a whisper.

The left corner of Damien's mouth crooked up. "Can I show you something?"

It took a moment for Zoe to realize he was gesturing at the glove compartment. "Oh yeah, sure." She held her breath as he reached across her body to retrieve a sheaf of papers from the compartment.

He stared down at it for a long moment, gripping it so tightly that his fingers made indentations in the paper's surface. "I told you that after Stanford, I wanted to pursue an MFA but decided to listen to my mom and get a software engineering job. Well, uh, I've been toying with the idea of applying for an MFA program lately. It's nothing serious," he quickly added as Zoe's eyes widened. "And I'm not expecting anything to come out of it. But I just finished my application essay and I'm editing it now. I carry a print copy around in my car so I can jot down ideas whenever inspiration strikes."

Zoe nodded, afraid that anything she said would disturb the charged atmosphere in the car. This was the most nervous she'd ever seen Damien, whose quiet self-assurance usually shone through naturally.

"I don't think the writing in this essay is great," he continued, his eyes fixed on a spot past Zoe's shoulder. "But hopefully it shows you what I mean about how people grow the most when they take uncomfortable risks."

Damien passed the sheaf of paper to her, waiting until her fingers closed around it before opening his door. "I'm going to step out and answer some emails. Just call me when you're done." Without waiting for a response, he quickly stepped out.

Zoe's eyes traced the curve of his back through the window. She would have betted anything that the "emails" were just an excuse for him to not be next to her as she read his work. She turned her eyes to the essay in her hands, delicately turning over the cover page:

When I was fifteen, I wrote my first line of code. *Hello world.*
When I was fourteen, my father walked out of mine.
Three months after my father abandoned our family and remarried, I discovered programming. Over the years, I've been told I have a natural aptitude for coding. I don't know if I'd call it aptitude, but I do know that from the very beginning, programming made sense to me. At its core, code is nothing but a series of logical commands that obey a common

syntax. Once I understood the syntax, I could string different commands together to produce different results—results that *I* wanted. If a line of code doesn't work, I know it's because there's a bug somewhere, and I can fix it. If a problem is too big, I can break it down into more manageable sections and tackle each one by one. It will take time and lots of frustration, but I can get there in the end if I work hard at it.

When people talk about artificial intelligence, the word *intelligence* refers to human intelligence. But human beings are not intelligent all the time, or even most of the time. We behave irrationally, swayed by whims and fancies beyond comprehension. Machines and programs don't do that—they behave as they are supposed to according to the code us humans write.

To this day, I don't know why my father just up and left our family. In my teenage years, I developed insomnia from lying awake every night, my brain raking through every word my father said to me and every twitch of his eyebrows in his last few days at home, trying to spot even a hint of the dissatisfaction that made him give up on us. But I couldn't. His was a language I could never understand, a behavior I could have never predicted until it happened. Was it because I wasn't a good enough son? Didn't share his interests? I could wonder for a lifetime and never know.

The pain hit Zoe so viscerally that it was as though she'd been punched, her heart squeezed in a choke hold in her chest. She looked at Damien on the other side of the car window. His back was turned toward her, his shoulders set in a rigid line, but Zoe felt like she was seeing him—*really* seeing him—for the first time.

An image of how Damien might have been as a teenager floated into her mind. The same dark eyes, but holding more innocence and openness than they did now. That quiet demeanor, but not yet that closed-off aloofness. Zoe inhaled deeply, holding back the urge to throw open the car door, run up to Damien, and give him a big hug—for his younger, bewildered self. She forced herself to read on.

Code—its predictability, consistency—was an anchor that I gripped onto when real life was so unstable. And for a long while, that was enough. I longed for human behaviors to be logical and relationships to be transparent, but I'd come to accept that even if that's not the case, I can still craft a controlled, curated world on my computer.

But one day in my senior year of college, my friends threw me a surprise birthday party—the first I'd ever had in my life. I never saw it coming; there was nothing in their behavior that made me suspect they were blowing up balloons and buying beer in bulk while I wasn't around. And that was the first time I realized that the human unpredictability that made my father leave without warning was the same unpredictability that inspired birthday surprises, unexpected friendships, and star-crossed romances. That party marked a turning point: I began to appreciate human whims and fancies, that what was uncontrollable and illogical could be beautiful. I began to search for a world outside of code. And I found that through writing.

Writing is not bound by strict syntax that flashes an error message if you color outside the lines. It does not progress from Stage A to Stage B, but can curve around and onto itself. A line of code arrives at the same end point every time it is run; a sentence of words strung together could be interpreted in a dozen different ways by a dozen different readers. This would have frustrated me in the past. But now, I'm teaching myself to embrace the uncertainty.

I still remember the very first essay I ever wrote in college for an English class that I'd willingly enrolled in out of interest and not just to fulfill a requirement. I labored over the essay for weeks, painstakingly combing through every line and taking days to deliberate between using a semicolon and an em dash, one word versus another. Unlike in code where I can isolate a bug and work on it without affecting the rest of the code, it's impossible to do that in writing. Changing just one punctuation mark can drastically change the whole feeling of a line.

I got a C+. My professor wrote: *The subject is well written, but I don't get a distinct sense of your writer's voice. It sounds emotional and clinical, almost as though you'd simply cobbled together a string of words from the thesaurus. There's nothing in it that would make me think,* Ah, Damien Scott wrote this.

It's hard to unpack a mindset that I've held so strongly for so long; it's hard not to panic when things don't go as planned and people don't behave as expected. My writing still reads too rigidly to me, my words still don't flow the way I'd like them to. But every time I put my pen to paper, I discover something new about myself and about the world around me. And that's why I continue writing; that's why I continue trying to explore who Damien Scott is, and how I can put a bit more of him, of myself, into my words every time I put pen to paper.

Zoe stared down at the pages lying on her lap, the neat, typed words blurring into a haze before her eyes. This time, she couldn't restrain herself. She stepped out of the car and before Damien could fully turn around at the sound of her footsteps, she'd thrown her arms around him.

He lurched back slightly in surprise, but the next moment, his arms were encircling her back. "Thank you," Zoe whispered into Damien's shoulder, feeling something within her settle as she breathed in the clean cotton scent of his shirt. "Thank you for letting me read it." *Thank you for trusting me.*

"I knew that if I ever showed it to someone else, you'd be the first," he said simply in return, his words slightly muffled against her hair.

Zoe pulled back to look him square in the face. "I get what you're trying to say now. Things that are worth doing are always hard. But just like how you kept writing although it doesn't come as naturally to you as coding, I can also make the most out of my FitPick job even though the Zoe from just a few months ago would never have expected herself to end up in tech." She pulled herself up to her fullest height and raised her chin. "This Aisha Monroe mess is a setback but I can still turn things around if I keep working at it."

Damien's face lit up with a rare smile. "Don't stop giving yourself the chance to try and fail, to learn and grow. It's okay to not have your shit together—no one does, no matter how much they look like they do on the surface."

Lillian does, Zoe thought immediately. But this moment with Damien was too perfect to ruin with any bitter thoughts. So Zoe merely nodded, allowing herself to savor the warmth and comfort of Damien's embrace for just a few moments longer before she had to confront reality again.

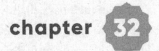

ZOE LEAPT TO her feet the moment Bill walked into FitPick's office the next day. He startled as she called out his name. "Zoe," he said, blinking as though he'd seen a mirage. "You're in early. It's not even eight."

"I really wanted to talk to you first thing today. I think I've figured out how we can deal with the whole ValleyVerified situation." Once Damien dropped her off at home yesterday, Zoe had parked herself at her desk to brainstorm how FitPick could turn the situation around. Despite Lillian's instructions, she wasn't about to stop working just so the COO could snag all the glory for leading FitPick out of this mess. Though when Damien and Austin texted her separately later that day to ask how she was doing, Zoe responded with a sleepy emoji.

Bill placed his backpack down and rubbed a hand over his face. "Look, about the ValleyVerified thing—"

"I know it seems bad, but if Kim Kardashian could turn her sex tape leak into a multimillion-dollar empire—"

"Rebecca Stiles published another article."

It was only then that Zoe noticed Bill's mouth was tight at the corners, his brows drawn into a line. Her words died in her throat.

"Can you come with me to the meeting room?"

"I'm not in trouble, am I?" Zoe tried joking, but Bill didn't respond and simply started walking toward the meeting room. Somehow, she found the strength to move her legs and follow behind him, but it felt like her limbs were moving on autopilot. Her mind raced as her stomach churned, turning her insides into a roiling mess. Bill had always insisted on calling it The Rook, no matter how corny everyone else thought the name was. That he wasn't doing so now meant something truly terrible must have happened. But what else could Rebecca Stiles write that was worse than what she published yesterday?

As they entered The Rook, Zoe's eyes fell on the laptop in Bill's hands. Her heart stuttered in her chest. This was it—Bill had prepared the paperwork for her employment termination. He was probably going to walk her through her severance package and what would happen to her unvested stock options. Had she even been working long enough for any of them to have vested?

Zoe tried taking a breath to calm herself down, but her throat felt so tight that every inhalation seemed to scape past her windpipe. She was being fired after only four months, but her rental lease was for a year. And what was she supposed to do now? Run back to New York and have everyone realize she failed?

Bill sat down at the head of the table. "Zoe, please, take a seat."

Wordlessly, she did as he said, feeling her legs buckle under her as she sank into a chair. It suddenly felt like the room was shrinking in on her.

Bill hesitated for a moment, then said in one swift sentence, "Zoe, Rebecca Stiles's latest article is about you."

FOR A LONG MOMENT, ZOE WAS SURE SHE MUST HAVE HEARD him wrong. But as if sensing her confusion, Bill nodded and said, "Yes, you. It came out twenty minutes ago. I saw it in my subscribers email, and Zoe—" His voice faltered. He took a deep breath before continuing, "Zoe, the article is not pleasant. It's a nasty piece of work that says far more about that woman and her lack of journalistic integrity than it ever could say about you. Everything's so poorly written—"

"Can I read it?"

"I don't know if that's a good idea—"

"I want to read it," Zoe said more forcefully, the words rasping out through her parched lips. "Please," she added when a small part of her—the part that wasn't completely frozen in shock— remembered she was speaking to her boss. But every other part of her was beyond caring. The only remotely coherent thought running through her head was: *Why me?*

"Okay," Bill said, still looking incredibly reluctant as he opened his laptop and pushed it in front of her. "Don't say I didn't warn you."

The devil wears pixels: Is this the true culprit of the FitPick saga?

BY: REBECCA STILES

So much of the fashion world is built on gatekeeping, but we want to break these gates down. We want people to feel comfortable experimenting, evolving, and evaluating their style in a public space—one that's supportive and not critical, welcoming and not judgmental."

Said Bill Lawrence, founder and CEO of FitPick, in an interview just two weeks ago with *S*, Asia's leading fashion magazine. His brainchild FitPick is an app that lets users create OOTD polls to crowdsource public fashion opinion. But those words have aged as well as Mark Zuckerberg's promise to WhatsApp's founders that he wouldn't mine their users' data after Facebook acquired WhatsApp.

Which is to say, not at all.

FitPick's See Yourself campaign was the hottest thing for a while until Aisha Monroe, fashion influencer and one of the campaign stars, was caught posting a FitPick outfit photo in which she had digitally edited her waist to make it look smaller. The saga opened a raging Pandora's box of whether it is ethical for FitPick to make money from letting women be evaluated like cattle.

Now, I can exclusively reveal that the mastermind of the infamous campaign is none other than FitPick's new vice president of marketing, Zoe Zeng, who has been working at the fashion startup for just over three months. According to my source, Zoe was previously a fashion writer at New York–based magazine *Chic*. A quick scroll through *Chic*'s online archives revealed that Zoe was responsible for a monthly *Hot or Not* series that asked readers to rate celebrities' red-carpet outfits and advice columns on scintillating topics such as 'what are the best jeans for your body type' and 'the best sunglasses for your face shape.' Her last *Chic* write-up before she joined FitPick was to celebrate the launch of a.l.r, a sustainable fashion brand that recently came under fire for only making their dresses in one size. Right, absolutely no gatekeeping at all.

Given Lawrence's admirable aim of democratizing fashion, I have to wonder why he decided to hire someone who had never worked in tech nor marketing before and whose entire pre-FitPick career was built on dictating to hundreds of thousands of women what's chic and what's not. Color me unsurprised that someone who used to regularly judge other women's outfits would be encouraging FitPick users to do the same.

In fact, my source tells me that Zoe is just as sartorially snobbish with the other workers in the office building where FitPick and three other startups are headquartered. "She swans around the building in her fancy outfits and looks down on the rest of us for only wearing T-shirts and jeans. She thinks she's so much better because she used to have a posh fashion career in New York and sees us as poorly dressed computer geeks."

In light of this, it becomes more understandable why Aisha succumbed to the pressure to edit her photo and preserve FitPick's picture-perfect facade.

And now with FitPick's powerful algorithms and rapidly growing platform at her fingertips, this *Chic*-tator of taste has become the click-tator of taste. Bill Lawrence might want to think more carefully about his future hires if he wants FitPick to keep looking good.

Verdict: FitPick—*fad*

Zoe Zeng—*fraud*

THE CLICK-TATOR OF TASTE? THE TRUE CULPRIT? SOMETHING prickled the back of Zoe's eyes, making her nose burn. Why would Rebecca Stiles write something so mean, so unkind? And who was that anonymous office source who threw out such nasty words? It could be anyone, maybe even the building receptionist.

There were now over a hundred comments under the article. The top one read: *LOL not surprised at all! I'm a model who worked with Zoe Zeng on a photo shoot once back when she was still in fashion. She told me at the photo shoot that I wouldn't be able to fit in the Dolce & Gabbana samples.*

The comment had garnered two hundred and thirty-seven Likes and a slew of replies. *OMG*, one netizen had written. *Do you have more tea to spill?*

Zoe bit down hard on her lower lip but it wasn't enough to stop tears from springing into her eyes, making the rest of the comments dissolve into a watery blur. She would never have implied anything negative about another person's body, not after those middle school years of lunchtimes spent jogging around the track as part of TAF Club (which stood for Trim and Fit, but mean kids would reverse the weight loss program's name into FAT). And she would have never suggested Dolce & Gabbana for any project, not after those racist ads they put out in 2014 that poked fun at the Chinese culture. Who could be coming up with lies like that to ruin her reputation?

"Zoe," Bill said, reaching out to grab her hands. The moistness on his palms against hers made Zoe's skin crawl, but she was too tired to move away. Every bit of strength left in her body was spent on keeping herself from bursting into tears.

"Hey, it's okay," he murmured, trying to catch her eye. Resolutely, she kept her face toward the ground, afraid that the tears barely kept at bay would come flooding out the moment she saw his expression of sympathy.

His tone hardened. "I'll demand a full retraction and apology from Rebecca Stiles. And don't think anything more about that quote." He didn't need to elaborate on which quote he was refer-ring to; it had been playing on repeat in Zoe's head, every word pounding like a jackhammer. "I'm sure she just made it up as clickbait."

Still keeping her eyes fixed on her feet, she gave a weak nod, one driven more by courtesy than any real conviction.

"Why don't you go back home?" Bill suggested gently. "And take some time off—with full pay, of course. Just until this whole thing blows over. I don't know why Rebecca Stiles has it out for you, but I'll do everything in my power to get to the bottom of this."

"Thanks," Zoe whispered, pulling her jacket more tightly around her body. In hindsight, it was laughable how eager she had been to get to work today to try to fix things. Now, this build-ing was the last place she wanted to be. There was someone here who hated her. Maybe even multiple someones.

As Zoe made her way to the exit, guided by Bill's hand on her shoulder, she passed by The Hook. Her eyes landed on a framed photo on one of the desks. Lillian, arm wrapped around her boy-friend, smiled back at her. Beneath the glint of the overhead lamp against the photo frame glass, her curved lips looked almost like a smirk.

chapter **33**

ZOE SEPARATED FROM Bill in the building lobby. She rushed down the steps leading outside the building, just as Damien came striding up. "Hey, where're you rushing off to—" His voice instantly softened as he met Zoe's red-rimmed eyes. "What's wrong?"

She shook her head, not trusting herself to speak. Although everyone else would surely hear about the article sooner or later, at least one silver lining had been that no one else besides Bill was around to witness her humiliation. But why did Damien have to choose this exact moment to come into work?

He straightened up as though he'd suddenly come to a decision. "Come on, let's get out of here. We'll go to Teaspoon." He gave her a cajoling smile as she remained rooted to the spot. "I promise to not even say anything about how squishy the pearls are."

Despite herself, Zoe felt the corners of her mouth tug up slightly. "Okay." The word left her parched mouth in a croak. "Lead the way."

THE BEST THING ABOUT GOING TO TEASPOON AT THIS TIME WAS that the office crowd had already left after securing their morning boba and the students from nearby Palo Alto High School had just gotten to school. So the store was blissfully empty when Zoe and Damien arrived. While Damien went to the counter to order, Zoe sat down at one of the small tables outside the store. She'd been there often enough that her phone automatically connected to Teaspoon's Wi-Fi, and it instantly started vibrating furiously in her hand as the notifications flooded in.

Missed calls from Cassie and Bjorn; a Slack message from Austin; and an email from Bram with the heading *WTF?!*.

Zoe buried her face in her hands, her head feeling as heavy as rocks. Her worst fears had come true: Everyone knew.

Damien arrived with their drinks soon after. He handed a red bean–laden matcha slush to Zoe and kept a plain black fruit tea—with nary a boba pearl—for himself. "Okay, do you want to talk about it?"

Might as well, since he would find out about it soon enough. "It will be easier if I show you." With one swipe, she cleared the cascade of phone notifications that were steadily increasing by the minute, then pulled up Rebecca Stiles's article. Silently, she passed her phone to Damien, and kept her attention fixed on her drink while he read it. The sweetness of the boba and the mechanical sips she took were enough to lull her into a state of pleasant emptiness, and it became easier to imagine that this was like any other day when she would sneak off to satisfy her boba craving during work.

The illusion—*delusion*—lasted right up until Damien slid her phone back to her. "That's fucked-up," he said quietly. "Don't let her get to you."

"Except she already did." Zoe laughed humorlessly. "She's absolutely trashed my reputation." The boba in her mouth suddenly tasted cloyingly sweet and she pushed the cup away. This might be the first time she hadn't drained a boba drink within five minutes.

Damien kept his eyes on her face. "I promise I won't let whoever's behind this get away with it. Do you have any clue who's out to get you?"

Zoe shrugged. "Could be anyone. Maybe the building receptionist, who sees me 'swan around' past her at least twice a day on my way in and out. Technically four times a day because I usually go on a boba run after lunch. Maybe even"—she swallowed as the memory of her first week struck her—"maybe it's Austin or Bram." She'd thought they were somewhat friends now, but maybe she was wrong. Maybe they had never let go of the bad impression they'd formed of her at the start.

She was relieved when Damien immediately shook his head. "No way. I know they can be . . . not easy to deal with at times, but Austin and Bram wouldn't do something shady like that. It has to be someone with a vendetta."

A thought struck Zoe. "It could be Wylan Watts!"

Damien squinted at her. "The CEO of Dreamcatcher? How does he even know you?"

"He cornered me in the building pantry the other day because his board chairman complimented our See Yourself campaign and he was salty when Lillian revealed it was me—"

Zoe's voice trailed off. Maybe Lillian hadn't been trying to credit her; maybe she had been planting the seed to *dis*credit her down the road and pin the Aisha Monroe debacle on her.

Clocking her change, Damien asked, "What's wrong?"

She met his concerned eyes. "It's Lillian," Zoe said quietly. "Lillian's the one who put Rebecca up to this."

Damien's eyes widened by a fraction. Silence stretched between the two of them, charged and heavy. Then he asked, "Do you have evidence?"

"I don't need evidence," Zoe bit out. "Lillian has hated me from the very beginning. And she finally saw her chance to throw me under the bus by going to Rebecca Stiles with this story idea. And it worked, didn't it? Now she gets to make herself look better than me by taking charge of fixing the mess." An edge crept into her voice as she spoke, a flicker of fire finally lighting within her and powering through her daze. "I'm not letting her get away with this. Bill needs to know about what she did."

Frowning, Damien leaned back in his seat, his drink still untouched on the table, the ice cubes half-melted. "Zoe, this is a very serious accusation. You can't just go to Bill unless you have some sort of proof."

Zoe tried to keep her voice even. "What happened to not letting Rebecca Stiles get away with this?"

"Rebecca Stiles was out of line for sure. But you can't be sure that Lillian has anything to do with this."

"I *am* sure."

Damien massaged his temples. "Okay, well, Bill is going to need something more than just your gut feeling. If not, it won't even make sense to him."

Zoe felt something within her snap as everything that had happened in the past hour rushed to the front of her mind. He was rubbing his head as though her lack of "sense" was giving him a headache. Even Damien, whom she thought she could count on, wasn't in her corner.

"I know that as an engineer, it's always about cold hard logic for you," she said, her voice every bit as cold and hard. "But life and people aren't always logical. Sometimes you just have to go with what your gut believes. I can't just sit back and let myself be walked over while I look for *proof.*"

"That's not what I'm saying. I just think you shouldn't do anything rash when you're upset."

"Upset?" she echoed with an incredulous laugh. Why was he acting like *she* was in the wrong? "Gee, Damien, I wonder why I would be upset. Maybe because not all of us are *emotional and clinical* robots."

The moment the words left her mouth, Zoe wanted to hit herself. Damien had finally trusted her enough to let her read his personal essay, and here she was throwing what he'd written back in his face, attacking him with his own vulnerability.

"I'm sorry—"

"I get where you're coming from," Damien interrupted, his voice calm and even like he was talking to one of his engineering contractors. "But if you start accusing people without proof, no one would take you seriously. You will just be letting Rebecca Stiles and all those idiots win because they want to see you get mad and lash out in public. So don't give in to your feelings; don't let them win."

Zoe clenched her jaw, any guilt swiftly evaporating. *No one would take me seriously,* or he *wouldn't take me seriously?* For once, couldn't Damien show just the smallest inkling of emotion? Offer some sign that he was actually on her side?

"If I don't fight back, *that* will be letting them win. Look, Damien, if you don't want to help me, fine. I am perfectly capable of defending myself," she said, leveling him with a defiant stare. "But don't try to hold me back."

Damien's eyes widened as she pushed her chair back and climbed to her feet, the screech of the chair's metal legs against the floor sounding extraordinarily loud in the still air. "I'm sorry, but I have to go now," Zoe said, longing for nothing more than to crawl into bed and forget this whole morning ever happened. "I'll Venmo you for the boba when I'm home."

He stood up, too, looking just as frustrated as she felt. "Forget about the boba cost. I—" He paused. "Zoe, I agree with you that there's something fishy going on here, but you will only be harming yourself if you say anything against Lillian now. She's the COO and Bill has known her far longer than he's known you. If it comes down to your word against hers, I don't think this will end well for you."

Zoe chuckled quietly over the sound of her heart splintering. "Or maybe you just don't want me to get Lillian into trouble because *you*'ve known her far longer than you've known me. She recommended you for this CTO job, didn't she? Well, it's nice to know where your priorities lie, Damien." She picked up her purse and pushed her chair in, averting her eyes from his. His gaze was so intense she could feel it scorching her skin. "I think we've said everything we need to. Goodbye."

ZOE HASTILY MUTED her television when knocks rang against her door. If she kept silent, maybe this person would think she wasn't home and leave her alone to wallow in peace. Who could it be anyway? The only person who knew her address was Damien.

An ache shot through Zoe's chest at that memory. That day had marked the first time she'd felt happy and confident since moving to the Bay Area. She'd single-handedly pulled off a successful pitch meeting that kickstarted the See Yourself campaign, and she'd spent the day with Damien, first being shown around the farmers' market, and then all his favorite spots in San Francisco. That day felt like a lifetime ago. Damien had dropped by two days earlier, but she hadn't opened the door then, either, not prepared to face him after their argument. He had finally left after five minutes of knocking and having his calls to her phone go unanswered.

But this time, it was Bernadette's voice that rang out. "Zoe! Open up. I know you're in there."

Zoe stayed quiet and curled deeper into her couch, but the knocking was relentless. At last, Zoe climbed to her feet and opened the door. Bernadette pushed her way into the living room, staunchly ignoring Zoe's grudging expression.

"How did you know I live here?" Zoe asked listlessly as she collapsed onto the couch again.

"Hello to you too," Bernadette said as she sat down next to Zoe with much better posture. "Did you forget you gave me your address for your Nordstrom delivery?"

"That was for sales purposes only! If you were a man, I'm pretty sure you'd have been arrested for stalking."

Bernadette waved those words away. "How else was I supposed to make sure you were still alive? Considering you've been ignoring all my texts and screening all my calls. You haven't even posted on Instagram once in the past week." Her voice softened at the sight of Zoe slumped over, swaddled in a thick blanket. "How are you feeling?"

"I feel peachy. Did you know that my name has now entered Urban Dictionary? To get *Zeng*-ed is to be criticized unironically by someone who has the same issue. For example, Aisha Monroe was Zeng-ed by Zoe Zeng for having a full stomach. Or, Miss Universe was Zeng-ed by Donald Trump in 2008 for being overweight."

"No such thing as bad publicity, right?" Bernadette offered, though without much conviction.

"There is when Mana-tee decides to make a graphic tee with the words *Have you been Zeng-ed?* on it. Or when *The Cut* decides to make me the poster girl for everything wrong with my generation. Have you read their article about me? *They chase picture-perfect, but has Zillennials' image obsession gone too far?*"

Bernadette's face creased into a grimace but Zoe pressed on, bolstered by an overwhelming sense of relief that she could finally unload everything onto someone else. "Or when my former magazine decides to scrub all my articles from their site and release a statement saying they do not condone or endorse my sentiments, which 'run counter to everything *Chic* stands for.'"

Zoe broke off as a lump formed in her throat. Out of everything that had happened so far, *Chic*'s press release was what had hurt most. She couldn't blame them for doing that, but did her former coworkers really imagine her capable of making those hurtful remarks about Aisha Monroe? Did Cassie and Bjorn? She hadn't answered their texts or calls, either, too afraid of what they might say if they got a hold of her.

Two slender arms wrapped around her and pulled her close. "Oh, babe." Zoe gratefully nestled into the warmth of Bernadette's body, letting the faint cinnamon notes of her friend's perfume soothe her. They reminded her of lazy afternoons with her mother, brewing black tea and adding way too much cinnamon. The memory of home, of warmth and comfort, was enough to make Zoe sniffle.

"Zoe, don't pay attention to those nasty things. And don't google yourself anymore."

"I don't," Zoe mumbled into Bernadette's shoulder. "But people found my Instagram and started bombarding me with comments. Most of the time, they're just being mean. Sometimes, I think they try to be nice though. Like, they'll say: *Ignore what* Teen Vogue *wrote about you! Them* Zeng-*ing you for being superficial says way more about them than you.* And that's how I found out about *Teen Vogue*'s op-ed about me."

"You need to turn off your social media accounts right now. Do you hear me?"

"I already have. Deactivated my Instagram, Twitter, and TikTok, and made my Facebook profile so private I can barely find myself."

"Good. I can't promise you everything will be okay, but I'll ride this out with you." Bernadette's voice gentled. "But Zoe, you can't hide out here forever."

"Technically, I can for at least two weeks on full-pay leave." She was initially only supposed to take a week off work, but Bill had extended her break when it became clear that the scandal was only gaining momentum. So for the past two weeks, she had been holed up at home, ignoring everyone's attempts to reach her. The only text she had sent was to Bill, thanking him for letting her take more time off. She hadn't even told him of her suspicion about Lillian. After all, Damien, who she'd thought was her friend, had ended up siding with Lillian, and Bill was even closer to the COO. Zoe wasn't prepared to have two people believe Lillian over her.

Bernadette sighed. "Your first time out of your hidey-hole can't be to work of all places." Her face lit up. "Hey, my fiancé's ending a big work project tonight and we're going out for dinner to celebrate. Come with us."

"Right, Bern. Because I *really* want to drag myself out of my hidey-hole to be a third wheel."

"Come on, you always say you want to meet him. Now's the time! Marcus is starting a new project on Monday, which means he won't get any free time until Christmas. And you need to be around people—all this wallowing isn't healthy." Her eyes darted to the frozen television screen. "Haven't you run out of *Love Island* episodes to watch already?"

"Bern, you don't get it. Everyone thinks I'm terrible or pitiful— and neither feels good. Whenever I talk to someone, it feels like there's this big elephant in the room and all I can think of is whether they agree with Rebecca Stiles's article that I'm a shallow snob."

"Good news for you: My fiancé doesn't know about your job. Trust me, the last thing Marcus wants to hear about when he gets home after a long day at work is more work, especially when it's someone else's. He just knows we met through Nordstrom. So no more excuses," Bernadette said firmly. "You're going to shower and put on that incredible Missoni dress you thrifted last time and I'll see you at Terun in Palo Alto at seven. And I'm not taking no for an answer."

Zoe glared at Bernadette, but her friend just gazed calmly back at her. Finally, Zoe huffed in resignation. "Okay, fine. But I'm not changing out of my pajamas."

Bernadette lifted up Zoe's blanket to take a look at her Karen Mabon dog-print sleep set. "Well then, it's a good thing they're cute."

BUT THAT NIGHT, WHEN ZOE REACHED TERUN, SHE FOUND ONLY Bernadette at the table the maître d' showed her to. "Sorry, Marcus got held up at work, but he'll be here soon. And despite how much I adore your pajamas, I have to say, I'm glad you went with my suggestion for the Missoni dress."

Zoe half smiled as she took her seat. "I like wearing an Italian brand to a pizzeria." Unbidden, the memory of the top comment on Rebecca Stiles's latest article popped into her mind, the one that accused her of size-shaming someone with a Dolce & Gabbana sample. Her chest tightened, but she forced herself to push that thought aside. At least for tonight, she would forget about all of that and focus on savoring the good food and good company. It would be a shame to waste a vintage Missoni slip dress on wallowing.

"Do you try to do the same when you visit restaurants serving other cuisines? Say, if you went to Jin Sho just next door, would you wear something from a Japanese brand?"

"Yes!" Zoe exclaimed, eager to focus on something else, especially when it concerned her favorite subject—fashion. "You know me—I never miss the chance to dress for a theme. There's this brand I've been obsessed with lately—Mukzin; they have the coolest retro prints. But if I know it's going to be a big meal, I might just go with Uniqlo since their clothes are loose-fitting. But look at you!" she said admiringly as she ran her eyes down Bernadette's outfit—a billowy blouse with shimmery gold threads tucked into tailored white pants. It wasn't the flashiest ensemble, but Bernadette pulled it off beautifully with her five-foot-eight frame. "You look amazing!"

Bernadette let out a silvery little laugh. "Stop it, you!" she said, but Zoe could tell she was pleased. "To be fair, you've mostly seen me either in my Nordstrom work outfits or my workout clothes when we go to Desk Step." A soft smile rose on her face. "But this is a big night for my fiancé, so I wanted to dress up to surprise him."

Zoe grinned. "I can see that. You're even wearing your engagement ring." Bernadette typically put it away so she wouldn't lose it at work or while working out. As the in-house band in a corner of the restaurant whipped up a jaunty little tune, Zoe leaned back in her seat, her shoulders loosening as the music and chatter of surrounding diners washed over her. It did feel good to be out again with a friend and enjoying life as someone her age should be doing.

Suddenly, Bernadette waved at someone over Zoe's shoulder. "He's here!"

Zoe stifled a grin. Her friend was a stunning woman, but Zoe had never seen Bernadette's face lit up so brightly before. Who was this man who could make even the preternaturally cool Bernadette Dubois so smitten?

She turned around. "Hi! I've heard so much about you—"

Her smile froze as her voice abruptly died. She knew this man. She walked past him at least five days a week. In real life, he was taller and slightly lankier than his photo made him out to be.

Because the man who had just approached their table, scooping Bernadette up in his arms and planting a firm kiss on her lips, was none other than Lillian's boyfriend.

"HEY, ZOE, RIGHT? I'M MARCUS."

It took Zoe a moment to register Marcus's outstretched arm, his smile now edged with a tinge of confusion the longer she let it dangle between them. Bernadette shot her a *What's going on?* look that made Zoe snap back to her senses.

She mustered a laugh that sounded extraordinarily high-pitched to her own ears. "Sorry! You reminded me of someone and I was busy trying to figure out who." Only half of that was a lie. "You don't happen to have a twin, do you?" she asked in her most casual voice.

"Not that I know of," he chuckled, making her heart sink. Zoe willed herself not to stiffen as Marcus slid into the chair next to hers. Was this man two-timing Bernadette and Lillian? But no cheater would ever bring an affair partner to a restaurant as conspicuous as Terun in downtown Palo Alto, which counted at least half its guests tonight among the Bay Area's tech and finance glitterati.

Did that mean he was cheating *on* Bernadette with Lillian? After all, Bernadette was the one wearing the engagement ring, and Lillian was just a "girlfriend." And if Lillian was capable of being a career wrecker, maybe she was capable of being a home-wrecker too.

But through her haze of anger, a prickle of doubt crept in. Would a woman like Lillian Mariko really be okay with being someone's side piece? Only one way to find out.

Zoe gave Bernadette and Marcus an apologetic smile. "Please excuse me. I need to use the restroom."

In the solitude of the restaurant's restroom, Zoe pulled up Lillian's contact in her phone. Before her resolve could abandon her, she typed: *Hey, can we meet tomorrow to talk about something?*, then clicked "Send."

chapter 35

ZOE WASN'T SURPRISED to find Lillian already at Starbucks when she got there. Of course the other woman would be early. Lillian must have come here straight from the office, but even after a full workday, she still looked more polished than Zoe, who had been resting at home for the past couple of weeks.

"Zoe, it's nice to see you again," Lillian said as Zoe slid into the chair opposite hers. "I bought a cold brew, but should we also order something to eat?"

"No, thanks," Zoe said shortly. This wasn't meant to be a friendly catch-up after all. She'd scheduled a meeting with Bill at FitPick's office after this so that she could finally share her suspicions about Lillian's backstabbing. But first, she needed to extract a confession from the other woman.

Lillian leaned forward. "You know, I was really glad to get your text yesterday. We have all been very concerned about you. I wanted to reach out earlier but Damien said you haven't been responding to his texts, so I figured you needed some space."

Zoe clenched her jaw. So Damien and Lillian had been discussing her while she was gone. Why did he think it was okay to share the status of their *private* communication with Lillian despite Zoe's misgivings about the COO? And the nerve of Lillian to act so concerned for her well-being when she was the one who orchestrated this entire mess.

"Lillian, cut the act."

Lillian frowned. "What act?"

Exasperated, Zoe gestured between them. "This! How you pretend you're holier than thou when you know perfectly well the shit you've pulled."

Beneath her furrowed brows, Lillian's eyes hardened. "Zoe, I have no idea what you're talking about. You told me to come here just so you could hurl accusations at me?"

If this had been a few weeks ago, Zoe would have backed down. Would have been the one to look away first and make her voice small as she mumbled an apology. But what did she have to lose now? She was basically out of a job and out of Silicon Valley. Lillian was no longer the boss whose good side she had to stay on.

So, Zoe leveled Lillian with a cool look. "I don't know what you have against me, but you seemed to have an issue with me from the very beginning. And don't bother lying because if you do, I'll make sure to tell everyone your so-called boyfriend is actually not who you make him out to be."

Zoe felt a flicker of grim satisfaction as her boss's face paled. "That's right. I know your boyfriend is engaged to another woman. You're not actually with him, are you? I don't know why you lied, but I'm sure everyone would love to know about it and what else you're capable of." Of course, there was no way she could bring herself to actually expose Lillian in case it put Bernadette in a tough spot. But Lillian didn't have to know that.

"You don't understand," Lillian said, her fingers tightening around her coffee cup. Her lips were so dry that her lipstick had sank into every ridge and crevice, only emphasizing the wrinkles further.

"I understand you were lying about that, which meant you were probably lying about many other things too." Zoe propped her elbows on the table, her eyes boring into Lillian. "So you might as well admit everything, including how you set me up."

Lillian's throat bobbed as she swallowed visibly. "It's because of Bill," she finally said, her voice dipping barely above a whisper.

Zoe couldn't rein in her snort. "Oh, let me guess—he told you to pretend you had a boyfriend? He told you to criticize me at every turn and throw me under the bus?"

"No, you don't understand. I pretended to have a boyfriend because I thought that was the only way I could get Bill to back off."

The words landed on the table between them like a grenade, instantly drowning out all the surrounding buzz in the café and turning everything in Zoe's head upside down. Zoe's eyes widened as she scoured the other woman's face for a hint of levity that she couldn't find. "What do you mean?" she finally asked.

Lillian lowered her eyes to the table, her shoulders hunched. Even though she looked as sleek as always on the outside, her clothes suddenly seemed to hang too big on her shrunken frame. "It was after our very first meeting with Logan Horossen," she said softly. "It was just us two then, staying overnight at the Ritz. That evening, we went for dinner together at Ophelia."

Zoe could picture the scene as it unfolded. The same dimly lit restaurant with its red-tinged lights, bathing diners in an oddly intimate ambience. Those small round tables that meant you had to sit close to your dining partners, your knees and shoulders a hair's breadth from theirs.

"Bill ordered wine and got a bit tipsy, but nothing too bad. After dinner, he asked me up to his room to strategize based on Logan Horossen's comments."

Goosebumps sprouted over Zoe's skin. The elevator rising up and up, bringing them one step closer to Bill's room. That fake money plant that was the first thing anyone saw when they stepped out of the elevator. The narrow hotel hallway with its beige carpet.

"I didn't have any reason not to trust him, so I went. And once we got to his room, he immediately collapsed on the only chair and told me to find a seat, so I had to sit on his bed. He dragged his chair closer to me, his laptop on his lap. It was okay at first—we really did review the meeting notes. But then he started touching my arm as he spoke. At some point, he grabbed my hand and pulled me toward him—"

The crack in Lillian's voice was like a dagger straight to Zoe's heart. Lillian was holding her head up high and her body straight, but her muscles looked so coiled that she seemed like she might shatter at the barest touch. "You don't have to talk about it if you don't want to," Zoe said softly, fighting the urge to wrap her arms around the other woman.

"No, I have to make sure you understand why I did what I did." Lillian let out a long exhale, but her shoulders remained tense. "I thought I imagined it at first and I just froze. But then he tried pulling me closer." She lowered her eyes to her hands, her fingers twisting around one another on the table. "Since that night, I've thought many times of what I should have done—I could have screamed at him or walked out and told someone."

With a humorless laugh, Lillian shook her head. "But in that moment, I panicked. All I did was tell Bill that I already had a boyfriend. I don't know why I said that, but it worked. Bill backed off and to this day, I still remember what he said. *Woah, sorry. I just lost my balance and grabbed you to stabilize myself.*"

Even though it was warm in Starbucks and she still had her coat on, a chill ran over Zoe, leaving goosebumps in its wake. She shuddered slightly, imagining Bill's big hands on her, running all over her body like it was property. "That's bullshit. He knew what he was doing."

"But he's still my boss and I would still have to see him every day," Lillian said quietly. "So I tried convincing myself that what he said was true. After all, he did have a lot to drink that night. Once I got home, I started worrying that Bill would see through my lie. So the next day, I brought a photo of me with a distant cousin to work and told everyone who asked it was my boyfriend. And then I just tried keeping out of Bill's way as much as possible. It's hard since we work so closely together, but I avoided putting myself in situations where we would be alone."

The realization hit Zoe like a lightning bolt: Marcus was Lillian's *cousin*; there had been nothing shady going on between them at all. Didn't Bernadette say months ago: "My fiancé's cousin is some boss lady at her company"? And Bram had said that after the first Logan Horossen meeting, Lillian stopped staying back late to work in the office with Bill, though she'd still continue to work from home in the evenings.

"And then what happened?" Zoe whispered.

"And then life went on," Lillian replied, her lips twisted in a rueful smile that made Zoe's heart ache. "All I can do now is make sure no one else would experience something similar. When I saw your text that night about the dress code, I immediately suspected that Bill had asked you out to dinner but not me so that he could be alone with you. I waited with my ear pressed against my door to hear when you two would be back so that I could step in before he trapped you in a compromising situation like he had done with me."

But it helps to be more alert so that you won't be caught in any compromising situations in the future. Back then, Zoe'd thought Lillian meant it as a pointed jibe about her carelessness, but now the words took on a whole new meaning. If Lillian hadn't come up with that excuse about wanting to borrow makeup wipes, she would have gone with Bill to his room, sat close to him—probably on his bed—to look at the projections sent by Logan's assistant, and things might have unfolded just as Lillian had feared.

Zoe's breathing shallowed. She never did end up seeing what Logan's assistant emailed over—not that night and not subsequently either. What if Bill had made the whole thing up just as a pretext to get her into his room? Trembling slightly, she wrapped her coat tighter around herself, but the coldness seemed to have burrowed beneath her skin and seeped into her bones, leaving her feeling more exposed than ever.

"I don't get it," she finally said. "I thought you disliked me."

"Disliked you?" Lillian echoed, looking bewildered. "Why would I dislike you when you've never done anything to me?" Her face colored slightly. "I know I can be rather . . . brusque. I can get so focused on a task that I neglect the people working on it. It's my fault for not being more considerate in my speech, and I apologize if I haven't been respectful of your ideas in the past."

Zoe blinked. Just twelve hours ago, she never would have imagined hearing an apology come out of Lillian Mariko's mouth. "I appreciate you saying that," she said honestly, "but something else that bothers me is how you would sometimes imply I'm not dressed or behaving properly."

Lillian sighed. "I'm sorry, I didn't realize that's how I was coming across. I was just trying to look out for you because many men in tech already don't take women seriously. And in my personal experience, they would happily misinterpret friendliness as a sign of your interest in them or the way you dress as an invitation to try their luck. I know this sounds like victim-blaming, but I just didn't want you attracting any attention you don't want. It's nothing against you personally; I also dress down at work so that people like Bill will see me as just a coworker there to do work and nothing else."

So *that* was why Lillian was always telling her to dress and conduct herself in a more businesslike manner. But why were *they* the ones who had to make themselves smaller and more invisible so that men like Bill could continue to strut around and intrude into other people's spaces?

"How can you even stand to work with Bill after all that?" Zoe asked.

Lillian cast her eyes down, her lashes fanning shadows over her pale cheeks. "Because that was the best move for my career. I spent years at Google, giving the company my all and working my way up to senior director, but then I got stuck. I was criticized for not being assertive enough, then criticized for being too aggressive. I was repeatedly passed over for promotions while the men around me rose steadily through the ranks. And from the stories I've heard, I would run into similar barriers at another big tech company. So when I met Bill at a networking event one day and he asked me to be his COO, I accepted even though FitPick was still so new. I thought that at least someone recognized my ability and was giving me a title I deserve."

She paused, fiddling with her straw. "And I've poured so much of my time and energy into FitPick. Right before the first Logan

Horossen meeting, I was in the office sixteen hours every day, even on weekends. I can't just give all that up now. I won't be valued as much at another company."

"Valued?" Zoe repeated incredulously, but softened her voice after hearing how it came out. "Sorry, I didn't mean it like that. I just don't think what Bill did to you was respectful."

"Yeah," Lillian said softly. "But he hasn't tried anything funny with me since I told him I have a boyfriend."

"That doesn't show he respects you; he respects your fictional boyfriend—a *man*—more than he respects you. And he hasn't had the opportunity to try anything else because you've been avoiding him. You still don't feel safe around him and I completely understand that. Even if he's not doing anything to you, he's got his eye on another woman—me, or the next one to come along."

Lillian's voice was low as she said, "Zoe, there's nothing I can do. Nothing *we* can do. Bill knows too many powerful people—powerful men—and at the end of the day, this industry is a boys' club. Those men will protect one another because many of them behave the same way. Who would believe me?"

Zoe sat up straighter. "I believe you," she said hotly. She had come to Starbucks prepared to hate Lillian, already thinking of what she could do to get the other woman back for what she had done. But the woman sitting across the table from her looked so shrunken and fragile at this moment; her expression was rigid as always, but now it seemed more like armor than deterrence, more like a self-defense mechanism than anything else.

"You might be the only one," sighed Lillian. "If anyone checks the cameras in the hotel hallway from that night, they will see me willingly following Bill into his room. It will become a case of 'he said, she said,' and Bill is much more charismatic so I'm sure everyone would take his side." Lillian's fingers flexed as though she was imagining them clenched in a fist.

Zoe's heart sank. "Not all of them are like that. There are good men in Silicon Valley."

"Sure," Lillian said, but Zoe could tell the other woman was just humoring her. "But most men at the top have done what Bill did, maybe even worse. What's more: They don't even think they're doing anything wrong. And I hate to say it but if we want to succeed in this industry, we have to play by the rules of those at the top. If we go up against Bill and lose, people will think of us at best as troublemakers and at worst as a liability. And word travels fast in Silicon Valley—no company will hire us again and no VC will risk investing in anything we're a part of."

Zoe's mouth clamped shut. Lillian sounded genuinely regretful, but there was a note of finality in her voice. "I understand," Zoe said through the lump in her throat. And she did. Silicon Valley was where Lillian had studied and always worked; tech was the industry she had wanted to be a part of since she was young. Lillian had given too much of herself and too much was at stake here for her to burn any bridges.

As Zoe's shoulders slumped, Lillian bit her lip. "Look, there's something else you should know. I'm not sure if I should say this because you're already dealing with so much, but"—she paused, a hesitant look on her face—"I think Bram was Rebecca Stiles's secret source. He was in the pantry when I passed by two afternoons ago, and I heard him say, 'Hi, Rebecca. Is now still a good time?'"

Zoe gripped the table to steady herself as her mind whirled. *No . . . not Bram.* They might have gotten off on the wrong foot at first, but they'd also gotten spiked bobas and played Catan together. He'd designated her his love and fashion guru.

She had thought they were friends.

Lillian's eyes were filled with sympathy. "It could be someone else named Rebecca," she offered without much conviction. "I wish I had more info, but Bram spoke too quietly from that point on for me to hear anything."

Did he do that because he was jealous? Disgruntled that her ideas were so valued by Bill even though she held a nontechnical role? Annoyed that someone with a "fluffy" fashion degree could actually contribute at a tech startup?

When Zoe still didn't say anything, Lillian moved closer and placed a tentative hand on her shoulder, letting her palm rest fully only after Zoe made no move to shrug it off. "I'm sorry, Zoe. You don't deserve any of that. Let me know if there's anything I can do. And in the meantime, just keep your head down and your wits about you, okay?"

Zoe nodded, but a new thought stopped her cold. She was supposed to meet Bill this evening in the office after everyone else was gone.

chapter 36

SHIT. I'M SUPPOSED to meet up with Bill tonight after work," Zoe groaned. "I wanted to—" Her mouth clamped shut. She couldn't possibly tell Lillian that the meeting with Bill would have been about her suspicions of the COO. "He, uh, wanted to discuss my situation, and I asked to do it after hours so I wouldn't run into anyone in the office."

"You have to cancel!" Lillian said. "Just say you're sick or something. Don't put yourself into a risky position like this where you're alone with him."

"But I will have to meet with him sooner or later. I'm supposed to go back to work any day now." Bernadette was right—she couldn't just hide away at home forever, especially since she was still getting paid. There were already rumors in the ValleyVerified community forum that she hadn't been seen at FitPick's office in two weeks, leading to gleeful speculations that she'd been fired.

"Even so, you shouldn't be alone with him." Lillian sat up

straight. "Let me go with you. I won't walk in with you in case that makes Bill suspicious. But I'll wait outside in the car and if I don't hear from you in thirty minutes, I'll go in and pretend I left something behind. Zoe, we can't take any chances here," she said firmly as Zoe opened her mouth to protest. Lillian's tone softened. "Please. I won't be able to sleep tonight if I don't know that you're okay."

Zoe gnawed on the inside of her cheek. The last thing she wanted to do was drag someone else into Bill's mess. But something about Lillian's earnest expression made her relent and accept the other woman's offer.

As they made plans for that night, the weight in Zoe's chest eased slightly for the first time. Regardless of what happened, at least the two of them were on the same team now—Lillian Mariko was definitely a person she would rather be on the same side with than against.

ZOE ARRIVED AT THE NOOK FIVE MINUTES BEFORE HER DESIG-nated 8 p.m. meeting time with Bill. But he was already waiting by the front door, giving her no time to run through a last-minute pep talk for herself or do some soothing breathing exercises.

She had on her Donna Karan military blazer with padded shoulders and jacquard cigarette pants because they always made her feel like she was wearing an armor of sorts. But any illusion of security evaporated the moment Bill spotted her.

"Zoe!" he exclaimed, covering the distance between them in a few big strides and enveloping her in a big embrace. Zoe felt herself stiffen but willed her muscles to relax. She couldn't let him sense anything was wrong. "How are you? We missed you around here!"

"I'm good!" Zoe chirped, matching Bill's bright tone. She took the chance to step out of his arms. "I mean, could be better, but—" She shrugged and Bill nodded understandingly. "Anyway, thanks for staying back late to meet with me."

"You know I'll always make time for one-on-ones with you, Zoe," Bill responded with a smile that sent goosebumps over Zoe's arms. "And just you wait—this will all blow over soon. But it's really great to see you again. Come, let's head to the office."

As she followed Bill, treading the familiar path to The Hook that she'd treaded hundreds of times, Zoe's heart was rocked with an unexpected pang. The past week spent holed up at home had been miserable and lonely, but not just because she was persona non grata in the Valley. To her surprise, she had missed work, missed the thrill of racking her head and hitting on a brainwave, missed the adrenaline rush of putting out fires, even missed the eye rolls she'd exchanged with Austin at Bram's predictable grumbles. Would she ever get all that back?

"It's so quiet now," Zoe commented, her voice breaking up the echo of their synchronized footsteps against the linoleum floor. There was no one else left in the office, leaving her alone with Bill for the first time since their dinner at Ophelia in San Francisco. She gripped her phone tighter, relieved that Lillian was just outside the building.

"Yeah, no one stays back as late as I do," Bill said as they arrived at the Hook. Zoe's chest tightened at the sight of Bram's Tesla Tequila bottle. How could she have ever trusted a backstabber like him? She'd even asked Bernadette for a favor to style him when Bernadette only worked with female clients.

Bill collapsed into his chair and gestured for Zoe to take the one right beside his—Lillian's. "Lillian used to stay back with me but then ditched me once she got a boyfriend."

Jerk. Zoe forced herself to keep smiling as Bill leaned forward, so close to Zoe that she could feel his breath against her face.

"So, Zoe, what did you want to see me about?"

Zoe inched back, her mind racing as her boss stared at her expectantly. It was supposed to be about Lillian, but she'd just found out a couple hours ago that everything she thought she knew about the other woman was wrong.

"Um, I just wanted to apologize for everything that has happened," she finally said. That much was true. After all, FitPick had been implicated by Rebecca Stiles's articles, too, and things couldn't have been easy for Bill as the CEO. "I'm sorry I brought so much bad press to the company. I should have insisted on reviewing Aisha Monroe's photos before she posted them, but things were going so well and I got complacent . . ."

"Don't apologize! This scandal was the best thing that could have happened to us."

He laughed as Zoe's mouth dropped open in surprise. "I guess you really have been underground, huh? You missed the big news: We've gained nearly a hundred thousand new users in the time you've been gone. Thanks to all the hoopla, so many more people have heard about us. All my old Kappa Sigma bros know my app now and our board of directors is very pleased with how things are looking. Drew Macklemore even says a Forbes 30 Under 30 is very possible."

Bill bestowed a glowing smile on a gobsmacked Zoe. "So your campaign totally paid off. Don't stop thinking outside the box, Zoe. Our business wouldn't have grown to what it is today if not for you seizing a black swan."

Her mind still reeling from the unexpected turn of events, Zoe asked, "What's a black swan?"

"Something unconventional and unexpected that turns out to

make a huge impact. You can take the safe approach, *or* you can choose to go out on a limb and try something that's never been done before. And it could flop or it could succeed beyond what you ever imagined. Lillian thought we should have stuck with SEO marketing and targeted ads like what most companies do, but you proposed something new and bold. And it paid off! Now, it's not wrong for Lillian to be cautious"—Bill said smoothly with his trademark diplomacy—"and that might be the best approach for certain situations, but a company with only cautious people would never get anywhere. So it's a good thing FitPick has some-one like you who dares to seize the black swans around here."

Zoe stared at Bill, something prickling in the back of her mind. *The black swans around here . . . swans around.* A hazy memory of those two words coming out of someone else's mouth began to take shape, growing more defined as the scene solidified in her mind. Bill and her in front of the framed photo of him at Burning Man. Him telling her that the festival was just—what were his exact words again?—*where the who's who of Silicon Valley swans around in a dick-measuring contest.*

Bill looked at her closely. "Zoe, are you okay?"

"Uh, one sec. I have to look something up." The moment she typed "Valley" into her phone's search bar, Rebecca Stiles's article about her in ValleyVerified popped up—as it had all seventy-two times she'd reread it over the past week.

After a few deft scrolls, her eyes landed on what she'd been looking for. "*She swans around the office in her fancy outfits and looks down on the rest of us for only wearing T-shirts and jeans.*"

There was a dull buzzing in her ears as Zoe forced herself to read the sentence again, and again, praying desperately every time that the words would have morphed into something different. Her head jerked up when she felt a hand touch her shoulder.

"Zoe, seriously, is something wrong?" Bill asked, brows knitted together.

Zoe shrugged Bill's hand off and forced herself to hold his gaze. "Bill," she said, hoping he couldn't hear the tremor in her voice. "Were you that anonymous source in Rebecca Stiles's article?"

Bill quickly took a step back, his eyes growing round. "What?" he sputtered. "No, of course not! Do you hear how ridiculous you sound?"

The next moment, his look of incredulity was replaced with a benevolent smile. "Zoe . . ." He said her name in a long, deep sigh, like a father who had just caught his teenage daughter sneaking out of the house at night. "I know you're going through a hard time now, so I'm going to let your little outburst slide. But it's not okay for you to take your frustration out on me. Like I said, I'll try my best to get to the bottom of this for you, but I can't help you if you're going to push me away and say crazy things."

From the corner of her eye, Zoe saw the framed photo on Lillian's desk. The one with Marcus, her cousin, whom she'd told everyone was her boyfriend so Bill would leave her alone.

And in that moment, Zoe knew beyond a shadow of a doubt that she was right. It wasn't just the fact that he'd used the same obscure phrase as the anonymous source Rebecca Stiles quoted, or his squirming, or his inability to meet her gaze. If it was Lillian on the receiving end of the accusation, she would have been shocked and aghast, but she wouldn't have tried to turn things around on her by calling her "ridiculous" or "crazy." Neither would Damien, or any other decent person.

Steeling herself, Zoe looked him straight in the eye. "You can deny it all you want, but I know it was you who fed Rebecca Stiles the information and called me a snob." She stepped forward as a fresh wave of anger spiked within her. "Do you know the number of hate comments I've gotten on social media because of that article?"

Bill rolled his eyes. "Oh my God, women like you are *obsessed* with social media. I'm sorry you lost Instagram followers, Zoe, but it's hardly the end of the world."

"Obsessed?" Zoe echoed, her voice rising and her hands balling into fists. "Bill, it's not about me losing followers on Instagram. It's about hundreds of strangers hurling every nasty name you can imagine at me. It's about having my reputation dragged through the mud just because you didn't want to own up to your mistakes—and in a town where reputation is everything. And you knew that, which was why you wanted to protect your own reputation by making me the scapegoat!" she exclaimed, the realization crystallizing in her mind.

Her throat tightened as every ugly word tossed her way over the past few days entered her mind. "You're the only one with something to gain from this and you didn't even try to defend me in public. You just happily let me take the blame that you set me up for. I bet you asked me to stay at home not because you genuinely care about me, but because you were trying to phase me out of the company. *You* planted those rumors in the ValleyVerified forum that I'd been fired."

Bill shifted in his chair, his eyes darting around the room. "Zoe, I don't know what you're trying to do here, but I don't have time to argue with you about this. You get to hide out at home, but I'm in the office every day, staying back late to put out fires. You weren't the only one who got called out, you know. I was mocked for not making better hires."

There was an edge to Bill's voice, a forcefulness that seemed like it was trying to overcompensate for something. Zoe scoffed.

"Of course you would ask Rebecca Stiles to put that in—it makes you seem less suspicious and reinforces the idea that *I* was the one who messed up, not you." She squared her shoulders, suddenly feeling ten feet tall as her scornful gaze bore down on him like bullets. Until finally, Bill threw his hands up.

"Zoe, what do you want me to do? You know that Logan Horossen is watching us closely, ready to pull out the moment he sees something he doesn't like? And this whole mess happens and no offense, but you're not even a C-suite executive—to Logan Horossen, you're dispensable. But if he starts doubting *me*, he's never going to invest in FitPick—he always says that a company is only as good as its CEO. So you had to take the heat for a bit, big deal. I heard Elon Musk is welcoming a new child soon; I'm sure whatever awful name he gives that poor kid will occupy ValleyVerified for at least the next two weeks. You'll be old news and we can all move on, richer than before once Logan Horossen makes his multimillion-dollar investment," he added pointedly.

Zoe's blood ran cold. Even as the suspicion had taken root in her mind, a part of her had prayed that she was wrong, that the man who had believed in her when she hadn't even believed in herself didn't stab a dagger in her back. "Bill, I don't want Logan Horossen's money, and I don't want to sacrifice my dignity so you can get it."

"Then what do you want? What's done is done. But if all goes well, you could end up wealthier than all of your friends. People would kill for this, do you realize? And now you want to make a mountain out of a molehill? No one likes a troublemaker, Zoe."

Zoe dug her fingers into her palms so she wouldn't give in to the temptation to slap the smirk off Bill's face. No wonder Lillian was so afraid of speaking up. "For starters, I want you to write in to ValleyVerified and admit what you did; I want my name to be cleared."

"Yeah, that's not going to happen." Bill rolled up the sleeves of his quarter zip and crossed his arms. "And if you try to escalate this, I'll deny everything. Who do you think people will believe? Me, a soon-to-be Forbes 30 Under 30 honoree, or you, whom people already think of as problematic and unqualified?" He stood up and looked down at her. "Maybe you don't realize this, Zoe, but it takes a certain hard streak to make it in this town. You women are too soft, and that's why most successful companies are run by men. Men like Drew Macklemore and Aswar Joshi, who are on our board, would understand why I did what I did, and I bet you they would have done the same. This town is full of people I know who will back me up, but you—you're on your own."

chapter 37

"WHAT WERE YOU thinking?" Bernadette exclaimed as she and Zoe walked out of Desk Step. Zoe had just finished recounting her meetings with Lillian and Bill. "Why would you go see your boss alone when you already know he's a nasty piece of work? He could have done something to you. And don't touch your face right after a workout," she added more sternly.

Zoe stopped in the middle of mopping the sweat off her forehead. The other woman was a staunch believer that touching your face too much would cause pimples to form. "Sorry, I wasn't expecting to sweat so much today." Probably because for once, with no work to do, she could concentrate fully on pounding away on the treadmill while everyone else was nose-deep in work on their laptops. Even Bernadette had forgone her usual water break to concentrate on "looking up something on AliExpress," she'd muttered absently when Zoe asked what she was working on.

"And yeah, that was not my brightest moment," Zoe admitted. "I was lucky he didn't try anything. But I was just so . . . so angry that I wasn't thinking straight. I hate how us women have to just keep quiet while the William Lawrences of the world get off scot-free!"

Bernadette stopped in her tracks. "Did you just say William Lawrence?"

"Yeah, but he usually goes by Bill."

"The man with the two first names!"

Zoe stared at her friend. "That was how he introduced himself to me. Do you know him?"

"Blond, kind of short—maybe five feet seven, has a young face?"

When Zoe nodded, Bernadette pulled her to the side of the street and out of human traffic. "He was a year ahead of me at USC. I was in a sorority and he was in a frat, so we crossed paths a few times in Greek life. But after he was suspended, I never heard or thought of him again. I didn't realize he was the Bill you kept talking about at work!"

"Wait, *suspended*?" Zoe gripped Bernadette's arm so tightly that the other woman winced. "Oh, sorry. But Bill told me he was a college dropout. And he's really proud of it too. The number of times he's compared himself to Jobs and Gates and Zuckerberg..."

Bernadette scoffed. "Oh, so that's the story he's been going around telling people? The whole thing was pretty hushed up on campus because his frat had powerful alumni that wanted to keep it under wraps, but word made its way around in the Greek community. Apparently, he created some sort of sleazy app that involved people in Greek life. I don't know the exact details though—" She snapped her fingers. "Hang on. I'm still good friends with one of my sorority sisters. Her husband was in the same frat as Bill. Let me call her and find out if he knows something."

She whipped out her phone and punched in a contact. "Hey babe! I'm doing great. How are you and Tristan? Oh, no way! He's so sweet to you! Mm-hmm, I have a quick question. Remember in our junior year when—I know, that feels like forever ago, right? Anyway, do you remember that scandal involving some guy from Tristan's frat? His name was William Lawrence, does that ring any bells?"

Zoe held her breath as Bernadette fell silent, waiting for a response. Her friend's face soon lit up. "Yes, yes! The man with the two first names—God, he really went around saying that to all the girls, huh? Anyway, do you remember what that scandal was? Would Tristan know? Oh, he's there right now? Yeah, I'd love to chat with him. Is it okay if I put him on speakerphone? Long story short: I know a few people who have been wronged by Bill and I think this would be very helpful for them to know."

Bernadette's friend must have given the affirmative because she pressed the "Speaker" button and beckoned Zoe to come closer. A man's voice crackled out. "Hey, Bern. Shauna tells me you want to hear about Bill's suspension?"

"Yeah, could you share what you know?"

"Sure. But disclaimer that it was six years ago so my memory's kind of hazy and most of what I know was heard through the grapevine. Um, there was this one guy that Bill was always hanging out with, I'm trying to remember his name—"

"Dune Macklemore?" Zoe offered.

"That's right—Dune! I can't believe I forgot him for a second; that guy's parties were legendary." Tristan paused, a note of wariness entering his voice. "Um, who are you?"

Bernadette opened her mouth but closed it when Zoe shook her head. *I've got it.* "I'm Zoe, Bernadette's friend, and I work at Bill's startup, FitPick. He did some things that really concerned me lately, so I want to get a better idea of his background."

"Oh yeah, he's still doing that app, huh? That's what he got suspended for."

Sirens began ringing in Zoe's head. Was FitPick a front for something illegal? Bernadette's face carried a horrified expression that probably mirrored hers. "I don't understand," Zoe said, fighting to keep her voice steady. "FitPick is an app that lets users upload outfit photos and poll the public on what to wear. What's so bad about that?"

"Ohh. My bad. Sorry, I misheard it as ChickPick. That was the name of Bill's app in college. He and Dune were big party guys and very into the ladies, if you get what I mean. Their senior year, they had a bet to see who could sleep with the most attractive sorority girls. And they decided to get the rest of the frat to rate the girls at USC and come up with a final attractiveness score for each person. I think they tried just a basic numerical rating at first—assign every girl a score from one to ten. But Dune made a fuss about one guy's eight could be another guy's five. So Bill made this app that scraped girls' Instagram accounts and put photos of two girls next to each other, and the guys would vote for the one they'd rather, uh, sleep with."

Bernadette clapped a hand over her mouth, her eyes wide. Tristan broke off with a small cough. "Um, I was only a pledge then, so I never got involved in any of that. But Bill wasn't exactly shy about it, you know? I think he was really proud of his coding work because he bragged about it to us pledges. And I guess word must have gotten out and the school administration heard about ChickPick. Before we knew it, Bill was gone. I guess he has now pivoted the app to something completely different, huh?"

"I guess so," Zoe said faintly, her mind whirling. She had to lean against a wall to steady herself as everything she thought she knew about her work came crashing down. The app that she had poured so much time, energy, and effort into promoting as a safe fashion space had been rooted in such seedy origins all along.

Tristan's voice surfaced in her ear again. "I might have an old email thread about this within my frat's mailing list because Bill was bragging about the app. Maybe I can dig it up if it's still there. I, uh, still use my student email to get student discounts when shopping online."

Zoe pushed herself into an upright position, a small hope flickering within her. "Those emails would be a big help." If Tristan could find it, it would be concrete proof that William Lawrence was not the holier-than-thou man he made himself out to be.

"Okay, but you won't tell him I gave it to you, right? I don't want to be on his bad side just in case his app makes it big and he becomes the next Zuckerberg or whatever. Who knows, he might give me a job someday."

Zoe and Bernadette exchanged an eye roll. "Yeah, this stays between us," Zoe said as pleasantly as possible.

Once Zoe gave Tristan her email address and hung up, she passed Bernadette's phone back to her and let out a long, deep exhale. "And now, we wait."

Less than ten minutes later, Zoe's phone buzzed.

———

[Forwarded from: tmack@alumni.usc.edu]

FROM: wlawrence@usc.edu
TO: kappasigma1314@usc.edu
DATE: 9/30/13
SUBJECT: SETTLE THIS DEBATE FOR ME AND DUNE

Who's fucked hotter bitches?! If you haven't voted already, go to https://www.chicksofsc.com and cast your vote so we can decide who the most bang-worthy chicks at SC are.

@ClaytonBeck: hey pres, can this count for my service points for this term? I guarantee all the guys will thank me for this.

Peace out mofos. Go touch some grass or something,
BLaw

[Forwarded from: tmack@alumni.usc.edu]

FROM: wlawrence@usc.edu
TO: kappasigma1314@usc.edu
DATE: 11/02/13
SUBJECT: DO YOUR CIVIC DUTY AND VOTE

7600 and counting votes in less than two months, yooooo. We vibin out here. My good man Eric told me it's discrimination to only include sorority chicks, so now every SC girl's photo is in there. Every vote counts, boys. And try to be fair for god's sake—don't do one girl dirty by putting up a photo of her in sweats next to another girl in a bikini.

And spread the word mofos,
BLaw

[Forwarded from: tmack@alumni.usc.edu]

FROM: wlawrence@usc.edu

TO: kappasigma1314@usc.edu

DATE: 1/14/14

SUBJECT: CHICKPICK

Yo dudes. If I hear one more story of a Cabo winter break trip, I'm gonna barf. Cabo is for plebs; real action is in Tulum.

Big news today: I'm renaming my app to ChickPick. Why, you ask? Easier to say, and the rhyme's more hooky. It was a close fight between that and HoePoll, but I only fuck with full rhymes.

So RIP to Chicks of SC 9/30/13–1/13/14. It lived a good life and saw more chicks than you mofos ever did,

BLaw

———————

[Forwarded from: tmack@alumni.usc.edu]

FROM: wlawrence@usc.edu

TO: kappasigma1314@usc.edu

DATE: 3/26/14

SUBJECT: My sincere apologies

Dear members of Kappa Sigma,

I would like to deeply apologize for the irresponsibility and disrespect I showed in developing the ChickPick app. What started as a mere prank soon grew beyond my original intention, and I cannot express how mortified and remorseful I am for the hurt I have caused my schoolmates as well as the damage wrought on our fraternity's good name. In light of this, I will be discontinuing the use of ChickPick on our campus immediately and voiding all user data. I will also be taking time away from school to reflect on my actions and how I can utilize my skills in technology for good as I've always dreamed of doing.

My sincere apologies once again.

Yours truly,
William Lawrence

"Holy. Shit." Bernadette looked up from Zoe's phone, slack-jawed.

"Yeah, holy shit. This is so much worse than I imagined—he sounds like an absolute douchebag." The taste of pennies filled Zoe's mouth. "I can't believe I once thought he was charming."

"Don't be hard on yourself. Charming men like him know just what to say and how to behave to get people on their side. You saw how he was able to convince thousands of his schoolmates to participate in something so nasty."

Zoe gestured at her phone. "But this means we have real proof of Bill's terrible behavior! We can prove to everyone that he has always been a pig."

Sighing, Bernadette ran a hand through her hair. "I'm afraid it's not that simple. When Evan Spiegel's frat emails were leaked, he just got a rap on the wrist and Snapchat's now more popular than ever before."

"Yeah, but even though his emails were douchey, too, they weren't about Snapchat. He was sexist but his app wasn't. But *these* emails"—Zoe gestured at her phone—"are about FitPick in its earliest form! No one can deny the link between FitPick and ChickPick when the app names are basically the same. They prove that a douchey guy created a douchey app, and now he's trying to build an entire business out of it by convincing girls everywhere it's a 'safe space.'"

"But Bill could just apologize and say it was locker room talk that doesn't reflect who he is now," Bernadette said quietly. "And the fact that FitPick *is* an outfit-polling and not a girl-polling app would help Bill's defense that he has turned over a new leaf. People forgive white men too easily."

Zoe stared down at the ground, her eyes fixed on a smudge of dirt. "So despite having concrete evidence in black and white that he's a jerk who sexually harasses women, we can't do anything?"

Bernadette laid a hand on her shoulder. "Babe, I'm here for you. I'm really frustrated, too, and I'm not even the one bearing the brunt of what Bill did. But he's a sneaky one. If we aren't strategic about how we expose him, he'll find some way to slither out of it. We have to hit him where he's not expecting."

Men like Drew Macklemore and Aswar Joshi, who are on our board, would understand why I did what I did, and I bet you they would have done the same.

Zoe straightened up, the glimmers of an idea taking shape in her mind. "I know just what he's not expecting. Or rather, *who* he's not expecting."

"ZOE, LET ME GET THIS STRAIGHT," BERNADETTE SAID ONCE ZOE
had finished laying out her plan. "You want to contact *the* Keira
White about this?"

"Yes! Bill looks down on her. In his words, she's nothing but
a gold digger who married well. But joke's on him because she
also happens to be one of FitPick's board members. It'll be poetic
justice when the only woman on the board is the one to make
sure he gets his just deserts and can't harass another woman again."

"I like the idea," Bernadette said slowly, "but how exactly are
we going to contact her?"

"Through email . . . Oh." A well-known public figure like Keira
White wasn't going to have her personal contact details listed
anywhere.

"Um, we could go through A Perfect 10 . . ." Zoe's voice trailed
off as the futility of the idea sank in. There was no way any request submitted through the organization's website contact form
would ever make it up to Keira White herself; some lowly assistant would have discarded it as a scam or fan mail long before that.

Bernadette sucked in a breath. "You realize that the only person who would have a board member's contact is . . . the CEO?"

"Damn."

The two of them looked at each other for a beat longer, before
Bernadette voiced what they were both thinking: "Well then, I
guess we're stuck."

chapter 38

THE RINGING OF her phone pierced the afternoon quietness in Zoe's apartment. She'd just been about to settle down for a nap after her strenuous Desk Step workout that morning and considered letting the call go to voicemail. But when she saw Bernadette was the caller, Zoe immediately picked up.

"Hey! Did Tristan say something else about Bill?"

"Have you seen ValleyVerified?"

Zoe snorted as she burrowed back under her comforter. "Yeah, I read it after breakfast every day for my daily dose of Zoe Zeng hate. No, I haven't. You were the one who told me to stop checking it, remember?"

There was a weird edge in Bernadette's voice. "Trust me, you're going to want to read this one. I'm sending you the link right now."

Frowning, Zoe pushed herself into an upright position in bed. Going back onto ValleyVerified was the last thing she wanted to do, but she'd never heard this note of urgency in her friend's voice before. So she placed Bernadette on speakerphone and dutifully clicked on the link, bracing herself for whatever Rebecca Stiles had to say about her this time.

With the poor Wi-Fi connection in her bedroom, it took a few moments for the page to load, but the title alone was enough to make Zoe's stomach sink.

Present and past coworkers of FitPick employee embroiled in Photoshop Phail say: "It felt right up her alley"

BY: REBECCA STILES

I n recent weeks, the name Zoe Zeng has become synonymous with the image-obsessed Generation Z, which some netizens have rebranded as Generation ZZ in her honor. Or should we say: dishonor?

The defining characteristic of Generation ZZ is a misalignment between the values they publicly tout on a soapbox and the values they actually practice in their personal lives. And for a while, Zoe Zeng, (former?) vice president of marketing at fashion startup FitPick, was the poster child for this hypocrisy.

For those living under a rock, Zoe came under fire for allegedly pressuring style influencer Aisha Monroe, whom she had engaged to be a spokesperson for FitPick's See Yourself campaign, to Photoshop a few images for Aisha's outfit poll on the FitPick app. More fuel was poured on the flames when another worker in Zoe's building wrote in anonymously to reveal that it seemed the *Chic*-tator had not changed her spots even after moving to the Bay Area from the Big Apple, where she used to be a fashion writer at *Chic*.

But since then, numerous individuals have reached out to me to unequivocally denounce the criticism targeted at Zoe. Bjorn Jefferson, a *Chic* lifestyle writer and Zoe's former coworker, wrote to me: "Every time I worry that I'm too big for something, she reassures me that clothes are meant to fit the body, not the other way round. She always suggested the magazine spotlight more topics that champion inclusivity and diversity. I can tell you straight up that Zoe is the most big-hearted and open-minded person ever. The kind of person who makes sure no one is ever picked last for a team and no one is squeezed off the sidewalk, you get me?"

Cassie Welks, a *Chic* stylist, was able to shed more light on Zoe's controversial editorial portfolio: "Most people don't know this but when you are starting out in the fashion industry, you have no control over what you write. You must follow every assignment the editors give you, or else you can kiss your dreams of making it goodbye. Zoe has confided to me several times that she was uncomfortable with what she was told to write, but her protests went unheeded by those above. In the end, it got to a point where she felt like she was compromising her integrity, so she decided to change jobs. We were all so sad to see her go, but also very excited for her new endeavor because Zoe genuinely believed in FitPick's mission to promote exploration and experimentation in fashion. It felt right up her alley."

And as for the tidbit that Zoe was "swanning around" FitPick's office building, looking down on her fellow tech workers' less stylish outfits? FitPick app developer Bram Chandra emphatically shot that down over a call with me: "I can't imagine Zoe doing that—ever. That's just not who she is as a person. She's very passionate about fashion and has a strong idea of what she likes, but she would never judge someone else for it. More often than not, it's us teasing her about her clothes—all in good fun, of course."

Also on the Zoom call was FitPick software engineer Austin Bishop. He concurred with Bram's assessment and added, "Really early on, Zoe actually pointed out that users might edit their photos. Unfortunately, we failed to heed her warning."

This new picture paints a different side to the Zoe Zeng of Generation ZZ fame, and one can't help but wonder if there's more to the FitPick saga than Aisha Monroe had led us to believe. That said, at the end of the day, this fight for greater body positivity goes far beyond one person or one business. If this is something you are interested in, check out Funny Face. Headquartered in Los Angeles, this startup promotes the use of funhouse mirrors over conventional plane mirrors in clothing stores so that shoppers are less likely to scrutinize their bodies critically.

"BABE, ARE YOU STILL THERE?"

It took Zoe a few moments to process Bernadette's voice crackling through her phone's speaker. "Yeah, still here," she said softly, barely able to get the words out over the lump in her throat.

Zoe stared at her laptop screen, the words blurring into a haze before her eyes. But a few jumped out at her. Bjorn Jefferson, Cassie Welks, Bram Chandra, Austin Bishop. Four names that she thought she'd never see in the same place, but they had all come together—for *her*.

Since the article condemning her was published, she hadn't spoken to any of them. Had screened all their calls and ignored all their messages. Couldn't bear the thought that the people whose opinions she valued now viewed her as a failure.

But here they were, standing up for her publicly. Bjorn and Cassie, who risked the *Chic* management's wrath to defend her, even though she had turned down their exclusive interview request. Bram and Austin, who dared to link their names to hers at a time when their company was already under intense scrutiny, when all along she had assumed they only thought of her as good for boba and board games.

"This Rebecca Stiles has some nerve, doesn't she? I noticed how she didn't mention she was the one who fanned the flames and wrote all that nonsense about you in the first place. And that clickbaity title—good lord."

Zoe felt the corners of her mouth turn up at the indignance in Bernadette's voice. Her eyes traced every curve and edge of the letters that made up her friends' names, as though just by doing so she could conjure the people themselves in front of her. Something hot flickered in her chest, warming her from the inside out. She wasn't alone—she had people in her corner who loved her for who she was. Who had been there for her from the very beginning.

THE MOMENT HER CALL WITH BERNADETTE ENDED, ZOE WENT TO her speed dial. As had been the case for the past two years, Bjorn was number two, and Cassie number one (arranged in order of who was more likely to be sober and answer their phone at any given time).

Zoe decided to try Cassie first. It was a Saturday afternoon so there was a not-low chance that Bjorn was still nursing a hangover.

"Zoe!" Cassie exclaimed the moment she answered the call. The knot in Zoe's chest loosened at the genuine pleasure in her friend's voice. "Bjorn is at my place too; he slept over after we went out last night. Okay if I put you on speaker?"

"Of course."

"Hey, Zee," came Bjorn's croak. "It's good to hear from you again. Wait, let's make this a video call. Just don't scream when you see me—I fell asleep before doing my twelve-step skin-care routine last night. But it's been ages since I've seen your face."

Zoe bit her lip. "I'm sorry. I know I've dropped the ball on communication lately."

Her friends' faces popped up on the screen—Cassie's looking as dewy as always; Bjorn's with his hair sticking up in tufts and what looked like a hickey on the side of his neck. "It's okay. We know you've been going through a lot," Cassie said soothingly, then more sternly to Bjorn: "I'm not giving you bagels until you finish chugging that entire glass of water."

Zoe couldn't help but smile as Bjorn replied with a shudder, "Please don't say chug around me when I'm hungover." A month ago, she would have been upset that she wasn't there with them on their night out, but now, she was just happy that she could still get a front-row seat to their antics.

"I miss you two," Zoe said softly. "I also wasn't sure if you wanted to hear from me."

Cassie's forehead creased into a frown. "Why would you think that?"

"I thought you two were upset with me because AI might

cause you to lose your jobs. And I work in Silicon Valley and FitPick uses AI—"

"Zee, I *was* mad that tech seems to be killing off jobs, maybe even mine," Bjorn admitted, looking chastised. "But that has nothing to do with you. You aren't your job."

You aren't your job. The four words echoed through Zoe's head. For as long as she could remember, even back when she was at *Chic*, her emotions had been so interwoven with her job. When work went well, she felt on top of the world. When work went badly, it was like being plunged into a ravine, all the self-doubt and self-blame creeping in. All she could think about then were the *what-if*s and *if-only*s. *What if I was skinnier or white? Would people in the fashion industry be more welcoming?* Which turned into, *If only I had a background in tech, then I could be more useful at work.*

"You're our best friend, Zee," Bjorn continued, his voice uncharacteristically gentle despite its hangover raspiness. "Maybe the three of us aren't as close as we used to be . . . What? I think it's time we speak openly with each other," he added in response to Cassie's exclamation, *Bjorn, you can't just say that!* "And that's just because we don't see one another as much as we used to. But at the end of the day, I know you have my back and I hope you know we always have yours too."

"Yeah, we care about your job because we care about you," Cassie said earnestly. "And we're rooting for your success at FitPick because we want you to be happy above all else."

Zoe gazed at her friends, their concerned expressions unmistakable even through the cracks on her phone screen. For months, she had held back around them, but all along, it had been because she'd projected her own insecurities onto their actions, convinced that they were judging her for her work because that was what she did to herself. Something ballooned in her chest, making her feel bigger and sturdier. She had people who loved her regardless of what her job was or how she performed, so maybe it was time she did the same for herself.

"But speaking of jobs," Bjorn continued, wincing slightly as he massaged his temple, "there's been another layoff in the fashion department."

Zoe's gut lurched. She scanned her friends' faces, but neither looked devastated, so it couldn't have been them. But there wasn't any opportunity to savor the relief as a rolodex of her former coworkers' faces ran through her mind. She hadn't been as close to anyone as she was to Bjorn and Cassie, but countless days of working overtime, deep into the night, had bonded them all—if not by choice then by circumstance. Each and every single person adored fashion with their whole heart.

"Who is it?" she finally dared to ask.

"Francesca."

"*Francesca Fraatz?*"

Cassie nodded, a small smirk dancing on her face. "The new owners did an editorial audit and found that under Francesca, most of our content is really simple, clickbaity stuff."

Comprehension dawned on Zoe. "Precisely the kind that their new AI program can easily create on its own."

"Yup, and in one-tenth of the time it would take us. So the owners gave Francesca a couple months to show she has more to offer, but she has never been editorially strong. She just got away with it because, well, anyone can write a listicle and I guess it helped that her mom was a German supermodel. But last week, they finally let her go and brought in a new guy to be the fashion editor. His name is Adam—"

"And he is *Hot* with a capital *h*," Bjorn purred.

"He's so much more open to us pitching new ideas—content and formats that computer programs still can't quite emulate. Now that the AI model is churning out those listicles and bite-sized pieces, we have more time to focus on long-form and more in-depth articles. In the next issue, I'm doing this debate piece with Rae where she argues that NFTs can help diversify fashion and I argue otherwise. And Zee, remember what you originally wrote for the a.I.r launch event?"

"How can I not?" Though it had never seen the light of day, that article was what had kickstarted her new job, journey, and life. In many ways, Francesca's rejection of it—rejection of *her*—had been a blessing in disguise. A blessing that she didn't have the perspective to appreciate at that time but did now that she had seen how much the world had to offer beyond fashion, and how much she had to offer beyond what she had previously thought herself capable of.

"I brought that up to Adam and he loves it! He wants to run it in the next issue with the angle of whether a brand can truly be called sustainable if it's not size inclusive. If you have time, we would love for you to rework it slightly—the bones of the article are already there, but including a few more brands besides just a.I.r would make it a more well-rounded piece. And of course, we would pay you the freelancer's rate. You up for that?"

Meeting Cassie and Bjorn's expectant gazes, Zoe didn't even hesitate. "I'm in." Just because she now worked in a different industry didn't mean the door to fashion publishing—her first love—was closed for good. If there was anything she had learned in the last few months, it was that she didn't have to pigeonhole herself. There were opportunities out there for her to explore and to embrace her many facets and interests.

Bjorn clapped and Cassie squealed "Perfect!" then cast an

apologetic look in Bjorn's direction as he grimaced. "Oops, sorry. Wait, no, I'm not sorry—I rubbed your back while you puked in my bathroom last night for Christ's sake. Drink more water!"

Zoe giggled as Bjorn reluctantly acquiesced. "Seriously, thank you both for everything you have done for me." Her throat tightened but she forced herself to go on. "I was very touched when I read what you two said about me in Rebecca Stiles's article."

"It was the least we could do for you," Cassie said. "But we can't take all the credit. You've got your coworker to thank for this."

"Bram and Austin? Yeah, I'm going to call them after this to thank them too."

"Oh no. I'm talking about that other guy. Bjorn, what was his name again?"

"Something sexy," he croaked out unhelpfully, wiping at his water-smeared lips.

There was a weird little flutter in Zoe's chest. "Damien? Damien Scott?"

"That's right!" Somehow, Bjorn found the strength to waggle his eyebrows suggestively. "Mm-hmm, why did your mind immediately jump to him when I said the person had a sexy name?"

Zoe rolled her eyes, hoping her friends wouldn't spot her pinking cheeks through the phone screen. "It's because he's the only other guy besides Bram and Austin at FitPick. And Bill, but *he*'s obviously not going to do something I would thank him for. Wait"—she narrowed her eyes at them—"How do you two know Damien? Why should I thank him?"

"Because he was the one who organized the article," Cassie explained. "He reached out to us over Instagram—"

"Yeah, I thought he was someone trying to scam me of money at first," Bjorn interrupted. "His profile was completely blank— no photos, not even a profile picture, and he wasn't following anyone. And he said he knew you, so I thought it was some schtick like, 'Oh your friend is stuck in Jamaica and needs money, please wire her half a million dollars through this link.'"

"It was a good thing *I* read his entire message instead of just stopping after the first line like Bjorn," Cassie said. "Damien said he knew you and that he knew we are your friends because apparently you've talked about us quite a bit"—she blew Zoe a kiss through the screen—"and that he had an idea for how we can help."

"In my defense, his empty Instagram account was extremely sus," Bjorn said. "I think he created it just to message us."

"It's because I told him people in fashion network via Instagram, not LinkedIn," Zoe said softly as guilt swept through her, hollowing a pit in her stomach. She'd accused Damien of being too logical and not empathetic enough. But all along, he'd been listening to her, remembering what she said, and looking out for her in his own way.

"Yeah, so Damien reached out and said he had an idea for helping to repair your reputation. He wanted to gather a bunch of people who have worked with you so we could show Rebecca Stiles that she's got the wrong idea of you. I know he gave her a quote, too, but she thought it wouldn't be as juicy since he's a C-suite executive—said it would sound too much like a company PR statement."

"And you two kept this a secret from me?"

"Damien asked us not to say anything," Cassie answered. "In case it didn't work, he didn't want to get your hopes up for nothing."

Something turned warm and gooey inside Zoe's chest. Damien had orchestrated everything behind the scenes, expecting no recognition and no thanks. He liked keeping to himself, but he had reached out to strangers on her behalf. He had even created an *Instagram* account. Damien wasn't the kind to sit around and hold her hand and tell her everything was going to be okay when it might not be, but he would do everything he could to try to make things okay. Just because he didn't react to a situation the same way she would didn't mean he didn't care about her.

And then Zoe's heart sank as the warmth she felt turned into cold, hard regret. If only she could tell him that she knew that now, that she was sorry for being so quick to judge him and shut him out. But after what she said about him the last time they saw each other, would Damien even want to see her again?

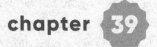

chapter 39

ZOE!" AUSTIN'S FACE loomed into view, so close to the camera that most of the screen was taken up by his nostrils. "You're alive!"

Zoe's face broke out into a big smile. Even though Austin's expression wasn't visible, the concern in his voice was unmistakable. "Thanks guys, for picking up this spontaneous FaceTime call. I've been okay."

"Lies!" screeched Bram from his segment on Zoe's screen. Then, to Austin: "Dude, move back a little. Zoe doesn't want to see a close-up of your big head."

"*My* big head? And what—you're Ryan Gosling just because you had one good date?"

Bram perked up. "Zoe, I have to tell you all about this woman I recently met on BaeArea. We had a great boba date and we're going to get dinner at Rosewood Sand Hill tonight. Which reminds me, Big Head here and I need you to settle a debate for us.

Can a person wear jeans to the Madera restaurant in Rosewood Sand Hill?"

Austin rolled his eyes. "Dude, for the last time, that place is Michelin-starred and has a dress code. Your jeans aren't okay."

"I saw a photo of Elon Musk in jeans—"

"Oh my God." Austin threw up his hands. "You aren't the richest man on the planet. Elon Musk could walk in naked to any place if he wanted to."

"Aha! But our debate wasn't about whether the dress code permitted jeans," Bram said triumphantly. "It was about whether Madera would let anyone wearing jeans in, and you just admitted that they let in Elon Musk, who is a human being as far as we know, although that is becoming increasingly debatable with his space obsession. But in the meantime, I win!"

Zoe burst out laughing as Bram stuck his tongue out and Austin shook his head in exasperation. God, it felt so good to laugh again.

"Zoe, see what I have to put up with?" Austin asked. "I need you back or Bram is actually going to drive me nuts."

"Yeah, we need you back at work so that we can have a third person for Catan. Just playing with Austin is boring," Bram said, shooting Austin a nasty side-eye. "Fuck the haters, Zoe. Everything they said about you is pure bullshit, so don't let them get you down."

"I know," replied Zoe, smiling at Bram's indignation on her behalf. "And thank you both for sticking up for me in the most recent ValleyVerified article." Her throat tightened. "I was very touched."

Austin waved his hand, looked slightly embarrassed. "Nah, don't thank us. We did it for our own sake. We need you here before Bram and I end up killing each other. So come back to FitPick and launch another brilliant campaign that will shut everyone up."

Zoe fiddled with a loose thread on her shirt as she looked into her coworkers'—no, her *friends'*—hopeful faces. As much as she wanted to, there was no way she could return to work at FitPick now, not after everything she'd found out about Bill. "I wish I could come back to work, but there are some things I have to do first."

An idea struck her. "You guys wouldn't happen to know how to contact Keira White, would you?" she asked casually, as though she and the famous philanthropic socialite were best friends.

"Oh yeah, absolutely. I have her on speed dial. We meet up every Sunday for yoga and bottomless mimosas," Bram deadpanned. "She's about to confess her love for me any day now."

"Plebians like us and Keira White don't exactly mix in the same circles," Austin said. "Oh, but she told Bill to hire me, so he would know how to get in touch with her. Ask him!"

It wasn't a surprise that they wouldn't have Keira White's contact. But Zoe still couldn't help the disappointment that washed over her. As for asking Bill for help? Over her dead body.

"You know, I think Lillian might know how to contact Keira," Bram suddenly said. "I overheard Bill telling her once that he would loop her into an email thread with Keira."

Zoe's eyes snapped to Bram's video square. "He did?"

"Apparently, Keira was asking too many dumb questions—Bill's words—about our technology and Bill got fed up with explaining the same thing over and over again, so he wanted Lillian to handle Keira."

Zoe coiled her shirt's loose thread around her finger so tightly that the flesh around it turned white. So there might be a way to reach out to Keira White after all and see if she could make sure Bill gets punished for his misdeeds. But Lillian had made it clear she wanted to wash her hands of the whole matter, and so that was that.

AFTER THE VIDEO CALL ENDED, AND DESPERATE FOR A CHANGE in scenery, Zoe headed to Nordstrom in Stanford Shopping Center to catch Bernadette on her lunch break. The two of them made their way to Go Fish Poke Bar as Zoe recounted her conversation with the two men. The outdoor mall was packed and all of the poke bar's tables were taken, but they managed to find an empty bench nearby.

"It's nice to hear Bram is having luck with the ladies," Bernadette said with a smile. She'd had a soft spot for him ever since he came to see her for a styling session and gave her her biggest sales commission to date. "But how come you can't just ask Lillian for Keira White's number? I thought you two were on good terms now."

Zoe drizzled unagi sauce over her poke mix as she thought about how to respond. While she'd told her friend almost everything that had gone down, she hadn't said much about Lillian except that she'd misunderstood her coworker who turned out to only have good intentions all along. Lillian's personal history with Bill was her business only, and Zoe knew the COO would be mortified if her cousin's fiancée found out that she'd been pretending Marcus was her boyfriend.

Finally, Zoe said, "Lillian said she doesn't want to get involved in this situation, and I want to respect that."

"Doesn't she realize what's at stake here?" Bernadette exclaimed as she speared a forkful of tuna. "She could be a huge help."

"I know." Zoe tossed the emptied unagi sauce packet into a nearby trash can and exhaled deeply. "Look, this isn't my story to tell, but Lillian has good reasons for wanting to stay out of it. Just trust me on this."

Frowning, Bernadette slowly chewed on her ahi tuna. "I do trust your judgment. But getting Keira White's email address wouldn't be involving Lillian per se. She just has to give a short string of alphanumeric characters, maybe with a few special characters tossed in, and then she will be out of this. It's all you from then on."

Zoe gazed at the stream of shoppers walking past them toward the colonnade of designer stores. Bernadette was right—there was no way anyone could trace any contact she made to Keira White back to Lillian. "Okay, I'll call her. It's worth a shot."

With Bernadette nodding encouragingly from the side, Zoe put down her barely eaten poke bowl and dialed Lillian's number. It rang, and rang, and rang. "I don't think she's—"

"Zoe?"

"Lillian! Um, hi." Zoe glanced at Bernadette for help, but all the other woman did was mouth "Ask her." "Um, I have something to ask you."

"What is it?" The note of wariness in Lillian's voice was unmistakable.

Zoe gritted her teeth and dared herself to ask: "If you have Keira White's personal email address, could you give it to me?"

She grimaced as the words left her mouth, registering how suspicious they sounded. "I know this seems weird but I just really think something should be done about Bill. He's creating a hostile situation at work and the board should know about it. And I have a stronger case against him now—one of his old college friends shared with me a bunch of emails sent by Bill in his senior year that proves he has always been a sleazy douchebag."

A beat of silence passed before Lillian said, "If those emails are legitimate, this would be something FitPick's board should look into. But why Keira White?"

"Because the men on the board have probably done some pretty terrible things, too, and will take Bill's side. Birds of a feather and all that. So Keira is the one most likely to listen. I can contact her myself since I know you don't want to be involved, but besides Bill, you're the only one who knows her email address."

There was a long pause, one that made Zoe's heart leap into her throat. "Zoe, I can't just give it to you," Lillian finally said. "Keira gave me her contact details to discuss work matters only and I can't betray her confidence by giving it out to anyone, no matter how well intentioned the request is."

Zoe slumped against the bench. Something must have shown on her face, because Bernadette laid a hand sympathetically on Zoe's arm. "I get it," Zoe said softly, her hand curling around her phone. "I don't want to put you in a tough spot."

"But I can contact Keira directly."

Zoe's body shot upright. "For real? But I thought you didn't want to be involved."

"I couldn't stop thinking about our previous conversation and realized you were right. I'm in a position where I could expose Bill for the person he truly is behind his golden boy facade and make sure he can't harass other women. So I'll do whatever I can to help you take him down, including emailing Keira White and sharing about what he did to me."

Zoe opened and closed her mouth a few times as she tried to come up with a response. From the sidelines, Bernadette was gesturing wildly, trying to catch her eye. *What's going on?*

"Lillian, you shouldn't feel pressured to share anything you don't want to. It shouldn't fall on you to right his wrongs."

"No, I *want* to do it. I can't just look the other way for the sake of my career; I can't live with myself if I do that."

Her heart lifting, Zoe tilted her head back and let the sunshine warm her cheeks. "All I can say is, any team is stronger with you on it." The corners of her mouth quirked up as Bernadette did a silent fist pump and pretended to wipe sweat off her brow in an exaggerated *phew* gesture.

"I'll contact Keira now and let you know what she says." Zoe couldn't see Lillian's expression, but there was a distinct smile in her voice that made Zoe's own smile widen.

Zoe felt like a weight had finally lifted off her shoulders. "Thank you, Lillian, really. I don't know if I can express that enough."

A quiet chuckle drifted down the line. "No, thank *you*. If not for you, I wouldn't have dared to take this step."

chapter 40

FTER ZOE HUNG up, Bernadette made a call of her own to work to call in sick for the rest of the afternoon. "What?" she asked as Zoe arched her brow in amusement. "There's no way I'm letting you wait for Lillian's update on your own."

Zoe leaned her head against the other woman's shoulder. "Thanks, Bern." If she was waiting alone, the anticipation would have driven her out of her mind, but her friend had turned out to be an absolute rock. Bernadette had been momentarily shocked upon learning that the same boss Zoe had grumbled about many times was none other than the cousin of her own fiancé, but she'd quickly shrugged it off. Given all the bombshell revelations the past couple of days, this one barely registered on the scale. And as Bernadette said blithely, "The Valley is just so damn small and everyone knows everyone else."

They soon finished their lunch, and as the afternoon sun grew more intense, they decided to abscond to their favorite juice shop for a cold refreshment. Zoe felt a little weird walking into Rejuice for the first time in a non-workout outfit. As the Rejuice counter worker handed Zoe her smoothie, she said, "Hey, I see in our system that you've come here five times in the last ten days. That entitles you to one free drink that you can claim the next time you come."

"Oh, thanks!" Zoe accepted her drink and made her way to a small table with Bernadette. She whispered to her friend, "Damn, I didn't realize I've been coming here so often." Then again, she had nothing better to do these days now that she was no longer going in to work. And come Monday, that would turn into a permanent situation when Bill fired her.

Within the next hour, as she and Bernadette sat at Rejuice, Zoe proceeded to down two Radiance Reboosts, one Good Vibes Tonic Water, and one protein Beauty Brownie laced with a hint of CBD—the latter a treat from Bernadette ("Babe, you *need* to relax," Bernadette said as she shoved the CBD-infused pastry into Zoe's hands. "Your nervous energy is making *me* nervous.").

But if anything, Zoe felt even more jittery than she did before. "Bern, can CBD give you heart palpitations?" she asked faintly.

Bernadette's eyes widened. "What?" She placed a hand on Zoe's bouncing knee. "Don't think too much about it."

"But this is taking so long. We've been here for hours."

"It's only been forty-five minutes," Bernadette said patiently.

Zoe's mouth clamped shut after a quick glance at Rejuice's clock showed that her friend was right. But it sure felt a lot longer than that.

"And it's probably taking so long because it's the weekend and Keira White, or her assistant, isn't checking their emails now. But once Lillian gets through to Keira, she'll know what to say. Lillian's a pro."

"But what if Bill was right? For all their talk about ethics and the greater good and making society a better place, it seems that what people in Silicon Valley care about most at the end of the day is money. Many of the biggest products were started for sleazy reasons. YouTube was created because people kept searching for Janet Jackson's nip slip; Google Images because of the fuss over J.Lo's revealing Versace dress. And FitPick is well on its way to becoming profitable—Bill can promise those board members more money than either Lillian or I can."

Bernadette took a sip of her own Radiance Reboost, which she had been drinking at a much more measured pace. "I can't deny that. But at least you'll know you have done everything you could."

Staring down at the Beauty Brownie crumbs scattered on her plate, Zoe let out a deep sigh. "That's the worst part—that I have done everything I could and it still isn't enough. And this is probably taking place all over Silicon Valley: men getting away with shitty things because they're protected by their privilege and other powerful men."

Bernadette nodded sympathetically. "Come on, babe, don't think more about it for now. Let's talk about something else."

Being in Rejuice reminded Zoe of their last Desk Step class together. "So, what were you searching for on AliExpress last time?"

"Oh, did I tell you I'm thinking of starting a crafting business?"

Zoe's eye snapped to her friend. Bernadette's tone was airy, but she was gripping her juice cup so tightly that her fingers left indentations in its surface. "No, you didn't! Bern, how long have you been thinking about this?"

Bernadette tucked a lock of hair behind her ear. For the first time since Zoe had known her friend, the other woman seemed slightly shy. "Not long. I mean, I enjoy styling, but at the end of the day, my job is still about respecting the shopper's vision and listening to what they want. Same goes for back when I worked in consulting. But with my own business, I get to create what I love and believe in," she said, her cheeks tinged with pink. "Maybe this won't go anywhere, but I figured I'd still give it a shot. You know?"

Behind her friend's seemingly nonchalant shrug, Zoe sensed something much deeper. "This is a fantastic idea, Bern. I've always thought you would make an incredible businesswoman, but I didn't want to say anything because I didn't want you to feel pressured. Have you thought of where you want to sell yet?"

"I think I'm going to start out small. Maybe just tell people I know first—"

"I'm going to be your first customer," Zoe declared.

Bernadette grinned. "All right, since you asked so nicely. And after that, maybe I'll go on Facebook Marketplace, or Etsy . . . take things one step at a time."

"Who knows—you might be stocked in Nordstrom someday! What are you thinking of selling?"

"Small trinkets, like pins and patches. I want to make a collection inspired by my own health journey. I've felt a lot of shame and embarrassment about not being able to conceive, but that doesn't make me less of a woman. I want to celebrate my ovaries even if they can't produce eggs."

"Well, you've always been an ovar-achiever," Zoe joked.

Bernadette's eyes lit up. "That's perfect! Can I use that? How awesome would an *Ovarachiever* pin be?"

"Be my guest! And what about—" They both startled at the sound of a phone ringing.

Her heart in her throat, Zoe reached for her phone, only to see Bernadette pick up her own. But her disappointment faded as Bernadette looked down at the caller ID and smiled. "Shauna again! Tristan must have found more dirt on Bill," she said before picking up the call.

"Babe, hi! Oh, Tristan wants to talk to me? Sure, put him on," Bernadette said, giving Zoe a small wink. "Hey, Tristan! Do you remember Zoe? She's next to me; can I put you on speaker—" Her smile faded. "What do you mean? No, Tristan, this is really important. I'm asking you to please reconsider."

The uncharacteristic note of desperation in her friend's voice made Zoe's stomach tighten. She mouthed, "What's going on?" to Bernadette, but the other woman was too focused on pleading with Tristan to answer. Finally, Bernadette sighed and said, "I get where you're coming from. But please call me if you change your mind."

She jabbed the "End Call" button so vehemently it made Zoe's eyebrows shoot up. "Bern, what's wrong?"

"Tristan doesn't want us to share the email transcripts with anyone else," Bernadette bit out. "Apparently, after our call earlier, he decided to go look up his old buddy William Lawrence. And of course, the first thing that pops up is that *Business Insider* article of FitPick's success. So Tristan decided he doesn't want to go up against Bill in any way."

Zoe squeezed her eyes shut, feeling her stomach sink to her feet. The emails Tristan had forwarded to them were the only concrete evidence they had of Bill's misdoings, their first breakthrough and the one thing that had gone right since this entire mess had begun. But now, Tristan had just ripped it all away. They were back to square one, with no other ideas or people to turn to.

Bernadette squeezed Zoe's hand. "Zoe, it's okay—"

"It's not okay," Zoe burst out, hearing her voice crack on the final word. "The entire Keira meeting hinges on this. She has no reason to believe us if we have no evidence, and Bill will charm his way out of it." She swiped her hands roughly across her eyes, mad at herself for wasting any tears on Bill Lawrence of all people. "I guess he was right after all. Men would always protect one another because they care more about aligning themselves with the ones in power than those who have been wronged."

Bernadette rubbed her hand in soothing circles on Zoe's back. "It's not the end of the road. I can appeal to Shauna to try to convince Tristan. I'll personally call every single person who was in USC's Greek community and ask if they have any information."

"Um, miss?" A tentative voice rang from behind them. It was the Rejuice counter girl, holding a steaming mug emblazoned with the shop's signature golden sun logo. "I couldn't help but notice that you seem rather upset. Maybe this will help you feel better. It's our Healing Heart Hojicha—on the house, of course."

Zoe quickly rubbed away any lingering wetness in her eyes. "Oh, thank you," she said, accepting the mug gratefully and taking a sip. The hot frothy drink slid down her throat, carrying with it a tinge of cinnamon and a comforting warmth. "This is really good."

The girl beamed. "I'm glad to hear that." She lowered her voice, her face turning somber. "Is this over a guy?"

Zoe and Bernadette exchanged a glance. "Yeah, you could say that," Zoe answered, before taking another gulp of the hojicha.

The girl nodded sympathetically. "I know what it feels like. When my ex broke up with me, I was devastated. Laid in bed and cried for weeks. But then I started working here and it really snapped me out of my funk. This is just such a soul-lifting place. Just breathe in deeply for me."

Bemused, Zoe and Bernadette nevertheless obliged, both

gamely taking a big inhale. "Do you smell that?" the Rejuice girl whispered. "Doesn't it just smell like good karma?"

All Zoe could detect was the cinnamon in her drink and something fruity in the air—maybe from the smoothies being blended or from an air freshener—but she nodded. "It does."

"Exactly! Don't let a guy get you down, sister. I'm rooting for you."

Strangely enough, maybe because the hojicha actually did contain magical healing properties, Zoe's heart felt just a little lighter as the Rejuice girl walked away. "I'm not going to give up. Even if Tristan doesn't change his mind, I'll find another way of proving Bill's creepy behavior."

And right at that moment, Zoe's phone rang.

This time, it was Lillian's name who appeared on Zoe's phone screen. Zoe stared down at it for a long moment. For all her bravado, was there anything else left for her to try if the attempt with Keira White turned out to be a dead end?

Only after Bernadette gave an encouraging nod at the phone did Zoe muster the nerve to answer her ringing phone. "Hey, Lillian. What did Keira say?" she asked, bracing herself for the answer.

"I didn't get to tell her what happened," Lillian replied. "I started saying that it concerns Bill's behavior, and she cut me off and said this shouldn't be discussed over the phone."

A hollow sensation crept into Zoe's chest. So that was it then. Bill would get away with everything after all.

"So she invited us to go over to her house this afternoon."

Zoe immediately sat up taller, hope flickering to life within her. She shot a thumbs-up at Bernadette, who was looking at her anxiously. "That's great . . . Wait, did you just say *us*?"

"I said another employee has email evidence that supports our claim, so Keira asked you to come along too."

Zoe sputtered. "But this is *Keira White*. She's appeared on the covers of *Vogue* and *Forbes*. My old boss at *Chic* absolutely worshipped her." Although Francesca Fraatz's adoration probably stemmed less from Keira White's philanthropic and fashion endeavors, and more from how she landed herself a billionaire husband at only twenty-five.

"And you're *Zoe Zeng*. You impressed none other than Logan Horossen with your marketing ideas and you didn't back down against Bill Lawrence. In fact, you inspired me to do the same. I think you can more than hold your own."

Zoe tipped her chin up and drained the remainder of her hojicha in one gulp. Just a week ago, she never could have imagined chatting away with Lillian on the phone and getting a pep talk from her. Even a billionaire supermodel-turned-philanthropist couldn't be nearly as intimidating as Lillian Mariko. Lillian was right—she, Zoe, would be just fine.

But her heart sank again as a new thought struck her. "Lillian, there's something you should know." Zoe swallowed. "The guy who told me about Bill's disgusting college emails? He doesn't want us to share them with anyone else."

A long silence stretched on the other end of the line. "That means we've lost our only piece of real evidence," Lillian finally said.

Zoe nodded, casting her eyes down at the table. "Yeah," she said softly. "Will Keira White even want to see us anymore? It looks really suspicious that we just somehow 'lost access' to the emails right after telling her we had them. She might think we made the whole thing up just to get a meeting with her. And if we made that up, we might have made up our accusations about Bill too." She nestled gratefully closer to Bernadette as her friend wrapped a comforting arm around Zoe's slumped shoulders.

Another stretch of silence passed, then Lillian said, "Even without the emails, we should at least make Keira White aware of what's going on. We can tell her everything we know, and then it's up to her whether she wants to believe us. But I'm not backing down if you aren't."

Zoe sat up straighter. "I'm not," she vowed. "I'm in this with you the whole way."

chapter 41

ZOE'S HEART COULDN'T stop thumping as she sat in Keira White's office a few hours later. She'd been relieved when the security guard at the driveway entrance had directed them not to the main mansion of Keira's sprawling estate, but to a smaller house at a far end of the backyard that Keira used as her office. At least things might be easier in a less intimidating environment.

However, even Keira's "studio" was at least six times bigger than Zoe's entire apartment. A Banksy painting hung in the bathroom that Zoe had ducked into to freshen up and give herself a pre-meeting pep talk. After she emerged, a housekeeper served her and Lillian freshly baked lemon biscuits and Earl Grey tea while they waited for Keira to finish a call in one of the other dozen rooms.

"Have you met her before?" she whispered to Lillian, who was nibbling daintily on a cookie. Meanwhile, Zoe's stomach felt too twisted in knots to digest anything.

"Just once when she dropped by the office." The COO let out a sound that was far too elegant to be described as a snort. "Bram was very excited. Apparently, Keira White was his teenage celebrity crush."

"What was she like?" Zoe had done a quick Google search of Keira White after leaving Rejuice, but the woman was surprisingly elusive even though she was one of the most photographed women in the world. She almost never gave interviews and when she did, it was mostly about fashion. Everything she'd said about A Perfect 10 was either through press releases or practiced speeches at galas.

Lillian furrowed her brows in thought. "Beautiful, obviously. And really tall. She was taller than Bill, which I don't think he liked. He looked slightly annoyed when she had to bend down to shake his hand. But she didn't speak much. She came with an entourage and one of the men with her, her business adviser, I think, did most of the talking. I remember Bill made fun of that afterward and said how it was obvious all the tech jargon flew over her head."

Zoe rolled her eyes. Of course Bill did. Still, this didn't tell her more about Keira beyond what her googling had already told her. Keira White seemed rather reserved; even if she believed them without the email evidence, would she really go out on a limb for them when it came to Bill?

A set of footsteps click-clacked down the hallway, growing louder as they neared the foyer. Zoe quickly straightened up. Lillian, whose posture was already perfect, dusted some invisible lint off her blouse just before Keira White appeared in the doorway.

She was dressed in a simple cashmere vest and matching lounge pants, a pair of cream-white sandals on her feet. Her hair was loose and her face bare, but Keira White looked like she'd barely aged a day since she took the fashion world by storm a decade ago as an eighteen-year-old transplant from Monaco.

"No need to stand," she said in her faintly accented English as Zoe and Lillian made a move to get up. She bent down to give both women a kiss on the cheek before taking the handsome leather wingback chair on the other side of the mahogany desk.

"Thank you for your patience," Keira said. "My call with my dear friend MacKenzie overran a little."

Zoe's eyes widened. This must be MacKenzie Scott that Keira was referring to. The tabloids had a field day after Keira was photographed entering MacKenzie's house not long after the news of her ex-husband's adultery broke out. *The scorned billionaire wives club?!* the headlines had screamed.

Keira crossed one leg over the other. "So, what is this about Bill?"

Zoe glanced at Lillian, waiting for the other woman to take the lead on the conversation. But Lillian simply raised a brow and gave her an encouraging look in return. *This is your story.*

With Keira White staring expectantly, Zoe had no choice but to swallow her nerves and begin her recount of what transpired between her and Bill. When she was done, Lillian launched into her own story of Bill's suspect behavior. Keira White listened attentively, but her face remained impassive throughout, as if she was simply listening to the weather report.

As Lillian spoke, tendrils of foreboding rose within Zoe. Fit-Pick was the first private company Keira had ever publicly backed on her own and not as one half of a power couple with her tech mogul ex-husband. Just as Bill had asked her to be a board member for the optics, it was very likely Keira had accepted the position to cement her own fledgling reputation in the intellectually snobbish tech industry. If FitPick failed, a significant portion of the blame might be thrown at her as the only woman on the board, so casting out the CEO would be just the kind of controversy Keira would want to avoid.

Once Lillian was done, desperation drove Zoe to blurt out, "I know this might sound far-fetched, but I swear, we're not making any of this up. We have no reason to. Bill was the one who gave me a job when I was feeling stuck in my old career. I felt so grateful toward him and I really wanted to believe the best of him. But I just don't want another woman to be caught in this same situation."

"I can second everything Zoe said," Lillian spoke up. "And there are emails proving that Bill was scummy even back in college. Our source didn't want us to share them openly, but maybe we could try asking him again, or find another source—"

Keira held up a hand. "Don't bother. I believe you."

She let out a silvery laugh as Zoe's eyes widened. "What, you think I haven't faced men like Bill before? Your jaws would drop if I listed all the famous politicians and businessmen who act like the pope in public but say and do the sleaziest things to women in private. Just because they think women are too timid to ever fight back. The unwanted advances I received only stopped after I married my former husband, and only because they respected his power, not mine."

Zoe stared at the beautiful woman sitting opposite her. It wasn't a surprise that the fashion industry was filled with predators. But it still felt like a slap to the face that even a woman as powerful as Keira White was still beholden to the power of men around her. Zoe could feel the same shock jarring her mind also rolling off Lillian, though both women kept quiet. Anything they could say felt too insufficient.

Keira clasped her hands together on the desk and looked down at her intertwined fingers. Her voice quieted. "I've seen all the ways men could make women feel small, and not just with outright harassment. I've heard all the things people said about me after I started A Perfect 10. They seemed to think I was just doing it for publicity, and that everything I was saying about wanting to give young immigrant girls like myself a better education was for show only." The corners of her mouth tautened. "My former husband told me I should have focused on a sexier cause, like breast cancer."

"What an asshole," Zoe mumbled. Her face reddened when both Keira and Lillian looked at her in surprise. "Sorry—"

"No, you're right. He's an asshole," Keira said, the ghost of a smirk flitting across her lips. "Not all of them are, but many. And we can't let them keep getting away with it. We'll show them how women can fight back."

Zoe and Lillian exchanged a look. For once, even the COO looked visibly excited. At last, they had someone powerful on their side, too, someone who could go head-to-head with Bill.

"But I can't guarantee anything," Keira said, her somber voice instantly subduing Zoe and Lillian's cheer. "I'll suggest a board vote to remove Bill as CEO, but Bill is on the board, too, and every member has one vote each despite how many shares they hold in FitPick. So if even one other person votes to keep Bill as CEO, the poll will be tied, and as president of the board, Drew Macklemore will get the decisive vote."

Zoe's smile wilted. She felt like she'd just been doused in cold water. "So you're saying that we would need all three other members of FitPick's board to vote for Bill's removal?"

"I'm afraid so."

Zoe dug her fingers into her palm but even the sharp prick of her nails couldn't quell her panic. "But Drew Macklemore is the father of one of Bill's best friends, and wasn't he accused of having sex with minors? And the other board member, Aswar Joshi— didn't that man oust one of his co-founders at Paylapa by just changing all the passwords and locking him out of the system? They are just as shady as Bill—they will definitely take his side." After all the hoops they'd jumped through to be heard, they still had to depend on other men for the final say. And there was no way Drew and Aswar would condemn him, not when that would mean an implicit admission of their own misdemeanors.

"Unfortunately, that's how it is," Keira said softly. "I feel just as upset about this as you do. But I'm not sure there's anything we can do beyond going to the board, especially with the lack of hard evidence. If we try to take this public, the other board members can easily say they've looked into the matter and found no wrongdoing on Bill's part. And the three of us will just look like scorned women kicking up a fuss for nothing."

Beneath the desk, Lillian pressed her hand lightly against Zoe's. "So what can we do now?" Lillian asked, in a voice far steadier than anything Zoe felt she could muster.

Keira breathed out a sigh so soft that Zoe might have missed it if she hadn't been waiting on tenterhooks for the other woman's answer. "All we can do is wait and hope for the best."

Zoe slumped back in her chair. This matter was out of her hands. But in the meantime, at least there was another wrong she could right. That she *had to* right.

chapter 42

A STRONG SENSE OF déjà vu washed over Zoe the moment she stepped into the California Avenue Farmers' Market. There was the dark blue awning of the Craftsmen and Wolves booth, and when she drew closer, she could see that this Sunday, the owner was polling market-goers on cups of whipped coffee mousse versus guava curd mousse. A few booths away was the Asian vegetables stand, with a sign hawking its seasonal produce: Japanese baby eggplants—four dollars per pound. The seller, his suntanned, wrinkled face stretched by a big smile, was stuffing a big Napa cabbage and a couple of lotus roots into a plastic bag for a waiting customer.

But Zoe barely had time to wallow in the nostalgia. Almost immediately, her eyes were drawn to the man standing a short distance away, his face half hidden in the shadows cast by the vegetable stand's awning. Zoe swallowed hard. She and Damien never did get around to buying their leafy greens that day, since they had to rush off to San Francisco. Or rather, *she* had to go up there, while Damien had only offered to give her a ride to help her. He had always been kind beneath his gruff exterior, but she had pushed him away in a moment of frustration. It was a wonder he had even agreed to meet her.

Damien lifted a hand in greeting when their eyes met over the bustling market crowd, but his face was inscrutable when she neared, giving no indication as to how he felt about seeing her again. Zoe steeled herself and gestured toward a quieter corner. "Shall we?"

The bustle of the farmers' market was fainter there. Without the distraction of the booths and other shoppers, Zoe suddenly became aware of how *alone* she and Damien were in that instant, the first time they'd seen each other since she'd stomped out of Teaspoon. He gazed at her, waiting for her to break the silence.

"Thanks for coming," she began, raising a hand to shield her eyes from the blazing sun overhead.

Damien did the same, such that it was impossible for her to make out his expression as he said, "It's okay. I would have come to the farmers' market anyway."

"Right. To buy your vegetables."

"Yes," he said, as though he had not been the one to tell her that, as though they hadn't wandered around the market together, their bodies just a hair's breadth apart. Even now, Zoe could still remember that tantalizing sliver of warmth from Damien's arm skimming hers.

Looking at his politely blank expression—the kind a person would give to someone who was just a coworker—made Zoe's stomach tighten. She dragged her eyes away from his face, her gaze landing on a booth over Damien's shoulder. The same flower stand where the owner had mistaken them as a couple, and now they were behaving like they barely knew each other.

"I just want to say I'm sorry," Zoe blurted out. The air between them was so charged with tension that it felt like her insides would burst out of her skin. "About how badly I reacted at Teaspoon. It wasn't right for me to take my frustration out on you. And you were right all along—the whole thing with Lillian turned out to be a misunderstanding." Boy, she had a lot to catch him up on, about Bill and everything else. But only if he would be willing to stick around to listen.

Damien scuffed his shoe against the ground. "Some of it is on me for not empathizing with your feelings. My default response when I encounter an obstacle is to enter problem-solving mode. But I forgot that other people have other ways of handling things." His eyes met hers. "I never meant to ignore your feelings, and I'm sorry if I made you feel that way."

A tentative smile flickered across Zoe's face. "So I guess we're even?"

Damien nodded once.

Zoe shifted from one foot to the other. Damien wasn't saying much; maybe he didn't even want to be here at all. But she still had one more thing to get off her chest.

She took a deep breath. "I know you reached out to my friends and organized that article defending me. I just want to say I'm very grateful. It's one of the nicest things anyone has ever done for me. So, thank you," she said softly. The last two words felt so inadequate after the lengths he'd gone to for her.

Damien shrugged. "It's no big deal."

It was like talking to a brick wall, but Zoe forged ahead: "I know you would have done it for anybody because that's just the kind of person you are, but it still means a lot to me."

"No, I wouldn't have," he said. He lowered his hand from his face, an uncharacteristic intensity in the depths of his eyes as he fixed them on Zoe's face. "Zoe, you aren't just anybody to me. You never were."

Zoe's breath caught in her throat. Instantly, all the noise around them faded, making the pounding of her heart even more obvious in her ears. And although throngs of people wandered around just a short distance away, it felt in that moment like they were the only ones there.

"But you were always so aloof," she squeaked. "And you always looked so stern with me . . . And whenever I invited you to hang out with me, Austin, and Bram, you almost always said no."

"I just didn't know where I stood with you," Damien admitted gruffly, now looking everywhere but at her. "You were so friendly and nice to everyone, and I thought you saw me as just a friend like you did with Austin and Bram. So I kept my distance in hopes that my feelings would fade with time, but after the ValleyVerified saga broke out, I couldn't stop worrying about you. And I realized I didn't like being in the office without you around."

He scrubbed a hand over his face and made a sound that sounded halfway between a laugh and a huff. "I'm in deeper than I ever realized. But it's not a big deal or anything. I'm not expecting you to return my feelings—"

His eyes flew to her face as she stepped forward, their bodies so close that she could see the amber flecks in his eyes, the sprinkling of freckles across his cheeks. Heat pooled in her stomach as the warmth of his body tinged her skin. "Damien, you're an idiot," she said quietly, seeing herself reflected in his eyes. "I've liked you since the beginning."

And then she reached out, grabbed a fistful of his shirt, and pulled him close. Instinctively, his arm encircled her waist, his hand splayed across the small of her back. He bent his head, she tipped up hers, and when their lips finally met, it felt both like a release and a restart.

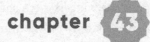

WHEN THEY FINALLY broke apart, both of them were breathing heavily. His right arm still looped around her waist, Damien reached out his left thumb and tentatively brushed it against Zoe's lips, a look of wonder on his face.

Suddenly, his hand stilled. "Zoe, you're vibrating."

Still lost in the sensation of the kiss, Zoe murmured, "Huh?" already longing to recapture his lips again.

"I mean, your skirt pocket is vibrating against my arm. I think someone is calling you."

Oh. Zoe drew back, her face red as she fumbled for her phone. She was so flustered that she answered without checking who the caller was, so her eyes jerked wide as Lillian's voice boomed into her ears. "Zoe, check ValleyVerified *now*."

At the note of urgency in Lillian's voice, Zoe's skin ran cold, the sweet respite of Damien's kiss forgotten as reality slammed back into her. "It's another Rebecca Stiles article, isn't it? How bad is it?"

There was a pause. "I think you should see it for yourself,"

Lillian finally said. "I'll send you the link. Call me back once you've read it."

Zoe couldn't hang up fast enough. She didn't realize how much her fingers were shaking until she managed to open Lillian's link only on the third try. Damien's breath skimmed her nape as he read her phone over her shoulder, and only his presence kept her knees from buckling.

FitPick's founder and CEO given the boot by board of directors

BY: REBECCA STILES

Has there ever been such a sharp turn of fortune for a startup before? FitPick, which for a while looked primed to be the next hot thing at the nexus of fashion and technology, has taken several hits to its nascent reputation lately.

First came InstaGate, where influencer Aisha Monroe was caught photoshopping a photo she uploaded onto FitPick—allegedly under pressure from Zoe Zeng, vice president of marketing at FitPick. While Zeng's coworkers at Fit-Pick and former coworkers at New York–based magazine *Chic* have spoken up in her defense, that did not save FitPick from the wrath of concerned parents and body image activists—all of whom are worried that the outfit polling app is promoting body dysmorphia and unrealistic beauty standards.

And now, I've learned that Bill Lawrence, the 27-year-old who founded FitPick while he was still in college and has drawn comparisons to other tech wunderkinds such as Mark Zuckerberg and Evan Spiegel, has been fired from his position as CEO in a unanimous vote by the other three members on the company's board of directors (Lawrence himself is on the board). He has been ordered to relinquish all his leadership duties, although he still holds a ten percent stake in FitPick.

While FitPick's board of directors—comprising Drew Macklemore, chairman of Macklemore Corporation; Aswar Joshi, CEO of Paylapa; and Keira White, founder of nonprofit organization A Perfect 10—did not disclose the reasons for the termination, there are rumors that the board has uncovered incriminating information that proves Lawrence's values are not aligned with the company's. Allegedly, his academic background was also called into question, with suspicions that he had not dropped out of the University of Southern California (USC) to build FitPick as he'd often claimed to the media, but that he had been suspended for inappropriate behavior.

When I reached out to Lawrence for comment, his only statement was, "I built FitPick from the ground up by myself. I believed in it for so many years when no one else did. But it seems as though now that I've finally managed to get it off the ground and achieve a sizable user base, the board has decided to take the company in a new direction that conflicts with my original vision. As such, I've decided to part ways with FitPick."

When asked for their thoughts on Lawrence's statement, FitPick's board offered no comment.

Only time will tell if removing Lawrence as CEO can turn around FitPick's future and revive its fledgling business, or if he had simply been scapegoated by a board who doesn't understand or have the patience for the topsy-turviness of running a startup.

ZOE PROMPTLY DIALED LILLIAN'S NUMBER. THE OTHER WOMAN picked up at once, almost as though she'd been waiting by her phone.

"You asshole!" Zoe exclaimed, remembering a beat too late that she was speaking to her COO. But she was too overwhelmed with relief to care. "You made it sound like it was another bad article that described me skinning puppies or something. You were totally messing with me."

"Sorry," Lillian answered with a laugh, not sounding sorry at all. "But isn't the relief that much sweeter once you realized the article was nowhere as bad as you'd feared?"

Zoe read the article again. The first time around, her heart had been in her throat as her eyes flew past the words, beelining straight for the part where Rebecca Stiles would reveal another devastating takedown of her. But now, she allowed herself to go more slowly, to let every word sink in since she no longer had to worry about what was coming next.

"Did you know this article was happening?" she asked Lillian once she was done.

"Nope. Keira called me twenty minutes ago to explain what happened. Apparently, the board convened an emergency meeting over the weekend to question Bill. He denied everything at first, including his sexual harassment toward us and how he threw you under the bus. Accused me of trying to stage a coup and you of taking your anger at the ValleyVerified article out on him."

"That's ridiculous," Zoe said, but less heatedly than she would have if she didn't already know the meeting's outcome. Seeing Damien's look of confusion and alarm, she mouthed, "I'll explain everything later." Poor guy. He didn't even know what his CEO—*former* CEO—had done; this must all be coming as a brutal shock.

"Right. But since we didn't have any concrete evidence, it seemed for a while that he was going to escape unscathed after all. But then Keira said that one thing they could do would be to check his academic records. So they reached out to USC, discovered he *did* lie about his suspension and that he was kicked out of school for sexual harassment."

"Hah! Even they can't deny how bad that is."

"Oh no. Even after all that, Drew Macklemore and Aswar Joshi were still inclined to just let things go. According to Keira, Bill actually said that the reason Facebook and Snapchat are both so big now was because the board stood by their founders even when their poor behavior in college was exposed. So those two men tried to make a case that Bill shouldn't be punished for something that happened years ago, and with FitPick going through so much turmoil, what the company needed was a stable leadership."

Zoe rolled her eyes. "Damn, that man is a smooth talker."

"Thankfully, Keira saw through it at once. But you know what board directors are like—all they care about at the end of the day is profits."

"You got that right," Zoe muttered as Logan Horossen's incredulous expression drifted into her mind. *And why should I care?*

"So instead of trying to convince them from a moral standpoint, Keira decided to speak their language. She argued that with ValleyVerified poking their nose into the company so much lately, it would only be a matter of time before they uncovered Bill's past. And the whole debacle around you could only distract the public for so long, so once people realized the shady things Bill did at school, there's no way any parent would be willing to let their children use the app because who knows what Bill might do with their photos and data?"

"Oh my God. Keira's brilliant. Serves Bill right for looking down on her."

"She is," Lillian agreed. "And once Drew Macklemore and Aswar Joshi heard that, they got spooked immediately. And as you know by now, Bill was kicked out of the company by a vote of three to one. And Keira White—bless her—tipped Rebecca Stiles off. She said she wanted to serve him a taste of his own medicine after what he did to you."

"Remind me to never get on Keira White's bad side," Zoe laughed.

Zoe leaned against Damien, savoring the feeling of his body around hers as she tried to process everything that had happened in the last two weeks and turned her world upside down. It was disappointing but not surprising that in the end, the only reason Bill got his just deserts was rooted in a practical cost-benefit analysis—that the board had decided the potential damage to the company's reputation was more relevant and more important than whatever Bill had done to her and Lillian. But at last, she could stop worrying about what new trick Bill had up his sleeve against them.

As though she knew what Zoe was thinking, Lillian's voice softened. "Zoe, Bill is gone. You can come back to work now." She paused. "But only if you want. I know you've been through a lot lately, so I don't blame you for wanting to take more time away."

A new thought struck Zoe. "What's going to happen now that Bill is gone? Will they hire a new CEO?"

"Actually, the reason Keira called me was to let me know that the board had decided to appoint me as interim CEO."

Zoe clapped a hand to her mouth. "Lillian! How could you have waited so long to tell me this? Congratulations! No one deserves this more than you. And I'm so proud you'll be my CEO," she said more quietly, wanting the full sincerity of her words to be conveyed. She giggled as Damien's eyes widened at the last line, her mind racing to plan how she would explain everything to him.

"Thank you, Zoe. But in any case, I'm only the interim CEO while the board looks for a long-term replacement for Bill. However, I wanted to ask you something."

"Go on."

Lillian cleared her throat. "I was hoping you would be my chief operating officer. I suggested it to Keira and she checked with the rest of the board, and everyone agrees with my proposal. They have been impressed with our marketing ideas so far. So . . . if you want the role, it's yours."

For a long moment, Zoe couldn't speak. Her fingers tightened around her phone. "I would love to," she finally said past the lump in her throat. Less than half a year ago, she'd given her notice at *Chic* because even though she loved fashion with all her heart, the industry never seemed to love her back quite as much, forcing her to smooth out her edges to fit in. She'd then moved to the tech industry—a roller-coaster ride that had also plunged her into her lowest professional moments, but had also shown her she could forge a new path for herself.

"It won't be easy," Lillian warned. "We'll need to work very hard to rescue the company's image and get ourselves on the right track. It's an uphill battle from here."

But she'd emerged from all the ups and downs stronger than before. Less starry-eyed than the Zoe Zeng from six months ago, but more self-assured in her ability to withstand whatever was thrown her way. This was a new beginning, a clean slate.

Zoe rolled her shoulders back and made sure to clearly enunciate every word as she replied to Lillian, "I am ready."

chapter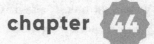

Three months later

"**H**AVE YOU GOT everything?"

"Uh, almost!" Zoe called out as she rushed around her bedroom to find her passport, almost tripping over a pair of Aquazurra sandals. *Hang on, these sandals are kind of cute.* She picked them up and flung them into her open suitcase on the bed before turning her attention back to her passport hunt. Maybe it was time she got a driver's license after all so that she could use it instead of her passport to check in for domestic flights.

Damien entered her room, frowning. "Your flight leaves in three hours."

"I only have to be at the airport two hours in advance if it's a domestic flight," Zoe countered, deciding in the moment to bring along a pair of zebra-print sunglasses. Everyone needs at least three pairs of backup sunglasses, right? Even if New York had been raining so much this spring that there was barely any sunshine.

"Anyway, what are you planning to do this weekend while I'm gone?" she quickly asked as Damien opened his mouth, no doubt gearing up to retort.

He shot her a look but thankfully went along with her subject change. "I've a submission for a short story due soon, so I'll be cranking that out. Then drinks with Austin and Bram tomorrow."

"I feel like you've been hanging out with them more after you left FitPick."

"Helps that I'm no longer their boss. So now they feel more comfortable complaining to me and chatting about their personal lives outside of work. I know way more than I ever wanted to about Bram's dating life."

Zoe looked up from her packing and grinned. "You know, the other day, Austin said something about how he realized he didn't give you enough credit while you were around. He said you make being CTO look far easier than it is."

After Bill's termination, the board had appointed Lillian as interim CEO while they looked for a replacement. All the shortlisted candidates were men with illustrious academic and work pedigrees, and all who appeared to Zoe to not truly understand what FitPick was really about. In the end, it was Keira White who convinced the other board members that Lillian had the experience and heart to run the company permanently. Once Lillian was officially designated the CEO, she had made Zoe the chief operating officer, Austin the chief technology officer after Damien left to focus on his writing, and Bram took on a new role of chief product officer.

"Austin's facing a completely different situation than I did. When I was CTO, I only had two people reporting to me, but don't you have six new engineers and two product designers in the office now? It's definitely tougher for him and Bram since they're managing more people. He needs to give himself more credit."

There was a hint of wistfulness in Damien's voice that made Zoe give him a longer look. "Do you ever miss working at FitPick?"

Damien furrowed his brows as he pondered her question. Zoe gently smoothed her thumb over the wrinkles in his forehead, a wave of fondness surging through her. That was one of the things she loved best about Damien—how he treated everything so thoughtfully and never made her feel like she was asking something dumb.

"I do miss it," he finally answered. "It was undeniably a special experience helping to build a product from the ground up. But I don't regret leaving. You know I've always wanted to be more focused on my writing, and thanks to Logan Horossen's investment, my FitPick stocks rose so much in value that I could finally afford to take a couple years off work and give writing a serious shot."

The corners of his lips curved up. "And my resignation meant I could ask you out at last."

Laughing, Zoe allowed herself to be swept into his arms, a buzz zipping through her stomach as it always did at the feel of his skin against hers. "That's definitely a silver lining. Lillian recently hired our first HR person and they came up with this rule that any non-platonic relationship with someone you directly manage must be disclosed. I think Lillian's just concerned another Bill situation might develop if there are no rules in place, especially in such a small company."

"That makes sense." Damien's expression turned stern. "But

Zoe, we *really* have to go soon. I bet Lillian's already at the airport waiting for you. Speak of the devil," he said with a tinge of smugness as a video call from Lillian popped up on Zoe's phone.

Shooting him an eye roll, Zoe accepted the call. "Zoe, are you still at home?" Lillian asked, raising her voice to be heard over all the noise on her end, including a faint automated voice reciting: *Last call for passengers for Flight 731 to Los Angeles.*

"Yeah. But I'm leaving soon, I promise!" Zoe replied, ignoring the skeptical quirk of her boyfriend's right brow.

"Oh, thank God. That you're still at home, I mean. I realized I forgot to bring the FitPick bracelets that we were planning to give away to the conference participants. If you have some at home, can you bring them along?"

"Of course," Zoe replied, throwing Damien a triumphant little smirk. "And I've also brought along fifty of Bernadette's enamel pins. I figured they would be cute as conference gifts too."

Three months ago, Bernadette had decided to turn her crafting hobby into a small business specializing in accessories that champion female empowerment. It had taken off after Keira White spotted Zoe wearing an *Ovarachiever* pin on her denim jacket and decided to make Bernadette's store the official gifts partner for her foundation. Every girl enrolled in A Perfect 10 would now receive a laptop case from Berni's Baubles emblazoned with the phrase *IT-Girl*.

"Great idea! I'm actually using one of her luggage tags. How's her business doing?" Lillian asked.

"Really good! She just got her first international order. Some woman from Singapore ordered the *Ovarachiever* and *Cuterus* pin set." Zoe mouthed a sheepish "thank you" to Damien as he handed her the pack of FitPick bracelets that he'd found buried beneath a pile of Bubble Wrap on her desk. "But Lillian, forgetting something doesn't seem like you," she joked, stuffing the bracelets into her suitcase and finally zipping it closed. "Who are you and what have you done with my CEO?"

Lillian groaned, the first time Zoe had ever heard such an inelegant sound leaving her CEO's mouth. "I know I'm super frazzled, but I'm just so nervous."

"Why would you be nervous? You've spoken at TechCrunch Disrupt before and this crowd isn't nearly as scary." The Fashion Institute of Technology was hosting its annual Changemaker conference and had invited FitPick to present on how they used data and artificial intelligence to analyze and leverage trends. An industry convention like this was just the kind of situation Lillian thrived in.

Lillian shook her head. "No, they are scarier. This is a fashion crowd and I know nothing about fashion." Her voice grew so small that Zoe had to increase her phone's volume to the max so she could still catch her boss's words over the airport bustle. "Those conference-goers are going to see through me in a second. What if my talk is so boring that they start walking out?"

Holding up a finger, Zoe let Damien know she would be out in a minute. It couldn't have been easy for someone as prideful as Lillian to admit an insecurity, so Zoe wanted to give the conversation her full attention. He nodded and picked up her suitcase to bring it to his car.

"Lillian, you are one of the most brilliant people I know, and you would be impressive at anything you put your mind to," Zoe said firmly. "What people in fashion appreciate more than anything else is a vision, and you have that in buckets. So just talk about your vision for FitPick and you will absolutely win them over."

As Lillian listened quietly, Zoe experienced a flash of disbelief. Just half a year ago, she would have never imagined being in the position to offer Lillian Mariko advice and comfort, or that Lillian would even be confiding in her in the first place. "I'm not dismissing your fears—I had major imposter syndrome, too, when I first joined FitPick. Some days, I'm still not sure what I, a former fashion writer, am doing in the tech industry. However, I've also learned that it's entirely possible to discover new passions and new strengths. But the only way to do so is to dare to step out of your comfort zone and not let yourself be pigeonholed. And for that matter, don't pigeonhole yourself."

There was a pause on the other end, then: "Zoe Zeng, since when did you become so wise?"

Zoe laughed. "Guess I picked up a few tricks from you, boss. But seriously, don't be nervous. Some of my fashion friends will be there, too, and I can't wait to introduce you to them." She'd already warned Bjorn not to overwhelm Lillian at their first meeting by badgering her for her brow routine.

"Okay." Lillian exhaled deeply. "Just get here soon, yeah?"

"I'm leaving right after this call," Zoe said, her eyes roving over her outerwear selection. Her coats would be too warm for spring, but her usual denim jacket wouldn't stand a chance against New York's April showers.

Lillian's voice drew her attention again. "Sounds good. Let me know when you're ten minutes away so I can grab you a Starbucks decaf."

"I love you," Zoe sighed.

"Don't let Damien hear you say that," Lillian said, nevertheless looking pleased.

Zoe's eyes lit up as Lillian's phone slid down slightly, the camera panning over Lillian's top. "Wait, is that the organza blouse you bought when we were thrift shopping in Mission last week?"

"Yeah, the one you said I would regret forever if I didn't buy.

And I paired it with the crepe wool trousers that you recommended." Lillian lowered her phone so her bottom half would be captured too. "What do you think?" she asked lightly, but Zoe could sense the trace of nerves behind her CEO's nonchalant facade.

"You look *amazing*! Like the ultimate girl boss. Anyway, I have to go now," Zoe said as Damien entered her house again. "I'll see you soon."

"Ready?" he asked.

She slipped her arm through his and nestled close to his body. "Yup."

With her other hand, she picked up her purse. As they walked past her closet, her eyes caught on an item hanging in the back.

The Patagonia vest she'd received on her first day at FitPick. The kind everyone in the Bay Area seemed to have, like some sort of unofficial work uniform. And that she'd sworn she would never wear in a million years.

Zoe slid it off the hanger and shrugged it on, the cool waterproof material sliding over her arms like a second skin. Its design was more functional than fun, but it fit perfectly and would keep her warm as she represented Silicon Valley—with style.

acknowledgments

亲爱的爸爸妈妈和爷爷奶奶，我最深刻的感激之情永远都是给你们的。我对故事的热爱来源于你们：在我还在上小学的时候，爸爸和我分享许多伟大的中国古典名著；妈妈则为我买下每一本我想要的书，并在我背英语单词时陪伴在我身边；爷爷奶奶，姥姥姥爷也陪我在儿童图书馆度过了无数个周末下午。正是因为你们一直在我身后默默支持，我才能够最终在硅谷学习和工作，得到了启发这个故事的宝贵经历。

To my editor, Angela, and everyone else at Berkley—Cat Barra, Jessica Mangicaro, Tina Joell, Lindsey Tulloch, Daniel Brount, Christine Legon, Sammy Rice, Heather Haase, Nicole Wayland—who helped bring this story out into the world. I owe each and every one of you a debt of gratitude for the time, energy, and love you gave to my books. From *The Fraud Squad* to *Valley Verified*, this has been the best ride because of you all, and I'm so honored to work with such an incredible team. I will always be proud to call myself a Berkley author.

Thank you to artist Natalie Shaw and art director Vi-An Nguyen, who created the most stunning cover. I want to steal Zoe's outfit on the cover so badly.

To my agent, Alex, who has always been my biggest champion. None of this would have been possible if you hadn't believed in me, and I am forever grateful that my gut instinct led me to you. And to the CAA team—Berni Barta, Ali Ehrlich, Jamie Stockton, Bianca Petcu, Kathryn Driscoll, Sophia Ungaro, Tessa Germaine—a big, big thank-you for all your tireless work and unwavering support. It's always an amazing experience working with a team of people who are each the best at what they do.

To my coworkers, who are far and away better than any character in this book. Thank you for being so incredibly supportive and encouraging of my writing. I lucked out with you bunch.

To the Ngos, who gave me a sense of family in a country where I don't have any family. It means more to me than you will ever know.

To my friends—those who write and those who don't—thank you for cheering me on through my writing journey, and also for reminding me that I'm more than that. The cast of Zoe's friends was inspired by each and every single one of you.

To C, who has been one of the best parts of my years in Silicon Valley. I hope we get to see a narwhal one day.

valley ✓ verified

KYLA ZHAO

discussion questions

1. Did you feel like Zoe made the right decision by leaving her fashion career for tech? Why or why not?

2. Have you ever made a career transition like Zoe did? How did it go for you, and what did you learn from the experience?

3. One of Zoe's big struggles after moving to Silicon Valley is loneliness from not knowing anyone and having no friends. Have you ever been in a similar situation, and if so, how did you handle it?

4. Did you identify with Zoe's feelings of imposter syndrome when she started her new job? How do you deal with imposter syndrome when you experience it?

5. Have you ever found yourself being put down or doubted by others, like what Zoe faced from her Fit-Pick coworkers? How did you navigate that?

6. What do you think of the way the book tackles issues of sexism and gender bias? Have you encountered such microaggressions in your life?

7. Tech billionaires and startups have been covered in the media more and more in recent years. In what ways did the book's portrayal of the tech industry in Silicon Valley surprise you, and in what ways did it fit with your expectations?

8. Zoe felt troubled by how she was growing apart from her old New York friends after she took on the job at FitPick that they couldn't relate to. Have you ever felt like you were drifting apart from a friend? How did you navigate that?

9. Zoe never thought she would become comfortable in the tech industry because she came from such a different background. Have you ever found yourself developing an interest or aptitude in a completely unexpected field?

10. Work plays a large part in the lives of Zoe, Lillian, and Bernadette. What do you think of each woman's relationship with her career, and can you relate to any of that?

11. Zoe and Lillian started off on the wrong foot, with each woman thinking the other was too dissimilar for them to get along. Yet they discovered eventually that they are stronger when they work together. Have you ever experienced a dynamic like that?

12. Would you want to work at FitPick? Why or why not?

A native Singaporean, **Kyla Zhao** came to California to study at Stanford University. She graduated in 2021 with a master's degree in communications and a bachelor's degree in psychology. Previously, she worked in fashion, writing for magazines like *Vogue* and *Harper's Bazaar* in Singapore. Now, she works at a tech company in Silicon Valley. She's still trying to understand why Californians love Patagonia and hiking so much.

VISIT KYLA ZHAO ONLINE

KylaZhao.com

Ready to find
your next great read?

Let us help.

Visit prh.com/nextread

Penguin
Random
House